FALCON BLUE

REBECCA LOCHLANN

ERINYES
PRESS

Falcon Blue

Internal design © 2018 Rebecca Lochlann, Erinyes Press
Cover design © 2018 Rebecca Lochlann, Erinyes Press

Trade Paperback:
ISBN-13: 978-0-9982678-1-4
ISBN-10: 0-9982678-1-3
Library of Congress Control Number: 2018905368

Published in the United States by Erinyes Press

Also available as an eBook:
ISBN-13: 978-0-9982678-0-7
ISBN-10: 0-9982678-0-5

For Mom

FALCON BLUE

REBECCA LOCHLANN

ERINYES
PRESS

BOOK SIX

THE CHILD OF THE ERINYES SERIES

MOTHER

Also By Rebecca Lochlann

THE FIRST REINCARNATION

Aodhàn Mackinnon told the story of Eamhair, Cailean, and Taranis in
The Sixth Labyrinth

He lied
Here is the truth

YOU HAVE SET THIS WORLD UPON ITS PATH, AND SO YOU WILL LIVE IT. YOU WILL WATCH IT UNFOLD, AND YOU WILL REMEMBER EVERYTHING YOU HAVE DONE...

~~~THE PROPHECY OF DAMASEN

Anamnesis

TARANIS WAS NINE WHEN THE MEMORIES CAME BACK.

Later, as he thought about it, he was certain the necklace caused it to happen—how, he could not say, but he was sure nonetheless.

You were wearing it when I found you, his mother told him. *In lean times I have been tempted to sell it, but I never could.*

Firelight gleamed against the silver; the blue stone in the center shimmered like a raindrop on a leaf. It was an exquisite thing. He had little doubt of its value, and was thankful the usually mercenary Breda had not bargained it away for a chicken or flagon of ale.

He fell asleep holding it and was awakened deep in the night by an onslaught of images, of shrieking guilt, of rage and helplessness, of loss and grief. His soul burned with the violence of the fire wind that decimated Crete.

Over and over again, he saw his hands snapping the neck of the fragile beauty he loved before falling to his knees and begging her to come back to life.

He lifted off his pallet, screaming. Breda thought he'd caught a plague and had him bled nearly to the point of death.

He clawed at his eyes and ears and begged everyone, anyone, to kill him. He tried to wrest the healer's blade from her, and had to have his wrists tied down.

By sunrise he lay senseless, staring dully, unable to respond to his mother, who bathed his brow with cool water as she cried, *Taranis? Can you hear me?*

The healer shook her head. She knew far more about midwifery than she did diseases of the mind.

Not until evening could he speak one hoarse word.

Aridela.

From that day on, his life was misery.

Mist shrouds our eyes and stoppers our tongues, a grey, damp silence broken only by the softest sigh, like a dawn breeze. We know not how many centuries pass: we feel not the flow of time, until She turns her far-seeing gaze to us. When we gasp and draw our first breath, we are newborns who never fought great wars, or loved deeply, or brought harm upon one another.

So the journey begins.
we are become Athene's wanderers...

~~~Selene of Phrygia

PART I

Confluence

Chapter 1

A JARRING *THUD* STRUCK THE EARTH SO CLOSE TO HER TOES THAT SHE FELT the vibration clear up her legs and into her stomach. Instinctively she sprang back, gasping as a smoky-warm snort added a spray of mucus to the tears on her cheeks.

She had a blurred impression of a horse's hoof and glossy black leg before she turned her face up. And up.

A man towered above her, astride the tallest horse she had ever seen. The hood draped over his head cast an opaque shadow; she saw little more than stern lips and a flash of blue.

The horse's muzzle was so close she could kiss it by barely leaning forward. Its hoof had almost crushed her foot.

Her attention shifted to the more pressing threat—a large, rangy wolf, hackles lifted, teeth bared.

Another instinctive step backward caused a stumble and too late, she felt the edge of the precipice disintegrate beneath her heel. She flailed, caught in the infinite juncture between recovery and the relentless pull of empty space.

Voiceless with horror, she silently, disbelievingly, screamed, *No!* Then, as her body succumbed to the pull, *Mother!*

But he was there, wrenching her to safety. How had he moved so fast? A strike of lightning could not have bested him.

As he released her, he said, "Your thoughts must be deep indeed, to keep you so unaware of what lies right before your nose."

Mouth open, heart drumming, she stared, still unable to see much beneath the cover of the man's hood. He was right. How had she not seen or heard any of these beings until she walked right into them?

Unless...they were not of this world. Could they have been conjured out of her mother's richly spun provinces, where divine entities lived inside trees, under water, and among the stars? It was entirely possible she hadn't seen or heard them because they hadn't been there until the exact instant she took that final step and her foot opened a rift between their domain and hers.

It was as likely a reason as any other.

He pushed off his hood and waited, arms crossed, as though he had all day to hear whatever she might say. His dark hair was drawn back from his face, revealing a raised white scar that curved around his left eye, extended across his cheek, and ended near his nose. He had no deliberate beard but had not shaved for such an amount of time that he soon would.

As she worked to catch her breath, overcome her shaking, and comprehend that she was going to live after all, her mind went on collecting details.

The man's gauntlets, worn leather jerkin, trousers, and hide boots had probably been black at one time, but had eroded here and there to grey. His quilted under-tunic was a muted greyish green, as was his cloak, in stark opposition to the highly polished silver knife hilt at his belt. The wolf, who continued to prickle and growl, was a mixture of black and silver, with a paler muzzle; a splash of white above each greenish-gold eye gave it a look of astonishment.

Behind her lay the unforgiving cliffs. The man stood before her. The wolf was faster than she could ever aspire to be. She was well and truly cornered.

Not wanting to test the wolf's patience, she remained as motionless as possible, but her rapid breathing proved difficult to control.

The man rightly deciphered her expression. "You need not be afraid." He turned slightly towards the wolf. "Vita." He raised one hand, just the barest lift of his fingers, and the creature subsided, licking its lips.

A bit impatiently, he asked, "Can you speak? Are you hurt?"

She tried to swallow. A stifling lump had formed in her throat, causing her voice to sound uneven. "I-I thank you, sir." Her curtsy was awkward—she knew it; she did not need the affirmation of the wolf closing its mouth and pricking its ears. *I'd like to see you do better after nearly falling to your death.*

Glancing behind her, she took in the sheer cliff and tumultuous sea so many fathoms below. There was the crumbled spot…a testament to her good fortune.

She turned back to the man and swiped at her face with both hands. The brief narrowing of his eyes made her suspect he saw more there than his horse's snot. "I think I might have been more than hurt, had you not moved so swiftly."

"Aye," he agreed. "Where have you come from? I haven't passed a farmstead in days. Dhu Rinn?"

"Nay. The fort." She waved vaguely.

He squinted into the westering sunlight. His forehead crinkled.

Simultaneously, she realized he was younger than he'd first appeared, and taller. She herself was one of the tallest women at Dunaedan, yet her line of sight was stuck at the level of his upper sternum. He might well be the tallest man she had ever encountered; unfortunately, she had encountered many.

"Fort?"

"Dunaedan. The chieftain there is called Bericus." A sudden burst of inspiration caused her to add, "He has *many* seasoned warriors."

If this stranger's intent was evil, it might help if he believed there were irascible men willing to defend her. If he wasn't inclined to mischief, then he should know he was riding towards an unfriendly fortress so he could change direction—any direction but north, which had nothing to offer but a cold, watery death. She owed him that much.

"How far?" His eyes seemed to absorb and reflect the sunset. "Can you get back before nightfall? I would not like to think of you stumbling again with no one to catch you."

She couldn't see the slightest sign of concern at her warning. In fact…could that twitch of the lips pass for a smile?

"I will be fine. I have walked by the sea my whole life. I would not have lost my balance, but I was so startled…."

"Maybe you carry a drop or two of kestrel blood, to wander these cliffs without bothering to look where you step. Can you fly, mistress?"

She searched for some sign of mockery, but his expression was once again inscrutable. "I have been compared to a stoat once or twice," she said faintly.

"Come. I will take you back."

5

"No." With any luck, the firm shake of her head would be enough to convince him to abandon his offer.

"Why not?"

Because you might harm me? She could be wrong, but she didn't think he would. *Because if Bericus or his men saw us together, he would have you slaughtered?* She was too embarrassed to admit that, though it was likely true—if not killed, surely beaten. Bericus considered every female at the fortress of Dunaedan his personal property, and had been known to punish his men for no more than an unguarded glance. She settled on, "I should not wish to delay you from your travels."

"Nonsense." He held out his hand, palm up, and she found herself placing her hand upon leather so shabby it was nearly as soft as a puppy's fur. He led her to the horse, put his hands on her waist, and lifted her, settling her on the saddle before vaulting up behind her. One hand reached past her in front to gather the reins and the other looped around her back, making it almost impossible not to lean against him.

She was so high off the ground! Her fear of falling revived, and she resisted a primal urge to seize the horse's luxurious mane in both fists.

The next instant brought an inexplicable sensation of safety, braced as she was with the man's arms around her, her side planted against his chest, both of them squeezed between the saddle horns. She probably should be on the verge of panic, since he could now ride off with her if he wished, but she wasn't.

She turned her face just enough to peek upward, and glimpsed the markedly defined outline of his lips and one bristly cheek. She was not accustomed to shaved faces on men. Those she knew might trim their beards once in a while, but not often. Much about her rescuer was different.

The scent of sun-warmed leather surrounded her, and something else. She breathed in, careful to be circumspect.

Every year, as summer gave way to winter and the air chilled, leaves scattered across the bare, windswept moor that surrounded Dunaedan—narrow, pointed leaves from the rowans that thrived in the cracks and crevices of the cliffs, the fatter, serrated leaves of thirsty alders that grew where they could alongside streams and rivers, the buttery yellow aspen leaves from mountain slopes at the southern edge of the moor, and rarely, a thick, scalloped leaf or two from the twisted bog birches over by the sea inlet called *Uisge Bealach*. She collected each and every one that came her way and kept them in her bedchamber. Their crackly autumn scent helped her imagine vast canopies and green-scented, mossy groves, where bear, boar, wolf, and elk abounded—like the places in her mother's stories.

As he reined the horse to the left, she became certain. That was the scent she detected—fallen leaves, with a suggestion of rain. Oddly, it felt both familiar and provocatively new.

She also noticed that the tunic he wore, though worn, was of very fine wool.

"Is this the right way?" he asked.

"Yes." How to warn him about the danger of being seen with her? It was too humiliating. "I did not know horses could grow this big," she said instead. "Your charger makes our horses look like sheep."

"He comes from a lost civilization." The man stroked his mount's crest and received a responsive shake of the head. "Bred for war. He is the tallest of my father's stallions."

"Anyone but you would need a ladder to mount him." She clutched one of the leather saddle prongs and relived with admiration the way he'd effortlessly vaulted up, swinging one leg over and dropping easily behind her.

"My bow brothers heard of a warhorse, bigger and stronger than anything we could find or breed here. It was said they fought in the Roman cavalry a century or more ago. They decided to search out this mythical beast and they let me go along, though I was only ten. We followed the story for a year, from place to place, and at last found a man who had heard of the breed, and another who knew someone...." He shrugged. "Rumor and legend brought us at last to a country where floods had driven everyone out at one time, but they returned after the waters receded and were farming there again. We were lucky to happen upon a village where the breeding of this horse was a sacred tradition, kept alive even through their exile. We bargained for three stallions and eight mares from the headman, with a promise to return seven foals to him. My Bharosa was the seventh foal born on our shores—I helped with his birth and wanted him, so we returned another."

Bharosa. What a remarkable name. And now she knew something else about the man. He was a warrior. The puckered scar curved like the blade of a sickle around his eye proclaimed as much, as did the sword hanging from his saddle and the bow on his back. "Does that name have a meaning?" Her mother put great stock in the meanings of names.

"It comes from a country in the east. In their language, it means 'Trust.'"

Fitting.

He looked down and she met his gaze. It was astonishing. The shoals at her beach were never this blue, not even on the clearest, brightest days. What distant land could he be from, where people had such eyes?

Suddenly she wished this ride could go on and on. But the horse ate up the turf swiftly, arching his neck, prancing and blowing and shaking his mane as though he loved the movement and the feel of his master's heels.

She centered her gaze between Bharosa's ears and gave herself a silent scold. It was only that she met this man on her own. She hadn't been dragged before him like braised piglet.

"What were your dark thoughts?" he asked.

She startled. His right arm tightened, and a peculiar tingling crept through her spine. "My thoughts?"

"Something so consumed you that you collided with my stallion's face."

Oh, he meant before. She relaxed. "I...nothing. I was...." She laughed. "Dreaming of sea gods."

Which was only partly true. Her mother had come into the kitchens that morning with one eye swelling shut and a purpling bruise erupting on her cheekbone. When asked what had happened, Ula replied, "What always happens, child? Help me with the soup."

Murder burned in the heart of Ula's daughter, intensifying with each day that she failed to protect the woman who bore her, the woman who drew their chieftain's wrath on purpose so his streak of cruelty would be spent before he turned his gaze to anyone else—especially her daughter.

She had been going over all her plots to spirit her mother away from this hated place. But each one, upon examination, fell apart. Ula was too slow, too weak; she couldn't travel by night, with little to no food. No one would dare hide them for fear of brutal reprisal. Bericus, lord of Dunaedan, would send out his men; two women traveling alone would be caught within a day.

She had been imagining slitting Bericus's throat, and pondering that she would have to kill his sons as well, and every one of his warriors except maybe Bran, the kindest of them.

She had been picturing every poison she knew that might end his life, but she couldn't be sure that Ula herself would not fall under suspicion, as she was Dunaedan's foremost herbalist and healer.

Finally, as she continued to wander along the edge of a lofty cliff above an ocean as turbulent as her rage, she desperately wished for Ula's magical seal-king. The king Ula had promised her when she was a little girl.

But instead of creating a useable plan or being rescued by an ocean monarch, she had ploughed into an immense stallion, a wolf that might still rip out her throat, and a warrior who sometimes shaved his face and whose speech held curious rounded accents. Perhaps he came from the land that invented the word *Bharosa*.

He guided the horse around a cluster of pointed rocks, a bit too close to the cliff edge to suit her.

"You laugh sweetly, mistress."

She was not quite sure if it was the cliff or his words that caused the quickening of her heartbeat.

They descended the incline and came abreast of the fishermen's mooring place. "Please." She gripped his wrist. "Let me down here. Dunaedan is just over the hill."

"I will take you all the way."

"That would be unwise."

He dismounted and again caught her at the waist, bringing her smoothly to the ground. When she stood before him, her hands on his forearms, he looked into her face, frowned, and tilted his head. "Are you certain?"

The man was built like one of the rock spires in the ocean—unbelievably tall and spare, as though the sea had eaten away everything but his core. There was not a single lintel at the fortress high enough for him to enter straight-backed.

"Yes." She detected an embarrassing breathlessness in her voice.

"May I have your name? I cannot call you 'Wanderer,' or 'Absent-Minded Girl.'"

"Eamhair. I am called…Eamhair."

At last he smiled. "Eamhair," he repeated, with a caressing trill of the 'r,' and stepped away. She stood to the side while he gathered the reins and mounted his stallion. The wolf, who had loped alongside the horse without making a sound this entire way, sat on its haunches and observed her, its expression now one of boredom.

"Fare well." She wanted to add, *Begone from this place if you value your life*, but was afraid such words might make him refuse to go.

She gathered the hem of her tunic in one hand to keep it from getting wet and skipped across the stream, stone to stone. At the summit of the hill beyond, she paused and looked back.

He still sat there, easy and relaxed on his restive, beautiful horse. She knew the stallion's name and the wolf's name but hadn't asked his. Why hadn't she? Now it was too late.

One of Ula's admonishments returned to her mind.

Tell your deepest secrets to trees; they will not betray you. Listen to water, for it will guide you truly. Let your gaze dwell upon the moon and you will be showered in wonder. Seek rainbows, Eamhair, and follow where they lead.

But, my child, trust no man.

She waved; he lifted a hand. Then she turned and left him.

Chapter 2

ONCE UPON A TIME, HARPALYCUS WAS A ROYAL PRINCE AND HEIR TO THE powerful throne of Tiryns.

So many centuries had passed since then he could no longer fashion a clear memory of Tiryns, or even see the face of his once-beloved sister, Iros.

He didn't like to admit it, even to himself, but the thing he had wanted most—immortality—had lost much of its relish. Everlasting life coupled with power and infinite riches had turned into a legacy of quicksilver—hard to hold and unpredictable. There were always those who wanted to steal his power and treasure, and were more than willing to murder him for it. In the effort to hold onto life he was often forced to lose power and wealth.

He was tired. He was bored. And he had been persistently ill for almost a year.

Sighing, he gazed at the barrier of evergreens running along the coast to the left of the boat. Mist wove through their crowns and branches like freezing exhalations, growing thicker the farther north they sailed. He had yet to glimpse anything else of this miserable land.

Gaius approached from the back of the boat. No doubt he had been secretly calling his master a lunatic since the morning Harpalycus ordered them out of warm and lively Constantinople, and forced them to spend two months journeying across glacial winter seas and frozen lands to an apparently uninhabited, eternally wet island manifesting nothing but endless primordial forests.

No matter. These bootlickers could think whatever they wished so long as they obeyed him. As long as they understood he would kill them if they gave him any less respect than they would offer his father, were they ever to be in that venerated man's presence.

"Lord." Gaius bowed. "We are running out of food and water. Do you intend to turn back soon?"

Someone was watching from within that opaque curtain. He knew it.

All his senses had heightened the instant he deferred to the overwhelming need to come here. He hadn't known what to expect and had naively assumed that Britannia, or Albion, or Caledonia—whatever they called the wretched place these days—had been somewhat civilized by its Roman conquerors. But every passing league made it easier to believe those old stories claiming the Romans had utterly failed to subdue the northern half of the island. Tales lived on, of bloodthirsty, tattooed savages who indulged in cannibalism, went about naked even in winter, and shared their women like swigs from a flask.

Damp mist filled his nose, carrying an undertone of rot. "Ah. And what is this?" He pointed.

It appeared the land was finally changing, curving into what looked like an enormous estuary or bay. "Bodotria," the helmsman informed him.

It resembled a colossal spout, pouring seawater into the loins of this country. "Go there," Harpalycus ordered.

Gaius bowed and retreated; Harpalycus watched him send his companions a discreet headshake.

The sun, weak as it was, moved ever downward in front of them and had vanished by the time they found a landing spot.

They disembarked. Harpalycus felt the pressure of his men's reluctance as they plunged into the close, shadowy forest.

"Lord, the men want to know what it is we search for."

"I cannot say yet." Harpalycus nearly laughed at the way his second-in-command's eyes bulged.

They were eating the stringy flesh of a badger. The meat was half raw, half burned, and they would still be hungry when it was gone.

"Eight days we have marched, lord. Can you not give us some idea?"

"I cannot."

"These trees have eyes." Gaius adjusted his sword belt and peered suspiciously in every direction.

The next day, they at last had a glimpse of humans—armed warriors with long, tangled hair, their faces and bare arms covered in blue.

"*Picti*," Gaius said, with no small amount of awe. "I heard of them when I was a boy, how they savaged the Romans."

Harpalycus motioned him to silence.

The men were camped beside a stream, laughing as they roasted game over two bright fires. Shaggy ponies grazed nearby. Harpalycus observed the scene for a while, determining which one was the leader by the respect he was shown. He gave the order for all but that one to be killed.

When the task was done—not without injury and death on his own side—and the leader bound and gagged before him, he ordered his companions to return to the boat and wait. There was, of course, argument, but it was lackluster, and in the end they obeyed. He knew they would wait no more than a few days before abandoning him. He didn't care.

Harpalycus drew his sword, watching the clench of his captive's jaw, the hatred in his eyes, the reflexive straining against leather bindings.

But when he put the tip of the blade against his own flesh, the man blinked and stilled. When Harpalycus drove the sword into his stomach, the prisoner's eyes widened and for the first time he looked fearful. He tried to scrabble away, but it was too late.

HARPALYCUS LAUGHED WEAKLY AS THE NAUSEA SETTLED, THE DIZZINESS retreated, and more details coalesced.

Fathna. That was this man's name. The guttural speech now made sense. One of the savages—*Udrost*—had bragged about his wife's latest lying in and the result—another son. Harpalycus was surprised to understand that daughters were more revered by these people. Udrost's tone had been a little regretful.

Harpalycus was now a ruler, a king over someplace called *Innse Orc*. Who would have thought coming to this sodden wilderness would elevate him from king's half-forgotten bastard to king in his own right? A king! But sovereigns in this barbaric place could know nothing of true luxury or the pleasures Harpalycus had enjoyed after he consumed the great Theoderic's only male offspring.

Now to determine if changing bodies had expunged the agonies that had eaten away at his health and forced him to come here. He dipped into this pagan mind again, seeking the untroubled dispassion, the jaded lethargy he had taken for granted until a year ago.

At first he thought he'd succeeded. The nausea that plagued him when he consumed another was retreating as it always did. The piercing headache and feverish shivering that had filled the last year with misery—gone. He searched for any sign of the worst symptom, the tingling, flooding anxiety that had ruined his sleep and drained his body and spirit of energy.

There was nothing. With each breath he felt better and better. He would have to wait and see if the nightmares were gone as well.

He had given up everything to come here. His adored *Basileuousa*, queen of cities, and his plan to confront his sire in Ravenna, consume him, and take his place, now that all the fighting was over. Truthfully, he would have given up far more than that to be rid of the tormenting afflictions. He had even considered relinquishing his immortality for the silence, the numbness, of death.

He turned his face to the dreary sky and howled his relief. But now what? He knew where his victim's fortress lay, hazily—far to the north, a cluster of islands rising out of a frenzied sea. But he wasn't journeying there—Fathna and his men had changed course and were headed for a nearby citadel called *Sgathag Creag*, which was his brother's seat of power. His older brother, who was...*Drost Gocinecht*. Fathna's mind produced a weathered bull of a man, covered in tattoos and silver. He was also a king—the king of the Northern Caledonii.

Fathna's memories revealed that a messenger from Drost had brought a summons, ordering Fathna away from his winter hunting to perform some service involving a rebellious chieftain.

Mounting one of the ponies, he set off, working out a story about the murdered men. It wasn't until he was ascending the hill to the fortress, with the scent of cooking fires in his nose and the bleating of sheep in his ears that his muscles again quaked. The agony was so extreme it pulled him off the pony and drove him to his knees, where he helplessly vomited.

He was not yet free.

Chapter 3

THE LONG, GLOOMY SHADOWS OF NIGHT TAPERED TO SCANTY INNUENDOS, giving Taranis a clearer view of the narrow gorge delaying his progress. It was filled with half-frozen water and enclosed on both sides by steeply slanted banks. Damp, weary, disheartened, and roundly cursing himself for undertaking this journey, he forced his aching legs to carry him up what felt like the fiftieth hill he'd scaled in the last two days, and trudged along an exposed ridge above the water.

When he reached the frigid, windswept summit, he paused to catch his breath.

He had been climbing and descending, climbing and descending for so long he could hardly fathom what he was looking at—a vast, barren expanse of rolling, uneven moorland, as though a giant had ground away all the mountains under his heel in an angry fit. Close to the far edge from where he stood—where land ended and a glittering ocean began—rising through grey threads of morning mist, stood a tower. A stone tower.

The wind carried echoes of hammering, an indecipherable shout or two, the bark of a dog, and the sweet smoke of peat fires.

It seemed a beam of light shot out of the tower's apex and momentarily blinded him. He shuddered at a sense of awakening from a long dreamless sleep to a morning of bright new hope, of renewed energy, to the belief that some broken part of his soul was suddenly healed.

The structure, rearing up through the mist so that it appeared to be floating above the ground, embodied all he had lost and all he had longed for since the instant the necklace brought back the memories.

Taranis had not crossed incalculable spans of mountains, valleys, fields, and rivers in vain. He had not come miserably close to starving, spent too many frosty nights without shelter, or almost lost his life in the fearsome pagan citadel of Sgathag Creag—*Dread Rock*— for nothing.

He had left his mother, his village, and everything he knew to find this place, without any certainty that it existed, half convinced it was nothing more than a madman's delusion.

All he had to do was walk down there and confront it—his nightmare, or his truth.

TIGHTENING THE ROPE THAT SERVED AS A BELT AND SWITCHING HIS STAFF to his right hand, Taranis strode boldly into the village like a real monk would. Beyond the cluster of bothies and workshops, tall fortress palisades loomed warningly.

He begged bread and milk from an aproned goodwife; she kindly provided both, and a hunk of cheese as well. Then he went straight to the priest at the little timber and thatch Christian church, where he offered his prepared story of being sent by his abbot from the famed priory known as Whithorn, the "White House." That he'd been specially chosen for a journey of conversion in the far north because he understood the languages. The priest's nose lifted and his brows lowered; he declared that everyone at Dunaedan had long been Christian—Lord Bericus demanded nothing less. And why had Taranis been sent out alone? Surely that was not how Whithorn did things in such dangerous times?

Taranis, ready for this oft-asked question, explained sorrowfully that vicious infidels had killed his companions many days ago. This earned the priest's sympathy, a clean habit of soft undyed wool, and the offer of a pallet to sleep on. There ensued some back and forth grumbling about the time of year, it being lamentably cold to be sent out on such a long, though important, journey. Could his abbot have not waited until spring? Would there not have been the same number of pagans to convert then?

Nodding his agreement, Taranis nevertheless spoke the expected platitudes of being an obedient servant who was happy to endure the weather in the name of God, which made the priest smile approvingly and pat his shoulder.

He gratefully donned the clean habit and told the priest goodbye, saying he would probably leave the area after a short rest and continue his journey, since there was no use for him at Dunaedan.

Nibbling cheese, he continued his exploration, searching for anything that would explain the dreams. He sent out silent thanks to his mother as he returned polite greetings, for she had grown up on the southwest coast of this land—the proud descendant of an ancient tribe called the Novantae, and had taught him the dialect she spoke as a child. These people had slightly different accents and a few obscure words, but it was similar enough that he could decipher most of it.

The villagers bowed. One after another asked for his blessing. He was offered more food and drink. But nothing other than the tower sparked any recognition.

Excitement degenerated into pessimism. Athene had done this. She and her sycophant, the bull-god Damasen, had yanked him out of peaceful death, shoved him into a savage land of constant war and privation, and forced every agonizing memory from Crete into his mind. Like a swarm of angry bees, they stung day and night.

For nineteen years he had suffered Athene's punishment. Yet, over time, the misery revealed lessons he had never understood as Chrysaleon. On Crete, he had enslaved himself to ambition. Glory meant all—and any means to achieve triumph was acceptable. But living again in this land, bereft of Aridela, of Menoetius, with no Pasithea or Gelanor or Bateia, without Alexiare, Selene, or Themiste—though those two had hated him—felt like being submerged in the ocean without being allowed to drown.

It was not the kingship or wealth, not the power or renown that gave his existence meaning. It wasn't even thwarting the king sacrifice or submerging Crete into Mycenae. It was the people he had known—the ones he had loved and those he had fought.

He had to admit he would shout with joy even to see Lycus the bull dancer, or his nemesis, Harpalycus of Tiryns. Someone…*anyone*…who could share a flask of ale and remember the enchantment of those days.

Dreams of the tower began shortly after the return of the Cretan memories. At first they were little more than broad strokes, but as the years passed, the dream unveiled depth and detail—high cliffs, narrow stone stacks like cathedrals created for sea-people, a cave with a yawning mouth, an expanse of restless ocean, and a wide inlet, so shallow in spots that at low tide it was hardly more than sand and mud.

When the dream had him in thrall, he was always struggling to reach the tower, clambering over rocks that cut his flesh, trudging through marshes and bogs, his efforts trapped in the slow, heavy motion that marked dreams with unfulfilled urgency, leaving him anxious and tired when he woke.

Now he stood in the midst of the dream, fully awake but still denied understanding.

Last spring, a newcomer entered the village near Whytchurch where Taranis and his mother lived, and expressed interest in finding a whore. He was promptly directed to Breda, who always knew where to acquire such things. But the man, who claimed to be a merchant, told her she was more beguiling than any girl she might produce; his flattery and a few bits of silver drew her out of retirement and Taranis was sent away. In fact, the two got along so well that he stayed a fortnight before moving on.

In the evenings, while Breda prepared the food he generously provided, he entertained them with stories of his travels. He described faraway lands that winter seldom touched, where the ocean was warm and free of tides. He told them about ancient cities buried beneath the surface of the ground, and said anyone could find treasure if he knew where to dig. He produced a gold ring from one of his many satchels, telling them he'd traded a valuable young stallion for it. It had a flat face with tiny carved divots; when pressed into a glob of mud a finely detailed picture appeared—a woman offering three round objects to the narrow-waisted male who knelt before her.

Taranis forced his expression to remain composed, though his grip on the cup he held tightened so much it would have shattered anything less than oak. He had to unlock his knuckles to reach out and take the ring. He pretended to examine it with nothing more than mild curiosity.

Of the three, only he knew the objects were apples, that the woman was a goddess, and the kneeling man a king. The gift of golden apples to the bull-king promised him safe passage to the garden of Hesperia after his noble sacrifice. This unassuming merchant had managed to acquire the most precious of artifacts—a bull-king's seal ring.

Chrysaleon had worn a ring like this. He had sailed that tideless sea from Mycenae to Knossos and back. Aridela had presented him with three golden apples on the night he was sworn to die.

All that he knew, all he had lived, was now a matter of treasure finding. He imagined sand drifting over the palace of Labyrinthos, the hollow roar of wind sweeping it into oblivion.

The places the merchant described sounded different yet in some ways the same. He spoke of seas that glowed in moonlight, of vast mountain ranges, of caves festooned with hanging stones and crystals.

Taranis and his mother exchanged a glance at that, and Taranis absently fingered the neck of his tunic. He had told her the necklace was ancient and priceless, and that it should never have been found, as it was hidden in a mountain cave far from any village or farm.

"All there follow the Christos these days," the merchant told them, "but in older times, many gods and goddesses were worshipped, who were sometimes generous, and other times vindictive. The natives love telling their stories. I suspect there are a few who still give those gods secret fealty."

Taranis yearned to slide the ring onto his middle finger. Instead, he returned it without comment. He swallowed to keep from shouting, *Those are the gods I know.*

Just as he thought his bones might erupt through his flesh, Breda asked the man if he'd ever seen a round stone tower set upon high sea cliffs.

For years, she had asked this question of wanderers passing through the area. No one had ever replied with more than a shrug or a puzzled shake of the head.

"I did see one of those once," the merchant said. "In Hibernia."

Breda glanced at Taranis. "But never in this land?"

The merchant pulled on his lower lip for a while before his face lit. "Oh aye, there is a fortress with a tower, as far north as a man can go without falling into the ocean. Dunaedan. When I was there they boasted every night in their hall of the man who built it—a Hibernian named Aedan who married a princess of the Caerini and became their chief. He built the tower to please her. The hall and palisades were timber, but as I understand, this Aedan grew tired of having to search for good wood, and so decided to make use of the stones from nearby ruins. He modeled his tower from what he thought they might have looked like before they crumbled away. This all happened long ago, before any of us were born. When I was there, Dunaedan's chieftain was a man named Bericus—the great grandson of this Aedan, or great

great grandson, or even farther removed, who knows? The tower was where Bericus kept his womenfolk."

The man happily quaffed ale as he relayed all the gossip he could remember from his time at the fort. "Bericus and the last of his tribe were overthrown a score or more years ago by Drost Gocinecht, the king of the northern Caledonii. The fortress, the village, its warriors and holdings, its tithes and output were annexed into Drost's, and Bericus's rule as a minor, petty chieftain—his very life—has continued only at his overlord's sufferance."

The merchant asked for more ale—said it would help him remember—and patted Breda's backside when she brought it to him. "Bericus killed Drost's eldest son in the fighting. Such things are to be expected, but after his victory, Drost claimed the lives of both of Bericus's sons as recompense. Bericus got on his knees and begged for mercy, saying his wife, who had just borne a daughter, had nearly died and would give him no more children.

"Now I can attest from personal experience that Drost Gocinecht is not a merciful king, but according to the men who shared these stories, he agreed on one condition not to put Bericus's sons to the sword. He demanded that Bericus keep his newly born daughter unwed and in reserve for Drost to do with as he wished when she came of age, and Bericus readily agreed."

The merchant's account played through Taranis's mind as he made his way towards the fortress. The closer he got, the more uneasy he grew; at the last instant, as the man in the gatehouse took notice of him, he veered off, leery of the pointed timbers, the ramparts, the sentries, and guardhouses. It bristled in war-like readiness, which struck him as odd in such an isolated place.

What were they afraid of? Much of their wariness must come from living under the thumb of the conquering warrior-king, Drost Gocinecht. On one unfortunate day about halfway through his journey, Taranis had been waylaid and taken before that man. The experience was one he barely survived. Since then, he'd prayed ardently that God spare him from ever again crossing paths with the king of the Caledonii.

He wandered along the cliffs until he came to a slope and followed it down to an inlet crowded with fishing boats. Men and boys were busy with various tasks, while women sorted the day's catch.

One wrinkled old man bowed as he passed. "Welcome, brother. We see few outsiders here at Dunaedan, much less men of the cloth."

"I follow God wherever he leads." The reply tripped smoothly off his tongue, having been used many times. "But it seems he arrived before me, and I have nothing to do."

"Ah, so you have met Father Bradan." The old man gave an almost toothless smile. "We have been converted here at Dunaedan for quite a number of years, though I am old enough to remember our druid. He, too, was a man of wisdom."

A flash of light drew Taranis's gaze to a steep, rocky bank on the west side of the inlet. "What is that?" He pointed at a cavity in the cliff wall.

"Nothing. A cave." The old man's nose wrinkled. "Carved out by the sea long before any of us were born."

"A cave?" Like a knot unraveling, warmth spread through his limbs. "Is there anything inside?"

"Not unless you reckon bird shit as something. It is nasty, brother. There are many caves in these cliffs."

A swirl of smoke appeared in the center of the cave mouth. It seemed to fuse and take shape, but the next instant it was gone.

The old man went on to the village and Taranis continued to explore. He passed above a sandy beach accented by blue-green shoals. Precipitous cliffs rose on the far side; just offshore a tall, narrow sea stack loomed; nearer to the beach, a wild jumble of treacherous, glistening boulders held their own against the roiling water. It was wild and pretty and the wind felt soft, cool rather than cold, which was a welcome change. He sat on the ground to rest, his back against a boulder, and so, when the girl came from the direction of the fort, she didn't see him. He watched her descend to the beach and wander, bending to examine stones or shells before she stepped close to the water. After some time, she leaned to the side and pulled off her headdress, tossing it carelessly to the sand and setting free two long, thick braids. She shook her head and unwrapped the ties, releasing a bright, coppery mass of hair that flowed past her hips. She filled her hands with it, shook her head again, and raised her face to the heavens as her hair streamed about her, following the whimsy of the breezes.

Taranis could not stop staring.

She continued to stand near the water, lifting the lower edge of her heavy tunic when the water threatened to dampen it, then all at once she turned and danced like a spirited foal. The breeze carried her laughter to his ears.

Eventually she pulled her hair over her shoulders, replaited it, and covered it again beneath the headdress. Picking up the shells she'd collected, she climbed to the plateau above the beach and walked away, towards the fort.

The girl's innocent, unaware actions affected him more than he would have expected. He allowed himself to fall into a reverie of twining and tangling himself in that burnished cataract of hair.

The day had grown old and the sun was setting when he returned to the boats. The fishermen and their women were leaving, headed for the fort and village. The tide was low; the boats rocked gently in their protected cove. But he hardly noticed. His gaze was locked on the cave. He didn't know why he needed to climb up there, but he had come too far not to finish.

It was not so high above an unruly pile of boulders. He used them to climb up and heaved himself over the edge, flattening his palms upon cold stone.

The stench made his eyes water. A pair of razorbills shrieked and flew out as he entered, the frightened beating of their wings loud in the enclosed space. The cave was no more than a basic half-moon, rock walls pocked with niches, almost all filled with nesting remains. Eggshells covered the ground along with a thick carpet of excrement.

No wonder it was undisturbed. It was disgusting.

The roof of the cave was too low for him to straighten completely. What had he expected? That glint could have been sunlight off a bird's feather, and the eddying wisp? Probably no more than smoke from one of the fishermen's fires, shaped by a breeze.

The rhythmic wash of the sea echoed off the walls.

He had almost convinced himself to leave when he saw two mice squeeze from a split in the rear wall, one after the other. They scurried down the rubble and ran from corner to corner before scrambling back up and vanishing into the split again.

He stepped closer. A draught of musty air puffed against his face. For the first time he noticed that while the walls to each side were dense black rock, this one was a chaotic patchwork of sand, stones, and pebbles. Intrigued, he put his fingers into the split and pulled. Stones and sand sloughed away; the flow of air increased. As he widened the split, the last of the sunlight revealed an open space. He crawled through, straightened, and extended his arms, hoping he wouldn't disturb bats or other unpleasant things. He had to rise up on his toes before he grazed the ceiling with the tips of his fingers, parts of which, he realized with growing fascination, were reinforced with stone blocks, as were the walls. He took a few steps more, into deep shadow. Certain he would soon run into a back wall, he felt his way forward, reminded vividly of his time in the underground labyrinth on Crete when he fought and nearly killed Lycus, the arrogant, ambitious bull-leaper.

The ocean was no more than a murmur now, giving way to the sound of his breathing and shuffling footsteps. Somewhere in the distance, water dripped.

The corridor went on and on. He felt it was leading him westward, back towards the fort. It must have taken years to construct. Could it be the remnants of an abandoned mine? The fisherman had claimed there was nothing in the cave but bird leavings. How was it possible that the people who lived here knew nothing of this singular achievement? Of course, the old man might have been lying.

After inching his way some distance farther, he discovered two offshoot corridors, one branching to the east and the other south. As he methodically felt his way around this junction, he stumbled over a ladder. It took him a long time and much stretching to find a square-shaped hole above his head. He propped the ladder into place and climbed, wishing he had a candle.

He emerged into another space. There was no light, but his hands told him that the floor and walls were completely enclosed in stone, rather than packed dirt. It was claustrophobic. He was only able to take two steps, both shoulders grazing the walls, before his foot collided with an obstruction. Bending, he ran his hands over the hindrance, and the one above it, and the one above that. A stone staircase. He ascended and soon came to a second flat space. His right hand brushed against a cold metal grip about waist high, and from there he discovered the outlines of a wooden portal, which reminded him of the rotted doors he had seen years ago in the ancient Roman fortress at Deva.

A couple of steps beyond this door, the staircase continued. The flat space was apparently a landing.

He pulled the metal handle. There was a click; something gave way and the panel opened. He tensed, ready to run. Before him was a chamber, dimly lit by several clay lamps on stands. Distant talk and laughter suggested a gathering of men.

He smelled onions, roasted meat, and other foodstuffs. Warily, he stepped over the threshold, scanning the room—a storeroom, perhaps —to make sure he was alone before turning to examine the panel. It was thick, yet he'd moved it with little effort, and it had opened soundlessly. While the side in the passageway was a framework of wood, this side was constructed of fitted stones that matched the rest of the wall. When closed, the seams would blend in and become invisible. The shelves affixed to this side of the door further disguised it, and moreover served to keep the floor in front clear. Holding onto the vertical edge, he moved the door, fascinated by whatever hidden mechanism made it swing so easily and quietly, but he was careful not to close it all the way as he saw no handle on the stone side, nothing to suggest how it could be opened from within this room.

The door was truly a marvel, but the food he'd consumed earlier was long gone and his stomach demanded he do something about it. He crossed to a table and grabbed two bannocks and a handful of almonds from the platters and bowls sitting there, stuffing one of the bannocks into his mouth immediately.

Approaching voices sent him running for safety. He used the iron handle to push the door closed and again heard a click as some hidden latch set. He waited, nervous and alert.

A woman laughed. There was some conversation he couldn't quite decipher, and the clatter of things being moved. Silence fell.

This must be the fortress of Dunaedan. He should retreat. There was no telling what they might do if he were caught.

But he was even more curious now. The steps continued. Where did they lead? The stale air suggested no one had been in here in a long time.

He felt much like Breda's old cat—the creature was always landing in thorny predicaments due to her inquisitive nature. He wavered, trying to convince himself to return to the cave, but he knew he wouldn't. Eventually, he shrugged and ascended.

Chapter 4

As Taranis pulled on the fifth door handle, he heard a man speak. "Bend over."

This was the first chamber he'd come to that was occupied.

"I don't like it that way," a woman said. "I want to lie in bed with you, look you in the eyes, and see you look at me."

"Bend over," the man repeated roughly. Taranis heard a cry of protest or pain, then nothing but grunts.

Taranis peered around the edge of the portal. A naked man, his back to Taranis, stood behind a woman who was bent over a bed, her arms outstretched. The man was pushing down on her spine with one hand as he thrust with his hips.

Taranis started to leave, but what the woman wailed made him pause.

"You do this so you can pretend I am your sister."

The man slapped her on the buttock. "I will cut out your tongue if you ever say that again."

He finished noisily, his head thrown back and his neck veins bulging before he slumped against the woman, but he didn't linger long. As he withdrew he slapped her again like one might a bothersome sheep and drank from a cup on a nearby table. Ale dribbled over his cheeks and through his beard.

She straightened, rearranging her gown. "I have loved you since I was a child, Nemausus." She wiped at the tears on her cheeks. "Why are you so odious, when I freely give everything you ask?"

The man pinched her chin. "You are in no way free to deny me whatever I want. I have had my fill of weeping women today. Get out."

Taranis didn't wait to see how their argument ended. He shut the portal and continued on, for the steps led ever upward in a spiral. The second door he'd opened had led into some sort of workroom, furnished with a long table, a brazier releasing pungent tendrils of smoke, and several stools and chairs. Wooden chests and parchments littered the table, held flat with smooth river stones. It appeared to be the sort of room where the lord of this place might conduct his official business. The third and fourth doors had opened into empty bedchambers.

He found yet another bedchamber at the next landing. A grey-haired woman lay snoring in a narrow bed.

By now he was convinced he was in Dunaedan's tower. It could be nothing else. He was climbing, unhindered, inside the actual structure he had dreamed of for nearly a score of years.

At last he came to the seventh and final door. Beyond this door there were no more stairs; the passageway ended in a wall of stone blocks. He pulled the iron grip and the timbered panel opened, but unlike the other rooms, his view was obstructed by a wall hanging. Most of the chambers he'd explored had them, probably to help keep in warmth. The weave was not tight; it was easy to part a few threads and peer through into another circular bedchamber, saved from utter darkness by three guttering candles and the embers in a brazier. The walls were draped with hangings, and rush mats insulated the stone floor. There was a curtained bed some distance from his vantage point. So far, it was about the same as the other bedchambers he'd seen.

He drew the weaving aside and entered, taking one step before pausing to listen, his senses drawn tight by now with strain.

His nose caught a faint but familiar scent. Instantly, his mind produced Aridela's face and memories of warm nights at her palace, in her opulent bed. He breathed in. When would he stop seeing her, hearing her voice, *smelling* her? Nineteen long years since the memories of Mycenae and Crete—*Kaphtor*—had hacked through his mind like axe blades through limbs. Since then he had known hardly anything but loneliness, guilt, and regret. He doubted that would ever change. It was his punishment, after all. Aridela's father, the bull-king Damasen, had condemned him to it.

The curse reverberated as if he were back in Alexiare's death chamber, hearing it for the first time. *You have set this world upon its path, and so you will live it. You will watch it unfold, and you alone will remember everything you have done.*

Emboldened by the silence, he advanced. But for the wall hangings, the room was rather barren, with only the bed, one chair, a wooden chest, and a single round table that looked as if it might once have been a wheel. He paused to examine the items on its surface: a cluster of dried wildflowers, a scattering of shells and stones, both halves of a broken bird's egg, a small skull, and a Bible. He opened the goatskin cover and admired the beautiful illustrations painted on fine vellum sheets. He had no trouble reading the Greek text. This was a priceless relic. How had it found its way here, to this desolate wilderness half a world away from its origin?

Picking up one of the candles, he drew back a corner of the bed curtain. Ah...the woman from the beach. In his mind he saw her unraveling her braids, shaking her head as if releasing a heavy burden.

Something else struck him and he was again pulled into memories of Crete. Aridela had slept in that position—on her side, mouth slightly open, one hand half-fisted beside her face.

The scent was stronger here.

Though he risked waking her, he brought the candle closer, holding his palm before the flame to keep it from glaring against her eyelids.

That scent. The way she was sleeping. He breathed in and closed his eyes, capitulating to indulgent fantasy.

Spicy night air drifted between the balcony pillars in Aridela's bedchamber. White draperies billowed. He gathered the queen of Crete's naked body against his and buried his nose in her hair.

I miss you.

Taranis opened his eyes, surprised to find his sight blurred by tears. The pain of his loneliness was terrible, yet he couldn't banish the memories of those days, before the Destruction, before Menoetius gave himself to the barley, before Aridela overheard Alexiare's damning confession.

The woman sighed. Her hand pressed closer to her face before relaxing, falling open. The candle flame sent dim illumination over the inside of her wrist.

Waves of ice flowed across his skin, followed by a nauseating flush of heat.

"Aridela." His whisper was magnified in the enclosed space and the candle flame leaped, throwing crazed shadows.

That mark. Aridela's birthmark, shaped like a bull's head.

He must put the candle down before he dropped it on her bed and set her on fire. Yet he remained.

What is happening? This woman looked nothing like his Cretan queen. Her skin was the color of cream, her hair gleaming like a freshly polished copper pot. She could have burned her wrist. He was allowing his imagination and the gaping hole in his heart too much power.

If only he could see her eyes. Then he would know.

He reached down and touched her hair. Light ran like flames along incandescent strands.

Despite his mind's silent warnings, he brushed the tips of his fingers against the mark.

She spoke. "Is it really you?"

He jerked backward, alarmed. But her eyes remained closed. Her words were slow and drawn out.

"My mother promised." After a brief silence, her head turned, first into her pillow then upward, towards the ceiling. Her eyelids trembled. "How do you breathe out of water?"

She is dreaming. He forced himself to retreat and once by the brazier, drew in and released several calming breaths. He clutched the necklace from Crete, wondering why it felt so hot.

If he woke her, she would be terrified. An unknown man looming above her bed? Undoubtedly she would scream. He could stop her, of course, with one hand, but the thought of her eyes glazed with terror....

Before he could push it away, the memory of Aridela's body slumping against his and the sound of her snapped neck roared in, raw and vivid. Shuddering, he set the candle on the chest and covered his face with his hands.

A soft rustle brought him out of his misery. He pivoted, afraid he'd awakened her after all. Nothing happened. Soundlessly, he returned and peered in. All lay in shadow but for a translucent cloud of purple, like a mist. Shooting through it was a dazzle of gold.

Her breathing was slow, even. She must be sleeping peacefully now. But even as he thought it, her breath caught. "What is your name, seolh-king?" she whispered.

Leave now, before fortune turns against you. He wasn't sure what his mind was suggesting, but he knew the advice was sound. Retreating to the open portal, he left the woman's bedchamber and pushed gently on the handle, listening to the tiny click of the latch as it set.

Chapter 5

THE AIR SMELLED DIFFERENT.

Eamhair got out of bed, sniffing. Many aromas filtered to her bedchamber, depending on the time of year and direction of the wind: moor grass, fish, malting barley from the brewery, roasting onions and spices from the kitchens, the reek of the pigsty, and the burning of the heather in some years, to keep it short and tender for grazing. Worst of all, when a strong wind blew from the south, she endured fumes from the tannery.

This was something else. Pushing her clothes chest beneath the narrow window, she climbed onto it, threw open the shutter, and rose up on her toes.

One day last summer, she'd slipped away from her duties to gather wildflowers not far from the seawaters of Uisge Bealach. It was windy, and storm clouds were building; as they engulfed her, they brought a distinct scent of approaching rain. What she smelled now was somewhat like that.

She closed her eyes. Now she smelled apples. Impossible!

The door to her chamber opened and Ula entered as she did every morning. "What are you doing up there?" She crossed to the brazier, added peat, and waved the smoke towards the open window.

"Good morrow, my mother." Eamhair conveyed a decent curtsy from her perch. "I smell something. I feel I have smelled it before, yet I cannot place it."

"You have a druid's nose. I can tell you these men would never catch such a subtle thing as a change in the air—unless it was blood. They are like ravens, the way they crave that smell."

"What could it be?"

"After we've finished prayers and fed the men, you can try to find it. I smell it too. It reminds me of the pine forests of my girlhood. They stretched so far you could walk a fortnight and not reach their limits."

"I long to see such a thing."

"This is a desolate place, starved of magic. I did glimpse a water spirit once—my people call them the *each-uisge*. It came up from one of the big sea lochs and cried at me. I think it was warning me of our defeat at the hands of Drost Gocinecht. I should have listened and run away. I was stronger in those days. I could have hidden. But it was nearly time for me to give birth to you, and after so many miscarriages, I was afraid of being alone when I went into labor."

Eamhair took her mother's extended hand and stepped off the chest. "Any woman would be."

Ula removed two woolen tunics from the chest and briskly shook them to dislodge any spiders and soften the wrinkles. "I am weary of beginning every day on my knees, pretending to honor a god I have never trusted. A god who hates us." She kept her voice low, for even here, at the top of the tower, even with the oak-hewn door closed, ears might be listening. "I have been thinking of a new story to tell you later, if we are left alone long enough. A story of my gods."

Eamhair loved her mother's stories. "Is it about Lugh?"

As she spoke she realized she was imagining Lugh—*of the flaming blue eyes*—as the wanderer who had kindly hauled her home on his tall stallion. In her mind he brandished the sword given to him by Manandán, Lord of the Sea—*The Answerer*—a weapon of such power that even the smallest wound from it inevitably proved fatal.

Ula nodded as she helped Eamhair dress. "His is a good story. You are drawn to Lugh because you, too, are bound to the sea. How I wish your father had not banned Lughnasadh. Some of my fondest memories are of the harvest festivals when I was young."

Eamhair adjusted a clean apron over her tunics and laced her leather shoes. "I remember you told me once that the stallion Manandán gave Lugh was tall, much taller than our horses, and that his mane and tail were made of sea foam."

The man's stallion had possessed a luxurious mane, with a forelock that draped flirtatiously across one large intelligent eye. The rest cascaded over his shoulders, almost to his knees. His tail had nearly reached the ground. Any woman would be overjoyed with such an abundance of hair as that horse possessed. She recalled the way he walked, lifting each hoof high, and how he arched his neck. So vain, and with good cause! It was easy to imagine his mane and tail being fashioned of spindrift.

Ula interrupted her thoughts. "Hurry, Eamhair, or Bericus will have something else to be angry about."

Eamhair tucked her braids under a veil as they hurried down the staircase.

"I would prefer to tell you more about the matriarch of my line." Ula leaned closer so she wouldn't be overheard. "The gods gifted her with a life of ten thousand years, so I have more stories than I could share in a decade. One of her names—the one I remember best—was Sorcha. Many knew her as the White Seer. She could change shape, and she could switch from female to male. It is written that she lived as a stag, a boar, and a sea eagle. She was the most dangerous of the gwiddonot, and in one life she was the famed Aife, Scathach's sister. She both hated and loved Cú Chulainn. But never did she enjoy life as much as when she lived in the sea, as a whale, a dolphin, an octopus, and a water horse, dancing among the tides with nothing to stop her but the earth. Why do I speak as though she is dead? I feel certain she lives on, somewhere, though we mortals can no longer see her."

"Why has magic been taken from us? Why did she have to go into hiding?"

"I don't know. There is a reason for everything—that is what I believe. She was the most acclaimed member of my tribe. I am proud to be her kin—as are you, being my child. She taught heroes and gave birth to others, men and women who have left their mark upon history." Ula squeezed Eamhair's arm then drew away as they entered the church. Bericus was suspicious of affection between women.

The intriguing scent teased through the psalms, vanishing and returning like a half-forgotten memory.

Under the watchful eye of Father Bradan, she and Ula obediently made the sign of the cross and bent their heads. Once that was finished, they were free to retire to the kitchens, where other women were already busy cutting bread, filling bowls with porridge, and piling meat left over from the night before.

Ula tended Brigit's flame before she did anything else, feeding it bits of sacred wood she bought from merchants and kept in a locked casket. She disguised the flame in the kitchens among the other fires, knowing that those who might destroy it would never see it for what it was. Men rarely entered this den of women, and if they did, one more fire meant nothing to them.

Jocosa, one of Dunaedan's most popular serving maids, came in with a basket of eggs, eager to share that Niall, Bericus's foremost archer and leader of his warriors, had returned from his morning rounds boasting of news.

Ula's brief nod gave Eamhair silent permission to sneak away and eavesdrop.

The fortress of Dunaedan possessed many chambers, nooks, and novelties. One such thing that only Eamhair and her mother knew about was an alcove above the timbered hall where the chieftain's men ate, drank, and socialized. A dusty old bearskin, rumored to have been hanging in that spot for a hundred years, disguised its presence; a staircase, hidden behind a wall at the back of the cooper's workshop, led up to it.

Eamhair was nine when she found the hidden door. She'd gone into the cooper's workroom to relay a message from her mother, but he was gone. While she waited for him, she stacked a disordered pile of iron rings against the back wall. When she had about ten neatly piled, she decided to see if she could climb them and touch the ceiling. She made it halfway before they toppled; as she flailed, her elbow struck the wall and the door opened, revealing an old wooden staircase. Wisely, she told no one but her mother of the discovery. Though she was only nine, she knew it would be taken away if anyone found out— the door mortared shut, the hiding place demolished.

Nowadays she had to bend over to avoid hitting her head as she passed through the portal, and step carefully, lest the rotted wood crumble under her weight.

Laughter and gossip rose to this spot, funneled perhaps by the way the walls curved inward at the ceiling. Even someone whispering could often be heard. Maybe Bericus's ancestor had constructed it that way on purpose.

Stepping over a nest of pink squirming newborn mice and a nervously squeaking mother, she peeked around the edge of the bearskin, drawing it back just enough to allow her to look down upon the long, smoky chamber without being seen. The boisterous shouting and coarse laughter were commonplace to her by now, so she ignored all that. The men drank, shoved, diced, wrestled, and made crude jokes she was not supposed to understand but did, and had for most of her life.

At first, the clamor drowned him out, but when Bericus slammed his ale jar onto the surface of the trestle table and roared, the hall grew quiet.

Niall rose, lifting his cup. "One of your turf-cutters, lord, a man called Cerdic, reported that an outsider has taken over the old hovel on the other side of Dhu Rinn, near the Point. Cerdic and a few others who have also spotted this interloper say a wolf follows him like a dog. They say he has the biggest warhorse they have ever seen—they claim it is seventeen hands at least. He has replaced the thatch and repaired some fencing."

It was her stranger! It had to be.

"So?" Eamhair watched her oldest brother, Nemausus, tip his jar and inspect its contents. He sounded half drunk already. "A peasant, hiding from his wife." There was a spurt of appreciative laughter. "We'll go along tomorrow and roust him out." He gulped in celebration of his own wit.

"This is no peasant," said Niall. "Weren't you listening? He has a stallion, *seventeen hands high*."

Bharosa.

"There is no horse in the world so tall."

"And a wolf."

Vita.

"A wolfhound. You know how stories grow in the telling."

Niall gave an irritated shrug. After a short silence, Bericus asked, "Well, Baron? Did you go and have a look?"

"I did, lord. No one was there, but there were signs. Hoof prints. And the repairs I mentioned. Someone has been there recently. Perhaps he was hunting."

"On *my* land?"

"I don't know. Possibly." The hovel lay beyond Bericus's authority, but of course Niall wouldn't dare correct him on the location of his boundaries.

"Did any of these men know his name?"

"No one I spoke to. They just saw him from afar."

There was a heavy, expectant pause as Bericus regarded Niall through squinted eyes and scraped the point of his dagger across the surface of the table. "Bring him to me," he said at last.

The man in the abandoned hovel east of Dhu Rinn was a mystery, and Bericus allowed no mysteries on the land he considered his own, though Drost Gocinecht, King of the Caledonii, would surely disagree.

Eamhair left the alcove and returned to the kitchens. A solitary man. A gigantic stallion. A wolf.... She'd believed the stranger who saved her from gruesome death had traveled on and was gone. She had experienced regret that made little sense.

You laugh sweetly, mistress.

As she fed peat to the fires and poured ale into pitchers, her mind wove fancies about his blue eyes, narrowed against the glare of the sun, the stubble on his cheeks, and the wicked scar beside his left eye. There had been that warm essence of leather when she sat upon his horse, and something else. She stopped pouring with an indrawn breath as realization swept over her. It was the same scent that had found a way through her window, and teased her into climbing onto her chest in search of it.

Was he hiding from a shrewish wife? Could he be a deserter from some tyrannical warlord?

She knew the hovel. It was quite remote, on the other side of Uisge Bealach, the wide sea inlet that marked the eastern boundary of her father's demesne—though of course the arrogant Bericus claimed the land beyond anyway. She had explored it once when Bericus and his sons went off hunting for several days, presenting her with rare and delightful freedom. The place was hardly more than a ruin, half buried among drifting sand dunes. She had invented stories about who built it—ancient seafaring people, or maybe even faeries, who used the hovel to creep out of their underground realms when they wanted to steal human babies and leave changelings behind.

It was a perfect place for someone seeking solitude—a desire she'd had her entire life. Solitude—to think her thoughts and choose her own course.

She was helping her mother prepare bannocks when Jocosa ran into the kitchens, crying that he had come. The foreigner was in the hall, conversing with Bericus.

"The chief has called for drink and food." Jocosa's cheeks bloomed with telltale color.

The women put a tray together. When it was ready, Eamhair saw

Jocosa smoothing her headdress and apron as she prepared to carry it in.

"You have too much to do." Eamhair seized the tray before the little maid could say a word and made off with it, throwing back, "Have a drink and warm yourself at the fire."

The hall was deserted but for the two men sitting at the chief's table on the dais. She walked towards them, between walls strung with shields and animal skins, past the bear hide that disguised her secret alcove, through pools of hazy sunlight filtering through greased, stretched parchment set over high windows. Hardly noticing the smoke of the hearth fires and charred smell of pork, she took the opportunity to study the stranger.

His face was turned away. She saw only part of one cheek and the back of his head. He wore no hood today and his cloak was pushed off his shoulders; Eamhair saw it was lined with supple fur—perhaps badger. His hair was confined with leather ties and silver clasps. As she approached, he removed his gauntlets and dropped them on the table.

No amount of blinking could erase the suggestion of a bluish haze curling around him. What was it? Could Bericus see it too? She had not noticed this on the cliffs.

The tension between the two almost sparked. Bericus's perusal was accusatory, the kind of boring stare that caused trepidation when it landed on her. Drumming his fingers on the table, he spoke in a tone that countenanced no deception. "One glance tells me you have seen battle. Do I hear something of Dalriada in your speech? Have you joined in the campaigns against Artorius, the man they call 'the Bear'?"

"I have fought in a few skirmishes," was the stranger's oblique reply, along with an inclination of the head.

"For Domangart? I have heard he is a worthy warrior as well as king."

"He can be, when he wishes."

Bericus's glower indicated this answer did not satisfy. "What do men call you then?"

"Cailean, lord."

"If you have been part of the fighting against Artorius, then you are an ally to Drost Gocinecht, who is my overlord these days. He would want me to treat you well. Unfortunately, you are a poacher and possibly a deserter, and you have trespassed on my land. But I feel generous, so I will give you a choice. Will you fight for me here at Dunaedan, or pay me for the game you have stolen? Yea or nay."

Ah. No man who lived and worked Bericus's land could refuse anything he asked. No woman either, if the truth were known.

Cailean sighed. "I am not a deserter, lord. I was wounded, and sent away to re—"

Eamhair set the tray on the table between them, gasping at an unexpected scuffle beneath her feet. She hadn't seen the wolf, disguised as it was by the table, the dim light, and its own dark pelt. It rose, its teeth gleaming, and she saw that it was, indeed, the same wolf. Unfriendly as ever. She froze.

Distracted by this interruption, Cailean gave her a perfunctory glance before returning his attention to the chief. The next instant his eyes snapped back, sharpening into a squint.

"No, Vita," he said. The wolf covered its teeth and dropped back beneath the table.

Heat crawled up Eamhair's neck and over her cheeks. She placed a dish piled with their best bread and meat before him and poured wine into the carved silver horn reserved for guests, watching him from the corner of her eye. When she finished, she bowed her head and murmured, "Dunaedan welcomes you."

He abruptly blinked and turned away.

"My daughter, Eamhair." There was a note of warning in Bericus's voice. Eamhair had heard it before—many times.

Cailean rose and bowed.

His height again struck her. He and his stallion were well matched.

"*Lady* Eamhair." The mockery was so subtle as to be nearly inaudible. He took her hand and kissed her knuckles. She curtsied, drawing in a breath at the shock-like tingle that radiated from his lips and fingers. Men had kissed her hand before, but she had never felt a kiss penetrate her flesh and flow into her blood like a thousand invisible lightning bolts.

He frowned too as he regarded her hand.

When he lifted his gaze, she saw that same unearthly glow. Dark, dark blue, his eyes were set beneath lowered brows that reminded her of an eagle's. It was hard to look away.

"You were saying?" Bericus spoke crisply. "A wound bothers you?"

"Nay." Cailean plucked one of his gauntlets from the table and worried it in his fist. "Not any longer."

"Then give me your answer."

Eamhair knew she risked drawing a rebuke or even a clout if she lingered. She walked away, breathless in the pause, sensing the warrior's awareness of her.

"I would be honored to serve you, lord," she heard him say just before she stepped out of earshot.

She smiled. "Cailean," she whispered.

Chapter 6

"THERE YOU GO AGAIN." BRAN RIPPED INTO A CHUNK OF SALTED MUTTON and chewed loudly. "I've already told you the trouble you're asking for."

Cailean averted his gaze from the chief's unaware daughter. Bran was too perceptive for his own good, but he was right—staring was dangerous.

Bran grinned. "You live like an old man. Come with me to the whorehouse, brother. Enough ale and what lies between a woman's legs will make you forget what you can never have."

Cailean tapped his heels against Bharosa's flanks. "You might be happy to sit and talk until the sun sets, but I would like to finish this chore. I'm starving and I didn't bring anything to eat."

With a mocking laugh, Bran kicked his own horse and they galloped out of Dunaedan's south gate to begin the usual morning circle around the fort, the village, and the land, checking for signs of invasion, poaching, flooding, pestilence, or any other problem that might put Bericus in a foul mood.

Bran didn't know it, but this was Cailean's second reconnaissance of the morning. It was his habit to patrol at dawn, as he liked the solitude, so he saw what everyone else missed—Eamhair stealing through the north gate most mornings and some evenings, if her father and brothers were occupied elsewhere. He had watched her race across the moor to the nearby cliffs and wander among them, quick, strong, sure-footed as a goat. She favored two little beaches to the east, where the water shifted between deep blue and iridescent green. He doubted many knew of these escapes, as the north gate was rarely sentried; who would attack from the north? The cliffs guarded things well enough.

Cailean hadn't lived at Dunaedan two days before receiving his first warning about Eamhair. *The chief or his sons will kill any one of us who dare speak to her without permission—even looking at her will get you the lash, and some say worse is done to her.* Bran had punched him on the shoulder. *If you value your manhood, you'll obey, as we all do.*

He was bothered by other tidbits he'd overheard. The possessiveness her father and brothers displayed was not, apparently, due to love but because Drost Gocinecht had claimed her when she was newly born. It was the payment he demanded for the loss of his son, whom Bericus had unwisely killed.

Did that mean Drost intended to marry her himself? Over a score of years had passed and Drost did not seem inclined to either marry the girl or release her so she could marry someone else.

Cailean and Bran paused on a hill above the little beach where Eamhair liked to spend time.

Bran rummaged through his pouch and brought out a squashed heel of rye bread. "You should know that no man has successfully tempted Bericus to part with his daughter, though many have tried."

Cailean watched foam caress the sand and said nothing.

"Well of course you know that, since she is still here. Still unwed. Still his well-protected, virgin daughter, though surrounded by men, and almost too old by now for anyone to want her."

"I have no interest in Bericus's daughter." Cailean spoke curtly.

Bran merely snorted this time, but it grated no less on Cailean's nerves. "Have you noticed that cup Bericus likes to drink from? The one with the red stones?"

"I have." The engraved copper cup was inset with three large rubies. It was something one would expect to see in the hand of a king. Of course he'd noticed it.

"A prince gave it to him. At least he claimed to be a prince. His skin was almost black, his clothing smooth and shiny as an eel's. He offered Bericus a chest filled with those stones. He called them *ratnaraj*. He told us how the warriors in his country cut themselves open at the groin, armpit, wrist, and throat, and insert shavings. They believe making the stones part of their flesh gives them invincibility in battle.

He had done it—we all saw the slivers under his skin. They also bury them beneath the foundations of their king-halls to bring luck and strength. That prince, and all his men, were covered in those stones—like blood turned to crystal," he said poetically, before snorting. "I suppose he could have been lying about being a prince, but he was rich. Of that I am certain, and he was willing to make Bericus rich as well. All Bericus had to do was give him Eamhair."

Cailean couldn't help but be intrigued. "Why journey so far and try to win a girl you have no chance of winning? Why does Bericus risk Drost Gocinecht's vengeance?"

"You truly do not understand? You should, for I swear you yourself have fallen head first into the legend—and without even a sip of the cursed ale. There is a look in your eyes, Dalriada, which I have seen before. The longer she is withheld, the more exotic she becomes, like one of those *ratnaraj* stones. She is a challenge no man can resist." He stuffed the bread into his mouth and went on talking around it. "And he hates Drost Gocinecht. I think one reason he does it is simple, foolish defiance. Aye, he will pay the price one day. I'm surprised Drost has let it go on this long."

"Is he an imbecile? She'll be the one who suffers the most."

But the king of the Caledonii lived far away and seldom visited, so Bericus went on brazenly dangling his virgin daughter before every man who happened through the area. According to Bran, he had been doing so since she was twelve, parading her, suggesting she could be won for the highest price, the most entertaining phrase, the richest gift, or an impressive feat. He never fully committed himself, but kept every arm ring, every gemstone, and every scrap of silver he was offered. He must be as rich as two kings by now, and still men came as if spellbound, longing to be the one who achieved triumph in a sea of castoffs.

Bran grunted at the idea of Eamhair suffering. "I cannot say for certain how it was done, but as soon as she was deemed old enough to marry, the tales multiplied. Bericus probably paid bards and merchants to spread stories about her. She is more glamour than woman now. Men come from near and far, not only from the land of the Britons, from Hibernia and your own Dalriada, but from much farther—Hispania, Armorica, Gaul—even farther than that, from places with names I cannot pronounce. Like that prince's homeland—I have forgotten what he called it. Some outlandish word."

It didn't matter in the end, whether Eamhair of Dunaedan was innocent or sinful, beautiful or ugly, whether she was of the purest bloodline or the worst. The challenge was all. What man did not dream of prying her from her avaricious father, of proudly displaying her like a hard-won war trophy?

Bran scratched crumbs from his beard and picked at his teeth with a grimy fingernail. "Every year the number of suitors increases. Bericus welcomes them, gives them food, drink, and a place to sleep. He suggests they will surely have a chance. But all are spurned eventually, no matter who they are or what they bid. He keeps their gifts and sends them on their way beggared and shamed." Shaking his head, he added, "I myself am immune, having known her since she was a squalling red-faced infant. You cannot want what you think of as a sister. Oh—and of course I never drink the ale."

Bran chattered on while Cailean succumbed to irritation.

Why am I here? I only meant to stay in that hovel a month or two, then light the beacon and go home.

But from the instant he looked into those dark eyes, he'd been trapped in a way, bound into Dunaedan's fate and hers.

Why hadn't she told him she was the chieftain's daughter?

Because Bericus is an arrogant, greedy fool.

Go home early, Cailean's father had said, planting a big, callused hand on his son's shoulder. *Rest. Let your mother and sister spoil you, and enjoy your harvest festival. Heal, son. Come back to me strong. I need you. Oh…and tell your mother—*

I know. You love her.

Cailean glanced at Bran, but knew he was safe. Bran was a friendly, honest, innocuous giant. He would never tell Bericus that Cailean had called him an imbecile.

As they passed the boundary cairns and started back to the fort, Bran offered the tidbit he'd held in reserve. "Some of us suspect Bericus is nursing another plan. We think he intends to collect as much silver as he can from these gullible suitors, and when he has enough, if that day ever comes, he will purchase an army to defeat Drost Gocinecht. Once Drost lies dead at his feet, he'll take Eamhair for himself or give her to one of his sons, in the ancient manner."

Startling fury erupted. Cailean's hands clenched; inadvertently he jerked the reins, causing Bharosa to shake his head in protest. Visions of sinking his blade into that bastard's gut flashed through his mind. In a voice gone hoarse, he said, "The Church banned such customs."

"Bericus cares only for himself and his sons. He uses the Christ for control. He would abandon religion tomorrow if it no longer served his needs." Bran bit his lips and scowled. "Once when Nemausus was drunk, he said something...."

"What?"

"He said every man who comes here wants to be the one to win the right of untying her blindfold, pulling off the headdress, and stripping her, bit by bit until nothing is left, and there is nowhere for her to hide. It was obvious to me he had spent a good amount of time picturing it."

Cailean gritted his teeth as they neared the fort, too angry to trust what might come out of his mouth.

Three times he'd glimpsed Eamhair on the cliffs. She was always alone. Did she have no friends? Not even a maidservant willing to walk with her? The women who followed his father's army were close and loyal, always sharing, laughing as they toiled, and offering comfort when one of their men died.

He was certain Eamhair's father knew nothing of her wanderings. Bericus would surely put a stop to it if he found out, for fear of a crafty suitor making off with her if not concern that she might fall into the ocean.

Cailean didn't want her to lose what might well be her only pleasure. He had watched her sing, draw designs in the snow, feed the birds, and climb among the rocks as though the test gave her joy. The seals allowed her to pet them, and barked mournfully when she left. He had witnessed her cuddle a white-furred stoat—had seen it lick her cheek. One morning, as the rising sun sent golden light careening across the water, she had torn off her ugly veil and loosened her hair, giving him a sight he would not soon forget. He knew few men could boast of ever seeing that radiant mass of waves, for her father made sure it was kept hidden beneath coverings that allowed no glimpse of it. Bericus forced all the females of Dunaedan, young and old, to garb themselves in dreary veils and bulky gowns. Cailean missed the riots of color he was accustomed to, the rich blues and greens, bright yellows and vivid crimsons, as well as the more tranquil shades of violets, creams, and pale oranges. At home, even the air had color.

Her stance when she went back to the fort was markedly different, her walk slow, her shoulders slumped. That glorious joy retreated, stuffed inside like it didn't exist.

He took to rising even earlier, waiting and following, circling like a predator. He would never allow her to know he was there, but if anything were to threaten her, he could quickly intervene.

This very morning, not knowing her father's newest warrior was observing her, she had climbed down to her beach, kilted up her skirts to mid-calf, and waded into the water, disappearing beyond a small protruding bluff. She was gone a long while. After she reappeared and returned to the fort, he went down and found a narrow cave, hidden from the main part of the beach. Its mouth pointed outward at the ocean, and it was only accessible by wading several steps across a sandy underwater bridge. A collection of shells and a crude wooden cup sat upon a natural ledge. The rocky floor was still wet from high tide.

A haven of sorts, where she spent her free time.

Several days after his reconnaissance with Bran, while rubbing down Bharosa, he remembered the dried rowanberries his mother had asked him to bring her for some remedy or other. He dug them out of his satchel and created a bracelet, strung with linen thread he begged from one of the maidservants. Early the next morning, he took it to the cave and left it beside the cup.

He would protect this strange, lonely girl, and her secrets, though he was not sure why.

Chapter 7

Eamhair scrambled down the slope to her beach. The sun hadn't quite risen, though a hazy blush showed her where to put her feet. Frost lay heavy over the rocks; the bentgrass was white and stiff, and crackled as she stepped on it.

She hurried across the sand and waded into the water, holding up her skirts. Though the whole coast felt as though it was encased in ice, she thought the water didn't seem as cold as the last time she had come.

The flat, angled stone near the center of the little cave was dry. She sat on it, pulling her knees to her chest and drawing her cloak close around her legs.

It was damp and chilly. If she'd stayed in bed, she would be warm right now. But this hour of the day was the only time she could readily escape Dunaedan. She wouldn't stay long—just until the sun rose. When Prime came, she would be sitting obediently beside her mother at the morning psalms.

The sun crested the horizon. A blaze of gold and scarlet shot across the ocean, illuminating frothy whitecaps. She sighed. She didn't want to go.

A quintuplet of seals left the water, passing by the cave mouth on their way to the beach. She kept motionless so they wouldn't notice her and was surprised when they squirmed past again in the opposite direction, vanishing quickly into the sea. Something had frightened them.

She heard male laughter and the yipping of a dog. What she saw when she rose and peered around the edge of the rock that hid her cave nearly made her gasp out loud and give herself away.

It was Cailean, and his wolf, and Bran, and a brawny warrior called Owain, who had wrestled Cailean when he first came to Dunaedan and Bericus was testing his skill.

As she watched, the three men stripped off their cloaks, boots, tunics, and leggings, tossing everything carelessly onto the sand. When all three were naked, yes *naked*, they waded and dove into the water, shouting at the glacial chill, laughing and calling each other crude names. The wolf joined them, yipping and leaping.

She suppressed a giggle. Three naked men, thinking themselves quite alone. And she must make sure they continued to think so. She kept still as stone, praying to Divine Brigit the wolf wouldn't catch her scent.

Gradually, as she watched them cavort, shouting and tussling like stags in a rut, their breath rising in clouds around their faces, her embarrassment receded and her fascination grew. Predators, all four, taking a rare respite from the daily work of hunting, killing, and guarding to splash, laugh, and release energy built up from being confined too long in a cramped, airless fortress. They were *beautiful*, their gloriously rippling muscles, wet, sleeked back hair, and white scars hypnotizing.

Cailean was not massive like Owain, nor hulking like Bran, but taller than either of them, leaner, built rather like his wolf. His hair was longer too; the winding plait fell clear to his buttocks. This was a new tidbit of knowledge for her, as he always kept it tucked beneath his clothing. A raised, reddened wound marred the flesh over his ribs.

He dove into the water and emerged without warning underneath Owain, tossing him up and over. They all three laughed as Owain surfaced, sputtering.

She stared her fill, expecting she would never see such a thing again as long as she lived.

Eamhair continued to wait after the men left, cautious of the wolf's sense of sight and smell.

As she prepared to wade across the dip between the cave and the beach, she glanced behind her and spotted something on the rock shelf, vividly red, bright even in the gloom. She returned and picked up an ornament she was certain had not been here before.

It was a bracelet crafted of dried rowanberries, each one pierced through its center and held in place with knotted thread, creating a continuous intertwined pattern like that favored by the Caledonii.

More than a few rowans survived in crevices along the cliffs. She and her mother had tried making wine from the berries, though it hadn't turned out well, and tinctures for stomachaches, which had worked better.

The bracelet was big enough to slide over her hand and halfway up her forearm. She crossed to the cave mouth where she could see it in the light. It was a beautiful thing; crafting it must have taken much patience.

Who had made it? Why had it been put in her cave? Had she been meant to find it? A shiver ran over the nape of her neck and across her shoulders. She felt as though someone was watching.

In all the years she had come this cave, she had never seen anyone else. No one had ever mentioned it or suggested they knew it was here.

But obviously, someone did know.

She held out her arm, admiring the workmanship.

One day, when your need is greatest, the king of the seolhs will appear, Ula had once promised. He would rescue her, Ula declared, from some unfathomable peril.

Had the seolh-king put the bracelet here, knowing she would find it?

Faery tales! she scoffed. *Ula invented that story to distract you when you were little and your brothers made you cry.*

She spoke severely to the ocean waves. "Eamhair, Ula's daughter, is sworn to Drost Gocinecht—*payment* for the loss of his son. If he decides he doesn't want her, she will be sold to another man of Bericus's choosing."

The ocean offered no argument.

She waded to the beach and ascended the slope, her gaze drawn again and again to the beauty and intricacy of the bracelet.

Hopefully, no one had noticed her absence except her mother. Ula noticed everything.

Chapter 8

TARANIS SET THE LAST PEBBLE IN PLACE AND DABBED MUD, AUGMENTED with sand, around it. He could never again use this entrance at the fishermen's cove, not without breaking down the wall he'd just finished sealing.

He picked up the clay lamp he'd taken from the fort and inspected his work. From this side, not a single speck of daylight penetrated. Later, he would climb up from the mooring area and check the outside. If no one knew of these tunnels—he'd decided they were originally intended as escape routes, and somehow, knowledge of them was lost —then disguising every entrance would help keep it that way. He wasn't sure why he wanted to preserve the secret. He did rather like being able to wander undetected through a fortress teeming with warriors. He liked eavesdropping. He especially liked standing at the bedside of the young woman and imagining her as Aridela, and had been doing that every night for the last half-month. He kept in reserve the possibility of revealing the existence of the tunnels to the chief of this place, but he had already overheard enough about Bericus to be wary of that idea. The man was unstable and bloodthirsty, and might be just as inclined to kill him for the information as reward him.

There were three tunnels—this one, which led to the staircase and door panels, another meandering south some distance beyond the village, and the longest, winding away to the east, an incredible structure carved through earth and rock, bolstered with massive stone blocks and further supported with thick oak archways.

Armed with his lamp, he had carefully examined each passage and determined the only recent footprints in the dirt were his own. The air was stuffy, and there were a few places where the shoring had caved in.

He had also learned a means of choking off the longest tunnel. At two different spots along that corridor, iron handles stuck out of the walls, one on either side. Taranis had fiddled with one and discovered that pulling it caused a rusty portal to slide down inside the wall, releasing an enormous cache of rubble and stones that barricaded half of the space. Were he to pull the opposite handle, he was sure the tunnel would fill completely. It was an ingenious method of stopping or slowing enemy pursuit.

The exit, hidden behind a tangle of stunted trees, thistles, and brush, led into a narrow cove—an offshoot of the wide, sandy sea inlet he had seen in his dream. That and the southern exit were so remote and well concealed that he decided to leave them, although he did further obscure the southern exit with stones. His explorations had convinced him no one and nothing other than wild pigs and perhaps a wolf or two had entered them in years. Besides, if he blocked all the entrances, the air would go bad, and if he did need to use them to escape, he couldn't.

The hidden doors inside the fortress were cunningly engineered. A divot in a seam on the upper left side released the catch when pushed, and reset with a nearly soundless click when the door closed. The builder had shrewdly placed the divot higher than most people could reach. Taranis had to stand on tiptoe and stretch as far as possible.

Satisfied with his pebble and mud work, he returned to the spot where he'd set up his bedding and supplies—wool blankets, sheep-skins, candles, lamps and flint, food and ale, and chests to keep every-thing safe from rats. He was confident he could hide here indefinitely. He couldn't decide whether or not to steal clothing; if he were discovered, his habit might offer protection from punishment, and was all he had left to identify him as a monk; the tonsure had completely grown out during his journey.

It was remarkable how he, an interloper, had stumbled upon some-thing so secret and valuable the very day he arrived, while the inhabi-tants who had lived here their entire lives remained unaware.

He thought of that smoke he'd glimpsed. It had vanished so

quickly he wasn't sure it had actually been there—but it had served to draw his eye, hadn't it?

The cave had appeared in every occurrence of his dream. And there was that inexplicable obsession to leave his home and search for the dream's source.

What good fortune that a traveling merchant, one with knowledge of Dunaedan, had happened upon Taranis's humble village, had asked for a prostitute, and had been sent to his mother.

I see Athene's hand in all of this.

The only thing he didn't like about living in the tunnels was the boredom. Time passed slowly as he waited for the relative freedom of night, when he could forage and explore.

To allay it somewhat, he would often climb the staircase, listening whenever he heard voices through the walls. Some he heard clearly, suggesting the speakers stood nearby, and others were incomprehensible. Laughter floated through as though there was no barrier at all.

This time, when he paused outside the storeroom, he heard a woman complaining about the absence of the chief's wife and daughter. *Lady Ula,* she said, *and that lazy chit, Eamhair. Where are they? There is so much to do.*

He climbed on, disinterested in the trials of kitchen wenches.

His mind strained towards the chamber at the top of the stairs. At this time of day the young woman was never in her bedchamber, but still he climbed. There was nothing else to do. Every now and then a new treasure appeared on her table.

What is your name, seolh-king?

He pondered what he knew. The woman collected trinkets from the land. Her sleep was lively with curiosities and fantastical creatures. She was likely torn between two religions—one ancient, exhaling from the land like mist, the other new, bound up inside buildings marked with crosses. Perhaps, in the privacy of her bedchamber, she prayed not to the Christos, but to older gods and goddesses.

How do you breathe out of water?

He rounded the last section of the staircase. Maybe she prayed to seolhs.

Aridela had always believed that Athene brought them together. She had believed in him as well, even when everyone else hated him. Until the end.

The room at the top of the tower was an irresistible lodestone mutating him to iron. It hinted at the gossamer enchantment of strong wine, a bewitching song, or a captivating story. Only in that chamber could he believe in the promise of impossible wishes.

EAMHAIR PULLED ULA ASIDE. "LOOK WHAT I FOUND." SHE HELD UP HER arm. "You made it, didn't you?"

"Nay." Ula frowned at the bracelet, watery-eyed.

"Who could have done it, if not you?" Eamhair's heartbeat quickened. *Could it have been the seolh-king?*

"A faery, maybe. It looks like their work. This is ready," Ula said to one of the maids, and gave her a platter piled with loaves of bread. "Take it to the hall before they eat each other, or worse, eat us." When the woman had gone, she sighed heavily. "Come along with me, Eamhair."

She led her daughter out of the kitchens, across the yard to the hall, into the tower and up the stone staircase to the top.

Closing the door behind them, she stirred the embers in the brazier and they sat near it on stools. "My bones hurt," she said. "This winter feels colder than usual. I long for warmth. I miss the drone of the corncrakes. One always knows summer is coming when the corncrakes come back from wherever they've been hiding."

It was obvious by her mother's grave expression and this need for privacy that she had something to say besides a complaint about the cold, so Eamhair wasn't surprised when Ula stated, "Four men have come. Bericus has ordered a feast for tomorrow night."

Eamhair's stomach turned and her pleasure in the bracelet was spoiled.

Whenever gossip and legend drew men to Dunaedan, Eamhair's smallest freedoms were revoked; she was locked in her bedchamber so would-be suitors could not accidentally catch a glimpse of her until the perfectly arranged point at the time of Bericus's choosing.

After years of practice, Bericus's men were adept in the methods of shaming suitors who displayed signs of parsimony. Those unfortunates were scorned and evicted, usually on their heads, at which point the warriors began the real work—escalating the manipulation and rivalry of those who remained. Much ale was consumed as competitive wagers drove the price higher. Only after the suitors were drunk and fleeced of everything they had or could lay their hands on, only then was Eamhair brought forth, like a precious icon on a sacred day. She was blindfolded "to protect her innocent mind," adorned in a special gown that revealed even as it disguised, and her hair was tucked away beneath a veil but for one gleaming lock allowed to curl over her breast, "to inflame the imagination."

Tucked against her father's arm like a plump young doe before starving men, Eamhair traversed the length of the hall, through silence so abrupt and complete she could hear the drumming of her heart and the rasp of her slippers through the rushes. Silence that vibrated with a beat of anticipation. Of lust. It would have been bad enough if the men staring at her would be gone come morning, but her father's men were there as well. Men who lived at Dunaedan, men she would occasionally speak to. For years, she had seen her humiliation reflected in their eyes.

When it was done, one of her brothers would return her to her bedchamber, taunting her with crude and graphic threats about how she would be sold to the richest, the most gullible.

Eamhair was twelve when the bartering started. As suitors appeared at Dunaedan's gates with ever increasing frequency and Bericus's greed swelled, Ula took her away to the cliffs where they would not be overheard. "I have a story for you," she said. Such an announcement usually thrilled Eamhair but not this time. Fear and anger issued from her mother in palpable waves.

"One year ago, I was approached by a young woman who asked for a love potion." She paused, staring out over the ocean. "I thought nothing of it. I often have such requests. A month later she returned, begging to be my apprentice, claiming someone would need to carry on my knowledge after I was gone. I thought that was wise, and took her into my confidence. I taught her many spells, along with healing arts. She was a good novice. The love potion was of particular interest to her—she begged to know exactly how I made it, so I showed her the combination of heather with yeast and honey and taught her the method of fermentation and the necessary spell casting. A few days later, she was found dead, her throat cut. I mourned her. But not long after, one of the kitchen maids told me she had seen my apprentice with Bericus, speaking in whispers. It made me suspicious so I cast a seeing spell. I saw Bericus and the old druid in a chamber, circled by pots and curling, half-burned parchments. I thought this strange, because Bericus had run him out of Dunaedan before you knew how to walk. I hadn't seen him in years and thought I would never see him again. The spell didn't show me the dead girl at all.

"I found the druid. I don't think Bericus knew that he and I had once been close. Even so, I had trouble getting him to confide in me. When he finally did, he told me the girl had been paid by Bericus to discover the secret of the love potion. After she gave it to him, he forced the old druid to decipher the formula and show him, step by step, how to make it. In fact, together they increased its power. Mine was a subtle help—a suggestion to the senses. What he concocted was a slave-maker."

Hesitantly, Ula admitted, "Bericus killed the girl, you see. He no longer needed her, and death prevented her from betraying him. Later, he again banished the druid—or something worse. I suspect my old friend is dead as well."

Eamhair hadn't understood. She wasn't yet thirteen when Ula made this confession; the parading was still new. "Why did he want your potion?" Even then she knew Bericus had no fondness for his wife, or interest in cultivating any love between them.

"He infuses it into the ale—special ale kept in reserve for the men who come here, seeking to win you. It winds down into the core of their bellies—it adds a shine to their sight and sends their blood pumping. By the time you are brought out, they are lost inside it, and what they see, as you pass before them, is not an ordinary young girl but the essence of all their desires—everything they have ever longed for."

Ula's story made everything clear. Magic was a natural thing. It was easy to believe Bericus would use it to further his own ends.

"Some of those men die here," Ula told her. "The potion blinds them, steals their reason. They burn, and in the burning are willing to tear down the tower to get to you. Bericus's warriors are always armed, always ready. Those who lose control are slaughtered and thrown from the cliffs. Those who don't are sent on their way, yet I suspect they are never the same. They only remember the perfect, untouched maiden with skin like milk and one curl of hair the color of a sunrise. That is how the saga was born, and that is how it keeps growing. Those rejected men spread Bericus's sorcery like fertile seed-pods. More men come, seeking this goddess among women—and they are not about to admit they were tricked." She stroked Eamhair's cheek, adding, "You are the loveliest being in the world to *me*, gifted and quick and able to see what is hidden in everything. But there is nothing about you, child, that a loutish man would be able to recognize as special. Their vision is not that refined."

Taking Eamhair's hands in her own, she made her point. "If any of these men—if any man—ever gets you alone, he will cajole you. He will speak gentle poetry and make his eyes soft. If you succumb to the flattery, Eamhair, you know what could happen. You could bear that man's child, or die trying to stop it. And where will he be, the one who had his way with you? Off in some other land boasting about how he had the girl no one else could touch. You will face your father and brothers alone." She shuddered. "It does not bear thinking of. Never allow these stories to turn your head, my love. You are a girl like any other, and you can be caught like any other. Guard your virginity as carefully as Bericus does. He and I are of one mind on this matter, but for different reasons—he wants to use you. I want to save you."

"I will never be fooled," Eamhair promised, and she never was. Ula knew what she was talking about. Through the years, Eamhair had been cornered—once by a traveling merchant, once in the granary by a suitor bolder and more devious than the others, and once by the most reckless of her father's men—a fellow by the name of Hadden, who was later put to death. None of them had ever tempted her and thankfully, none forced the issue. Ula gave weight to her warning by taking Eamhair along to help with labor and birthings, not just to the lying in of the village women, but also Dunaedan's whores. Seeing women labor and often die, listening to so many bewail and curse their fate, watching small children lose their joy early, grow pinched from hunger and neglect, thoroughly jaded whatever romantic ideas Eamhair might have begun to entertain as she grew older.

No matter how soft the eyes, gentle the words, or handsome the face, Eamhair walled away her heart and remained virgin. Some called her aloof and proud. They couldn't know she was afraid. She didn't want to be torn from someone she loved and placed in the hands of a stranger, who could do whatever he wished with her.

All this ran through her mind as she sat with Ula at the brazier in her chamber. She heard the noise and bustle of slaves and servants making preparations outside the tower. Tomorrow the hall would ring with music. Extra candles would be lit. There would be roasted pig, their finest bread made from double-boulted flour, plates of cheese, and pastry pies steaming with succulent game birds. Eamhair heard the alewife barking orders as the oak casks were carried to the hall— one filled with concocted ale for the suitors, another for the men of Dunaedan.

And she would be led out like a fatted calf at the autumn fair.

Ula's chin quivered. Tears filled her eyes. "Bericus and your brothers have conjured a powerful illusion, and the men who come here are truly under the spell before they ever arrive. Sometimes I doubt he needs the cursed potion to achieve his ends."

Running a hand over the rowanberry bracelet, she said, "You say you found this?" At Eamhair's nod, she added thoughtfully, "I suppose a faery may have woven it—they love to play tricks. But it could have been the seolh-king himself." She rubbed away the tears, sighing. "Does he not realize the danger you're in? Not only from your father and brothers. Drost Gocinecht is sure to wreak vengeance upon Bericus for this trickery. I fear that day more than any other, Eamhair. He will burn this fortress and everyone who lives here to ashes. How I wish the seolh-king would come and take you away."

"But Mother, I don't want to be separated from you. Not ever."

"You would be safe, Eamhair. That is all that matters to me. I wish he would appear now. Today. Fear for you has stolen any comfort I have ever known."

Behind the wall hanging, Taranis watched and listened. So this was the chief's wife, and the girl who so intrigued him was the chief's daughter. *Eamhair.* Unfortunately, Eamhair had her back to him. He hadn't yet seen her eyes.

The bedchamber door flew open and a bearded young man entered.

"Ah, you're here, little wealth maker. Father sent me to lock you up. You," he added, glancing coldly at the older woman, "why are you here? There is much to do before tomorrow and you must supervise."

Both women rose from their stools. The older one hugged the younger.

"Come, Mother." The man scowled.

Sniffling, the older woman allowed herself to be pulled away. She and the man left, and Taranis heard a bolt being fastened on the outside of the door.

The girl sighed and faced the brazier, holding out her hands to the heat, but she soon left the fire and dragged the wooden chest beneath her only window, an opening no wider than her shoulders, shuttered to keep out the chill. She climbed onto the chest, threw open the shutter, and rose up on her toes. Grasping the lower edge of the window with her hands, she leaned out as far as she could.

He heard her speak. "I want to be free."

For the second time, the Cretan necklace grew hot—hot enough that he had to lift it off his skin.

He pitied her. She was dejected and the man had locked her in.

There was nothing more to see here. He should allow her some privacy, but instead of leaving he pulled the fibers in the wall hanging farther apart so he could continue watching her.

Fastening the shutter, she climbed off the chest and returned to the brazier. She rubbed her arms as she contemplated the embers.

Time passed; he waited, willing her to lift her head. Finally she did, absently gazing at the wall hanging that disguised his presence.

Ricocheting blasts of shock, disbelief, and joy thrashed through his limbs. He only dimly realized he was shaking, and released the wall hanging, fearful he would give away his presence. He stumbled backward, holding in wheezing breaths, fighting to recover some semblance of composure as he shut the portal.

His legs quavered as though they had turned to water. He slumped onto the landing, his back against the portal, and pressed his face to his knees.

"Aridela," he whispered. "Aridela. Aridela."

He tried to stand and could not—he tumbled down the steps to the next landing, knowing he had to get away from that door, or the girl at the brazier would hear his raving and think she was going mad.

After some time he got to his feet and ran down the narrow spiraling stairs. He fell through the hole and raced into the longest tunnel, where at last he could allow himself to laugh without restraint, to sob, groan, and shiver.

This is why I came here. This is why Athene sent the dreams. So I would search and find Aridela.

She had helped him! She was offering him a chance of redemption.

He fell onto his back, rolling and laughing helplessly. "Aridela," he said, the sound of her name making him feel drunk.

It was only much, much later that he sat up, wiping tears from his face, and began to question his conviction.

The girl looked nothing like Aridela. Her skin was not Aridela's dusky hue but fair, her hair not black as deepest night but bright, almost vermillion in candlelight. The girl was statuesque, quite different from Aridela's small-boned frame, and she did not manifest Aridela's consummate demeanor of courage and authority.

But there was that mark on her wrist. And Aridela's scent. The instant he'd entered Eamhair's bedchamber, he'd smelled it.

Finally...there were the eyes. Those eyes had ripped him from this place and sent him backward in time and far away, across the ocean to the isle of Crete.

Another woman's body, yes. But Aridela's eyes.

Chapter 9

IT WAS EARLY. THE AIR, SNAPPING WITH FROST, WAS BLACK IN THESE HOURS before dawn, the ocean aggravated. Taranis knew the water would be bitterly cold—cold enough to kill him. He dreaded going in.

Nevertheless, he would. There was no other way.

He stalked from one end of the beach to the other, going over every word, putting it all together.

I wish your seolh-king would come and take you away.

But Mother, I don't want to be separated from you.

He released a low laugh. Eamhair's mother had taught her that magic was real. Both women believed the king of the seolhs was coming to take Eamhair away. Ula wanted this to happen. She saw it as a salvation.

"I, too, am a believer," he said out loud. He fell to his knees and closed his eyes. "Potnia Athene. You brought me here." He lay face-down on the cold sand, his arms outstretched, his fingertips immersed in the icy ocean. "You placed me with Breda when I was a baby so I would learn the language these people speak, so I would understand them, and they, me. You filled my nights with dreams of the tower. You brought the merchant who told me where to find it. I thank you, Lady, for your forgiveness. Your generosity. This time I vow to you I will make no mistakes. I will do whatever you ask of me. I will sing your praises until the end of my days. I will never forget that you led me to her."

Nothing happened to make him think she was listening, but his exultation flowed on, unabated. He rose and climbed almost to the summit above the beach, keeping low so that if Eamhair came, she wouldn't see him.

Yesterday, a man had locked her in her chamber for some reason, prompting him to take a terrible risk. Monk or no, if he was caught anywhere near Eamhair's bedchamber, he would surely be put to death.

In the blackest hours, he crept out of the tunnels and up the tower stairs to the top. Sure enough, a heavy iron bolt barred the oak portal. He released it, hoping she would rise, test her door, and come to the beach. But if she did not, no matter. She would eventually, and he would wait every morning for the rest of his life if necessary. For as long as it took to be reunited with her.

THE LAUDS BELLS WOKE EAMHAIR AND SHE LAY FOR A WHILE, THINKING OF the seolh and what her mother had said. She should try sending a new song across the waves. Perhaps it would charm him enough to take notice. But if she couldn't even leave her chamber, he would never hear her pleas. Without much expectation, she rose and tried the door, surprised and gladdened when it opened. Ula must have come during the night and thrown the bolt. She knew how much her daughter hated being confined.

This was a sign. She was meant to make this effort. Throwing on two of her warmest tunics and a heavy cloak, she slipped down the stairs and kept to the shadows until she reached the north gate. All was deserted and she soon reached the slope leading down to her beach.

She knew she didn't have long. When the Prime bells rang, someone would come to fetch her, and if that person found her door unlocked and her chamber deserted, both she and Ula would be punished. A guard would be placed on the steps to prevent any future escapes.

She would stay just long enough to sing one song.

Crimson brilliance edged the eastern horizon. The sky was no longer black but silver grey. She ran down the slope and stood near the water, breathing the crisp winter air. Closing her eyes, she imagined a place of freedom, where no suitors existed, no Bericus, no sadistic brothers. She even allowed herself to revisit the whimsical empire she had invented as a child. It lay deep in the ocean—but not so deep the sunlight couldn't reach it. There were towers and pinnacles, and it was peopled with gentle seolh folk.

When she opened her eyes, a man was coming out of the sea. A large man with powerful shoulders, his black hair running with seawater, dripping from his beard, and streaming over his torso, which was naked but for a striking silver and blue ornament. Water soaked his black leggings, making them cling like skin.

She backed up, stumbling, yet couldn't turn away to flee.

He waded out, walked up to her, and took her hands. His were freezing cold.

"I have come," he said. "I have found you."

The light of the rising sun reflected off his wet skin, causing a hazy red sheen to form around him, like the auras that circled the moon when a storm was brewing.

Her mouth opened but she remained speechless. Where had she heard that voice before?

In dreams.

He dropped to one knee and stared into her eyes. "Aridela," he said, and kissed her knuckles.

"I-I am Eamhair. Daughter of Bericus, chief of these lands." She swallowed. "Who-who are you?"

He rose. Staring into her face, he repeated brokenly, "Aridela," and stroked the back of his hand across her cheek.

"If that is a name, you have mistaken me for someone else. Who are you?"

"You know who I am."

For the first time in her life, Eamhair thought she might faint. Her throat was tight, her stomach queasy. "My mother promised you would come, but so much time has passed. I told myself she invented you to give me courage. I stopped believing." Her head bent. "Forgive me, seolh-king."

He was majestic, this sea creature. She sensed he could be deadly. Yet he lifted her chin as carefully as if she were a newly budded flower.

"I must make plans," he said, "but I will come to you again. Tonight."

"I-I am well guarded. No one can get to me but through my father's men."

"Stone…wood…men. These are the impotent tools of the feeble. Go back, Eamhair, before you are missed. Tell no one what you have seen here." Drawing her hands up, he kissed them again with his cold blue lips before turning and wading into the sea, farther, farther, until the ocean frothed around his shoulders. He looked back at her once then he dived and was gone.

Chapter 10

EAMHAIR'S BEDCHAMBER WAS EMPTY. CURIOUS. SHE HAD GIVEN TARANIS the impression that she was almost always kept there, locked up and guarded.

Distant laughter, shouting, and singing drifted from the hall below. Music too, a lively drumbeat, a harp, and the airy sound of pipes.

The noise had been going on for a long time, so when it stopped abruptly, Taranis noticed.

Complete silence now but for a single drum's slow, repeating beat.

He waited. Everything remained quiet but for the drum.

Crossing to her bed, he idly picked up a pillow and held it to his nose, breathing in the intoxicating aroma of musk, along with the mellow scent of bedstraw.

He turned the pillow over. Embroidered there was a boat—*the* boat—its high, curved stern and prow easily recognizable. Restless waves surrounded the hull, and worked onto the prow was a figurehead—a woman's face and torso. She stared into his eyes.

Apprehension flooded him. Another of his dreams come to life. Had Eamhair embroidered that? Were they sharing the same dreams?

His unease was severed by a commotion. Furious screaming, thunks and thuds and a man shouting obscenities.

He raced for the tunnel. Once safely inside, he held the door ready and squinted through the wall hanging. It would be difficult for anyone to see him, but he kept a tight grip on the iron handle, ready to melt away if necessary.

A man pushed Eamhair into the room—the man Taranis had seen having sex in a lower chamber the first day he came to Dunaedan.

Holding onto her arm, the man ripped the veil off her head, dropped it, and seized her braids. She cried out as he used them to jerk her head brutally. He released her arm and waved a strip of cloth in front of her face.

"You had to see that old man," he said. "He may be as withered as a corpse, but some part of him clings to life, and you know what part that is, don't you? What's worse, do you think? A man who will stick his prick in you four or five times a day or one who can only paw at you and wish he could?" He laughed and slapped her backside.

She tried to pry his hand from her hair. "Let go of me!"

Unmoved, he continued his taunts. "We will marry you off one day, when some fool offers enough silver to satisfy us. That fool will take the only thing that makes you worth feeding." He forced his free hand between her legs. "He will rut with you and force you to shit out his spawn, if he has half a wit, until you are used up and about as tasty as worn-out leather. Or we may murder him after we have his riches, and share you among ourselves."

She released a tight, frenzied hiss. Her fist came out and struck him on the chin. The blow was hard enough to propel his head backward, but he recovered and punished her by pulling on her braids and pinching her breasts until she screamed. Laughing again, he shoved her to the floor and stood over her, fondling his crotch, before he sneered and left. Taranis heard the heavy grate of the bolt being thrown. He clutched handfuls of the habit he had put back on after coming out of the sea—mostly for its warmth—and swallowed a lump of relief that nothing worse had happened.

Eamhair remained on the floor. He fought the urge to go to her, to comfort her, but he knew he must wait until he was sure no one else was going to burst in.

After some time she rose unsteadily. She straightened her gown before crossing to the door, where she tried the latch. When the door wouldn't open, she slammed both fists against the wood and rested her forehead against it.

She remained there awhile, silent. He sensed the rage coursing through her. But at last she sighed and straightened. She went to the brazier and held out her hands to warm them.

Fortune favors the bold, he told himself as he left the tunnel and edged around the wall hanging.

She hadn't heard him. She went on staring at the brazier, scowling.

"Are you cold, my lady?" he asked.

She swiveled with an indrawn breath and lost her balance. He leaped forward, catching her arm and waist and steadying her. She had almost fallen into the brazier, and would have burned herself at least.

He remained close to her, one hand on her arm, the other on her waist, like a lover. "I promised I would come. Would you rather I go?"

It was hard not to notice how her breasts lifted and fell rapidly beneath the thin, revealing gown. The tips were hardened. It was cold in this chamber, despite the brazier. One bright lock of hair curled artfully over her right breast, rising and falling with her breathing. It was oddly erotic.

Her eyes were shiny-bright with tears. "No, seolh-king." Awe and wonder played across her face. "Only you could breach this chamber. You have come as my mother promised—as you promised. Have you...hidden your seal skin somewhere?" Her puzzled gaze traveled over the monk's robe.

"You're shivering." He pulled one of the furs off the bed and placed it on her shoulders, drawing it close in front. "I stole this habit so I wouldn't draw too much notice if anyone saw me."

Her brows lowered again. "Ah, I see. That was shrewd." Her gaze upon his face was fixated. Slowly, hesitantly, she said, "The fire makes jewels of your eyes...like sunlight through a wave."

Aridela's words. It all came back in a flood, the night of the fire-wind. She had tricked her women and found a way to spend time alone with him. They had built a fire in a meadow and had enjoyed brief intimacy before the catastrophe that changed everything forever.

She remembers!

Tears blurred his vision. He shuddered, hating to show such weakness, but utterly incapable of exerting control over these physical reactions.

Her hand extended towards his face but stopped and retreated before touching him. "Am I foolish to trust you? Are you really the seolh-king? Why now? Why have you come *now*?"

No, she does not remember me.

It was agonizing. What would happen if he told her of their past together? Would the telling make her remember?

Instinct had directed everything he'd done since the night he had seen that mark on her wrist. Now he stood before her without any answers to her questions. What words did she need to soothe her fears and keep her believing?

Help me, Athene. Show me what to say.

Breda had told stories when he was little about the seolh people, ageless myths that claimed male seolhs had unexplainable power over human women. When a girl shed seven tears into the sea, a seolh would respond. He would come onto land, transforming into the likeness of a man. He would entice, seduce, and take her as his wife. The stories always ended with the seolh abandoning his human love for the overwhelming call of the sea.

His mind whirled. He had performed an elaborate trick to convince her he was a seolh. She had believed, there by the sea, but he saw from her expression that since then, she had questioned her belief.

He had to throw himself completely into the spell he'd created and make her belief unassailable.

Aridela. You live and breathe in the same world with me. I will do whatever I must to exert power over you. I will never leave this place, even if it means my death.

"You are not foolish," he said. "I am here to save you from harm." He knelt. "I would lay down my life for you gladly, Eamhair, but that is not my plan. I want to take you with me, far from here, to my world, where you will be safe."

Her breasts were again rising and falling rapidly. She tucked her lower lip under her teeth and tears spilled over her cheeks. "At first I believed you would come right away," she said. "I was so impatient! I watched. I called. I sang. Did you hear my songs?" She knelt too and bowed her head.

He touched her hair. "You have been lost to me...for so long." His ears filled with fearsome thrumming. "I've found you. I've found you...Aridela."

"My name is Eamhair, lord." She raised her face, smiling shyly through her tears. "What is 'Aridela'? A title of some kind? I hear the accent of your people, but you speak our language well. I will try my best to learn yours." Her expression was no longer wary.

His past swam before him as he stared into her eyes—Aridela's eyes, dark and fathomless, kind and mystical. Grave, clear, and wise. The eyes of a goddess. Somewhere in this body, Aridela lived on.

"That man who brought you in here—"

"My brother. Nemausus."

"Is he using you as some kind of bait, Eamhair?"

She lowered her face again. Her shoulders rose as if she was trying to fold into herself. In a small voice, she said, "He and my father mean to sell me, once they find a man rich enough. They blindfold me and parade me before the suitors who come with offers. So far, none have passed their tests."

He couldn't help thinking of Aridela—the woman men genuflected to and revered. But in this life, her only worth lay in how much profit her father could make off her.

Shaking off her sadness, she jumped to her feet. "I cannot wait to tell my mother. Promise you will bring her with us. I cannot leave without her. Will you take us into the ocean and change us into beings like yourself? She has always—"

He rose too, and placed his hands on her shoulders. "Nay, stop, Eamhair. Tell no one you have seen me. This must be our secret for now. I must have time to...plan how best to spirit you away from here."

"I—of...course I will do whatever you say. But my mother's faith has never wavered. She suffers, mighty seolh-king. Promise you will save her too...."

Could he take the chance? No. An older woman would see through his ruse instantly. "I—I will try. But I can make no promises. Not yet."

She stared, her expression betraying her dismay. Then her face cleared. "You don't understand. She was given knowledge of you long before I was. Let us warm ourselves, lord, and I will tell you the story of how I learned about you—of how I knew you would come. I was eight years old, you see, and had just met Drost Gocinecht for the first time."

Moon bull, King bull, Lord bull,
Dance with me...

~~~*The Song of the Bullring*

A Woman's Secret

"Mama, Mama…"

"I've been looking for you, Eamhair. This was no time to wander off, with Drost Gocinecht and his men appearing like a carbuncle. You know I rely upon you. So does every other woman here. Would you want to see them whipped because breakfast was not served quickly enough?"

Eamhair faltered under her mother's annoyed gaze, but only for an instant. "Nemausus says Drost Gocinecht is going to take me away and make me his wife."

Shock widened Ula's eyes. "Nay. It is too soon."

She yanked Eamhair against her stained, onion-scented apron in a hard embrace, but soon put her daughter at arm's length with a shaky laugh. "Oh, child," she said, "he is tormenting you. You should know that by now."

"But Ossian said it too, and Father is angry."

"Of course he is. There is only one thing your father hates more than Drost Gocinecht, and that is Drost Gocinecht appearing unexpectedly after a night of heavy drinking. There, can you hear him bellowing? We must get these platters into the hall. Hungry men are like wounded boars—very dangerous. You stay here. Help fill the pitchers and keep the stew from burning. I don't want Drost or any of his men to get a glimpse of you."

"He already has!"

"What? How?"

"I-I was going out the north gate, and there he was. He and Luned —they were—they were against the wall." The two were rutting like pigs, yet that hadn't stopped Drost from spotting her. He reached out and clamped his enormous hand over her shoulder. She tried to twist free but couldn't. His grip was like iron.

Ula's face whitened. "What did he do?"

"He asked my name. I was too afraid to lie."

"Is that all?"

"N-nay." Eamhair shivered. The Caledonii king, even in the gloom of pre-dawn, was an alarming sight with his intricate tattoos, weathered skin, and long, loose hair, interwoven with plaits and silver balls. He'd grasped her chin and turned her face from side to side with fingers that were scratchy, dry as barley husks. His cold gaze examined her like a hungry eagle eyeing a fat hen. "He asked me how old I am, if I have ever been sick, and if I can ride. I answered. Then he laughed and let me go."

Ula put one hand on the worktable and leaned on it. The other she pressed to her eyes. "No, no."

Eamhair's shivering intensified, though the kitchens were warm with the cooking fires and frantic rush of serving maids.

Ula straightened and spoke briskly. "Fetch one of my headdresses and cover your hair. You know how angry your father would be if he saw you." She clasped Eamhair's arms and shook her. "Come straight back. You should not have been trying to sneak out—especially with those men here!"

"Yes, Mama." Eamhair went off, hearing Ula mutter, *Not even Drost Gocinecht would ravish an eight-year-old child.*

When she returned Ula said nothing but grabbed her daughter by the hand and took her out of Dunaedan through the north gate, the same one Eamhair had tried to use earlier. They walked to Eamhair's favorite little beach, where not even the stone tower on the east end of the fortress could be seen.

By the time they reached the fine damp sand, with the vast, thundering ocean spread before them horizon to horizon, Eamhair's heart was racing, not only because of such an unaccustomed and abrupt abandonment of their chores, but because of her mother's somber expression.

Ula led Eamhair to the water's edge, keeping hold of her hand. "I had difficulty giving birth to you," she said. "You refused to come out of me for two days and nights."

"Will it be like that for me?" Eamhair thought of the king—how fearfully large and wild he was, like the giant mythical stag on the wall hanging that had come with Ula from her father's hearth as part of her dowry.

"Not if I have a say." Ula squeezed Eamhair's hand. "Now listen. While I waited and labored, I dreamed. I was not always asleep when these dreams came to me."

Eamhair nodded. She, too, had many dreams—dreams she usually remembered, though she didn't understand them. Sometimes they came when she was awake. Not often, but sometimes.

"I dreamed of a woman," Ula said. "A tall, bare-breasted woman, wearing a crown. She told me I was giving birth to a girl—a special girl, who would one day lead warriors."

"Me?"

"You."

Fear sprouted deep inside.

"She told me you would never be alone, even if I am gone, for she had charged a king to serve you, to help and protect you."

"Who is he? Where is he? What does he look like?"

"I know none of those things. The dream woman came to me at the Point, out of a thick sea mist, in a white boat that danced upon the waves, so I expect that means he will come from the sea, too. It is true that I was born in the forest, but the coast was not far and my people revered the water. I was raised on stories of sea creatures—of their abilities, their strength, their love of music and poetry."

"A king from the sea...."

"I have had years to think about those dreams, and yes, I believe your protector will come from the deep blue abyss, from the coldest depths beyond the reach of any light. No doubt he will be of the seolh dynasty. My tribe believed that seolhs could change into human form at will. In the dream, my sight was filled with blue—every shade of blue we have ever seen in the sea, all laced together. I tasted the color blue in my mouth."

"Like bilberries?"

"Yes, with a bit of salt. Bilberries and seaweed."

They laughed. "One day, Eamhair, when your need is greatest, he will appear. This is what I was shown as I labored to bring you to life.

So you see, you have no need to fear Drost Gocinecht or any mortal man."

"Why can't he come now?" Eamhair wanted to meet this king of the seolhs. Her need was already great. She hated her father and brothers. They were cruel to everyone, but most of all to Ula. When this king came, she would find a way to make him protect Ula too.

But she soon realized what it meant that he hadn't yet come. Sometime, maybe tonight, maybe far in the future, her need would be weightier than it was now. Her imagination formed monsters with jagged teeth, snarling mouths, and burning eyes.

"Rulers cannot spend all their time with little girls," Ula said. "They have many important things to do."

She veered onto another subject, distracting Eamhair from anxiety. "My mother made me promise that if I ever had a daughter, I would name her Olwyn. Her favorite stories were Olwyn's; they say she was so fragile that white lilies grew in her footprints." She snorted her disgust. "At first I agreed, but after two sons and many miscarriages, I finally had you, a daughter I could love, who could carry on my secrets and the folklore of my tribe. And so I refused! I did not want you to be pure and dull and meek. I wanted my daughter to be strong. Eamhair, I named you. Swift as a river flowing into the ocean, fleet of foot, quick of mind. My darling. My light."

This impassioned speech kept Eamhair silent awhile. "Do all children have their own seal-king?" she finally asked.

Ula shook her head, laughing. "No one but Eamhair, daughter of Ula. Now listen to me. You must never tell your father or brothers about this. It is a woman's secret. Our secret."

Chapter 11

Taranis wove his fingers between Eamhair's, lost in the thrill of touching her, and of the story her mother told her—that she would be saved from servitude to Drost Gocinecht by a creature-king from the sea.

He had come close to losing his life in Drost Gocinecht's stone fortress. He understood how frightened the child Eamhair must have been by that colossal barbarian.

"Everything changed that day," she said. "I was eight years old, and it was the first time I knew hope." She regarded him with delicious interest. "What am I to call you, lord?"

Touching her hand caused a sensation he could not help but notice. It was as though sparks from a fire flowed between them, drawing up the fine hairs at the nape of his neck. As he moved his fingertips across hers, she frowned—was she feeling the same thing?

Unable to stop himself, he brought her wrist up and kissed the mark there. A dizzying tide of emotion flowed over him.

"Taranis." The prickling increased as he flattened his palm against hers. It was an amazing stroke of good fortune that she believed him to be this seal king. At the same time, her conviction that he was a shape-changing savior made everything unbearably worse.

In true measure of budding trust, she allowed him to lie here next to her on the bed, covered with warm sheepskins, but her gaze held no flirtation or desire—not the slightest hint that she thought of him as a man.

And oh, he longed for her to think of him as a man.

If only she could remember how they had once loved each other, how they could not get enough of each other and were always stealing away from their obligations in order to be alone.

All he had endured to get here was worth it. He had found Aridela. He was not alone in this foreign era and place, which seemed both more primitive than Crete and less, at the same time.

Aridela! Alive, lying next to him! If he had to pretend to be this seolh-king, he would, gladly, and confess the truth later, when she was his again. After he won her loyalty, as he had on Crete. After he found a way to make her remember, as he did.

"I see color around you," she said. "Like a cloud. A red cloud."

Taranis peered down at his chest. He saw nothing, but he did remember a wash of color swirling above her that first night. What sorcery was this?

She ran her hand above his shoulder, her gaze following. "I have never seen such a thing before…except…." She trailed off. "Tell me of your world."

He rubbed the mark on her wrist. "Sunlight slants through the water, bright and shifting, then growing dim. Deeper, fathoms down, the light comes from rainbows. My world is filled with pearls and shells, coral and gold—a wealth of gold and silver, my lady, enough to make the richest king envious."

She clapped, her whole face radiant. "How beautiful it sounds. I wish I could see it now."

He smiled. "You cannot hold your breath so long."

"I often dream of sinking into rainbows, and in the dream I can breathe." Her expression turned wistful. "You will change us, seolh-king? So that we can live under water like you do?"

He looked away from her, hating to steal that delight and damage her trust. "I will. Or I will live with you on land. Things will be different now I am here, but there are many problems to solve. I ask you to be patient."

"Will it hurt?"

"I would never harm you."

"Do you miss your home?"

"Yes. The only happiness I have is here, now, with you."

"I understand. There are…a few here I would miss if I left."

He blurted, "You remind me of my wife."

"You have a wife? Where is she? You should be with her, Taranis. Am I keeping you from her?"

"She is close tonight."

"Could she not come with you?"

"We are trapped between worlds; she in one, I in another. She does not remember me."

Her eyes turned luminous. He felt her empathy surround him like a balm. It made him want to spill every hidden truth.

"Tell me of her," she said.

"She was a queen."

"A queen! So my mother was right to call you king."

"Once I was the Gold Lion of Mycenae. But where I am from, kings are not as important as queens."

"Not as important," she whispered.

It must be unimaginable for a girl in this place, under the thumb of such men as those he had seen, to believe. "She once led us into battle. Our lives depended on the outcome." He swallowed, trying to regain control over his voice. "It was a decisive triumph. She killed the leader as he tried to kill me."

"I have heard of women who fight alongside their men. So your wife is a warrior?"

"A ruthless warrior, if she has to be. But that is not her nature."

"What does she look like?"

"Long black hair," he said. "Eyes much like yours. She was small, like her brethren, shorter than you, yet strong." He bit his lip as the night of the cataclysm returned to his mind in its full horror. "There was a...disaster." He traced her cheek with one finger. "The earth shook. Everything burned—even the air. Palaces and cities were destroyed. She led her people back from that. It took years, but eventually, all was as it had been." Sighing, he added, "Yet nothing was ever the same."

"I am sorry that you must live without her. If I can help you be with her again, I will."

He had sunk so deeply into his memories he hardly heard. "She once danced with a bull. She let it fling her over its head, and all the while she laughed. She knew no fear. I will love her in every life, in death, and on the other side of death."

He pressed his fingertips against the silver pendant hidden beneath his tunic.

Labyrinthos. Phaistos. Mycenae. Tiryns. We believed those wondrous places would last forever, but all memory of them is gone. Forgotten. The fortresses of mammoth stone, the sailing ships. Statues of marble and gypsum. The marketplaces, where anything that could be imagined could be purchased. The pageantry and traditions, ceremonies and festivals, the portents and rites. Crowds in the stands screaming as brave leapers danced with angry bulls. How we laughed and wept. How we loved and hated, schemed and tricked.

I alone carry the memories of all that. She remembers nothing.

He looked into this woman's eyes. So like Aridela's yet different because there was no awareness of the queen she had once been. No recollection of how she loved Chrysaleon, king of Mycenae, in defiance of her mother and her council, how she changed ancient custom, or how fiercely she protected those she loved.

The elation that infused him with bright joy diminished under the heavy weight of loss that could never be undone.

He closed his fist around the pendant, feeling its subtle heat.

How had it come to be here? Was it a sign, or happenstance?

No. If there was one thing he could be certain of, it was that the necklace had not appeared by chance.

Everything else fell away before Eamhair's gaze. Those eyes were all that mattered.

I will rip the stars from the heavens. I will maim every living being between here and Powys if that is what it takes. I will have you, no matter what price I must pay.

Somehow, I will bring you back to me, Aridela.

Chapter 12

EAMHAIR WAS AFRAID TO LET THE SEOLH-KING GO, AFRAID SHE WOULD wake in the morning and find it had been nothing but a dream. *You are real?* she asked desperately.

Did you not shed seven tears into the sea? He kissed the back of her hand, bid her peaceful sleep, and melted into the shadows. *I will not leave you.* His voice was a beguiling force, making her imagine things that embarrassed yet lured her. Finally, she understood Ula's warnings about the power in a man's seduction, and felt sympathy toward those who paid a terrible price for capitulating to love.

Throwing off the sheepskins, she ran to the wall and pressed her hands against the cold masonry, but there was nothing. Taranis had vanished through unbroken stone.

Too wrought to sleep, she climbed back into bed, hugged her knees to her chest, and watched the flames in the brazier. Her mind recreated the scrape of his callused palms and fingers against hers. That was peculiar, now that he was gone and she could think. Why would a being from the ocean have the coarse hands of a laborer?

And his voice...that voice...low and somewhat breathy, rough like wood smoke in the throat. She had missed some of his story, so mesmerized had she been by it, and the way his eyes alternately flashed with joy, narrowed in laughter, and clouded in sorrow.

She glanced at the window. The Lauds bells hadn't yet rung but soon they would. With the rising of the sun, her mother would come and they would be expected to attend morning prayers, bow their heads at a litany of their failures, and make the indelible sign of the cross over their breasts.

She rubbed her eyes. What of Cailean? She secretly believed he had only agreed to become Bericus's man in order to be near her, though they never spoke, other than to say good morrow now and then.

Maybe you carry a drop or two of kestrel blood in your veins, to wander these cliffs without bothering to look where you step. Can you fly, mistress?

Her mother insisted that Eamhair's destiny was to go with the seolh-king. Eamhair assumed this meant she would be his bride. But Taranis already had a wife, one he loved deeply. Eamhair would not be bound, body and soul. It was a relief. Perhaps she could convince him to take Cailean as well as Ula.

For the first time in her life, Eamhair found herself being drawn not to one but two men, each with his own unique alchemy.

Splinters were forming in the tower around her heart.

Sometimes, when she was trotted out before the suitors, she could see through the strip of cloth. Bericus allowed some—those willing to make it worth his while—to kiss the back of her hand. That old man Nemausus had taunted her about had done so. She could still feel those dry, cold lips against her skin, and the eel-like touch of his tongue.

The seolh would change everything. Bericus would have to find another way to increase his wealth.

She rose and tested her door. Again it was unlocked. Even as she sent thanks to her mother, Eamhair was relieved Ula hadn't come in to catch her daughter lying in bed with a man, no matter how innocent it was. Had that happened, they would have been forced to tell her the truth.

She changed from the revealing gown to her usual warm clothes and a cloak and escaped from the tower, keeping to the shadows as she made her way to the north gate. From there it was easy. She ran across the open moor and waded to the cave.

A setting half-moon showered the ocean in a froth of white light. She sat in her usual spot and released her anger to the sea, sending it into the waves and inhaling new confidence as she imagined a future filled with sunlight, rainbows, coral, and enough gold and silver to make the richest king envious.

CAILEAN PAUSED AT THE CAVE MOUTH. EAMHAIR WAS THERE, MUFFLED IN A cloak, one cheek resting on her knees. She didn't move. But as he took another step and his boot caused loose stones to shift, she raised her head and blinked at him sleepily.

"Lady Eamhair. Forgive me. I didn't know anyone would be here. I will leave you to your solitude."

But as he turned, she said, "Don't. Don't go."

He looked at her, one brow lifted.

"The cave does not belong to me. There is room enough for both of us, if you wish to stay."

He inclined his head and sat in a dry spot near the mouth, his back against the wall, one leg bent so he could rest his forearm upon his knee. "I like to come here and look at the ocean."

"I do as well."

Her tone suggested she didn't mind his presence, and what she said next relaxed him farther.

"I can finally talk to you."

"Yes, finally," he said with a smile.

"How do you like serving my father?"

"It passes the time."

"You have nothing better to do?"

"Nay, lady," he said. "Nothing at all."

He watched her take that in. She pinkened a little.

"And now you are his baron."

"Aye." Niall, the previous leader, had fallen out of one of the gatehouses while drunk and promptly expired. Bericus replaced him with Cailean, which some of the other men celebrated as a wise choice and some grumbled about.

The surface of the ocean transformed as the angle of the sun changed. The waves turned a burnished shade of crimson.

He watched it, instead of her, as he said, "I was in the hall last night."

Her voice was hard as obsidian. "And did you—drink anything?"

"A foul, watered down brew," he said casually. "Bericus keeps the finest ale separate, for those men he turns into beggars." He sifted a few pebbles through his fingers. "Why do you stay here? You could go anywhere you want, make a life for yourself, and answer to no one."

A drop of water fell from the ceiling and splashed against her temple. She blotted it with a corner of her cloak. "My mother follows the old religion. You cannot tell anyone that." The frown that accompanied this statement was formidable.

"I will say nothing."

"She raised me in the old ways, to listen to the stars. To honor the spirits in spring buds, and ocean waves, and tree sap. To flow with the clouds and read the message in the eyes of a doe." She looked past him, out at the waves. "My mother is everything to me. She has kept my soul alive. When I was afraid, she offered me hope, in this place where there is none."

He waited, knowing there was more.

"I stay for her. I allow him to parade me for her. Bericus learned early on that he could coerce my obedience by threatening her." She wiped absently at her temple again. "Ula gave me life, and has given me all of herself ever since. I will never leave her to my father's mercy."

She stared at him, and he saw the challenge in her eyes.

"I have my own secrets from Bericus," he said. "My father follows the Christos, but I do not. My mother, like yours, does not. Your secrets are safe with me, Eamhair."

Her shoulders relaxed. "In this cave, I hear gods and goddesses singing in the tides and wind. I can almost see them. Sometimes I think I am so well hidden that they don't realize a mortal is watching. They come out and wrestle. They twist and spiral, splash and foam. At first there are many, but they always merge into one. A woman. A crowned goddess, both stern and sad." She lifted her hands to indicate the rough-hewn walls. "This cave is more home to me than Dunaedan. The cliffs, where I can feel the wind and sea spray, are where I would live, if I had a choice. But I have no choice in anything."

"Bericus has netted himself a seolh and stolen her skin." Cailean was only partially teasing. He didn't understand why she startled at his words, and sent him a penetrating glance. He smiled to put her at ease. *She is as capricious as a newly caged bird. I would gentle her as I do Vita or Bharosa, with a soft voice and stroking, if only I could.*

EAMHAIR COMPOSED HER FEATURES. IT WAS NOTHING, A COINCIDENCE, YET Ula had taught her that all things were entwined; what seemed coincidences were not, and should be examined for their true message. Later, she would ponder it.

Cailean watched her, but this was something she could not share. She had promised. Sighing, she rose. "We should return to our obligations," she said, wanting to say the opposite. *I wish we could spend our lives here together.*

"Aye, time to don a mask and play the fool." He stood, holding out a hand, and looked pleased when she placed hers upon his gauntlet. He helped her across the watery divot and onto the beach. It was bitterly cold. Her breath steamed and though she wore a cloak, she shivered. It had been warmer in the cave.

He kept on holding her hand as they made their way up to the plateau.

She was a little ahead of him when he stopped her. She turned, questioning with her expression.

"About the hall," he said. "I swear, if you would bend your head and bow your shoulders, no more men would come. If you would cringe and weep, your torment would end. But you won't do that, will you? It is your pride, Eamhair. That is what brings them, and what keeps reigniting the legend, sending its fire across the seas. You walk before them like a lioness, and you make them feel...alive. More than alive. Like nothing can defeat them."

He made her sound grand! Not the cow her brothers called her. Shyly, she asked, "Lioness? What is that?"

"I would I could show you." His hand pulled hers, gently but inexorably drawing her closer. She allowed it, but with resistance, for part of her understood everything was about to change.

His brows lifted; his smile was resigned. "Aye, a lioness," he said as he bent his head and kissed her.

She closed her eyes and leaned in, surrendering to his immutable strength, to the warmth coming off his body and the taste of his mouth, like the air inside a cloud. He held the back of her neck and tucked her hand between their bodies, and she felt the swift, steady beat of his heart.

His kiss was thorough and confident. It pulverized the protective barrier she had long cultivated.

He released her mouth and looked into her face with such tenderness it was frightening. She had to say something to get past all the dizzying emotion. "You have much practice at this game I think," she said breathlessly.

"Game?" He frowned.

"You have done this before."

"Truly, I have been at war so long I'd forgotten there were 'games' such as this."

Ashamed, she admitted, "You frighten me."

He blinked. His frown deepened. "That is the last thing I would do."

"Aye, I know. But that first day—on the cliffs—you breached the defenses I have hidden behind all my life. That frightens me, for I have long trusted them to keep me out of trouble."

The remarkable blue glow in his eyes intensified, and she felt again a tingling vibration between their hands. She shivered. "Are you...a druid?"

"I can only tell you that I felt the same. There is something about you...." He kissed her again. She rose up on her toes and put her arm around his neck to let him know that she hadn't meant it—it was no game.

Outside Dunaedan's gate, where they no longer touched for fear of being seen, he stopped her again.

"Eamhair, if ever you need me, I am here."

The way he spoke her name lingered after he was gone, how his tongue rolled the 'r,' caressing it like naked flesh.

She went in to attend her morning duties, imagining what a lioness looked like.

Chapter 13

CAILEAN LEFT THE HALL, PREFERRING SOLITUDE AND THE STILL COLDNESS of night to the noise, heat, and smoke inside. He was staring up at the stars, lost in thoughts of Eamhair and his home when a shout disrupted the silence.

"My brother!"

Instinct sent him stepping quickly backwards, saving him from the scrabbling reach of a dirty, bloody-faced man in a monk's robe. Vita bared her teeth and snarled.

She calmed when Cailean placed his hand on her head, but her low, protesting whine made clear her disagreement.

"Menoetius!"

The guard who had lost hold of the prisoner threw him to the ground, slamming his boot against the man's spine. "Sorry, Baron," he said. "I wasn't expecting that."

"And if he'd had a knife, I would be dead."

Flushing, the guard kicked the prisoner in the ribs. "Get up, oaf."

The monk came to his feet, still staring at Cailean.

What had he said? *My brother. Menoetius.* What did that mean? "Put him in the pit." Cailean turned as one of Dunaedan's many serving maids approached, a pretty, flaxen-haired woman named Viviana.

"Lord Bericus sent me to find—" she said, but got no farther, for again the man tore free of his captor.

"Look at me! I know I don't look the same, but can you not remember? Mycenae. Our father, Idómeneus—our sister, Bateia."

Vita clamped down on the monk's outstretched wrist. He recoiled, cursing.

The maid screeched. Cailean put a reassuring hand on her arm and gave a quiet order.

The wolf released the monk, but remained between him and Cailean, fur bristling. A snarl lingered; she watched every movement he made with cold, rapacious eyes.

Two more warriors ran forward with torches. Together, they and the first guard wrestled the prisoner away.

Cailean watched as they lugged him to the hole and threw him in. There was a dull thud as he landed, and a howl—either from him or one of the other prisoners he landed on.

Three men it took to restrain him—a monk!

He walked over and looked down. What was that? He blinked, but the reddish haze didn't disappear. It was dim, but he'd swear that faint glimmer outlined one of the prisoners.

Viviana joined him at the edge. "Bless you, lord." She touched the back of his hand. "Who knows what that madman would have done if you had not protected me?"

Cailean glanced at her but immediately returned his gaze to the pit.

"I'm sorry." The guard kept his head bent. "He is strong, that one."

"He does seem strong for a monk," Cailean said. "Do you see that?" He pointed.

"What, lord?"

"The light. That color."

"I see nothing down there but blackness. Shall I fetch a torch?"

"No. It's gone now."

"I think this is the man Drost Gocinecht has been seeking," one of the other warriors said. "He admitted his name is Taranis."

"Really. Bericus will like that."

"What did he call you?"

"I've already lost it." *Why did he act like we know each other? He must be a lunatic, or he thinks to trick me.* Yet those words had felt familiar in some way. *Mycenae. Idómeneus. Bateia.*

Drost Gocinecht, king of the Caledonii, had sent messengers to every corner of his realm and even promised a reward for the capture of the monk named Taranis. Apparently the man had murdered Drost's baby daughter.

Cailean was good with faces. If he had ever seen Taranis the monk, he would remember. He didn't. He hadn't.

A shiver ran over him. The scent of roasting meat made his mouth water. His mind turned to food, ale, and a warm fire.

Maybe he would catch a glimpse of Eamhair—depending on what Bericus wanted of him.

"Lord Bericus sent you to find me?" he asked the maidservant, who was now fluttering her lashes and smiling in that way women the world over used when they were volunteering intimacies.

With a soft word to the four-legged creature poised beside him, he led the way back to the hall.

MORNING BROUGHT GREY, WATERY LIGHT TO THE PIT.

Taranis had shivered all night, with nothing but filth to sit on and cold stone against his back. Water dripped through the iron grate above and ran down the back of his neck. He couldn't escape it; the other prisoners had already taken every spot that provided protection. Rats and spiders crawled across his feet and the wolf bite on his wrist throbbed. He was lucky. The beast could have crushed his bones and would have, if Menoetius hadn't ordered it away. He also felt lingering aches from every kick he'd received.

He had to get out of here. Eamhair would be expecting him. What would she think if he never appeared again? Or worse, saw him roped to other criminals like a common, lowborn thief?

Why had he been taken? What did they think him guilty of? He cursed himself for openly entering the village this evening, his intent twofold—to check the other side of his pebble and mud sealing work, and to visit Father Bradan with some tale of spending the last fortnight traveling along the coast converting wherever he could. He'd planned to get the garrulous priest talking, and maybe learn more about Bericus, his sons, and this "parading" they forced Eamhair to endure.

Had Eamhair realized he was a fraud, and told someone of his appearance in her bedchamber? What else could it be?

Something hit him on the head. Cringing, he looked up. A woman stood at the rim, dropping in hunks of stale bread. The other prisoners burst into motion, seizing every crumb before Taranis had gathered his wits.

He didn't have the strength or will to fight for a share. He let his face drop back to his knees, telling himself he couldn't eat anyway, not with this stink of unwashed bodies and excrement. As a woodcutter, he was accustomed to the clean, sharp aroma of shaved wood and the airy green scent of forests. This cramped confinement with filthy humans was unendurable.

"Here."

Taranis looked up again. A skinny, lank-haired man held out a green-brown lump of oat bread.

Taranis took it and shoved it in his mouth with a muttered, "I thank you." The bread was dry and hard, but he was so hungry he hardly noticed.

Another glance at the kindhearted soul left him fighting off a sickening shudder. He saw past the dirt and greasy hair. "A-Alexiare!" He grabbed the man's forearm with his uninjured hand.

Spots leaped across his eyesight and he drifted into a brief trance. The pit felt as though it was rolling, tumbling like a boulder down a hill, sending him spinning into vertigo. At the bottom lay the white boat with the woman carved in the prow. Her dispassionate eyes were turned upwards to him; he clutched at every root and stone and weed he passed, certain if he fell into that boat he would die.

This man's reaction wasn't any better than Menoetius's the night before. He scrambled away, muttering, "Leave me alone."

Taranis slid out of the humming illusion. He swallowed the last of the bread, coughing as it stuck in his throat. "Don't—don't you know me?" he asked when he could speak. Excitement drained away for the second time. Aridela, Menoetius, and now Alexiare. All three together in this far-flung place, at the same time. And none of them knew who he was.

It was clear to him who *they* were, though they looked nothing like they had in the old days—but for the eyes. Oh, yes, he had recognized Aridela's eyes in Eamhair's face, and Menoetius's, though they were bluer than before, and now, Alexiare's.

Why could they not see Chrysaleon, prince of Mycenae, in his?

Isn't it more likely Chrysaleon is a dream that has taken you over and turned you mad? You think you can see people who have been dead for centuries, if they ever existed. The necklace poisoned you.

He surreptitiously made sure it was well hidden beneath his robe. This putrid group would joyfully crush his skull for such a trinket.

Logic and reason returned. He was not mad. Surely madness could not be so exquisitely detailed. But it had been a mistake to confront

Menoetius and Alexiare. All he had accomplished was to turn them against him. It had been such a shock—though meeting Aridela in the body of Eamhair should have prepared him.

His brother! His most loyal follower! In that instant, he discarded the bad blood Chrysaleon and Menoetius had built up between them, or how he'd cursed and mocked Alexiare at the end, and ordered him to hurry up and die.

At least I did not frighten away Aridela.

"That's the thanks ye get," said a woman in a dirty gown with a large tear at the shoulder.

One of the other prisoners pointed at him with his crust. "Are you the one who cut the throat of Drost Gocinecht's baby daughter?"

"*What?*" Taranis questioned his imperfect understanding of the man's speech.

"His messenger said it was a monk, and here you are."

"I-I have never seen his daughter."

The man chewed awhile before he asked, "So what is your crime then, stranger?"

"No one told me. I was kicked in the head for asking." Taranis wasn't about to admit he'd found a secret tunnel leading into the bedchamber of Bericus's daughter, or that he'd reclined on her bed, held her hand, and coaxed her into believing him a creature from the sea. Certainly not that he'd entertained heated, determined thoughts of seducing her.

The man waited, but when Taranis said no more, he stuffed the crust into his mouth and spoke as he chewed. "Can't say I hold with killing children—not even that bastard's. Bericus will happily collect the reward on your head. I would not choose to be you, brother."

"I have killed no one."

"Can you prove your innocence? If not, you'd best begin your final prayers. I suspect your death will be most unpleasant."

Rather than respond to the goad, Taranis shrugged and pretended to lose interest. He turned his head and stared at the rough stone wall as he sent his mind racing backward.

It had been Breda's suggestion to disguise himself as a monk for his journey. Monks enjoyed the same freedom and safety when crossing through guarded lands as did traders and bards, and monks from Saint Ninian's white stone chapel were being sent out in increasing numbers, charged with the task of conversion.

Drawn to the control, order, and power that was the foundation of the new Christ religion, he had sworn himself to it when he was four-teen. He liked Breda's idea and knew he could speak convincingly about its beliefs.

He set out on an aged donkey, resisting the urge to rub the prickly tonsure his mother had shaved onto his scalp. He had nothing but two extra habits practical Breda had acquired, and a loaf of bread; he begged for food as he went and encountered few people until many days into his travels, when a score of armed, tattooed warriors emerged from the forest on either side of his path. They fingered the sleeves of his robe and spoke in a garbled language he understood no word of. In the end they would not release him. When he protested, they pointed spears at his chest and herded him off course to Drost Gocinecht's northern stronghold of Sgathag Creag, not a prisoner exactly, but not free to continue on his own way, either.

Drost was an imposing figure, from his attire—a sleeveless quilted knee-length tunic that mocked the cold and woolen leggings bound in strips of leather, to his prominent beard and the vivid blue whorls and animal patterns pricked into his flesh. Gleaming silver bands around his massive arms made his wealth obvious. All his limbs were thickly muscled, as though he trained for war every day. His queen, Cadha, was also impressive, with her splendidly bared breasts, painted eyes, and hair partially plaited with blue and silver baubles. She appeared to enjoy nothing more than twirling knives like a juggler and gazing upon her court with languid eyes. Taranis watched her instantly size him up and dismiss him as uninteresting, which annoyed him.

Drost was fluent in Taranis's native tongue, having spent much time in the south battling Artorius, the famed bear-king of Britain. Unfortunately, that also meant he viewed Taranis as an enemy. Taranis had to swiftly explain where he was going and why. He assured Drost he had never been attached to Artorius's armies, or any army. He told his prepared story of traveling through the northern lands to share the Word of God and bring the promise of Heaven to men everywhere. Then he offered to share the Word with Drost.

The king acted slightly amused yet politely willing and invited Taranis to stay at Sgathag Creag as his guest. Beautiful, half-naked women flocked around him at the evening meal. They were difficult to resist, especially when they placed their hands on his thighs and leaned in to kiss his neck. He had to tamp down his urges again and again. Something about Drost sent warnings through his mind, perhaps the way he watched without seeming to, or smiled without sincerity. Taranis knew he couldn't take the chance of yielding to lust, for this well-traveled man, though pagan, was probably aware of the strict vows of chastity to which monks adhered.

These were goddess lands with mysterious traditions, not so different from Aridela's country, where Athene ruled supreme. He must be careful.

All went well for a few days. Taranis and Drost walked the grounds, talking of the Christ and other things, like sheep shearing, brewing ale, and the ongoing fight with the Britons.

On the third night he was given mead to drink. He'd enjoyed all kinds of mead growing up, but this had a queer, bitter flavor. He didn't like it, but after half a cupful, his tongue numbed and he no longer noticed. The next morning he woke bleary-eyed, head thumping, with two naked women he recognized as the queen's handmaids. His recollections of the night were cloudy. Had he boasted of his life as a king, and how his ancient name meant *Gold Lion?* Perhaps he had only dreamed of saying those things. When the women woke and chattered to him, he realized it didn't matter. They knew nothing of his language and he knew nothing of theirs, so even if he had spouted his secrets, they would not understand.

Relieved, he tried to communicate that they should say nothing of their night of debauchery with the monk. They giggled as they mimicked him, placing their fingers over their lips, and he finally gave up.

Drost acted no differently that day or the next. Taranis's apprehension lessened.

But on the third day after he misplaced his judgment and lay with the queen's handmaids, everything went sour. Taranis watched Cadha rebuke her husband's advances at the feasting table, apparently because she was more interested in another man, and a sudden, seething rage spiraled out of thin air and overtook him. As if from a distance, Taranis heard his voice ring through the hall as he rose. He stated that the One True God demanded a woman's absolute fidelity and submissive obedience. Rather than shutting his mouth after these insults, he struck the table with his fist and added that men were lords over every creature of the earth and sea—females most of all, as their natures were deficient and inclined to sin. His final statement declared that the freedom the Caledonii men allowed their women would be their downfall.

The hall fell into tense silence as those who did not understand this outsider's language grew wary, mostly due to Drost's thunderous expression. The queen spoke to Drost and he replied. Her cold gaze turned to Taranis; her nostrils dilated. Her women muttered and brandished their knives.

His head cleared somewhat and, baffled, he glared at his cup. He had been most careful since the other night, and had sipped only a small amount of the bitter mead. Yet again his tongue had loosened, and again his head was spinning. What was in this evil drink?

As Drost rose from his throne, Taranis heard laughter from somewhere beyond his sight, but before he could search out the one who found his rant so amusing, Drost was ordering him to leave his table and his stronghold, unless he wished to be skinned alive by his wife and her women.

Taranis didn't even try to reacquire the donkey. He walked—almost ran—through the night, and only when the sun was high in the heavens the next day did he feel free of hostile eyes. Had the mead been one of the crafty king's tests? He *had* watched the monk's outburst with a brief expression of delighted satisfaction, hadn't he?

Thanking the Christ for his life, Taranis set out again on his original purpose, and at long last, weary and footsore, he looked down upon Dunaedan and dared contemplate a happy ending.

Finding the tunnels and Aridela had flooded him with the old arrogant assurance of glory and triumph. Blessed lady Athene had sparked the dreams, brought him here, and showed him a way to be with her.

He remembered the vow he'd given Aridela on Crete. *Not even death can part us.* And it had not. Their bond was unbreakable.

But now he squatted in a stinking pit, facing accusations of murder, helpless and separated from her yet again.

Had he been wrong about Athene? *You will remember and despair,* the bull-king Damasen had declared. Was she dangling the shining prize of happiness so she could snatch it away?

Forgive me, he thought hastily, and from habit made the sign of the cross before he remembered he was praying to a much older deity. *It is hard for me to trust, Lady. I will be better.*

No doubt Menoetius was here to again challenge everything Chrysaleon wanted to save. He had seen the cloud around his half brother—dark as twilight and pale as dawn. What could that have been? Was it linked to the violet-gold mist hovering above Eamhair that first night, and the colored light she claimed to have seen upon him? Was Athene causing it?

There was no color around the slumped form of Alexiare on the other side of the pit.

Alexiare was Chrysaleon's man, through and through, never an ally to the goddess. Why had she returned him?

Taranis had been brought back to life and reunited with those people he had known on Crete. At first it had felt like a gift—a second chance for happiness. But with Athene, one could never be certain. What did his future hold? Every step, every thought, every gesture, seemed beyond his control, fraught with chance and possible chaos.

Chapter 14

A ROUGH GRATING SOUND STARTLED TARANIS OUT OF A RESTLESS DOZE. The iron bars were being lifted. A shadow appeared in the shape of a person's head and shoulders.

The other prisoners were already standing.

"Be quick," came the command from above. A crude ladder slid down.

Each prisoner scrambled up, Alexiare among them.

Taranis rose. He would take his chances and try to keep close to Alexiare, rather than waiting in this hole for Drost's questionable mercy.

TARANIS FOLLOWED UNOBTRUSIVELY AS THE MAN HE KNEW AS ALEXIARE headed toward the ocean. The other prisoners scattered like a hive of uncovered insects.

Before long they came to the mooring place. Alexiare untied a line holding the farthest boat and pushed against the prow.

"Help me if you're coming."

Taranis shoved on the other side and the boat slid off the shingle. They leaped in and rowed, fighting the incoming wash until it finally softened and they caught a current flowing eastward. The boat sprang towards safety and freedom.

"Who got us out of there?" Taranis asked after Alexiare set the sail to catch the cold night wind.

"A brother to one of the men. We have to get as far as we can before morning. I'm told the leader of those warriors is an uncommon hunter."

"What was your crime?"

Alexiare paused. "Does it matter?" He shrugged. "We are both murderers now. Any of us they catch will be hanged or worse. They won't care which one actually killed the guard."

"Where do you mean to go?"

"Innse Orc. But for the missing boat, it will be hard for them to track us. Even if they do realize we stole the boat, it's a big ocean, and a long coastline."

"Innse Orc?"

"A cluster of islands. You'll see when the sun comes up. There are many places a man can hide among them."

"It sounds like a good plan."

"I am glad you approve." After some time of silence, Alexiare asked, "Why did you think you knew me?"

Taranis didn't want to risk angering him again. "You resemble someone I once knew, but I was half senseless from being beaten."

Alexiare appeared to accept the answer. "It is good to know a madman has not joined me on this boat." He fiddled with the sail. "Sleep if you can. We are fortunate on the weather, if it lasts."

Taranis didn't think he could sleep, but he closed his eyes and when a choppy wave jolted him, he realized by the position of the sun that hours had passed. Alexiare sat with his hand on the tiller, staring into the distance. The waves were high, but not unbearably so, and crisp winds sent them skimming along at a good pace.

His spirits rose. Now if only they could find land and build a fire. He was chilled to the marrow of his bones.

Alexiare took his turn sleeping while Taranis manned the tiller and kept them on course. The day passed slowly, with no food and only one skin of water someone had left in the boat.

"What is your name?" Alexiare asked later, after he woke.

"Taranis. And you, my friend?"

"Winoc." After a pause, he asked, "Did you murder Drost Gocinecht's child?"

"I swear I did not."

"I have helped you. Now you must help me. If you are guilty, you and I need to part company as soon as we land, brother, for he will never stop searching for you, and I'd rather not get caught up in that."

"I swear upon God's face. I did insult the king of the Caledonii. He banished me and I left his fortress. I never saw his daughter."

"Killing a child is surely not something a monk would do." Winoc glanced at Taranis's robes.

"I am no monk," Taranis blurted. He cursed inwardly. This was *not* Alexiare, yet he was babbling as though the old man still knew him.

Winoc looked puzzled. "You are not?"

"I disguised myself as one in order to travel the length and breadth of this land. It was my mother's idea. She thought it would lend me safety."

"It appears to have done the opposite."

Again, Taranis had to fight the urge to divulge every one of his secrets to this stranger he remembered as his most ardent supporter. "I am grateful to the man who got us out of that pit, for my future was sure to be grim and short."

Winoc drank a few sips of water and wiped his mouth. "When the powerful decide to persecute, there is little a man can do to defend himself. It is best to simply disappear."

The heavens had purpled into twilight when the island Winoc sought loomed before them. At first Taranis was sure they could never land—the coastline was astounding in its beauty but also daunting—cliffs reaching to the heavens, and black, gnarled stacks, boulders, and frenzied, unwelcoming seas.

"We cannot land here!" Taranis shouted over the roar of the surf.

"You veered too far north, but I know what to do. I grew up here." Winoc took over and aimed southwards; in time, the high precipices collapsed into sloping hills and the sea grew calmer. Winoc steered them into a dim inlet, littered with so many boulders Taranis was sure they would end up on the sea floor. They pulled down the sail and Taranis rowed while Winoc leaned over the prow and guided him to a place where they could heave the boat out of the water. Once landed, it was well hidden by boulders and rock walls.

"See?" Winoc said. "A man born to it can bring a boat in here. Come, Taranis. A year ago, I had a mother, a wife, and a babe soon to be born. I am anxious to see how they have fared."

Taranis scrambled behind his guide until they reached high, flat ground and set off northward, following the coastline.

During the time Winoc had been asleep, Taranis had watched him.

Was this truly Alexiare? Why was he so certain, when the man looked completely different? It was the same with Menoetius and Aridela. Only the eyes were similar. That and something nebulous, sensed rather than seen.

There *had* to be a way to return their memories. Somehow he would find it.

Chapter 15

CAILEAN WAS FURIOUS.

Every prisoner...gone. The guard's throat slit. A few suspected it had been done by one of Bericus's own men out of jealousy, designed to make Cailean look bad in the chieftain's eyes.

He rounded up a score of warriors and they set out in pursuit. Two of the prisoners were recaptured within a day. Another was caught the next.

A fisherman came to the fort, complaining of his boat being stolen. Cailean interrogated the recaptured prisoners until one of them confessed that the man called Winoc hailed from Innse Orc—the nearest isle.

Cailean, shadowed by Vita, walked to the cliffs and stared at the mist-veiled smudge in the far distance. Bran interrupted him to report that another escaped prisoner had been found.

That left only two. The perverted merchant, "Winoc," accused of trying to bugger the tanner's twelve-year-old son, and the monk—the killer of Drost Gocinecht's daughter, probably the most valuable criminal ever to be imprisoned at Dunaedan.

The lunatic who had called Cailean his brother.

There was no help for it. He would have to set sail for Innse Orc. But not without talking to Eamhair first.

In the morning, Cailean stuck a raven's feather between two timbers at the north gate, the sign he and Eamhair used to suggest a meeting in the sea cave.

Snow was falling, thick and silent. Not a good send off, but Bericus would hold with no delay. He wanted that monk, and would make Cailean suffer if he was not retrieved.

Last night, after stuffing himself on venison and impatiently beckoning to a serving woman, Bericus had leaned close. As the girl refilled his vessel with a third helping of ale, he slurred through noxious fumes of onion and sour drink that he would give Cailean his daughter if the monk was returned.

Cailean waited in the cave a long while, clenching and unclenching his hands in their leather gauntlets. He should have just gone. The sooner he went, the sooner he might return.

Thankfully, Bericus, his sons, and most of his men had drunk their frustration away the night before, and would sleep later than usual.

Bericus lies to every man who comes here. He makes them believe they will walk away with Eamhair in their possession. He takes their bribes and they wake from the poison ale to find themselves alone and destitute. The only difference between them and you is that you cannot blame the ale.

Still, his imagination could not be completely quelled.

She appeared at last, dwarfed by her voluminous cloak, hooded against the snow, her cheeks blushed from the cold. For an instant, in the dim light of pre-dawn, he saw an aura around her, the color of violets shot through with golden speckles.

He felt sick with dread and premonition. Raised by a woman like his mother, he couldn't dismiss it as unimportant.

She entered the cave, throwing back her furred hood, her breath clouding around her head. Her teeth chattered and her lips were bluish. "Oh," she said, "that water is cold."

Vita allowed her to approach without protest, which was interesting.

"Your father has charged me with an important mission," he said. "I am to find the last two men who escaped from the pit the other night. One is a murderer, and Bericus especially wants him."

"In this storm? Alone? Where—how long...?"

"Not alone. Seven of us. I don't know how long we'll be." He walked to the cave mouth and looked out at the waves. "It has been suggested," he said slowly, turning back to her, "that success will make it worth any danger or discomfort."

Her brows lifted, betraying her dismay. "Bericus allows a feast on the night of the solstice. There is music and dancing—and of course prayers, now that we celebrate Christ's day of birth at the same time. Will you be back by then?"

"I will do my best."

"I—I will miss you…Cailean."

Her words sent spears of light shooting through his heart and diluted his apprehension. He pulled the gauntlet from his right hand and removed his ring, a heavy silver circle woven in the distinctive knotwork long perfected among his people. His mother had given it to him when he was nine, the year he left his home to go to his father. He placed it against her palm and closed her fingers over it. "Take care while I am gone." He added, "Why are you not wearing gloves? You are so cold." He lifted her hand and blew on her knuckles.

Tears welled in her eyes. "I will not fear for you." She rested her free hand on his forearm. "A man who commands the love and loyalty of a wolf could never be bested by a mere murderer."

He felt again the inexplicable sensation he had first experienced in Bericus's hall, like flashes of lightning running from his skin to hers.

"Eamhair." He wanted to say something that would make her his, keep her true, no matter how long it took to find that cursed prisoner.

But what if he didn't come back? What if he died? He didn't know why he felt such foreboding, but he did, and he knew it would be unfair to ask anything of her. Besides, her father and Drost Gocinecht had utter control over whom she would spend her life with. "Do you know the Point, beyond Dhu Rinn, where the sand is deep? As far north as you can walk?"

"Yes."

"If you were to go there and light a fire, a boat would come for you. Men I trust would take you to my mother, and she would give you her protection. You would be safe."

"Why are you telling me this? Are you—are you not coming back?"

"I plan to. But if something were to delay me…or prevent me…I want you to go to my mother. Promise."

She nodded slowly. "You have my promise. But only if I can take *my* mother."

"Yes, of course you can. She would be most welcome."

"How long will you be gone?"

"I cannot know. Vita will watch over you."

"I think you expect trouble."

He gave a careless shrug. "No more so than any fleeing criminal would give, and less than a battle. It is you I worry about."

She hesitated. "I will keep to the kitchens and my needlework. I'll make no more noise than a mouse. Bericus will forget he has a daughter."

Cailean knew better than that, but he let it go.

He kissed her hard and held her, breathing in the gentle scent that made him feel as though he was in a dream. "*Donnah*," he whispered.

"What does that mean?"

"I will tell you someday."

An hour later, he and six carefully chosen archers set out to sea in one of Bericus's war-boats, its green-dyed sail marked with the chief's signet—a double-peaked rock and the head of a stag.

He looked back as they rowed out of the inlet.

She was standing near the water's edge, part of a cluster of waving women. Vita pressed against her right leg. Her left hand was fisted; he knew his ring lay warm and safe against her palm. He sent back a silent plea. *Divine Lady, allow nothing to part us.*

YOU WILL BEG FOR DEATH, BUT DEATH WILL REFUSE YOU...

~~~THE PROPHECY OF SELENE

I Will Name You After The
God Of Thunder

BREDA THE PROSTITUTE VENTURED FORTH WITH SOME TREPIDATION TO SEE how much damage the storm had caused. She hoped she might find something of value, or at the very least wood she could take home, dry out, and burn in her cooking fire.

She found a child.

It had poured rain for three days before the clouds finally shredded, coming apart like thistledown. Hazy hiccupping rays of sunlight illuminated a thousand pools of murky water; sodden barley heads tried to unbend. Frogs emerged from their hiding places, droning happily in a sudden luxury of midges, and every leaf in the forest shook off clinging dew.

The river had erupted, joining with the rain to scour a wide swath of destruction. Breda picked her way through debris, marveling at the changes wrought in what had been a lush valley of ancient forests and fertile farmland. As she shivered in the damp morning chill, her gaze passed over then rebounded to what looked like a motionless chalk-white hand thrusting from a tangle of severed tree branches. She ran to it, yanking at flotsam, muttering her shock and pity. The boy must have been tossed, thrown, and pummeled until the surge had enough of him and vomited him out amongst rocks and other wreckage.

Where was his mother? She searched as the sun climbed, turning the air to muggy syrup, but found no other bodies. It was odd. She knew everyone in the village, but she had never seen this boy. He appeared to be five or six years old; only Gwawr had a child that age, and this was not Gwawr's son.

She returned, gently removing a twig from his hair. His flesh was cold, covered with bruises, blood, and muck.

Poor thing. How he must have suffered. How frightened he must have been. She would carry his broken corpse to her bothy and bury him beneath the yew. She caught herself thinking maybe she could ask one of the nuns to bless him before she remembered that the nuns would not speak to her. They lifted their skirts and scurried the other way if they saw her coming, like she was the Devil himself.

Reaching down, she swabbed a glob of slimy river mud from his eye, gasping when his mouth opened and he released a weak, angry whimper.

"Alive!" she cried. "You're alive, little one." She picked him up and cradled him, holding his cold wet cheek to her throat. "Ah, you are a strong boy. I will try to make you well. And if you live, I will name you Taranis ap Taranis, after the god of thunder, for you surely deserve it."

Chapter 16

TARANIS WAS STILL THINKING OF BREDA THE NEXT MORNING AS HE DONNED the trousers, wool shirt, and tunic given to him by the gypsies. Reveling in the much-needed warmth they helped generate, he tossed the monk's habit into the fire pit and watched with angry pleasure as the flames consumed it. Winoc was right—the robe had brought bad luck.

His thoughts fell into a gloomy place where he never saw Breda or Eamhair again, and neither ever knew why.

Before long Winoc's mother joined him. When he and Winoc arrived at the encampment, deep in the night, she had awakened and come to greet her son; her gaze upon Taranis was perceptive, and had made him uneasy. After Winoc went off to reunite with his wife and baby, she engaged him in conversation, enticing him with bread and salted mutton. They sat by the warmth of the fire and talked until the sun came up.

"Thank you, Mistress Eseld, for these." He gestured at the clothing.

She waved off his thanks and went right back to what they had talked about the night before. "You were telling me this woman—Breda—is not your true mother?"

"Nay, she is not."

"She is a...?"

"Whore. I spent much of my youth being sent away so she could earn what she needed to feed us. We did eat better than many."

"And so, Taranis, you have no knowledge of where you were born, or what birth name you were given."

Why does she care about my troubles? He shook his head. "Breda told me all she knew when I was old enough. She oft-repeated the story. Now and again I try to imagine who gave birth to me—if she tried to save me and died, and was washed away. No body was ever found."

Eseld laid down thick woven mats and they sat near the fire. The other members of her tribe kept their distance, only glancing over every now and then from other fire pits.

"You constantly watch my son," she said after some time of silence. She placed her hand near Taranis's wrist as he started. "Even now, you hardly take your eyes off him."

"He seems familiar to me."

"You do know him."

Taranis wasn't sure what to say. He regarded her warily.

"Are you not a visionary?" She laughed. "Do you not remember the lives you have lived before this one?"

"How...how do you know that?"

Her bracelets chimed as she lifted her arms. "I see colors around those who have lived before. You are one. My son is another. You knew him in that other life. Your colors blend when you are near each other."

Taranis sought out Winoc, but again saw no color—nothing. And still he couldn't understand why Athene would bring his old slave, her proven enemy, back to life. But here they were, and how, but for Athene, could he have found his way to Winoc or Eseld, a woman who apparently had the ability to see the innermost truths he so needed to have explained?

Once he had prayed to no god but Poseidon. Could the bearded lord of thunder still be alive and watching, playing a part, perhaps in competition with Athene? That would make Alexiare's presence easier to understand.

He rejected the idea with scorn. Any help he might give Poseidon credit for had been weak and indifferent. No, he would put his trust in Athene, the goddess of golden Crete, and equally in the Christos. Why couldn't Christ be as real as the others he remembered so well? With the demise of the last of the goddess lands, the door was flung open to newer gods, or a god, one who encompassed all the violence and jealousy of the many gods he had once worshipped. He could truthfully say he helped it happen, when he broke Aridela's neck and sent Crete into darkness.

The power of the Christ god and his priests was immense and ever expanding. The part of Chrysaleon that lived on inside Taranis couldn't help being inspired. It was too bad, though, that the new god hated anything joyous and demanded that his people be always grieving and begging absolution for even the smallest sins. At least the old gods knew how to make merry once in a while.

Flames leaped in Eseld's black eyes. "I have come close to death from those who name me devil or cursed. So I move from place to place and keep away from towns and villages. For now, I live here." She waved fondly at the wagons and tents. Taranis thought it a poor subsistence, but the people laughed and chattered as they went about their daily chores. The children played happily. Winoc had told him the band moved from island to island, and preferred being able to quickly pack up and vanish.

Last evening, as he followed Winoc on the long walk to his mother's nomadic tribe, he observed that most of the island's terrain was windswept moorland, with the occasional stunted tree, bare humped hills, and boulders protruding from the ground like bleached bones. But the camp was situated in a deep, crooked valley not far from the ocean, blessed with fresh water from a racing burn, sheltered by steep hills and set in a cozy clearing surrounded by a wood so thick that even in winter, stripped of leaves, the tangle of rowan, hazel, and birch trees offered excellent concealment.

"Can you tell me why I remember and he does not?" Taranis motioned towards Winoc, who was lifting the baby from his wife's arms.

She sobered and shook her head. "I will cast the bones, if you like."

His breath caught.

She smiled—her gaze missed little. "Tell me about your other life."

It was hard to speak of it. For years he had believed he was turning into a gibbering fool. But now he had seen Menoetius, and Alexiare, and Aridela herself. Now he knew the necklace had brought him truth.

"I ruled over two kingdoms. Winoc was my slave. In those days he was called Alexiare." Lower, he said, "He was the only man I genuinely trusted."

She said nothing, but her gaze grew even more intent.

"My queen from that life is alive as well. I have seen her, talked to her. And my half brother. I saw him at Bericus's fort, just before I found Winoc. For a time, we were all in the same place, a few steps from each other. But none of them remember me." Desolation flooded him. "I feel I am sinking in a bog, watching the sky for the last time."

"Take heart, Taranis."

"In that life...the queen...my wife...died. It was...my doing." The words chafed his throat like the prickles on a blackberry stem. "I would give my life to change that. I would give anything. *Do* anything. Why would I be here now, but to earn forgiveness for that crime?"

Her brows drew together. Her gaze riveted on him, as though she was seeing something he wasn't certain he wanted her to see.

"Is that all?" she asked when he said no more.

He swallowed. "After she died, I took a few trinkets that reminded me of her and hid them in a cave. But somehow, one of those trinkets is here." He pulled the necklace out from under his tunic. "My mother says I was wearing it when she found me."

Hesitantly at first, he related how the necklace had forced the Cretan memories into his mind.

"Yours is an intriguing story." Closing her eyes, she touched the blue stone at the center of the pendant. Instantly her brows descended and her mouth tensed. After a short interval of silence, her eyes flew open.

"You saw."

She swallowed. "I-I did."

He faltered but forced himself to speak. "Now you know how I was cursed. So was Winoc, by powerful women. By a goddess."

"Every time I have looked at my son since the day he was born, I have seen this curse, like a cloud wrapped around him. I saw it in your necklace. I see it upon you now."

He could think of nothing to say, no words of defense that would have any meaning.

"I am ready," she said, and stood.

Taranis stood too. "You can bring back his memories?"

"I will try." Eseld went off and soon returned with another mat under her arm, a bowl holding her divinatory bones, and a leather pouch. In her other hand she held a shriveled, slimy black thing, dotted with green mold.

"Forgive me." She glanced at the object. "I did not know you were coming, or that I would have need of the energy in these. This one is spoiled, as you can see, and I have none preserved."

"What is it?" He grimaced at the odor.

"Some call them dream flowers. See how it resembles a woman's breast?"

A dying hag's breast, maybe.

"This is all that is left of my harvest from several months back. I usually dry what I find but I did not this year. I hope my sister will have some. But I warn you, Taranis. What you desire is no small thing. As powerful as these mushrooms are, they may not be strong enough to grant your wish."

"The priestesses on Kaphtor—Crete—used such things to commune with the gods and see the future." An ancient saying floated through his mind. *They can drink everything Mother Gaia drinks and suffer no ill effects.* "Lady," he said fervently, "I swear a god has led me to you. I will thank them all, so I offend none."

"Try to sleep. Tomorrow morning, I will find my sister. Tonight I will cast the bones, and when I return, I will tell you what I can."

Taranis glanced at Winoc, who still hovered near his wife. They were talking and playing with the baby.

He was as far from tired as he had ever been, but Eseld handed him a blanket, indicating their conversation was done for now.

He went off, imagining a joyous reunion with Alexiare, Menoetius, and most of all, Aridela.

ESELD LEFT AT DAWN, TAKING ONE OF THE YOUNGER GIRLS WITH HER. Taranis watched them go, already impatient, skeptical that a rotted mushroom could possibly have the kind of potency needed to resurrect memories buried for two millennia. But his thoughts soon returned to Eamhair.

Seeking distraction, he left the encampment, came to the edge of the wood, and hiked up a steep slope to a windy plateau, where he could hear the ocean thundering. He followed the roar to the cliffs and gazed westward. To Dunaedan. Gloomy snow clouds blocked any glimpse of the headland. Had she given up on ever seeing him again? What of Menoetius? How had he come to be at Dunaedan? Had dreams or memories driven him there, too?

Nearly three days passed before Eseld returned. Her sister's tribe had moved and it took time to find them. She opened her pouch and dropped several grey-brown mushrooms into Taranis's hand. "In the morning, break them up and mix them into Winoc's gruel."

These had no smell or mold, other than a bluish tinge. The nipple Eseld had tried to show him on the rotted one was more pronounced on these. Still, Taranis couldn't help asking, "They won't kill him, will they?"

"No." Her brows furrowed. "But I expect they will make him ill."

Anticipation dried the inside of his mouth and kept him awake most of the night. Rising early, he collected two bowls of porridge from the women who were cooking, tore and stirred the mushrooms into one and took them to Winoc and his wife. They were just waking, and thanked him. Taranis sat nearby, holding Winoc's baby boy on his knee while they ate.

Winoc shoveled the porridge into his mouth as though he hadn't eaten in months. He grimaced once or twice, but went on eating until he finished the last spoonful.

Later though, he complained of belly pain. Soon he was vomiting. Taranis exchanged glances with Eseld, who was overseeing the roasting of a pig at the central fire pit. He brought the empty bowls to her, hoping she would share what she had divined when she cast the bones, but she put him off.

Winoc staggered away, saying he thought he was going to die. His wife started to follow but Taranis intervened, saying he would tend her mate, so she could remain near the fire with their son.

"What is happening to me?" Winoc's voice was hoarse and halting. "That porridge. It tasted off."

Taranis brought him water from the stream.

Another length of time passed; Winoc wavered in and out of consciousness, groaning when he woke then lapsing into feeble silence. "The Lady," he muttered. "Her eyes...."

Taranis began to worry that Winoc might indeed expire.

Sunlight struggled through thick, swiftly building clouds, and the wind turned severe. The storm Taranis had seen massed over Dunaedan's point had reached them.

Winoc straightened, his eyes red and watering. His face, which had been greenish, suffused to scarlet. "My lord," he whispered, and bent his head.

Taranis stared. "What?"

Winoc remained silent.

Losing patience, Taranis rose. "Stand up and face me. What is it?"

Winoc stumbled to his feet. He kept one hand pressed to his

stomach and his face ran with sweat. "I remember," he said, not looking directly at Taranis. "Please—water."

Taranis handed him the skin. Winoc drank and poured a good measure over his head. Swiping the back of his hand across his eyes, he said, "It runs through my mind like a firestorm. Everything, my lord. My lord...Chrysaleon, son of Idómeneus, king of Mycenae and Kaphtor."

Taranis sucked in a breath. Legions of white sparks exploded, disrupting his sight; his ears roared. For an instant, he thought he too might lose consciousness.

Winoc teetered. He extended his arms, seeking his balance. "Ah, yes, at last I understand. I must sit, my lord. I feel unsteady."

Taranis nodded and took his arm. "Let us move away where we won't be overheard." Leaving the forest, they crossed the moor until they came to a cluster of tall boulders, almost like a lopsided circle of standing stones. They sat, bracing themselves against two of the stones. Winoc drank, drank again, and continued to shudder.

"I am a trader," he said shakily. "I have traveled most of my life, and have seen many things, but it was different when I came to Bericus's holdings. Something forced me to stay—a need I cannot explain. It would not release me. When I slept, I dreamed of that place. I saw it as clearly as I did when I stood outside the gate at the fort and for the first time, looked up at its tower—like a beacon! When I walked through the village, I knew I had found the place of my dreams. But I didn't know why I was there, why it was important. I had no memory of you. The dreams were frightening, my lord, violent and bloody. In each one, there was a white boat, with a bare-breasted woman at the prow, a *living* woman, my lord, trapped in the wood, and when she looked at me, it felt as though my flesh burned. I expected to see this boat at Dunaedan, but I did not."

Taranis could not speak for many heartbeats. Finally he said, "I have dreamed of that boat. That woman. I, too, dreamed of Dunaedan, and was compelled to go there, no matter the cost."

"Please tell me of your life, my lord."

Taranis showed Winoc the necklace and told his story. They tried to imagine how it could have come to this far-removed place and time. He told Winoc the details of his own compulsive journey, but just as he started to share the most wondrous tidbit of all, that he had found Aridela in the body of Bericus's daughter, he stopped. His throat closed. He couldn't reveal that part, not yet.

Winoc rubbed his cheeks. "It is her doing, my lord. Athene. It has to be. But why has she forged herself to a boat?"

This was nearly too much for Taranis. Fear crawled over his skin. To postpone thinking of it, he said, "Tell me what got you thrown in the pit."

Winoc picked up a pebble and juggled it from one hand to the other. "I had nothing to eat so I stole a bannock from a hut in the village. A woman saw me and screamed, which brought Bericus's warriors. They caught me—they on horseback, me not. I had no chance."

"A bannock?" The man was lying; everything about his expression and voice betrayed it. The trust Taranis instinctively wanted to give Winoc retreated a step or two. "You were thrown in the pit over a hunk of bread?"

"Have you not heard about Bericus, how mean-hearted he is?" Winoc threw the rock. "A man rode up. Not any ordinary man. High, high above me on his stallion, and that wolf by his side. Bericus's premiere warrior, the leader of his war band, I was soon to learn. Hatred ran through me. I never felt such a thing before toward anyone. In that instant, I knew what brought me to Dunaedan. It was to kill this man they call Cailean of Dalriada, even though I did not know him, or why such hatred burned within me. But now I do. He is Menoetius! I cannot explain how I know this, but I am certain. He barely glanced at me without any sign of recognition. I was shackled and helpless. I could not even attempt to harm him, but if you command it, I will go back. I will find a way." He rubbed his eyelids, then his forehead. "Once, at Mycenae, I cast a spell and was given a vision. A woman spoke. 'Gold and obsidian, lion and bull, they are forged,' she said. When I looked at Cailean—Menoetius—I knew I had to kill him, and now, I know why. To protect you. My lord, without doubt we are embroiled still in the events of Kaphtor and your kingship—the curse still works its doom against us. His death is the only way to escape the fate he brings with him through the ages."

Taranis bent his head and closed his eyes against stomach churning dizziness. *I am not mad. At least…I am not mad alone.*

But relief diminished as he thought, *Again? I must kill my brother…again?*

"Did you know he was there, my lord? Have you seen him too?"

Taranis opened his eyes. "Why must he die? He has done nothing to me here. Nay, I want to return his memories as I have done with you. I want you both with me. Perhaps, together, we can defeat these curses." He couldn't bring himself to confess he was now Athene's contrite follower, or that he believed she had forgiven him. Not with that gleam of vengeance in Winoc's eyes.

Winoc said nothing, which caused Taranis alarm. "What is it?"

"You imprisoned your brother in the labyrinth. You murdered him. You want him to remember that?"

"It was not murder. He volunteered to die."

"Bringing back his memories will also bring back the rivalry between you, the bad blood, the jealousy, the love you both bore for Queen Aridela. I advise against it, my lord."

Taranis's thoughts tangled in confusion, anger, and perhaps strongest of all, grief. "What am I to do then with this knowledge?"

Winoc shook his head wearily. "It is the curse." He drank more water. "Selene's curse. *You and your master will wander. Glimpses of joy will be ripped from you. You will beg for death but death will refuse you. You will follow...and follow...without end.*"

"I remember." Taranis remembered the other curse too—the one Aridela's father had leveled against him. *Until you honor your vow, you will carry the burden of all your deceptions, and they will grow heavy.*

Those curses were coming true. He alone had suffered the weight of the memories until now. He had begged for death that night, and nearly every day since.

How could he honor his vow? Crete was gone, at least the Crete he had known. How could he do anything to earn forgiveness, with Labyrinthos buried in sand?

Tears streamed over Winoc's cheeks. "What have we done, my lord? What will become of us?"

Before Taranis could think of an answer, the first arrow hissed past his temple and sank into Winoc's right eye.

Arms flailing, Winoc flew backward and landed flat on the ground. His left eye opened wide and slowly faded into blankness.

As Taranis gaped, an arrow whistled past his ear; another grazed his shoulder, leaving a bloody notch. He stumbled to his feet, shielding his face and head as arrows thudded around him.

He heard screaming from the gypsy settlement and ran towards it, away from his unseen attackers.

Chapter 17

THREE OF BERICUS'S MEN RETURNED FROM THE SOUTH, WHERE THEY HAD been helping their overlord in the fight against Artorius's Britons for several years. Drost Gocinecht had originally conscripted eighteen; fifteen would never again fight anywhere.

Eamhair listened from her hiding place as the newly arrived men shouted over each other in their eagerness to tell of the Pendragon and how it had been, fighting his well-trained warriors. Again and again they brought up the size of the horses—much like Cailean's stallion— and enviously described the Saxon mail shirts most of them wore, and how Artorius could always be seen, for he rose head and shoulders above other men.

After thoroughly chronicling those topics, they moved on to the Blue Falcon—as tall as Artorius and always at his side. He was rumored to be the war-leader's lover, son, or bodyguard; no one knew the nature of their relationship, but they had *seen* the glow of blue said to surround him in battle—a mystical thing no enemy weapon could penetrate. Their voices grew hushed as they spoke of his lethal sword, *Ravange*, how it never bent or shattered like ordinary blades. His deadly charges were discussed at length, and how he could string three arrows at once and strike three separate targets while astride his galloping mount. It was a common claim that the Falcon and his unstoppable beast had slaughtered over a thousand men.

Awed whispers rumbled through the hall. *Artorius! Blue Falcon....*

Someone asked what the Falcon's name was, but none of the warriors knew. They had never heard him called anything but his title.

They went on to conjecture about the Blue Falcon vanishing after a particularly fierce battle, two years back. Apparently he never returned. No one knew if he had been killed, captured, or had deserted. Desertion was doubtful, as Artorius had crushed the enemy and won the day. The victory had been so overwhelming that there had been no fighting since, but for minor skirmishes. That was why the survivors had been allowed to come home at last.

These three men had best learn how to disguise their pensive expressions, or Bericus would have them hanging from the palisades. They seemingly longed to abandon Dunaedan and offer their lives to the legendary Artorius, who was reputed to be half-Roman, half-native, and protected by powerful magic. The glory of it must make their sword-hands itch.

Eamhair allowed her imagination free rein. Artorius, growling and massive as a real bear, his companion as swift and pitiless as a diving falcon.

How she would love a glimpse of such mythical warriors. Her own hand prickled, though she had never wielded anything heavier, weapon wise, than a filleting knife.

BARE BRANCHES WHIPPED TARANIS'S FACE AS HE RACED THROUGH THE forest and burst into the clearing. At the same time, the storm turned monstrous. Rain no longer fell but slashed; wicked lightning branched across the sky. Thunder shook the ground in one deafening roar after another.

Holding Winoc's son in her arms, Eseld was dazed and stumbling, though she had no obvious wounds. Other women were trying to shield themselves and their children from deadly arrows. At least seven men lay on the ground, dying or dead.

Taranis grabbed Eseld's arm. He'd noted the arrows were coming from the north, from warriors hidden among the trees, so he pulled her to the west.

"Who is it?" she cried. "I saw no one."

Bericus's men—it had to be. Maybe led by Menoetius. *Cailean of Dalriada*, Winoc had named him. He should have realized Menoetius would piece together what he and Winoc had done, and where they went.

"These trees will aid those who hunt us," Eseld said. "We must get to the cliffs, where there are caves. My people have hidden in them for centuries."

He followed her lead, plotting as they ran and climbed. If he could get back to the stolen boat, the attackers would follow. It was the only way to save what remained of these people. He owed Winoc that much.

They raced across the open moor, using boulders as cover. Taranis glanced behind them. So far, he saw no archers. Perhaps he and Eseld had eluded them in the forest, but the baby's wailing would surely give them away.

"Can you make it stop crying?" he asked. Eseld put the babe to her shoulder and tried to soothe him.

They came to a barely-discernable goat path leading over the cliff's edge and took it, sliding on icy mud. Taranis's heart pounded. One misstep and he would plummet to cold, certain death in the ocean. Soon they arrived at a cave. They went inside, their gasps echoing against the damp walls.

"Where is Winoc?" she asked, when she could speak.

"He-he was killed. I am sorry."

She was quiet for a time, rubbing her eyes. "I always knew he would not live to be old. But it is hard, Taranis, to lose a child, even when you know it is coming before it should."

He could think of nothing to say that would give comfort. He, too, would miss Winoc.

"His wife was killed as well," she said. She patted the baby and kissed its cheek. "I am all this one has left."

Another of the tribe scrabbled in, panting, bleeding from two separate wounds. He insisted no one had seen him.

They could do nothing but wait, listen to the deafening ocean, and worry about being discovered.

Hours later, during a lull in the downpour, Taranis returned to the camp. He found Winoc's dead wife and about ten others. Maybe the rest had escaped and were hiding. There was no sign of their attackers.

"They've gone," he said when he got back to the cave. "But wait here overnight to be certain. I know who pursues us. He tracks as well in this life as he did thousands of years ago."

"You're leaving?" Eseld asked.

"It's me he wants."

"But this storm…." The other survivor glanced outside. "And it is nearly nightfall. Where will you go?"

"Taranis—" Eseld put her hand on his forearm. "The bones showed that you must return to the other part of your dream. Therein lies your destiny."

His throat closed, and he could only nod. He had never considered going anywhere else.

Later, when he recovered the boat, after he emerged from the cove through some miracle, as he was tossed like a leaf between waves of savage height and fury, he cursed the idiocy that had brought him to this end. But living his entire life inland, among green hills and forests, he could not have been prepared for an ocean seized by madness. Now he would die, and the other part of his dream—*Aridela*—would never know he'd died trying to return to her.

As if to prove the point, the highest wave yet soared above him, giving him an eternal, heart-stopping pause to watch his death coming before it crashed, throwing him out of the little craft and breaking it to bits.

THE STORM THAT BEGAN WHEN EAMHAIR WATCHED CAILEAN SAIL FROM Dunaedan continued, plaguing the coast for two more days before finally drifting away to the east. The air remained cold; layers of mist clung to the cliffs, but it was fresh and calm after the continuous terrible booming of the sea.

Eamhair left the fort as soon as the weather cleared, wanting to see how her beach had fared. She had named it "Beach of the seal-people," when she was little, as the seals favored it. She loved imagining what each seal would look like as a man or woman. Something about the air at the beach was different—breathing caused an energizing wakefulness and a shiver on the back of the neck. Sometimes she would turn, certain of movement out of the corner of her eye, her mind telling her that a shape was forming out of sea spray and mist—an arched gateway, she thought—but so far, no matter how fast she pivoted, it always vanished before she actually saw anything, and so she was never sure if it had been there or not.

The plateau was muddy; her leather shoes and the bottom of her tunic and cloak were soon soiled, but she didn't care.

She stood near the shoreline, surveying the frothy water. Earlier, she'd scratched the ninth line in the stone beneath the window in her chamber. Nine days since she last saw the seolh.

I will not leave you, he'd promised. But he had. His arrival, after years of waiting, had amazed and shocked her, had lifted her from despair. His stories were enthralling. He made her believe her pain, and Ula's, would soon be nothing but memories. His presence resurrected her belief in miracles.

As she stood on the beach and thought her thoughts, a trio of sleek wet heads appeared near the shore. All six eyes were trained upon her. She made no movement. The seals swam closer and hauled out, only about the length of two tall men away from her. Having come to some decision marking her as no threat, they ignored her as they rolled, shaking their fat, spotted bodies, and spoke to each other in grunts and snorts and raspy coughing.

Eamhair well knew that seals were not usually so fearless, unless, of course, there was a boat with a tempting catch of fish. "You are very brave," she said, carefully modulating her voice. Only one of the seals even glanced at her—a weanling, smaller than the other two, with a sweet, puppy-like face and sleepy eyes.

A shiver ran over her and she rubbed her arms. "How do you live like you do? I know you have much fat, but still. Do you not ever feel the cold?"

Now the smaller one leveled her with more than a glance. It rolled again, staring at her the whole while, until it lay on its stomach, its head and tail lifted in the manner common among its clan. When she did not speak again, it barked and scooted towards her.

She wasn't sure if it was trying to frighten her away or merely curious, but she held her ground. It stopped just out of reach, lifted its head again, and inspected her.

"I think if you became a man, your eyes would be silver."

Was it listening? The way its mouth closed suggested alert surprise.

"And I think, if you became a man, you would shed all that blubber. You would be tall and thin. And your hair would be long and silver, like your eyes." She realized she was now describing the children of the Goddess Danu, and so mixing up Ula's stories, but she was no bard. She shrugged. "Yes, that is what I think."

The seal didn't move, but as Eamhair watched, the light around the creature diffused into a soft alabaster mist. Her heartbeat quickened and she held her breath.

Nothing happened. The sun inched higher, the seal continued to stare, and the ocean washed against the shore.

Perhaps a song might sway him. She began an old lullaby meant to send children to sleep. *"Sweet young bear, all alone..."*

The other two seals stopped preening and looked at her.

Where is your mother, where is your father?
Are you alone in the deep dark woods,
Cry for your mother, cry for your father,
None to show you what to do. None to show you what to do.

A lump formed in her throat and her eyesight blurred. Had she angered Taranis? Not for the first time, she mulled over every word they had shared, but could think of nothing—except for that change in his expression when he spoke of his wife. At first he'd seemed happy, until he admitted Eamhair reminded him of her, and all happiness fled from his face.

He left his golden palace in the ocean, assumed the awkward legs and arms of a man, for her. He took her hands in his and promised everything would be different, and in that instant he transcended from seolh or man into hero. Guardian. Savior.

His disappearance was an acute blow. She was glad she hadn't broken her word and told her mother of him. At least Ula didn't have to feel this ache of betrayal and new, keen-edged desperation.

She took two steps and sat down on a dry stone. The seals watched her do this, but none took fright. The smaller male scooted closer, but showed no aggression. Slowly, she held out one hand, palm up. "Are you going to change?" It would be wondrous if he did, but she had a feeling such things were only done in private.

Making a soft bleating sound rather like a sheep, he heaved forward and rested his snout in her hand.

"You are a handsome lad." She stroked his whiskers and his smooth damp head.

The thought struck with abrupt force. She drew in a breath. "Is it you, Taranis? Are you trapped, unable to change for some reason? Is that why I have not seen you?"

There was no way to tell. Though bright and intelligent, his eyes gave no indication that he was anything other than a seal.

"It is hard to be the one left behind. Hard to be the one not knowing what has happened, or why."

The seal bobbed its head and snorted.

"I fear for Cailean as well. Every day it worsens. Have you seen him? Has he come to harm out there, in your ocean? The storm was so terrible. It was cruel of my father to send them out in that."

Viscous membranes slid halfway across the seal's eyes. Perhaps she was boring him with her rambling, but there was no one else she could talk to.

"I prayed, morning and night, to my mother's gods and Bericus's too, that he and the others found a sheltered cove or harbor some-where. Vita—do you know Vita?—has been watching. I think she would sense if Cailean were dead. I think she would mourn him, and show it somehow. But today, when I passed behind her, she barely looked at me then went right on watching."

Shading her eyes with her free hand, Eamhair searched the sea too as seabirds wheeled and shrieked overhead.

She kept Cailean's silver ring on a leather cord around her neck, hidden beneath her clothing. Now she pulled the cord over her head and held up the ring, cradling it in both hands like an offering.

The seal's gaze followed the movement of her hands.

"Never in my life, and it has been a long life, seal, a score of years plus two—most women my age are mothers of three or four children—never have I desired any man, yet now I am drawn to two at the same time. Father Bradan would have something to say about that. He would chastise me and order me to make the sign of the cross and speak many prayers. No doubt he would inform my father, and I would be locked away in the tower, never to see you again, or feel sunlight on my face."

The seal rolled over, sneezed, and scratched his round barrel chest with the claws on one flipper.

"I am drawn to both, yes." She put the ring back around her neck and under her tunic. "But not in the same way. Taranis, your king, is a creature of wonder. I am certain he has much more power than an ordinary seal." She laughed at the seal's comical bobbing and the way it flipped upright. "Do not be jealous. He held my hands and promised to take me away from Bericus. But then he vanished without a word. How I wish you could tell me what happened. Is he gone forever?"

The seal did not speak.

"And there is Cailean. A man of quick decisions and, I think, unshakable resolve. A man who won the friendship of a wolf—and that cannot be an easy feat."

The seal gave a piercing bark. Eamhair nodded solemnly. "You want me to speak of no man but Taranis, is that it? You are a loyal subject. Alas, I think I am in love with him—Cailean, I mean." She glanced around to make sure she was still alone but for her bulky companions and the birds, for such confessions were risky to say aloud, not only for herself but for Cailean as well. "When he looks at me, I forget my mother's warnings. I want to follow him into one of the barns, lie down with him in the straw, and do all those things I promised my mother I would never do. Long ago, I built a stone tower around my heart to match the one I live in, but now it is falling apart. Every piece that crumbles away leaves a wound. It is painful, my friend."

She scratched the seal's cheek. Beneath its coarse outer hair, it felt soft and warm as a baby.

If Cailean would return, she could accept the seolh's desertion. Cailean might not have the power to spirit her away to an underwater palace or anywhere else that Bericus could not find, but his companionship—she wasn't sure what else to call it—would bring secret joy to her forlorn existence. Carrying on with one of Bericus's warriors right under his nose might even prove a rewarding, albeit perilous, game.

That last morning, Cailean's eyes had carried a millennia's worth of longing in them.

Wait for me.

Since she was eight years old she had wished for the seolh-king, longed for the promise of a miraculous escape. Now, when she thought of vanishing with the seolh, she was torn—almost physically reluctant. What if Cailean came back and she was gone? He would never understand.

Taranis might simply be busy making plans, preparing a refuge—perhaps perfecting the method of transforming her into a creature that could survive in the ocean. Such things were surely difficult. If he did return, and if he agreed to save Ula as well, she had no choice. She would go with him, and no matter what he asked of her she would submit.

One of the most confusing things was that when she considered what he might ask, she was not unmoved. Her feelings for Taranis were harder to understand than her feelings for Cailean. Trying to separate them was like unraveling hopelessly snarled threads.

"Am I faithless? A loose woman, a slut, a doxy?" She met the seal's big dark gaze. He looked as surprised as she felt. "I never knew how many words there are to heap shame upon us."

She thought of Nia and Luned and the other brothel women who serviced her father's warriors. The idea of doing such things turned her stomach.

It turned their stomachs as well, of course. There was no question that mating without affection or love aged the women and made them hard. But when stomachs weren't turned from doing unsavory things, they had a way of relentlessly demanding food.

"You are too young to ask," she said. "Forgive my indelicacy."

Without offering a single sign of forgiveness or reassurance, the seal turned away and undulated back to his comrades. They made grunting noises that seemed to convey agreement and all three heaved into the water and vanished.

If—*when*—Cailean returned, she must tell him of the seolh. It was the only way.

She flung the grain she'd brought. The birds flocked around her in a noisy, happy squall.

To whatever god would listen, she prayed. *Please return my father's men, and their leader, alive and whole.*

Chapter 18

WITH THE HELP OF THE CROFTER'S WIFE, TARANIS PROPPED HIS SHOULDERS against the wall of the bothy and accepted the soup she offered, grateful for the hot wooden bowl fresh from the cauldron over the fire. He couldn't seem to stay warm after his near drowning.

His head ached. His nose and lungs burned. Muscles he'd never known he had throbbed, and his right thigh bore bruises from groin to knee. But he was alive.

The woman had never heard of Dunaedan, but from what she did say, that Innse Orc was just off the coast, he realized he needed to go west to get back to Eamhair.

He glanced at the makeshift pallet next to his, which held the only other storm survivor these villagers had found. Cailean.

Of course. It was Athene's doing, it had to be. Taranis watched his unconscious half brother, wishing he knew what the Lady wanted of them.

So far, Bericus's proud war leader hadn't awakened, though this morning his legs and arms were twitching restlessly and his skin was flushed with fever. The crofter's wife said he'd suffered deep gashes across his shoulder and chest, and worrisome bruising on one temple.

The people of this village had searched the coast after the storm, but had only found one other, and he was dead.

If Cailean survived his wounds and the infection setting in, he would hold Taranis responsible for his dead men, as well as for the deaths of the gypsies on Innse Orc.

No matter how badly his leg hurt, he must leave soon.

EAMHAIR HAD HEARD MOST OF THE BROTHEL WOMEN'S STORIES BEFORE SHE was old enough to understand all the words. Several had taken her aside when her monthly courses began, to add their warnings to Ula's.

"I was raped when I was thirteen," Luned confided as she combed Eamhair's hair. "By seven boys. You cannot imagine how much it hurt —how much I bled—how I was ripped inside, over and over again. If anyone heard me screaming, they did nothing. Before that day, I was as respectable as any of Dunaedan's goodwives or their virgin daughters. But my mother was dead—" She squeezed Eamhair's shoulders. "You are lucky to have your mother still, Eamhair.

"They knew who to attack—which girls had no protection. Afterward, I was scorned. Even stoned." She tapped the scar on her cheekbone. "It was either the whorehouse or starve. My father and his new wife wanted nothing to do with me. I have never started a baby. I know what those boys did destroyed any chance of it. And for that, at least, I am grateful."

Nia was Eamhair's age and had long displayed fondness for the chieftain's only daughter. "Some of Bericus's men prefer the illusion of rape," she said. "They pretend I am a virgin and they are forcing their will upon me. I am ordered to weep and cry and strike them with my fists. That is the only way they find pleasure. Watch out for those men, Eamhair." She whispered their names.

Nia had given birth to three children, children who hung in the corners at the whorehouse like mice, their only companions the other bastards. She used what little she was given to feed and clothe them, but had no expectation that they would grow up with any kindness or compassion. "Look at that one," she said once. "He resembles Niall a bit, but sometimes he looks more like Owain. The way he acts? Ossian." She spit on the floor. "That frightens me more than anything."

Boys and men were something to fear—hardly different from a boar or wolf. Eamhair knew from a young age where not to go. She knew when to enter the dovecote for eggs and dung, the brewery to help with ale making, the barns to feed the horses, and the pigsty to scatter the scraps, and when going to those places might prove disastrous—even deadly. Instinctively, she became adept at sliding around the edges of things, keeping her face lowered, and never speaking or drawing attention.

Years passed in this manner before she realized none of it was necessary. It was fear of Bericus, Nemausus, and Ossian that kept her safe, not her own efforts. She could have walked from one end of Dunaedan's hall to the other naked, and none of those men would have dared say a word. They would have turned their faces away from the sight of her body.

Eamhair never really knew what intimidation Bericus used. But whatever it was, every one of his men, and every man in the village, and every one of those men's sons, knew better than to lay a hand on Eamhair, daughter of Bericus.

ULA CAME INTO THE BREWERY AND GESTURED. "HELP ME, EAMHAIR. NIA has gone into labor and the midwife has the gripe."

Eamhair handed the mashing rake to one of the other women, changed her apron, and tucked several locks of hair back under her veil as she went along with Ula to the whorehouse.

Nia's labor—which, if successful, would culminate in baby number four—continued all that day and night. Eamhair and her mother napped as they could, between labor pains.

During one of the lulls, Ula took Eamhair aside. "I am unsure whether I should tell you this. You know Bericus. It is probably a lie."

"What has he done now?"

"He offered to give you to Cailean in marriage if Cailean manages to recapture that last escaped prisoner. That is where the baron went you know, to find the man and bring him back."

Eamhair, along with many others, had gathered at the fishermen's inlet to watch the war boat sail away. Cailean looked back from the stern, and when he saw her, he seemed to stop searching. But she couldn't be certain, as the boat was already halfway out of the cove and it was snowing heavily. *An important mission*, he'd said in the cave. *Success will make it worth any discomfort.*

She leaped up and danced around the stuffy little room. "Cailean's wife! I am to be Cailean's wife!"

"If he finds that man," her mother warned, but she smiled too. "I suppose if you have to marry, it might as well be him rather than one of these outsiders."

"Oh, Mother. You like him. You know you do."

"He's not as bad as most."

Eamhair stopped dancing as she remembered how long Cailean had been gone. Ten days. Ten days with no message. No sign. He could be—she forced her mind to veer off from the image of him blank-eyed and open-mouthed at the bottom of the sea.

"Tomorrow is the solstice feast," she said. "I so wanted to dance with him."

"Looking for a man who doesn't want to be found can take time. And he may still return before then."

Desperate to change the course of her thoughts, Eamhair pulled out his ring. "Look, Mother."

"What is this? I have seen this before." Ula's gaze met Eamhair's. "It is Dalriada's!"

"He gave it to me."

"Oh-ho, so the two of you have already planned a future together, have you?"

"Not really. I think he only means for me to keep it while he's gone."

Ula laughed. "He would not have given it to you, child, but that he wants you to keep it forever."

Later, Nia's pained moan woke Eamhair from an exhausted doze, subsuming the seolh-king's vow. *I will love her in every life, in death, and on the other side of death.*

At daybreak the poor woman was finally delivered of a healthy son. Ula said she would remain awhile, and told Eamhair to go and get some sleep.

But Eamhair, still exultant, was drawn by the crisp cool air and streaming yellow rays from the rising sun, and decided to share her happiness with the ocean before seeking her bed.

She watched the sea change colors as the sun rose higher, and apologized to the birds for not bringing any grain.

She was returning to the fort when she felt the ground tremble. She turned to see clouds of snow and a thundering mass of riders; before she had a chance to flee, she was trapped in a tight circle of horsemen, their mounts blowing and snorting. One of them carried a banner displaying an open-mouthed boar's head with long, deadly tusks.

She frowned at the way they looked at her and laughed. None of her father's men would dare speak about her in such a manner. She tried to walk on, but the horses blocked every attempt. Who were they? Why were they on her father's land, and where were his warriors to rout them? For the first time she was sorry that the north rampart had no sentries.

If Cailean were here...but he was not.

"Let me pass," she commanded.

"But why?" said the man barring her way. "When it gives me so much more pleasure to sit here and look at you?" He maneuvered his horse sideways as she tried to slip around him.

Another asked, "Are you some freeman's doxy? Does he let you wander unprotected when he's sleeping? A fool, I call him."

Two more men rode up. The one in front wore black leather embossed with the same boar's head. For an instant she thought it was Cailean, and her heartbeat quickened.

But this man was heftier than Cailean, his hair shorter, his bearing colder. When he saw her he reined his horse viciously, swung off, and approached.

All the crude vulgarity vanished. The horsemen backed their mounts away, giving this new arrival a wide berth.

He stopped before her. His unblinking stare made her flush and look away as she worked to hide growing fear. She did not like to think what might happen if her father's warriors did not come soon.

"And who is this?" he said.

None of the men said anything, so she did. "I am Eamhair, daughter of Bericus, chief of Dunaedan."

His brow lifted and his gaze traveled slowly over her. "Well, well. The famed Eamhair."

She scowled and clenched her hands. "Are these your men? They are hindering me."

"I am sorry. They usually have better manners."

From the corner of her eye, she saw several of them exchange uneasy glances. She suspected that, much like her father, their leader was quick to impose punishment when he was displeased.

The odor of burned ashes hung around him. It wasn't pleasant, nor was his emotionless regard. But he was young—about the same age as Cailean, she would guess, well dressed, obviously a man of power and control.

"I am Fathna." He offered a stiff, almost mocking bow. "Sometimes called The Boar."

Eamhair curtsied, as duty demanded.

"I have business with your father." He motioned to the man who had ridden at his side. "You come with me." To the others, he said, "Go back to the inlet and signal the boats. Two of you take my brother's horses and return them to him."

He held out his arm. "I shall escort you to the safety of your hall, Lady Eamhair."

"I am in no need—"

He cut her off with an arrogant wave. "I insist. As you have seen, things can turn hazardous without warning, even on land controlled by your father." He pursed his lips and his demeanor turned speculative. "It is peculiar, him allowing you to walk out here...alone. Rather negligent."

She had better be careful. If this Fathna were to question her father's laxity, she could find herself under so restrictive a guard that she might never again have the opportunity to dance at the edge of the ocean.

With some effort, she pasted on a more friendly expression.

They walked around to the main south gate, Fathna regaling her with stories of his sprawling stronghold on Innse Orc, where, he said, the cliffs rose as high, if not higher, than those she knew so well, and of the ancient city of Constantinople, and Frankish Paris, and other fantastical places she half believed he invented as he spoke. His companion walked a little behind them and said nothing.

She took them to the hall, gave them over to her father, and escaped at last, gratefully and wearily.

Isle of cloud, moon's stronghold,
See your death come in spears of gold...

~~~The Prophecy of Aridela

You Wasted Your Water

THE HIGH PRIESTESS OF KAPHTOR SAT AT A TABLE IN HER LABYRINTH sanctuary, meditating upon a clump of long golden hair.

Earlier, as she washed and prepared Queen Aridela's body for burial, she'd noticed that one hand was locked into a fist. When she pried it open, the hair fell out.

Only one person on the island of Kaphtor had hair like this.

Everyone believed Aridela broke her neck when she fell down a set of stairs.

Themiste wound the hair around her index finger, around her middle finger, then around her thumb. It glimmered in the lamplight.

The hair formed pictures in her mind. It recalled events she would rather forget. She saw Chrysaleon's face turned upwards, grimacing as he held her against the shrine wall and pounded into her, an act of lust neither could resist.

But her beloved daughter, Pasithea, had come from that day, so she didn't completely regret her weakness.

For some unknown reason, Aridela had ripped a handful of hair from Chrysaleon's scalp, and died so quickly afterward that her fist never relaxed.

Gently placing the hair on the table, Themiste picked up her reed stylus.

What is Chrysaleon's obligation? she wrote. *To die. If he will not walk willingly to his death I will drag him there.*

She gazed at the words, chewing on the dull end of her writing instrument.

This is my last entry in the Oracle Logs, she wrote.

I must rectify my sins. I must silence the call of my queen's blood, and earn my place at her side in lives to come.

"Aridela." Themiste spoke softly into the shadows. "Never again will I fail you."

I will not fail again, she wrote.

She dropped the stylus and picked up Chrysaleon's hair.

Betrayal cannot birth from nothing. It weaves backward and forward, into and out of the thread of life and death, of faith and love, of envy and desire.

Aridela's father had whispered those words into her ear. She had never forgotten.

It was true. Betrayal never came from nothing.

She formed the hair into an elegant curl. She knotted it and held it against her cheek. She tasted it, pulling it slowly across her tongue as she thought her thoughts.

Rusa stared at Themiste, unimpressed by her mature dignity or her many titles: Oracle, Minos, Moon-Being, and Keeper of the Prophecies.

"Are you willing to assist me?" Themiste asked. "You will have to subdue someone of importance. You might have to kill him."

"I have killed before, and will do so again, as long as you make it worth my while."

"Then come with me."

First she took him to the underground shrine, where she retrieved a knife made of bone. From there they traversed narrow passageways and steps before coming to an inconspicuous door. When she pulled the handle a portal opened, revealing an opulent chamber. Chrysaleon was sitting at a table, legs sprawled, head on his arms, lost in a drunken stupor.

Themiste nodded at her companion. *This is the one.*

Rusa smiled. Before the woman could change her mind, he caught up a dagger from the table and stabbed himself in the chest. He wanted death to come swiftly, for that would make the consuming easier. It must be done before Themiste could intervene. Fighting an agonizing haze of pain, he seized Chrysaleon's forearm.

"What are you doing?" he heard the woman shout. He threw his head backward, groaning as the inner pull began.

Long ago he'd tried to consume Aridela and had been thwarted by a terrifying apparition—a woman with a spear, engulfed in a blinding nimbus. As he sought to annihilate Chrysaleon it happened again. White light flared and a spear tip appeared, aimed directly at his face. Gripping the haft was a stern-faced woman. Her voice ricocheted through his head. *Release him!*

Reverberating female voices added their commands. *YOU WILL NOT! Back AWAY! Cursed man!*

His flesh burned. Behind the divine handmaid he saw shadows and gaunt, unholy faces dripping hot green slime.

Chrysaleon lurched to his feet, breaking Rusa's hold. The king looked terrible—thin, red eyed. Nothing remained of the proud warrior of Mycenae.

Four guards flooded in, weapons drawn. Weakened by pain, confusion, and blood loss, Rusa was quickly overpowered. Why was he not dead? Surely the knife had pierced his heart. He tried to lift a hand, seeking to touch one of the guards, but he couldn't. His legs and forearms were trapped beneath their leather sandals.

The guards willingly immobilized Rusa, but were hesitant to lay hands upon the high priestess.

Wild-eyed, Chrysaleon stared at Rusa, at the wound in his chest. His gaze veered to Themiste.

Rusa saw the exact instant Chrysaleon put it together. Chrysaleon *knew* Rusa was Harpalycus. Somehow, he knew.

The king's gaze moved on to the open portal. He glared at Themiste, who stared back defiantly.

"Bind and gag her," he ordered. Two of the guards reluctantly obeyed.

Chrysaleon motioned toward Rusa. "Secure his hands behind him and take him to the healer. Tell her to make certain he does not die. Do not—*do not*—let him touch you."

The healer succeeded in keeping him alive. She told him he was fortunate—the blade missed his heart. He'd been careless, in too much of a hurry, eager to feel his essence plunder Chrysaleon's body.

He lost track of the days. At some point, the healer's care turned cold and bitter. She called him the murderer of Kaphtor's holy high priestess. She conveyed with relish that he would pray for his own end long before it would be granted.

After his fingernails were pulled out, after he was strangled, after the soles of his feet were charred and he had been raped by five different men, he was taken to the deepest, coldest, blackest part of the labyrinth and thrown in an oppressive cell where the rats never stopped scrabbling and biting.

He knew he would die there, starved and alone. It was almost exactly what he had tried to do to Chrysaleon years before.

But the guards came again, carrying flaming torches that made his eyes water. Their talk and laughter caused his ears to ring after so long in silence. He was shoved into a bronze cage, taken to the marketplace in Knossos, and put on display. Four armed warriors kept anyone from coming close enough for him to touch.

By day the sun beat upon him. The nights were cold. He was given no food or water. Children threw rocks and ran off, laughing.

He grew weaker. His wounds festered.

Salvation came in the form of a compassionate woman. He woke from a stupor, hearing her say, "Let me give him a last taste of water. He is nearly dead. What can it hurt? It will ease his passing."

Gruffly, the guard said, "Be quick—and don't touch him."

He could hardly believe how his fortunes had changed. The woman pushed a skin of water through the bars of his cage. He reached out as though to take it, but latched onto her thin wrist instead.

The woman released a choked cry. Harpalycus was so close to death that he was able to take over her body instantly. By the time the guard yanked her away Harpalycus was inside her. She swayed and dropped to the ground, vomiting.

"What is wrong with you?" the guard asked. She could not reply. She was too sick. "Send word to the king," she heard. "The prisoner is dead."

The guard shoved the skin into her hands as she rose unsteadily. "You wasted your water on this one, old woman. You need it far more than he."

She staggered away, hatred springing, stronger, stronger with each step, like an approaching storm's poisonous cloud demanding vengeance....

Chapter 19

Harpalycus pondered those bygone events as he walked beside Eamhair. His memory of the Cretan marketplace was vivid—the dust and heat during the day, the shivering chill at night, faraway bells calling the priestesses to their prayers and rituals, the laughter and ridicule from ragged boys, the pain of stones striking his flesh.

Since that day, he had deceived everyone, starting with Chrysaleon himself, who never once suspected the old woman who brought him his wine was really the enemy he believed dead. Far too trustingly, he drank and drank and drank in an effort to expunge the loss of his beloved Aridela. Harpalycus was there, in that old woman's body, when Chrysaleon died, choking on his own vomit.

Before suspicion of poison could take hold, Harpalycus abandoned Crete and began an endless celebration of every luxury the world had to offer, every perversion, every manner of power and glory.

For over two thousand years, he led campaigns and ruled. He burned, enslaved, tortured, laid waste. He had raped so many he could never begin to remember all their faces, even if he cared to. He amassed fortune after fortune, to the point where he lost track of his wealth, and where he had stashed it all. Whenever death came chasing, he evaded it by consuming another hapless victim.

It was easy—so long as a living human was near enough to touch, and he himself was near death. Sometimes he consumed the body of a king, and sometimes a slave—whatever was necessary to survive.

In the beginning, his plans were lofty. When he ruled the entire world and was worshipped as a god, he would maintain a harem of young, strong men to consume whenever he wished. He would change bodies with his mood, a black-haired youth today, a flaxen-haired one the next. It would be like donning new clothes. But the goal had not materialized. It was not that easy to consume great men: they were guarded and never alone. His fortunes went up and down with every body he usurped. He had learned to accept it, to be satisfied with vast hidden wealth and the means to indulge his passions, always with an eye towards glory and fame.

Not once had he expected to encounter his old adversary, alive after so many centuries.

The monk from the land of the Britons was Chrysaleon of Mycenae. The man Harpalycus hated more than any other. Chrysaleon, the man who used Harpalycus's sister Iros then had her strangled so she could not interfere with his great passion for Aridela.

Harpalycus had always listened to his instincts and obeyed them. They had saved him many times.

After consuming Fathna, the Boar of Innse Orc, and making his way to Sgathag Creag, he'd played the part of the king's brother while continuing to search for the source of the compulsion that had wreaked havoc with his life. He felt he was close, but only when the monk appeared on his braying donkey, as a headache stabbed and a hum deafened his hearing, only when his body convulsed and he glimpsed a spectral aura around the man, did he finally understand.

Harpalycus kept his distance. If he recognized Chrysaleon, or Chrysaleon's essence inside the monk, Chrysaleon might well recognize him too.

He observed from the safety of shadows, from behind posts and pillars. He took his meals away from the feasting hall and tried to fathom how the prince of Mycenae could be here. Had he learned Harpalycus's secret of traveling from body to body?

The man mostly played the part of a humble monk but for flashes of arrogance that were pure Chrysaleon. Why was he appearing only now, after two millennia? Harpalycus had forgotten about his loathsome competitor eons ago but for infrequent dreams, and believed him moldered to dust.

He decided to test his suspicion and enlisted a few of Queen Cadha's women—women Fathna had established intimate relationships with, and the herbalist, who produced a container of dried, pointed leaves. She promised that just one, crushed into the monk's drink, would blacken his senses and make him agreeable to suggestion.

It had worked. Fathna listened to the monk babble while thrusting away at the maids. *I am no monk. I am a king,* the clod said more than once, which made Fathna laugh, *and the queen of Crete was mine.*

She was mine too, once, Fathna thought. *And you could do nothing about it.*

Now Harpalycus stood face to face with that queen, the one woman, of all the women he had ever known, who had bested him. Who had come notably close to ending his life. When he remembered how close, on that battlefield at Amnisos, it sent a shudder down his spine.

He recognized Aridela within this young female, just as he recognized Chrysaleon. He did not understand, but he *knew,* and after confirming things at Drost's fortress, it was easier to accept.

For several breaths he stared, too shocked to do anything else, and waited for her to scream his ancient name, but she didn't. Her expression held wariness and reserve, but no recognition.

He examined the girl, Eamhair, all the way to her father's fortress. It was something in the eyes, and yet, more—almost as though a veneer of her proud, queenly face overlay this one like a veil made of memory. He had also known her by the sudden trembling that overtook his muscles, the nausea that erupted in his stomach, the stake-like pain stabbing his temples, and that transient white cloud that rippled around her. He knew it beyond any doubt when he took her arm. He *smelled* her. This woman had the same scent he had come to know so well when Aridela was his prisoner of war. He would never forget it, not if ten thousand years passed.

And so Harpalycus of Tiryns learned that it was more than happenstance that brought him from the civilized entertainments of Constantinople to this barren, lonely place filled with grunting savages.

How many more from his past were here? Perhaps next he might stumble upon his own father, Lycomedes, or his sister, Iros.

Drost Gocinecht had sent Fathna to Dunaedan to subdue its troublesome chief. He had long been aware of Bericus's plots and had chosen to do nothing, preferring to allow the fool to follow in the steps of the Christos and get himself crucified.

But lately his spies were informing him that Bericus had begun

recruiting mercenaries. No longer was he a somewhat amusing, irri-
tating thorn. Now he was becoming a threat.

The fact that Bericus had captured the murderer of Drost's
daughter made things even more convenient. Fathna would discipline
Dunaedan's chief—kill him if necessary—definitely confiscate his
wealth—and return Taranis for torture and death.

How could these two wraiths from his past be alive? Harpalycus
vividly remembered Aridela's corpse being paraded through Knossos
after she broke her neck falling down a set of steps—what an ignoble
end for such an illustrious woman—and being laid to rest in a gilded
sarcophagus. She was certainly dead—before burial her body had been
displayed immersed in a fortune of gold and ivory. Women had
swarmed around her, weeping, tearing their hair.

They entered the hall. Eamhair led him to a garishly carved and
painted chair on the dais and presented him to her father. Bericus
frowned at their approach, his suspicious gaze going from his
daughter to the man beside her, but when she introduced him and told
a brief, kinder version of their meeting, he relaxed. The barest flicker of
a smile passed over his lips.

Bericus thought he had another weakling he could fleece.

Giving himself a mental shake, Harpalycus released the past,
cloaked himself in the guise of Fathna, and bowed.

"Come slake your thirst," Bericus said, gesturing. "Share news of
the world beyond my lands."

Eamhair curtsied and left, no doubt off to do the things women did
in this time and place—weaving, cooking, mending, feeding the livestock and treating the sick. Her eyes held nothing of what she had once
been—a powerful ruler who performed the thirteen sacrifices, rallied
her people, made judgments, leaped over the backs of wild bulls...and
fought in battle as she'd done at Amnisos, alongside Chrysaleon and
his half brother.

Now she lived or died at her father's decree.

A serving woman brought ale. Fathna watched the exchanged
glance between the two, and the woman's nearly invisible nod.

After she walked away, Fathna spun his lie. "My original purpose
in coming here was to ask your permission to harbor my boats at your
river mouth while my men and I hunt the lands south of yours. But
now...there is another matter."

"Yes?" Bericus couldn't quite disguise his glee.

"That lady...the one who so kindly brought me to you." Fathna glanced at the doorway where Eamhair had gone.

"My daughter."

"Is she wife to some fortunate man?"

"She is unmarried. Untouched. I see you have discerned her quality. She has been taught every womanly refinement."

"Her virtues are evident."

"The man who aspires to win such a prize must show me how well he can care for her."

"Indeed."

"Though many have tried, none have yet convinced me. It would take a man singular in every way to do that."

Eamhair was renowned as much for her father's jealous possessiveness as for her legendary beauty—which now that Fathna had seen her, was not exceptional. Her face had pleasant symmetry and her bearing was dignified; that was the most he could give her, outside the eyes, which possessed Aridela's unparalleled dark intensity. He had slept with lovelier women—wild, feral women—at Sgathag Creag, and the whores in Constantinople were compellingly exotic and sinful. Bericus had to be utilizing some trick on all these men.

Yet he could not deny there was something. Perhaps it was Aridela's spirit. Without exception she was the most...fiercely *burning* woman he had ever known, in any era.

Fathna merely glanced at the cup sitting before him before pushing it away.

Bericus's eyes narrowed.

Many a rumor suggested that no matter who came to this remote outpost with offers of marriage, no matter how enormous the offered bride price, or how highborn the suitor, Bericus always found a way to turn him down. This pattern had been endlessly repeated. Drost had even heard the predictions that someday Bericus's wife would inexplicably die and the daughter, willing or not, would take her place.

It was logical. Eamhair was years past the age when most girls were married. Many rich men had made offers, yet she remained at Dunaedan, *untouched,* as Bericus so proudly claimed.

Fathna smiled idly at Bericus while he constructed his next move.

Shortly after Taranis the monk fled Drost Gocinecht's fortress, Drost's three-year-old daughter was found lifeless behind the granary, her throat cut.

A weeping Fathna carried the limp body into Drost's hall, telling a tale of glimpsing the monk as he ran away with a bloody knife.

Amidst the screaming of the girl's mother and other women, Drost sent out two hundred warriors, ordering them to bring back the murderer. Had any of them found Taranis as Fathna expected, the man would be dead for certain by now—after a long interlude of the same kind of torture Harpalycus had suffered on Crete. The pleasure of imagining that made killing the child more than worthwhile. She'd had a special fondness for her uncle, and had accompanied him without qualm or protest when he asked.

But Taranis, the canny fox, had somehow evaded the searchers, only to be captured here, in this place, where Aridela lived. It could not be coincidence.

Did Taranis know of Eamhair? Could he see that other within her different body? Had he been drawn here, the same way Harpalycus had been drawn from Constantinople?

Elation filled him. He was glad Taranis hadn't been captured right away and sent back to Sgathag Creag.

Instead of returning Taranis to Drost for punishment, Fathna would take the monk to Innse Orc and present him to his new, properly disciplined wife. He would force Chrysaleon to watch, as he had once forced Lycus to watch on Crete.

After months of humiliation, Fathna would strangle him. He would drive an iron blade through his heart and throat. He would burn the corpse until not a sliver of bone was left.

He would use every method he had ever heard of to make certain Chrysaleon of Mycenae could never again appear in this world.

His resolve intensified. "I understand your dilemma, Lord Bericus, but I am certain I heard that Drost Gocinecht long ago reserved her for himself."

"Bah. Three things, my lord. First, Drost only ordered me not to marry her to anyone without his permission. That does not mean he wants her, and that was years ago. I doubt he even remembers. Secondly, I would have no trouble convincing him to release her from any betrothal he thinks I owe him. After all, the man has what—five wives? What does he need with another? Although I would wager my Eamhair is far more beautiful, skilled, and obedient than any damsel he has ever possessed."

"And your third point?"

"Eamhair is *my* daughter, to do with as *I* wish, and I will never relinquish my rights as a father—not to any man. Do not worry—if I choose to marry her to another, I can always find a way. I can tell Drost she died, for instance. Or that she gave herself to some churl, and no longer has any value."

"Why are you telling me this?"

"Are you not interested in her?"

"You must know I will inform my brother of everything you have said."

"Who is your brother, and why would he care what I do with the girl?"

Fathna widened his smile, baring his teeth like a wolf on the scent. "You do not know that I, Fathna Gocinecht, the Boar-King of Innse Orc, am Drost Gocinecht's brother? He mentioned your daughter to me just before I left his court. I assure you, he has not forgotten."

Bericus's face went white. Fathna glanced again at the ale cup and waited for the protests to run out, for the man to realize he was trapped in an inescapable corner of his own making.

Both Bericus and Drost Gocinecht were going to lose their pretty little commodity. And if Drost became angry, Harpalycus could easily abandon Fathna's body for another—but not before he enjoyed Aridela in this new body, thoroughly and beyond repair.

"My visit here is twofold," Fathna added as Bericus spluttered into silence. "My brother ordered me to take charge of the prisoner who murdered his daughter."

"I-I...that is a problem, my lord."

Fathna frowned. "Why?"

"Well, he—I—he—"

"What is it?" But Fathna knew instinctively what Bericus found so hard to say. Rage erupted like lava in his veins.

"He—escaped." Bericus swiped at his forehead. "My best warriors are hunting him as we speak. I will have him again, and soon, I swear."

Because Bericus was responsible for ruining Fathna's sport, the chieftain would suffer. He would pay Fathna to take Eamhair. He would pay dearly.

The rest of the bargain was dealt with apace and to Fathna's satisfaction.

Chapter 20

"Eamhair! Oh, Eamhair, my child."

Eamhair woke slowly. Her mother sat on the bed next to her, weeping. The skin around her left eye was swollen and turning purple.

"What...what happened?" Eamhair sat up, rubbing her eyes.

Ula embraced her. "You're to be given to that man. He has won you, my lambling, and you're to be wed on the morrow! Bericus said he was tricked—then he hit me, but that is nothing new."

"Man? What man?"

"He is a king or chief from the isles of Innse Orc. It is not so far, is it? Maybe we will see each other again." She sucked in a miserable sob.

"Him! Oh, no, Mother, he frightens me."

Ula shook her head, sniffed, and patted Eamhair's shoulder.

"How did he do it? Father has turned down so many. And what about Cailean?"

"Bran told me your father tried to refuse, but the man said something no one could hear, and your father turned white about the eyes. Bran thinks he threatened Bericus somehow, and it worked. You are to be given with no bride price at all. In fact, it looks as though Bericus will pay *him*." Tears poured down her cheeks. "I have never seen Bericus so ferocious. All the women are in hiding."

It had finally happened. She was to be married. The devil from Innse Orc who called himself the Boar would take her away from her mother.

"Bran said his purpose in coming here was to fetch that prisoner—the one Drost Gocinecht wants so badly. But he saw you, and decided he wanted you as well. He has given Bericus a fortnight to recapture the man. Who knows what will happen if Bericus fails!"

Eamhair held Cailean's ring and wept. *Goodbye to you, Cailean, and all my hopes for love with you.*

CLOTHED IN COARSE LEGGINGS AND A PATCHED TUNIC PROVIDED BY THE crofter's wife, Taranis pushed doggedly westward, hardly pausing to beg for food or to sleep.

If Cailean recovered, the woman would tell him about the other survivor; a description might make him realize his prey was still alive. With luck, maybe he would assume Taranis had run the opposite direction from Dunaedan.

Cailean couldn't know that Taranis had no choice. He had to return. Aridela was there.

Now that he was believed a murderer, no one at Dunaedan could see him. He would have to be ready to murder in truth to keep his presence a secret. He decided to go directly to the hidden tunnel entrance at Uisge Bealach, and make his way to Eamhair's bedchamber.

He reached the inlet, exhausted and hungry, two days after setting out, shortly after sunset, and used one of the currachs stored there to row across. As he neared the wide beach on the west side he drew up, alarmed by the scent of roasting game, the sight of a small fire, and the silhouetted forms of men crouched around it.

Hoping there was no sentry, he landed at the southern edge of the beach, well beyond the reach of the firelight, and stole closer.

At first their conversation was fairly bland. They talked about Drost Gocinecht, his grand fortress, his beautiful wives, and their own sexual escapades while there.

They reached for their weapons and jumped to their feet as another man rode up, but relaxed when he called out. He swung off his horse and accepted a flagon of ale and a sizzling chunk of meat.

He tore into the meat and spoke around it. "The Boar has won the hand of Lady Eamhair."

Taranis stiffened. He held his breath; his heartbeat drummed so loudly it almost obliterated the low voice.

"You jest," one of the men said.

Another man whistled and yet another snorted.

"And they have lost the monk. Fathna has given Bericus a fortnight to bring him back. Did you send for the boats?"

"Aye. They will anchor at the mouth of this inlet."

"Fathna says he will join us at daybreak and we're to sail home."

"Will the lady be sailing with us?"

"Nay, she is to become Fathna's wife by proxy and await our return. Uurguist—you have been given the honor."

One of the men looked surprised and sheepish. Laughter erupted. He was punched, slapped, and teased. There were suggestions about what he might do behind Fathna's back.

Eventually, they returned to the other topic. "What if they don't find the monk?"

"I imagine Bericus will be tortured in his stead, don't you?"

One of the men said, "I thought the girl was marked for Drost. How is it she is now being given to Fathna?"

"I don't know. She is a juicy little gosling, though. Too bad. She won't be when he is finished with her."

Taranis edged away. He waded through the frigid shallows separating the beach from the rest of the shoreline and scrambled into the tunnel. His hands were shaking—he could barely strike a spark for the lamp he'd left there. Once he could see his way, he raced towards Dunaedan.

Jocosa brought orders from Bericus. Eamhair was to remain in her bedchamber while Ula prepared whatever was needed for her daughter's wedding, which would take place the next evening.

Ula hugged Eamhair before she followed Jocosa out of the room. "Something will happen," she whispered. "I have never prayed so hard. The seolh-king will come, or something else—perhaps your baron will return and put a stop to this."

Eamhair returned her mother's embrace but could not share her confidence. *Fourteen days since I last saw Taranis. Did he find his wife and return to his palace beneath the sea? He has either forgotten or abandoned me.*

She tried to overcome fear by following her usual routine. Changing into her nightshift, she placed the tunic she had been wearing over the top of the clothes chest and on a whim, removed the cord holding Cailean's ring from around her neck. "I will not wear this while my father sells me to another," she said, and placed it next to the rowanberry bracelet in the coffer where she kept her scant collection of adornments.

One token from Cailean, one from Taranis. Nothing from the king of Innse Orc, who would soon own her.

He will come when your need is greatest, Ula had vowed. How could her need ever be greater than it was now?

Her control broke as she laced up the front of the shift. Futility and despair overwhelmed her and she flung herself onto the bed, weeping into her pillow.

The entire time Fathna had walked with her she struggled against nausea. He had placed her hand on his forearm and covered it with his so that she could not remove it. Even through the leather of his gauntlet his touch had sickened her.

He would take her to Innse Orc, islands she had always heard were bitterly cold and even more barren than Dunaedan. She would never again see her mother.

And she would be at his mercy—she and any children she bore. Something about him warned her he was no better than Bericus, and likely much worse.

"Why do you weep, Eamhair?"

Gasping, she sat up and stared into the recesses beyond the ember glow, searching for those deep tones of sorrow and promise.

"Taranis!"

Moonlight showered in from the narrow window, illuminating him as he approached her bed. He looked so different, dressed as a man instead of a monk, that she drew in a startled breath and questioned her sight. To cover her confusion, she said, "My father has pledged me to the king of Innse Orc. Will you not come to him? Tell him you are taking me away."

"It is true? You are to be wed?"

"Can you not hear them in the hall, celebrating?"

They listened to the shouts, drunken laughter, and barking dogs.

He sat next to her, twisting her braid around one hand, rubbing away her tears with the other.

"He came here to confiscate some criminal for Drost Gocinecht, but the man escaped. Fathna of Innse Orc has given my father a half-month to find him. I am to become his wife tomorrow."

"I didn't want to tell you and dampen your belief, Eamhair, but my powers were lost when I came out of the sea. There is nothing I can do, I have no—"

The sound of footsteps pounding on the stairs outside her door drew her gaze. She felt his hands release her as the bolt was thrown and the latch lifted. As mysteriously as he'd appeared, he was gone.

Her brother Ossian came in, followed by one of the maidservants—Viviana, Nemausus's pretty, flaxen-haired lover, and no friend to Eamhair.

"Why do you disturb my sleep?" Eamhair asked.

Ossian grinned. "Viviana is going to stay here with you—in case you think to vault from the tower walls and kill yourself."

He carried in a straw-filled pallet for the servant and left, bolting the door from the outside.

Viviana gave Eamhair an annoyed stare. She sat on a stool beside the brazier, lit several candles, and plucked at some embroidery, saying nothing.

Eamhair glanced longingly at the wall where Taranis had vanished, but he did not return.

Chapter 21

Nemausus burst into Eamhair's chamber and clamped down on her arm. "The king of Innse Orc is anxious to have you." He thrust his hips forward, pulling her close and laughing as he released her.

He wanted to see fear, so she showed none. "Insolent bitch," he growled, and slapped her. He went out, leaving her to spend the day with sulky, indifferent Viviana. The only information Viviana would give was that her betrothed had insisted on a pagan ceremony, so men had been sent in search of a druid, and the old Stone near the cliffs was being straightened and cleaned.

She stared at the wall where Taranis came and went, but the sun traveled across the sky without any sign of him. Perhaps he meant to go directly to the hall and confront her father there. But the day passed without any sound of fighting or argument from below.

Viviana is going to stay here with you — in case you think to vault from the tower walls and kill yourself.

When the time came, Viviana laced Eamhair into her wedding gown and her brothers escorted her downstairs. She was surprised and relieved to learn Fathna was not there. He had sailed that morning for his island home, leaving one of his men to wed her by proxy. No reason was given for his disinterest in personally marrying his chosen bride.

She looked around the smoky hall, decorated for the solstice with candles and evergreen boughs. Later there would be music. The harp and drum were already in place on the dais. Before Cailean left, she had dared imagine dancing with him. Maybe sneaking a sip or two of wine. She had even envisioned him pulling her into a corner to steal a kiss.

In case you think to vault from the tower walls and kill yourself.

Eamhair's father had run the old druid out years ago, but there was another local man who, before he converted to the new religion, had apprenticed with him. He was rounded up and ordered to perform the rite.

It was done first, to avoid raising the ire of Father Bradan.

Eamhair and the proxy, Bericus and Ula, Eamhair's two brothers, the druid apprentice, and two guards were the only attendants. Everyone else was sent to wait at the church in the village.

She and the proxy, whose name she was never told, knelt at the moss-covered Druid Stone. The apprentice called on the spirits of wind, fire, water, and air for harmony and fertility. He walked around them, sprinkling wine, and wrapped a scarlet cloth around their wrists —scarlet for virgin blood and her husband's virility.

Rune stones were carved, signifying that any betrayal by either husband or wife would bring supernatural retribution. The stones were thrown into the sea where they would lie beyond the reach of human interference.

With Bericus and his sons watching, Eamhair and Ula could exchange only a glance. Eamhair was whisked off to the church for the Christian wedding insisted on by her father. Two maidservants held the train of the embroidered blue gown her mother had long ago created, and another straightened her gauzy watchet blue veil.

When it was done, she tried to remember any word of what the druid or the priest had said, but could not.

Was it only a day since she'd helped deliver Nia's baby? Only a day since she danced around Nia's tiny chamber and fancied Bericus giving her to Cailean?

She thought of going to Nia and confiding her fear and anger. Nia would understand. But she was still recovering from childbirth and wrapped up in her baby, though she had no idea who the father was. It would be selfish to dampen her friend's short respite.

The wedding party returned to the hall for the combined wedding and solstice feast. Both hearths blazed and the minstrels had arrived. Roasted pork, meat pies, smoked salmon, venison, and grouse graced the trestle tables, and there were lighter offerings of herbed mussels, caramelized onions, roasted carrots, and three different types of cheese. The kitchen maids had even baked delicately sweet cakes from oats, nuts, and heather honey. Bericus must want to impress the man who had bested him, or at least he did not want to anger him, for all of this did not come cheaply.

The warriors and the proxy proceeded to get drunk. Singing accompanied the harp and drums and pipes. The hall was smoky and loud as men tried to outdo each other in boasting and storytelling. Women ran from man to man, filling ale pots and giggling as they were flirted with.

In case you think to vault from the tower walls and kill yourself. Kill yourself.

No one noticed when Eamhair left.

SHE PAUSED JUST LONG ENOUGH TO COVER HERSELF IN A CLOAK ONE OF THE maids had left on a peg in the storeroom. Her thoughts offered up one escape idea after another before falling into despairing wishes that she could retreat to a time before this day.

The seolh was not coming. He would have done so by now if he meant to. She and her mother were too much trouble after all. *My powers were lost,* he'd said before they were interrupted. If that was true, perhaps he could not save her.

The music and singing grew fainter until there was nothing but the sound of the ocean. *Come to me,* it sighed. *I will shelter you.*

She stumbled. Instinctively, she used her arms to break her fall; her palms struck the ground and pain shot through her wrists. She stayed there, on her hands and knees, thinking this might be her last chance to weep, but what good would that do? Her eyes remained dry.

At some point she got up and continued, not knowing or caring how close or how far she was from the edge of the cliff. She paused once to stare into the setting sun's radiant center until her sight was subsumed into sparks and fiery streaks.

Fathna of Innse Orc. She knew nothing of him, but his face caused her instincts to shriek and her stomach to heave. She saw him in her mind like a looming demon, his mouth next to her ear.

I swear by Poseidon I will never tire of you.

Chapter 22

TARANIS REMAINED ON THE LANDING OUTSIDE OF EAMHAIR'S BEDCHAMBER, toying with the idea of entering after the woman—Viviana, he heard Eamhair's brother call her—fell asleep. He could kill her and spirit Eamhair away into the tunnels. No one would ever find them.

But he hesitated. Confessing he had used concealed tunnels and hidden stairs to get to her would destroy her belief in his power. She expected him to intervene, to stop the wedding, to save her and her mother. Discovering he was nothing more than a man who had found a clandestine way into her bedchamber would spoil everything he'd worked to create. And what if she found out he was the missing criminal accused of butchering a three-year-old girl?

Still, he forced himself to consider it from every angle. They could remain in the tunnels until Bericus and his warriors gave up. Then they could make their way south, back to Breda. Surely they would never be found there.

But she would probably refuse to go without her mother. It would rouse too much suspicion and a more determined effort to find them if Ula vanished as well.

Ossian and Nemausus returned to her chamber and told her it was time. She was to be taken to the Druid Stone. He raced down the steps and left the tunnel by the south entrance, pulling his hood close to his face and making a wide berth around the village, which seemed deserted anyway.

There she was, wearing a blue gown and walking in the midst of a group that included armed guards. He watched as she knelt beside a man. Some kind of ceremony ensued. After it was completed, she and the others crossed to the nearby cliffs and threw something into the sea.

There was no way to get to her. She was taken back to the village.

He trudged to the mooring place and climbed up to the cave, where he sat and stared at one of the most dramatic sunsets he had ever seen. A heavy sea mist formed along the edge of land, picking up the deeply crimson conflagration and giving the suggestion that sky and ocean were one.

His thoughts circled. Her voice, asking for his help. Her eyes, spilling over with tears.

He sifted pebbles and tossed them, listening as they hit the stones below. He needed to keep his hands and mind busy or he might attempt to break down one of the hidden doors and lay waste to Bericus's fort, as much as he could before he died.

Could he follow Eamhair to Innse Orc? But how would he ever see her there? Would there be convenient caves and secret passages? Would she have her own bedchamber, or would she share her husband's?

Snatches of music carried on the wind. The wedding celebration had begun. It continued as the sun dropped and Taranis grew more despondent.

A woman walked onto the point on the other side of the cove. He could shout and she would hear. She approached the edge and stopped, staring at the ocean, grasping the hood under her chin to keep the wind from blowing it off. The cloak she wore didn't look substantial enough to keep her warm if she spent much time out here.

She turned and started back, tripped, and fell. She remained there on her hands and knees for some time before rising and wandering on, weaving as though blind. Taranis shook his head. These cliffs were no place for a woman so drunk she could hardly walk.

Showing himself was dangerous. She might have seen him when he came to the village as a monk, and remember that he'd been accused of murder. She could scream or tell someone. He turned away, deciding to ignore her. But as she continued, stumbling now and then, he changed his mind. He would follow and intervene if need be. Perhaps if he helped her, she might return the favor by taking a message to Eamhair.

Taranis leaped from the cave mouth to the rocks, waded across the stream, and climbed up to the cliffs, keeping a discreet distance between them.

THE WOMAN PASSED THE LITTLE BEACH WHERE TARANIS HAD COME OUT OF the sea to trick Eamhair, and went right to the edge of the cliffs beyond. A few birds circled, shrieking, but she didn't look up.

She must have recovered her wits. She stood without swaying, and appeared to be simply admiring the sunset.

There was a sudden sensation against the back of his neck, like an exhale. He swiveled.

When you ask it, you will have my forgiveness.

The cliffs, the woman, the birds—all blurred as though veiled in mist. Several breaths passed before he remembered he had heard those exact words in the labyrinth on Crete, the night he sought to become Crete's bull-king.

The woman turned her face to the heavens, clenched both hands into fists, and shouted, "My fate is my own! No one shall take it from me!" She ripped off her cloak and the blue veil, dropping them on the ground.

Taranis started forward, propelled by exploding terror as he recognized the gown and the voice.

But he was too late.

Crying out wordlessly, he stopped at the edge and stared. He couldn't see anything until the fog thinned. There—a sodden blue mass billowed and collapsed as it took on water.

He swallowed and leaped, fully expecting to be crushed on the rocks below.

THE WATER WAS SO ICY THAT FOR SOME AWFUL LENGTH OF TIME, TARANIS couldn't draw a breath. He choked even as he flailed, dove, and dove again. His muscles numbed. All too soon he would sink.

Thick, waterlogged fabric brushed against his arm. He filled his hands with it and hauled. Eamhair appeared, grey as a ghost, her eyes closed, her body limp. He set out, following the different sound the water made as it beat at open space rather than solid rock.

The tide pushed them in; he staggered onto the beach, only half aware of the intense red sunlight that set the whole coast inside a gemstone.

She coughed; a runnel of seawater trickled from her mouth. He put her down on soft sand in a sheltered spot between a sheer overhang and a line of boulders that formed a decent windbreak. He felt her arms and legs, searching for wounds or broken bones, noting absently the many bruises, some purple, some green, some yellow, and remembered how Nemausus had casually struck her. Her lips were grey-blue and there was a small cut on her cheekbone. Nothing appeared to be broken yet her eyelids fluttered before falling into stillness and her breathing was negligible. When her eyes did open they stared without recognition. He feared something inside had shattered from the force of hitting the water, or perhaps in her mind she had already left this world.

He glanced at the water, where countless rocks protruded like teeth. How was she alive? How was he?

She tried to speak but hoarse coughing stopped her. At last she croaked, "You."

He tucked her hands into his. They were so cold. All he could think to do was stretch over her and rub her arms and shoulders.

Wait—wasn't there a cloak? Before she jumped, she'd discarded it. With any luck, it would still be on the cliff. With a word of reassurance, he climbed to the plateau, willing his sluggish mind to remember where it lay. Every step sent his blood pumping more smoothly, and by the time he collected the garment from the ground he didn't feel quite so frozen. He brought it back and wrapped her in the healing warmth of dry wool.

"Can you hear me, Eamhair?" He leaned close, rubbing her hands.

The air around him turned violet and gold; he tasted it on his tongue, like ripe blackberries and the sweetest honeyed pears.

She didn't move. Her eyes were closed, her skin deathly pale. "Eamhair—look at me."

He put his arms around her and lifted her, pressing her cheek to his throat. "Aridela."

She said something. Supporting the back of her head, he leaned away so he could look into her face. Her eyes were open but her gaze was unfocused.

"I thought you would come sooner," she said, her voice almost a sigh. "Then I no longer believed you would come at all."

He tried to swallow and couldn't. His throat was raw.

She blinked several times. He watched her struggle to come back to her body. Lifting her hand, she placed her index finger on his cheek, beneath his eye, and trailed it down to his beard, her gaze following. "If you hadn't come to me on the beach that day, I think I would have been obedient, for my mother's sake. I would have gone with Fathna. But you did come. My mother didn't lie about you. She always said you would appear when I needed you most, and you came just before Fathna. But nothing happened the way I thought it would. You didn't take us away. You didn't stop them from marrying me to him. I decided to die. At least that would be my choice. And there would be nothing they could do about it."

"Oh, Eamhair." His strength drained away. It wasn't Fathna. It wasn't even her father. It was him. He was to blame for this.

She frowned. "Your eyes. Your voice...they call to me...in dreams."

"Aridela. My Aridela. You have been lost to me for so long."

"Why do you call me that? Is it your lost queen you see when you look into my face? Do you wish I was her?" One of her hands slid around his neck and the other touched the tears on his cheeks. "Do not weep, seolh-king," she said, though her own eyes filled with tears.

He lowered his head and kissed her. Her lips moved. Memories flooded, dimming the terror of diving into the frost-bound ocean, of fighting to find her before they both drowned or froze. Now his heart pounded for a different reason.

Lifting off her slightly, he opened the cloak and pulled up the wet gown and shift.

The ghost of Winoc shouted a warning at the back of his mind, but he let his racing heart and soaring exultation drown it out. It had ever been that way, the slave Alexiare giving unwelcome admonitions, Chrysaleon dismissing them.

He covered her face with kisses. "Do not die, not again," he whispered against her mouth. "I cannot bear to lose you again."

He poised himself against her, holding back, waiting for her eyes to open, to look into his. They did, slowly. Languidly. *She wants me.*

"I left my home for you," he said. "I came to this place of bitter cold and men who would kill me on sight." His hands tightened on her arms. "You chose death over becoming a man's slave. Because you love *me*. You and I have to be together. If we stay together, death has no power over us."

"Did you bring me out of the sea?"

"Yes." He kissed her jaw, her neck, and the lobe of her ear. Her skin was as sweet as water to a starved, thirsty man.

"I—I am not his. I cannot be his. I cannot. That man from Innse Orc." Her brows furrowed. "Cailean will not let this stand. He will kill my father, or my father will kill him. Will you save Cailean, Taranis? I will never ask anything else of you, if only you will save my mother and Cailean. I cannot bear to lose them."

Jealousy and hatred flared, blackening his sight, warping his desire. What was wrong with her? How could she kiss him while thinking of another man? How could she speak his name so sadly?

Cailean! *Menoetius!*

"Do not say his name!" He sank into her, groaning, not in joy but misery. "You are mine. Tonight. Every night. Forever."

It was not easy. He had to push hard. It felt like an attack, not an act of love. From the beginning, Aridela had always been ready, willing, her body drawing his in, her embraces making him feel like a god. Eamhair's body was the opposite, dry and unwilling, rejecting him.

She cried out and fought. He knew he was hurting her, but he didn't stop. *She will remember me, and how we loved each other.* He held down her arms and thrust, again and again, until he spent himself inside her.

"Aridela," he said, shuddering.

She arched away as he withdrew. Her chest contracted in an audible sob. "Do not call me that. I am not her, and I am glad of it."

Time passed. He listened to the unbridled drumming of her heart. "For-forgive me. Forgive me, Eamhair."

She made no reply, but her chest again contracted.

If only, oh if only he could have given her Eseld's mushroom. She would not be terrified. She would not feel as if she had been...raped. She would remember. She would put her arms around him and welcome him as Aridela had always done.

But what was the use in wishing? It was too late now for that.

She said nothing. Shudder after shudder ran through her. Each one felt like a blade through his stomach.

He found the courage to look into her face. "I should not have done that. But he—he is not—not anyone you should care about. You and I are all that matters."

She stared at him and there was, at last, real awareness. Her voice was hard as stone. "And what of your wife?"

For the length of a kiss she had seemed willing, responsive. Had she been imagining another man in his place, as he had been imagining another woman?

She did not remember him, or their life together on Crete. She was not Aridela. She was Eamhair, a virgin until this night. He rolled off her and arranged her gown so her legs were covered. He folded the cloak over her to help keep her warm. He did all these things silently while inside, he fought off a tirade of disbelief and condemnation.

She sat up, looking at the beach and out to the misty ocean. "How have I come to be here?"

He smoothed a clinging lock of hair off her cheek, trying to be gentle and non-threatening. "You jumped from the cliff. Don't you remember? You would have drowned...had I not brought you back."

The mad shrieking and tearing of the Erinyes wormed around the edges of his mind, seeking a way through. He sucked in a breath, another, and another, short inhalations that didn't ease the sense of choking. He had to keep calm. Later, he could hate himself for what he had done, and try to think of a way to earn her forgiveness. For now he had to hold the monsters off. He rose abruptly, keeping hold of her hand. "Can you stand? You need to go back before they start searching for you."

Distantly, she said, "I am no longer pure. It was the only thing about me my father valued."

He pulled her up, fastening the cloak and covering her hair with the hood. "You have strength enough to fight them. You are a queen. A queen would never let herself be used like a sheep to sacrifice."

"No. I suppose there are many things...a queen would not allow."

He gritted his teeth and helped her climb to the plateau, acutely aware of the awkward way she walked, as if trying to hold her legs apart. She had been so dry his prick still felt inflamed; she was surely suffering too—worse since he'd torn her virgin barrier.

The sun had long since set. Moonlight turned the clouds of mist to undulating mounds, like sand dunes stretching to the farthest horizon.

She stopped well beyond where the fortress guards could see or hear. Her teeth chattered; she was shivering. How miserably cold she must be. "Fathna," she stammered. "The...the king of Innse Orc. He could kill me for what you took." She looked past him into the dark. "I began this day as Fathna's chattel. Now I am yours. Your whore, I suppose. You say you love me, yet you did nothing to stop my father and brothers. All day, I waited. I prayed you would come. But you did not."

"Me, alone, against your father, your brothers, and all his warriors? Eamhair, I do love you, more than you know. I will find a way—we will be together. That is all that matters."

"No," was all she said, and he was left to wonder which of his declarations she denied.

Anger erupted and he shook her. Why couldn't she see? Why was she fighting him? Aridela had always believed in him...until the end.

She wrenched away. "If I refuse Fathna, my father will beat me. Maybe banish me. His impure daughter. Or he might harm my mother. That has always worked for him. Will you come with me now? Tell my father you are taking me—and my mother—to your empire beneath the sea."

"They will kill me. They think me an outlaw."

Her brows rose. "You are leaving me to Fathna and whatever mercy he chooses to give or withhold?"

"Men know I am different. They will always seek to destroy me."

After a moment of silence, she said dully, "The woman spoke the truth."

"What woman?"

"On the cliffs. She told me you had taken me from my path and changed my destiny. I thought you could save me, but you cannot, or will not. Now I will die."

There had been no woman on the cliffs. She was imagining things. Yet there was an instant...just before she jumped.... "You will not die," he said with all the force he could muster. "I will come for you, Eamhair, as soon as I can." Pushing back her hood, he removed his necklace and put it over her head, tucking the pendant beneath her tunic. "Here is my token. It is my most prized possession, for it was once yours. I will come, Eamhair. We still have time before the king returns. You will not die."

"But you will not go in with me now...."

"If I do they'll murder me. Then you will have no protection— none, and there will be nothing to stop that man from making you his property. Give me time."

After a long interlude of silence, she said, "Very well. I will face them alone."

She left him without looking back.

Chapter 23

BERICUS WAS DRUNK. THEY ALL WERE. HIS GAZE TRAVELED OVER EAMHAIR and hardened. "Where have you been? Swimming in the ocean?"

Nemausus laughed. The proxy looked at her, bleary-eyed, as if he couldn't remember who she was.

"Give the man compensation for whatever he paid you, Father," she said. "I cannot be his wife."

Nemausus snorted into his mug. "Shall I have her flogged?"

"What is she talking about? She spends too much time with her bitch of a mother. They prattle endlessly and drive me mad." Scowling, Bericus smashed his fist against the table then swept a platter of meat onto the floor. The dogs raced to fight and snarl over this unexpected feast.

Eamhair's head was spinning. The noise in the hall echoed and the flames in the cresset lamps glared. She could not fully recall going to the cliffs, or jumping, as Taranis claimed she had, though judging from her state, it could be true. What he had done after was all too vivid. Her mind would not stop replaying it, and the place between her legs burned.

She dug her nails into her palms but could not focus, or halt the sense that her head was floating above the smoky hall, separate from her body. She was certain all the blood had seeped from her veins, leaving nothing but empty skin consumed by frost.

Why would any woman seek such hideous, painful intimacies?

Even worse, he could have bred a child upon her. She knew babies didn't come every time a man had his way, but she had heard enough women lamenting that they had tried to prevent it and failed, and warn others to beware the stiff prick, unless they wanted another mouth to feed.

Would she give birth to a seolh, only part human? Would he long for two worlds, and be forever sad and lonely?

There were ways to tell if a woman had been with a man. If she went to the northern king now, he would know. She would be lucky if he only repudiated her. Killing her would be his right. He might come back to Dunaedan and kill her father and mother for lying to him.

She was accustomed to betrayals from men. Still, she reeled at the abandonment of the seolh-king, though every story about them warned they would always desert their human lovers for the lure of the sea. He had won her trust far too easily. Not only had he attacked her, he balked at confronting Bericus and the others. He left her to do that on her own.

Would he keep the promise he made at the gate? Her faith lay like a scatter of broken icicles at her feet, dependent on the whim of the sun.

"Get to your bedchamber," said her father roughly. "You will be off to your husband before the month is finished. You should be grateful. I have made you a queen."

She stiffened her spine and forced an expression of fearless confidence. "I am another man's wife already. I cannot be Fathna's wife too."

Nemausus leaped from the bench and came around the end of the table. She stared at him, refusing to cower. In one swift movement, he grabbed her by the hair and jerked her off balance.

"Get her out of here!" Bericus was red-faced. The proxy squinted from one to the other, frowning.

As Nemausus yanked her from the hall, she heard Bericus reassuring him. "She must have had too much ale. Her brother will see to her, and she'll be obedient come morning—of course she is not married! She has been well sheltered."

She fought Nemausus all the way up the stairs, but he was too strong. At her door he twisted her arm. "You better not have opened your legs to some wretch. If you have, I swear you'll not live to see another full moon."

He locked her in.

Taranis heard Eamhair's accusation again and again. *You are leaving me to Fathna and whatever mercy he chooses to give or withhold?*

He had never hated himself more.

To be reborn after two millennia. To find not only Menoetius and Alexiare, but also *Aridela*. To be presented with the opportunity to make right his ancient crimes. And what had he done? From the instant he'd recognized her inside the body of that girl, he hadn't stopped plotting. He'd done nothing differently.

He had used her belief in magic to trick her. He told lie after lie. When she was most vulnerable, he forced himself on her.

Every time he thought of going to her, he had to swallow the scald of bile. He could not face her. He didn't have the courage.

Once more he allowed himself to imagine what it would have been like if he had given her the mushroom. Her eyes, joyous with recognition. Her tears, her kisses, her laughter. Then he pushed those fantasies away forever.

Athene, you bitch! You play with us still. You blind me with hope and rip it away.

He had instantly known Menoetius, Alexiare, and Aridela, though all three resided in unfamiliar bodies. Something caused that. *She* caused it. As Winoc had warned, she was moving them to her will.

I never would have attacked Eamhair on my own. Athene forced me to do what I did.

But he had done such things as Chrysaleon. It was his right as a conquering prince and warrior.

He felt her eyes boring into his head. He flattened his hands against his skull, pressing, longing to extinguish the memory of what he'd done.

Athene had brought him to Eamhair. He had too easily believed she was giving him a second chance. It had been no more than a trick, designed to make him suffer Aridela's loss once more.

He wept for those three happy days at Phaistos before the cataclysm. Three short days of shared love and intimacy.

Uttering the vilest curses he knew, he overturned his sleeping pallet, threw the coffer of food, and shattered the lamps against the tunnel walls. It did no good to weep like a child at the unfairness of things. He must be strong—stronger than the Bitch. He now knew beyond doubt that she was aligned against him.

You have made an enemy of me, Potnia Athene. You had better never bring me back again, for I will not stop until I have wiped you from the memory of every mortal who lives or will live.

Lost ages ago, on a hot day at the Cretan bullring, Aridela held up her necklace. *Damasen had it made. Some say it comes from a lake of silver on the moon.*

It cast a spell over him as it swayed from her fingertips, a spell that continued unabated.

"This is no time to be afraid," he whispered. "If you are going to take vengeance upon a goddess, remember—fortune favors the bold."

OSSIAN BROUGHT THREE WOMEN—VIVIANA, JOCOSA, AND THE VILLAGE midwife—into Eamhair's chamber, rudely waking her from the exhausted sleep she had drifted into after hours of reliving the many horrors of the previous day. Together, Ossian and Viviana overpowered her; Ossian bound her wrists and threw her onto the bed. He pushed on her shoulders while Viviana and Jocosa held down her legs so the midwife could examine her. There was pity in Jocosa's eyes, but none in Viviana's.

"Your suspicion was right," the midwife said. "There are bruises and blood, and I smell a man's leavings. She could be with child, but there is no way to tell—not for a few months."

Ossian slapped Eamhair until the midwife protested, which brought his fist to her cheek. She fell, cursing him.

Eamhair was locked in with no fire, food, or water. This deliberate prison they made of her bedchamber was just another way of showing her that she was their property to do with as they wished. Even Bericus's slaves had more freedom.

She wanted to escape, but even more, she longed to stand and fight. Ula had told her that in the old religion, no woman could be forced to marry against her will. But Bericus followed no laws other than his own, and those Drost forced upon him.

Rising from bed, she crossed to her coffer and took out the bracelet of red rowanberries. It was impossible to reconcile the artisan who devised this harmonious pattern of berries and thread with the angry male who had assaulted her.

Her mother's promise wove through her thoughts. *The dream woman told me she had charged a king to serve you, to help and protect you.*

He will come from the deep blue abyss, from the coldest depths beyond the reach of any light.

Her recollection of leaving the celebration and going to the cliffs remained elusive. Clarity began when Taranis carried her out of the ocean and into a world bathed in crimson radiance. Seawater cascaded over his face and shoulders. He had looked down into her face, and at that instant was in every way a magical creature of the sea.

How could he have known she was on the cliffs, or what she intended, if he did not have extraordinary power?

Mostly what she remembered of their joining was the stinging, the shock, and his labored breathing, almost as though *he* were in pain. He was the seolh-king, the one she had waited for her whole life. But what he had done—was this the way of seolhs? Had it been no more than what, to him, was common?

She almost crushed the bracelet. It would be easy—it was quite delicate. She wanted to destroy it, and with it, all memory of him. But in the end, she replaced it in the coffer and shut the lid.

Never again would she look to Taranis for salvation. She hated him now. She would keep the bracelet as a reminder of how foolish it was to give trust before it was earned.

Chapter 24

No one brought food or drink to Eamhair's chamber the next day, either. It was nothing new. She would be expected to beg forgiveness and display obedience after a period of isolation, cold, and hunger. She tried to distract her thoughts by making up stories to go with the illustrations in the Bible one of the suitors had presented to her father. He hadn't cared about it since he couldn't read, so he'd let her take it. She couldn't read either, but liked looking at the depictions of the Christos and his worshippers.

The worst part of these punishments was always thirst, but at last she fell asleep, only to endure nightmares of a figure heavy upon her, unrecognizable until a shaft of light showed her Fathna's face. When she woke, she felt suffocated in the odor of ashes and a voice. *I hope you never lose your hatred.*

The next day she was given another chance, but she kept her spine straight and again refused to be Fathna's wife.

This time the proxy was sober. "I warn you, Lady Eamhair. Fathna of Innse Orc is not a man you want to anger."

She met his gaze steadily. "I am not a beast to be caged."

"You are a cow!" Nemausus shouted. "You have been in a cage your entire miserable life, and now we have sold you. You are nothing —snail slime. The king of Innse Orc's property. We could just as easily give you to a leper."

He rushed at her, balling his fist, but the proxy intercepted him.

"She is young," he said gently. "She is afraid, as any innocent girl would be. Perhaps she does not understand this honor." He lifted his arms and looked around the hall. "Here, you are merely the chief's daughter, and subject to an overlord. On Innse Orc, you will be Queen Eamhair, subject to none but the king."

"I will not go."

While Nemausus cursed and slammed his fist against his palm, the proxy sent an inquiring glance around the hall. "Where is this husband? Why is he not here to claim you? Why does he not protect you from unwanted suitors?"

"He—will come."

A lifted brow and puzzled frown made clear the proxy's doubt. "I think if he were an honorable man, he would be here already." He glanced at Bericus, who was shaking his head and breathing like a bull. "I pray, for your sake, Bericus, that your daughter has not allowed herself to be seduced by some stable boy. If my master believes, even for an instant, that you have lied, you will regret it more than you can fathom."

So her father and brothers had not told the proxy of the midwife's declaration. She almost laughed. They still thought they could pull off their fraud.

Bericus gestured and Nemausus again removed her from the hall. For once he made no taunts as he pushed and prodded her to her bedchamber. He said nothing until they reached her door; once there he put his face close to hers and wrenched her arms so brutally she whimpered. "If you bring war down upon us, you bitch, I will shred the skin from your bones with my bare hands."

The door slammed and she was again left with only the scornful Viviana for company.

She lay in bed, her knees curled against her chest, and wept.

Deep in the night, she jerked at the pendant Taranis had placed around her neck. The chain snapped. She dropped it on the floor and turned her back on it.

THE RINGING OF LAUDS WOKE EAMHAIR. SHE LAY STILL, LISTENING TO AN odd rustling before carefully lifting her head. Through a gap in the bed curtain she saw Viviana standing beside her table, a candle in one hand. The other was buried in the coffer where Eamhair kept her trinkets and treasures. As she watched, Viviana brought out Cailean's ring. She set down the candle, slid the ring on her middle finger, and held out her hand, turning it so the candlelight gleamed against the silver.

"Put that down!" Eamhair threw off the furs and jumped out of bed.

Viviana whirled but quickly recovered. "Why should I? I think I will sell it. You're away to be a queen, if your new husband does not kill you first. Surely you will be given more treasure than I will ever see."

Eamhair ran forward; Viviana put out her hands but Eamhair caught her wrist and twisted, causing Viviana to screech.

Jerking hard on the woman's finger, Eamhair pulled off the ring. She mimicked Nemausus's method of intimidation by putting her face almost against Viviana's and making her voice low and menacing. "If you ever touch anything of mine again, I will rip out every one of your fingers—one by one."

Viviana shrank back, cursing, her eyes shining with hard, bright fear. Eamhair knew the woman would never again pry into her coffer.

She returned to her bed, but it was hard to release the anger. Even after Viviana's movements stilled, Eamhair stared into the gloom, turning Cailean's ring over and over in her palm. She was surprised by the burning heat of her rage, but it also made her think. How could she keep this from happening again? The thin leather cord she had used before was still in her clothes chest. The next time Viviana went to the privy, she would use it to fasten the ring around her forearm, beneath her clothing. That way, it could not be taken unless she was senseless or dead.

Gradually she became aware of a glow rising from the side of the bed. She peered over the edge. The fire in the brazier was nearly depleted, yet the necklace flashed. Wheeling beams of light came off it like sunrays.

It was once yours.

She picked it up and ran her fingers over the raised blue stone. What had Taranis meant by that? She had only seen this necklace once. He'd been wearing it when he came out of the sea.

How she wished she could cut his voice from her mind! She hated the way it intruded, speaking of love as he forced himself upon her like a beast.

She felt the broken link in the chain. For some reason she could not understand, she cared about the cursed thing. She threaded it as best she could around the next link and pushed the ends together. Tomorrow, she would work on it again, when she had more light—and whatever privacy she could manage.

She put it around her neck.

You and I will be together, Taranis had promised.

She wanted nothing less than that, but even now, after what he had done, she would go with him—if it meant her mother would be saved.

Chapter 25

OF THE ORIGINAL SEVEN WHO VOYAGED TO INNSE ORC IN SEARCH OF THE escaped prisoners, all but two were lost when their boat capsized and sank off the coast. Cailean didn't know who the other survivor was, since he recovered and left while Cailean was unconscious. The village woman's indifferent description matched several of his warriors. He wanted to get back to Dunaedan and discover who had dumped him at the mercy of strangers. Not one of his bow brothers would have done that.

He was astonished to discover seven days had passed. His cloudy memory produced a splintered chunk of hide-covered timber pitching toward his head, but nothing else. The goodwife said he still had a fever, and was fortunate to be alive. She fed him fish stew and told him she and her husband were off to join the solstice festivities in the village.

Bericus allows a feast on the night of the solstice. Will you be back by then? Eamhair's expressive face had held such hope.

He lay on the pallet after the woman and her husband left, impatiently clenching his fists, wishing he knew a way to transport himself to Dunaedan in the blink of an eye. What was Eamhair doing? Was she angry, or worse, did she believe him dead?

Curse that cocksucking, murderous monk. If not for him, Cailean would be dancing with her right now.

He tried to stand but soon collapsed, stabbed by sparkling dizziness, nausea, and a pounding heartbeat.

The fever was not finished with him. It returned twice more. He was not well enough to start his journey until ten torturous days later.

The woman brought him his own sword, which had remained strapped to his hip throughout the near drowning. He thanked her and promised she would be rewarded for her honesty and kindly care.

THE SMOKE OF COOKING FIRES AND STENCH OF THE TANNERY REACHED Cailean's nose before he saw the fort. As he topped the final hill and started down, he spotted the minute forms of villagers, and soon a dog or two was barking at him. He hated everything about Dunaedan, but the anticipation of seeing Eamhair made him happy, even though he knew he would have to face Bericus and confess he had failed to recapture the escaped murderer.

The trek to Dunaedan that should have taken two days took six, due to excruciating headaches and a snowfall so deep it rose to his knees most of the way. He was glad to see the windswept headland of Dunaedan was nearly bare of snow, though the wind gusts were cutting.

Vita charged through the heath like a ghostly shadow, jumping upon Cailean and licking his face, whining and growling her joy.

Several villagers spotted him and shouted. More ran up to offer greetings.

Everything appeared exactly the same as when he'd left, yet it wasn't.

He was being surreptitiously studied. Perhaps he'd been replaced and they were worried about his reaction.

He headed for the smithy. Gede liked to talk. They had enjoyed several amiable conversations about metalworking. The blacksmith was outside, yet as he approached, the fellow lowered his head and vanished into his forge.

Uneasiness quickened Cailean's strides. He stood outside and called.

The silence from within stretched out until Cailean was ready to curse. Finally the man emerged, wiping his hands on a grimy rag. "I am glad to see you alive, Baron."

Cailean felt Gede wanted to add something to the end of that, but had stopped himself.

Gede's shaggy bay mare snorted and sidestepped as far as she could from Vita. Cailean gentled her with a few words and a stroke or two on her soft nose. "How has Dunaedan fared in my absence?"

"You—you have been gone a long while."

Cailean dropped all pretense. "What has happened?"

"It is not my place to say. I don't want the chief—"

"Gede—"

"It is Lady Eamhair."

"Tell me. Now."

Gede spoke in a rush. "A man came through while you were gone. No one knows exactly what he did, whether he tricked Bericus, paid him, or threatened him. I think he threatened him, because it became known that he is a king—and that is not all. He is Drost Gocinecht's brother. You know as well as I how Bericus has used his daughter as a bribe behind Drost's back. In this case, I think Bericus himself was extorted. Anyway, the girl was given to him. There was a ceremony—"

Cailean coughed to clear his throat. "She is gone?"

"It's only gossip, you understand, my lord. But I have it from my wife, who heard from the kitchen maids, that she refused the man, and claimed she was already married."

"What!"

"She has been beaten." Gede's shoulders hunched and his mouth turned down. He rubbed his eyes with the rag. "The midwife proclaimed her...defiled...and warned her father she might have a babe growing inside her. They tried to hide this but it came out, and the king's proxy left, promising war with Bericus."

"Where is she? Tell me quickly."

Taking a deep breath, Gede said, "She was to be taken to the cliffs at sunrise. To be killed if she did not provide the name of the man who ruined her. Her new husband, you see, gave Bericus a fortnight to find the monk accused of killing Drost's child. That fortnight has come and gone. I have heard Bericus is very much afraid of the man, and hopes to placate him through any means necessary—even executing his own daughter. Did you find the monk, Baron?"

This last was shouted, for Cailean had already jumped upon the pony and kicked it away.

Damn Gede for wasting so much time.

V<small>ITA ARRIVED BEFORE</small> C<small>AILEAN.</small> H<small>ER LOOSE PACING AND SOFT SNARL KEPT</small> the frightened horses at bay, no matter how Nemausus and Ossian kicked them.

Cailean brought the pony to a halt and drew his sword.

Eamhair lay like a dead mackerel across Ossian's lap. Cailean eyed her, keeping his face expressionless though inside, he trembled with fear. Blood dripped steadily off her left hand.

"Dalriada," said Nemausus. "Finally returned, just in time to see our whore of a sister receive justice."

"Is she alive?"

"For now." Ossian used the veil to pull up her head so Cailean could see her face. It was bruised and bloody, her left eye swollen shut. "And she will go on living if she tells us the name of the man who spoiled her. If she won't, it's over the cliff at the Judgment Stone."

"Let her go." The pony shied, not liking the presence of the wolf or the way Cailean sawed at the reins.

Ossian glanced at Nemausus. "Bran said he thought our baron was sweet on Eamhair."

"If you want to live," Cailean said, "let her go."

Nemausus edged his horse closer to Ossian's. "You have no say in this. Go back to the fort—you found that prisoner, didn't you? My father is counting on it."

"Let her go," Cailean said, "while you still can."

"Who do you think you are? Wait—are *you* the one who had her?"

"Vita," Cailean said. "To me."

The wolf hesitated, glancing from Cailean to the brothers, before she obeyed.

Ossian laughed and Nemausus bared his sword. Both kicked their horses. Cailean pivoted the pony sideways and thrust his blade into the breast of the horse Nemausus rode. It screamed and fell as Vita lunged for the other horse's throat. Nemausus leaped free and Ossian followed, pulling Eamhair with him. Dragging her by the upper arms, the two brothers retreated as Cailean dismounted and approached, ordering Vita to stay at his side.

Eamhair moaned and lifted her head. She looked at him, her good eye half-closed. He thought she mouthed something, but he couldn't hear what.

Cailean had an urge to kill himself for not preventing this. But at least he was here now, and she was not dead. Not yet.

She tried to struggle but they were too strong and she was only half conscious. She slumped, obviously at the end of her strength.

Nemausus placed the tip of his sword at Eamhair's stomach. "Back away, Dalriada, or watch her guts spill."

Ossian brandished a seax. "Put down your weapon if you want her to live. But whatever happens, my father will have your head for interfering. Who do you think sent us here? It is his wish."

"He commanded this?" Cailean couldn't believe it. He knew Bericus was ruthless, but Eamhair was his daughter.

They meant their threats. They would do it. He shoved his sword into the ground.

The brothers exchanged a glance. Nemausus laughed as they threw Eamhair over the cliff.

PART II

Sanctuary

Chapter 1

SAND, SOFT AS LAMB'S WOOL AND SPARKLING LIKE STARDUST, STRETCHED away on both sides as far as Eamhair could see. Before her there was rippling movement—a vast body of water giving off glinting reflections of moonlight.

She took one step. Another. There was not a breath of wind. She felt alone and small until she saw two shapes against the silver white sand and recognized Bharosa and Vita. "Come, come," she said, bending a little and clapping her hands, but neither one approached or made any movement other than Vita perking her ears.

"Why are you here? Where is Cailean? Where is your master, Vita?" Neither animal moved. They just watched her.

As she turned to search for Cailean, she spotted a white boat floating beyond the reef, half hidden behind a cloud suffused in a myriad of colors.

She recognized the boat. She had seen it many times in dreams. Eagerly, she drew up the hem of the loose shift she wore and waded into the shallows but the boat was beyond reach, where the water was black and deep. The sail swelled and the water around the hull was wild and frothy, yet the boat remained still, as though tied by unseen lines to the sea floor.

Carved into the prow was the naked torso and head of a woman. As Eamhair waded nearer, the woman turned. Her eyes made Eamhair want to laugh and weep.

The cloud around the boat swirled into the shape of a man. Silver bands circled his forehead and arms in intricate designs like the ring Cailean had given her. His hair fell unbound to his shoulders. As he held out his hand, she watched him shift and spiral, at first well-formed then fluid as water, his hair varying between short and long, light and dark.

Will you come with me?

She was not sure. She did not know this man. He was familiar in one breath, a stranger the next.

Even as her mind warned her to be careful, she struggled through ever-deeper water to get to him.

But the boat evaporated and nothing remained but the woman's gentle refusal.

Not yet.

EVERYTHING WAS DISTORTED, AS THOUGH THE WORLD AND ALL SHE HAD ever known lay beneath the surface of a wind-rippled loch. Voices came and went. White light flashed before softening into cool green shadows. There was a delicious smell of vegetation. Eamhair heard the sound of hooves striking earth and the occasional equine snort. She felt herself swaying rhythmically, but arms held her and her head rested against a sturdy shoulder. She was safe.

THE MOANING WOULD NOT STOP. SOME POOR CREATURE WAS SUFFERING. Why was it not given succor or put out of its misery?

Drink. Blue eyes, intent and uncompromising as a raptor's.

Menoetius, why have you come to me as Velchanos?

Then nothing.

KILL ME. IF YOU CARE AT ALL ABOUT ME, KILL ME, I BEG YOU.

We will not kill you, Eamhair. Someday you will laugh again. Drink. It will dull the pain.

I AM HERE, BELOVED. NEVER THINK I HAVE ABANDONED YOU.

This voice was different from the others. It was that woman's—the woman carved into the prow of the boat. She came slowly into focus. First her eyes—large, rimmed with black lashes, the irises grey, silver, and blue, blending like the ribbons that hung sometimes in winter skies, her golden crown as ephemeral as spindrift.

The woman looked nothing like Ula, yet Eamhair was drawn to her in the same way she was drawn to her mother.

Go and live as all women do. Make their stories your story, so that one day, they will know you as one of their own.

Chapter 2

I WILL HAVE VICTORY.

The words echoed as Eamhair woke.

Her left ankle and wrist throbbed in unison with the ache in her ribs. Pain was everywhere, and stiffness, as though she hadn't moved in a month.

Had she gone blind? She could see nothing.

She remembered her brothers bursting into her bedchamber and propelling her down the stairs, taunting her about how they meant to toss her into the ocean like a dead cat. At a particularly narrow turn her head slammed against the wall; she remembered nothing after that until she was on the cliffs. Wind blew against her face, clearing her mind somewhat as Ossian pulled her off his horse.

Cailean had been there, hadn't he? But her brothers wouldn't allow him to intervene.

Was she at the bottom of the sea? Was she dead?

Her ears detected movement. There was the scent of leather, and… what else?

A distant drift of rain, cool and alive. An approaching storm. Her mind formed a picture of a man lying beside her on piles of fur.

You'll tether me like a goat? That is your image of victory?

I will have victory, Aridela.

A weight settled nearby and she instinctively lashed out. She could not make a fist of her left hand, so she struck with her right, groaning at the pain that bit through her chest but punching anyway. She would not give in to her brothers. Not again, no matter how much it hurt, no matter if it killed her.

Her wrist was captured in a grip she could not break no matter how hard she twisted and fought. An arm went around her. She was pulled against a body—a man's body.

"Eamhair, I will not harm you, but you might harm yourself. You have broken ribs. Please don't fight me."

The voice was alarmed yet hushed.

Her struggles faltered. "Cailean?"

"Aye. Only me." He released her, moved away, and returned. The edge of a cup touched her lips. "Will you drink? It will help with the pain."

She did, and was carefully returned to a reclining position.

"What—how—"

"Rest. You are safe. You need do nothing but get well."

A hand stroked the side of her face. "You are safe."

She closed her eyes and succumbed to the dark.

WHEN NEXT SHE WOKE, SHE REALIZED WITH SOME RELIEF THAT SHE HAD not gone blind. She lay in a bed, in a small chamber. Sunlight streamed through a perfectly round, open window edged in patterned wood. A warm whiff of air teased one of the shutters, causing it to drift lazily.

Her gaze moved on. The bed sat higher than the floor, as if on a dais; a column at each corner supported a dome and curtains, which were tied back. She saw another room through an arch in the wall, illuminated more brightly than hers. There was a hearth with something suspended over it—like a circle of stones, rather like Dunaedan's round tower in miniature, and an iron ring hanging from the ceiling holding seventeen unlit candles. Dust motes floated, glittering like fine particles of snow.

A grey striped cat sat in the center of the doorway beyond the hearth. It jumped, spitting, as a man and dog came in. The dog merely glanced at the cat as it passed, and her mind corrected her. Not a dog. A wolf.

The man carried an armful of wood, which he placed next to the hearth before glancing into the anteroom. Seeing she was awake, he came in and sat beside her, lifting a bowl from a table by the bed.

It took time to place him. *My father's baron,* she thought, seeing a badger pelt flecked with snow, and his leather-clad hand pulling her closer.

Asterion.

Her mind cleared a little. *Cailean of Dalriada, the warrior with a wolf.*

She flattened her palm against his chest, digging with her fingertips. Tears spilled, running over her temples and into her hair.

He set the bowl down and wiped at her tears. "You're alive," he said. "I have you. You are safe, Eamhair."

"What—what happened?"

He hesitated. "Just rest."

She wanted to argue, but couldn't. She was already floating away.

There was dampness in the air the next time she woke. A low fire burned in the other room; she heard rain striking the roof. Cailean was sitting beside her. Hadn't he done that before? She thought so, but was sure of nothing.

He put his arm around her shoulders, lifting her and tucking a roll of fur behind her back. "You need to eat."

The change of position sent an unpleasant stinging through her ribs. She pressed her right hand against them but quickly removed it as even slight pressure enhanced the pain.

A bandage wrapped around her head interfered with the sight in her left eye and rubbed against her eyelid. Her left wrist was bandaged as well, and restrained with strips of wood. Bruising extended from under the bandage, up her arm and over the back of her hand. She wore a loose brown tunic, one she had never seen before. It was softer than any cloth she had ever felt in her life.

She met his gaze.

"I will answer all your questions," he said, "but will you eat first? I've made stew." He left her to go out to the hearth, where he dipped something from the suspended cauldron into a bowl. He returned and sat beside her again.

Whatever he'd brought had a delectable aroma. One bite and she wanted to tip the bowl and gulp it down like a starving dog. "What is this?" The chunks of meat were so tender they almost melted on her tongue.

"Rabbit."

"Rabbit! I have heard of rabbits. But I've never seen one."

"Our traders brought them from the Romans long ago. They do well here."

It was wonderful stew, thick with carrots, onion, garlic, and beans. She tried her best to take small, circumspect bites, but was so hungry it was hard to be polite.

Under his satisfied gaze, she said, "I feel as though I haven't eaten in a year."

"It has been…a few days." He offered her a cup of goat's milk and she drank voraciously.

After her stomach was satisfied, she said, "Please tell me everything."

He set the bowl on the table. "Your ankle and wrist are broken, and a rib—one at least, but more likely two or three. You have a few cuts and bruises, but now that you're awake and eating, I have no doubt you'll soon recover."

His grave expression was difficult to meet. She looked away, concentrating.

The forced marriage. Her refusal. The beatings. The—the rape. Her stomach twisted and her heart veered into irregular pummeling. She sucked in a shaky breath.

"They threw me over the cliff." Her uninjured hand clenched as she remembered falling. Thankfully, she had no memory of landing.

"They believe you dead. I thought you were too, the whole time I was climbing down to you."

"But I was not."

"Nay, you were not. They would know it too, but they didn't bother to make certain. I suppose they didn't think anyone could survive such a fall. They didn't understand how strong you are."

"You saved me."

"Not by myself. The village healer has been here every day."

"Where am I? What is this place?"

"This? A little bothy I built long ago, a place to stay when I want solitude."

"So this is…your…bed?" She felt her face heat. Knowing he would see made it worse.

He replied gravely. "I wanted you near. You know, in some countries, if you save someone's life, they belong to you."

Yes, her mind instantly replied, but shyness kept her from saying it. Instead she said, "Really?"

His eyes narrowed, just briefly, but she wondered if she had revealed more than she meant to.

"I also have land in Armorica, given to me by my father. When you are better, if you want, I will take you there." He rose and picked up the dishes from the table. "I will never let them hurt you again, Eamhair."

She didn't think she had ever believed a man's words so easily or quickly. Relief washed through her. Knowing Cailean would protect her made it possible to return to sleep with a full stomach and no dreams at all.

Chapter 3

TARANIS SMASHED HIS FISTS AGAINST HIS TEMPLES AND HOWLED.

After that there was a lost interlude of foggy, unbearable despair.

I might as well have thrown her myself. Again she is dead, and again it is my doing.

He left his hiding place and ran to the cliffs, though he didn't know which cliff they had thrown her from. He searched throughout the night, and several times nearly brought himself to the same fate.

If I had taken her back to the fort after I carried her out of the sea, instead of....

"Raping her!" he screamed. He fell to his knees, sobbing.

Why was I brought here? To again cause her death? Could even Athene be that cruel?

He stumbled up and down, over rocks, into icy pools. Once, as he hung from a rocky pinnacle with the water frothing below, he began to laugh and couldn't stop. If anyone saw him, they would believe him a madman. He thought so himself.

But he found no corpse.

The fact that she'd been tossed off the cliffs like so much rubbish was not the only thing he'd overheard. The kitchen wenches had also been aflutter about what the midwife had told Nemausus and Ossian. That Eamhair was no longer a virgin and could even be with child. Viviana had been most eager to spread that bit of gossip.

If she had lived, would she have borne my child?

Aridela had never successfully carried a babe. The idea that Eamhair might have conceived was agony on top of agony. She would surely have forgiven him if she had given birth. She would have agreed to flee with him. They would have been together, and eventually, he would have made her happy.

As he stared, trying to decide if the sea had pulled her body out where it could never be found, he saw a wavering above the water, as if heat was rising from it. He blinked and it vanished.

He studied the spot. Once more the air changed, a brief flicker of rainbows before it disappeared, and this time, though he stared until his eyes watered, it didn't return.

For the last fortnight she'd been locked in her chamber, and not always guarded. He could have gone to her, begged her to give him another chance. If only he'd had some warning, a premonition that her father could be so ruthless to his own child.

He could have saved her. Instead he had cowered in the tunnels, afraid of her judgment. Afraid of what she might say to him—of the hatred that might have blazed from her eyes.

He ran up the hidden staircase to her cold, empty bedchamber and threw himself onto the bed, seeking her scent.

Only when he heard steps and the bolt being thrown did he force himself up and away, yielding to the primal need to save his own despicable skin.

Chapter 4

EAMHAIR WOKE CLEAR-HEADED AT LAST, ABLE TO RECALL THE DAY HER brothers threw her over the cliffs. She could now relive the agony of her bones breaking as she struck the rocks, and of shivering, half in, half out of freezing water, and drifting from consciousness to a place of cold black anguish. There was another memory too, of a woman sitting beside her, weeping. Obviously that was a dream.

She drew the bed linens up to her nose. They smelled heathery and clean, and the fur blanket, folded away at the foot of the bed, was incredibly soft and supple. She stretched carefully and ran her right hand over the space beside her as she imagined Cailean lying there, perhaps looking at her with that faint smile of his, one arm curled beneath his head, the other resting on her stomach.

He walked into the room then, severing her fantasy. She must be improving, to have the energy for such thoughts.

"How long has it been?" she asked. "Since…the cliffs?"

His regard was somber. "Ten days."

So much time gone, though in her mind no more than a few days had passed.

He brought a bowl of hot oat porridge. She insisted on sitting up by herself, to see if she could, and took the bowl from him. Her efforts were awkward but she succeeded. He looked pleased, which gave her an absurd sense of accomplishment.

"My sister will want to see this. Do you remember anything yet?"

"I think so, though I don't know what is real and what is caused from fever. Your sister?"

"Rhalanse. She is apprenticed to the healer, and has been helping us care for you."

"Will you thank her for me?"

"You can do it yourself, when you meet her."

He brought a pitcher full of cold water from a nearby stream. She was unbearably thirsty and drank cup after cup until the pitcher was empty. As she returned the cup to him, she looked into his face and was struck by a fleeting image.

He sat on the edge of the bed. "What is it?"

"I was in such pain, and you were looking down at me. Your eyes were like an eagle's, and oh—you talked to me. You kept me in my body and made me want to fight. You promised I would live."

She stopped, confused and shy, but he gave her a reassuring smile as he set the cup and pitcher on the table. "You have been awake, but at first I was never sure if you could hear me."

Relieved, she laughed, which caused a stab of pain—though she was certain the pain was less severe than before.

He massaged the fingers on her good hand. "I prayed to whomever I thought might listen—the Christos, Mithras, Eir and her Greek sister, Hygeia, Brigit, the Tuath Dé, the Lady of the Stars. Whomever I thought might keep your heart beating."

She had never heard of four of those deities, but rather than reveal such ignorance, she asked, "Were you not afraid the others would be angry? I have been taught that Christ is jealous, and tolerates no worship of other gods."

"You are alive, and I am here with you. I am content."

She liked the way he had of saying much with few words, and dared ask, "Who is the Lady of the Stars?"

"My mother's patron goddess. You will probably hear her sworn to, or at, on occasion."

His irreverent humor put her further at ease, giving her the confidence to make more confessions. "I'm sure I dreamed this, but there was a boat—a white boat. The figurehead was a woman. She looked at me."

Drawing the fine soft edge of the bed linens between her fingers, she tried to recall more details. "Once, long ago, my mother told me about a dream she had. There was a white boat and a woman who made her a promise. It meant so much to her. I embroidered it on a pillow."

He said nothing but tilted his head to one side, rather like Vita did when trying to understand what was being said to her.

As she looked at him, she remembered the necklace. She felt for it at her throat and glanced at the table but it wasn't there either. "I was wearing a necklace, Cailean. Did you see it?"

"No. There was no necklace." His gaze left hers briefly and she wondered why.

"Perhaps it was lost. The chain was broken, and I repaired it badly." She shrugged but inside, hidden from this man who had saved her, a pang of loss reared, followed by disgust. Loss—over the necklace, or Taranis? He was the cause of every pain she felt when she moved. He was the reason for her near death. He was to blame for her lying in this bed, bandaged and splinted. Because of him, she knew what it felt like to hurtle through the air, watching death reach inexorably for her and helpless to stop it.

Could she be any more feeble-minded?

She would be glad to never see that necklace again. Really, she would.

Chapter 5

Jocosa could not escape the gossip. Since Eamhair's death, it never ceased. It had come to the point where she dreaded going to sleep.

Frightening sounds emanated from the walls, especially at night, which added to the ominous atmosphere. The maids conjectured that Eamhair's angry spirit wanted vengeance. The eerie howling several claimed they had heard in the storeroom off the hall had made them all afraid of going in there alone, and there were other rooms as well where sobbing or thudding was heard—most notably Eamhair's bedchamber.

One of the wizened elders had ideas. "It is the tower. The old chief used the stones from an ancient place. He didn't realize he was bringing the spirits of that place too."

"Why have they been silent until now?" Jocosa asked.

The old woman clicked her tongue. "Bericus's murdered daughter raises them against us. The Druids warned Aedan not to dismantle those stones, and that if he did, Dunaedan would suffer. He would not listen, and his male descendants, including Bericus, have been angry, vindictive men—cursed, one and all."

"Bericus was not so evil when he was younger," one of the other women said. "Nor were his sons. Something has made them so."

"It is the work of spirits, and I tell you now, it will get worse until they are appeased."

"How can he appease them?"

"He should tear down the tower and return the stones. But he won't. He could at least salvage his daughter's bones and show them the respect they deserve. Poor wee girl."

Ula came in and they stopped talking. Jocosa had never seen such a terrible change in any person. Ula was broken, a phantom of what she had been before her daughter was so spitefully slaughtered. They all pitied her, but they were also a little afraid of her, for her eyes had taken on a hot, fiendish sheen that made them uneasy.

A FORTNIGHT AFTER EAMHAIR WAS THROWN FROM THE CLIFFS AT Dunaedan, Cailean saw telltale signs that his patient was chafing at her bed rest. She made no complaint but spoke less, stared often at the window and doorway, and though she probably didn't realize it, released a few wistful sighs.

He knew from his years on the war trail that a bath made everything better, so he built up the fire and heated water from the stream. When it was ready he helped her scrub her arms and face, and offered to carry her outside where they could wash her hair without making a mess. She agreed shyly and he took her from the bothy for the first time, to a large arbor roofed with oakwood latticework. He placed her on a stool beneath the hanging roses and purple-flowered vines he'd cultivated to climb over the trellis, seating her so she could look out toward a sea of harebells, red clover, and poppies, and beyond that, the depthless green forest. He had used this view to renew himself after deprivation and bloodshed; he hoped it would bolster her spirits as well.

At first she was speechless. Her mouth fell open before curving into a smile. "I could weep," she said. "I never knew—*never*—that the world had such beauty. Oh, Cailean." Her awe left him both pleased and grieving that her life up until now had been so bleak.

He put himself to the task of washing her hair, using buckets of warm water and slivers of soap, rich with oils and scented of honey, woodbine, and heather.

Those copious tresses gleamed like the skin of an eel when he poured water over her head. As her hair dried, it curled and sprang up, catching at the sunlight that filtered through the beams.

She stretched her arms over her head, much like the cat that sat nearby, alternately cleaning its fur and observing. Cailean started to warn her, but too late. She winced and quickly lowered her arms.

"It takes so long to heal," she said.

Cailean dropped onto a nearby log. "I have had wounds that take forever to stop aching. It is tiresome."

"How is it so warm? You said it has only been half a month since you brought me here, but it feels like summer. Deep summer."

Not knowing how much his mother would forgive him for sharing, he answered vaguely. "The seasons are different here than at Dunaedan."

As of yet, he had not spoken to Meraud, though he had no doubt she knew he was here, and not alone. He was a bit surprised she was allowing him such a long period of liberty.

As if she'd read his thoughts, Eamhair asked, "Where is your mother? Will I meet her? What of your sister? You said she was here, but I don't remember. Will they be angry with you for spending so much time with me? Surely they want to see you." Her fair skin betrayed her with a blush, as it often did. "Forgive me. I ask too many questions."

He suppressed a smile. "You will meet them. I wanted you to feel stronger first. My mother can be…formidable."

She was d—his mind refused to utter the word. *Dying,* he substituted. *Now look at her. Did the ribbons do it, or my mother, or something else?* Eamhair thought it was taking a long time to heal, but in truth, her recovery was miraculous, especially considering the instant, just as the island came into view, when she stopped breathing and he no longer felt even the suggestion of a heartbeat.

He had never learned all of his mother's secrets or powers, but this? Did she have enough power to bring a shattered girl back to life, without even seeing her?

That fall from the cliffs ought to have crushed Eamhair beyond recognition, yet she had only a few broken bones and bruises. And how had he climbed down to her? His memory provided images of sheer wet rock, an unfathomable distance, and few footholds.

"Bring me a boat!" he'd shouted at Gede, who had come after him and was standing on the precipice, wringing his hands and wailing —*the poor lass, poor helpless lass*—while Vita paced.

Gede had promised to bring one to the spot where the ocean flowed into Uisge Bealach, *though she be dead, lord, she cannot have survived.*

The air changed as he reached Eamhair, in the way a violent spring storm could lift the hair on the back of the neck just before a strike of lightning. He looked everywhere, suspecting Nemausus and Ossian had returned, but there was no one and nothing other than a lone sea eagle circling overhead. He gathered her in his arms and carried her along the shoreline, clambering over rocks and splashing through water until he came to a place where he could scramble up to the high moor and over to the inlet. True to his word, Gede was waiting for him with Vita and a currach. Cailean placed her inside and rowed swiftly across then carried her to the hovel he'd stayed in before becoming Bericus's man, for that was where he'd left his war chest and medicinal paraphernalia. He staunched the worst of the bleeding before leaving her to race to the Point, where he lit the beacon fire.

The sailors arrived that night and helped him carry Eamhair and the war chest to the boat. Had Eamhair retained enough awareness to see and remember it in some fashion?

A shiver ran across the back of his neck. The other possibility was that he and Eamhair were having dreams in common, for he, too, had dreamed of a white boat with a living woman as a figurehead. In his dream, he always stood at the prow, facing the waves before them with his arm around the woman's neck. She often spoke to him, but he never could remember what she'd said when he woke.

Gede claimed Eamhair had refused the man her father gave her to with the assertion that she was already another man's wife.

She must have lied in an attempt to stop an unwanted marriage.

But there was that other talk—the midwife declaring her sullied, and warning that she could have a child sprouting inside her.

"Did I ask you to kill me, Cailean?"

He pulled himself out of gloomy contemplation. "You were in pain."

She hitched a shoulder. "Well I think I might live after all, so thank you for refusing."

He smiled, and so did she.

CAILEAN CARRIED EAMHAIR OUTSIDE EVERY DAY AFTER THAT SO SHE COULD sit in his pergula, surrounded by the scent of flowers and ripening apples.

Her color was returning, her bruises fading, her appetite improving. "Where has this food come from?" she asked between bites of crusty bread and goat cheese.

"People bring it."

Her brows lifted. "Why?"

"They are generous, and they care about you."

"But—how do they know I am here, and alive? If they know, will not my father and brothers find out as well?"

"We are nowhere near Dunaedan. Your father will never find you here. Never."

Relief lightened her face. She closed her eyes and turned her face towards the sun, leaning back on her good hand. The bruise on her left cheekbone was more yellow now than purple, and the cut on her forehead, right at the hairline, was nicely scabbed. Blood had flowed profusely from that cut the day he scooped her off the rocks; anguish and fear nearly paralyzed him when he felt the grating of the broken ribs, as he bound the ankle and wrist and pressed cloth to one wound after another. He'd put away his rage and concentrated on keeping her alive—one more hour, just until sunset, into the night, waiting and sending desperate pleas outward—to his mother, to the sailors, to the island itself.

Hurry. Hurry. Please hurry.

"There are sand dunes not far from here. I will take you tomorrow. Walking through sand will strengthen your ankle."

"I want to get stronger. I'm sure you're tired of hauling me around like a log."

I would carry you forever, he thought, but said nothing.

Vita got up from her resting place in the shade and padded over, thrusting her nose against Eamhair's good arm until she got what she wanted, a scratch about the ears. The wolf stood quietly until Eamhair stopped scratching. Lifting a paw, she scraped it across Eamhair's thigh.

"Vita," Cailean said reprovingly. She backed away with a plaintive whine. "Do you know, she has never been friendly to anyone. She merely tolerates my father, and has bitten several of my men." He didn't miss the way she dipped her head—probably trying to hide another blush—and opened her hand so that Vita would nuzzle her palm.

"How did you befriend each other?" she asked.

"I was scouting. It was winter, and night was falling. I was hungry, and cold, and careless. Too young, trying to impress the more seasoned men. A pack of wolves attacked me. I killed the leader and the rest ran away, but I was badly wounded and couldn't walk. I expected them to come back and finish me off. After awhile I heard whining, and here came this cub out of the grass, right up to me. I put her in the crook of my arm, thinking we could die there together."

"But you didn't."

"Around dawn I heard horses. I wasn't sure I should call out—the area was thick with Saxons—but thankfully, they were my brothers in arms. They'd found my horse and were searching for me."

"And?"

"I fed Vita milk and kept her by my sickbed. She chose to stay with me, and grew into a good fighter. She has saved my life more than once."

"So is that where you were before you came to Dunaedan? Fighting?"

"Aye."

She looked at him, brows furrowed, more questions forming just behind her lips, but she didn't ask them. He guessed something in his face warned her off. He was torn—wanting to tell her everything, but honor-bound not to, on more than one front.

When next he went out, he picked some late summer wildflowers, which he presented with a flourish that made her laugh, then he went off to fish for their evening meal.

She was still sitting in the same spot, Vita by her side, when he returned with two brown trout. He hesitated some distance away, caught by something in the set of her shoulders, and the way she was fingering the blossoms on her lap. It was nothing overt, yet he sensed melancholy; the suspicion strengthened when he approached and her face brightened into a smile that didn't quite erase the bleakness in her eyes.

She praised his catch, but he was not fooled and decided to meet whatever it was head on. "You are sad, Eamhair."

Pressing her bandaged hand against her ribs, she said softly, "I would not share my silly disappointments. Not with a noble warrior such as you."

"Please." He dropped the trout onto his cleaning stone and sat on the ground on the other side from Vita, who raised her head to regard him, her tail thumping.

"I wasn't given a bride's wreath." Though she laughed as she said it, he thought he saw a shimmer of tears in her eyes. "The village women should have braided me one from the flowers around Dunaedan. I have done so for other brides. Any proper wedding would be held when flowers bloom in abundance, not winter, when all things slumber."

She drew in a breath. "I had a gown—my mother made it when I was fourteen, and everyone thought Drost Gocinecht would soon come to claim me. But no wreath for my hair."

He'd been so certain she hadn't wanted to marry the king of Innse Orc. Hadn't she refused? It was because she steadfastly continued to refuse the man that her brothers threw her over the cliff. He forced himself to stifle his many questions. He knew they would sound angry —or worse, jealous.

"I think it foretold how wrong it all was, how unhappy I would have been as wife to Fathna of Innse Orc. A bride's wreath is a humble thing, yet it is a symbol, is it not, Cailean? A symbol of new life, of future happiness."

"I never thought about it," he said, though now that he was, he remembered how the women attached to his father's army fussed over gowns and flowers when one of them married.

"I know I am too old to worry about such things. And now, because of my defiance and...sins, I will never have a home, or children, or a hearth of my own." All sign of laughter vanished. "I have done every-thing that was required of me, all my life, until that day, yet none of it mattered in the end. Only my refusal to be bartered, and—"

"And?"

Color bloomed across her cheeks. She caressed the flower petals in her lap.

"Eamhair?" he asked gently.

But she said nothing and only shook her head, once, decisively.

He wanted to say, *I would have you, and be happy for it until the day I die*. But he stopped himself. She had been through so much. She needed time to heal, both inwardly and out. Twice they had kissed, but still, he knew she wasn't ready for such declarations. More than anything else, she needed to learn how to be free.

And when she learned, she might well refuse to shackle herself to any man, ever again.

He glanced at her arm. Hidden under the sleeve was his silver ring. He could just see the bulge of the leather strap that held it. Knowing it was there, had been there, perhaps ever since he placed it in her hand, kept his hope alive.

"You have a hearth if you want it. Do you remember me telling you about my land in Armorica? It is a beautiful farm, with pastures, meadows, and deep woods. In spring the land is covered with white anemones and purple violets. The soil is fertile. There is a walled fort that has long needed a mistress." He reached out to Vita so she would come to him. When she did, he stroked her forehead and she dropped to the ground beside him, placing her muzzle on his thigh. "Your father and brothers think you dead. This is your chance to have a life of your own, and never again be persecuted."

He watched brief delight fade into sadness. "It sounds wondrous."

Her words conveyed what he wished for, but her tone held no pleasure. What was worrying her?

"It makes Dunaedan seem a wasteland," he said, hoping to find out. "I have wondered why your ancestor—Aedan—chose such a barren place to build his fortress."

"He didn't need fertile land. He was the chief of the Caerini. His people provided for him and his family. I have been told that he chose that spot because it is awe-inspiring. Now of course the best of what is grown goes to Drost. Bericus gets part of whatever is left, and the people, for all their labor, often go hungry. In bad years, we at the fort go hungry as well." She paused to look up at the drifting purple flowers, and he watched narrow shafts of sunlight skip across her face. "I love Dunaedan. It has shown me its secret places, and given me many treasures. It isn't beautiful in the way you describe, but it is…exciting. The sea has moods without number. It is never the same as it was the day before. When I stand on the cliffs and feel it thunder, I know how small my beating heart really is, like a bird must feel when we trap it in our hands. I know what it is to see into the incalculable past and glimpse the infinite future."

Cailean ground his fingertips into his palms to keep from reaching out and touching her knee. He bit the inside of his cheek to stop from declaring her the most enchanting being he had ever encountered.

And when it came to enchanted beings, he knew more than most.

The golden mist he had seen floating around her from time to time —especially when he first brought her here and she was in such agonizing pain—magnified, competing with the glare of the setting sun.

"I would be dead if not for you." Again he saw a transient shine in her eyes before she blinked. "These complaints are petty trifles. I should not have allowed them purchase in my mind, much less should I have spoken them."

"They are not trifles. They are profound, and put men's preoccupation with war and destruction to shame."

There was awkward silence as she looked at him, startled, then blinked and stared at the corner pillar.

"Is there someone, a woman, who holds your heart?" Her voice was small, rushed, her glance fleeting before it again slid away.

Has she forgotten how I kissed her? She must think it did not matter to me. The only men she has known are brutes. "I am a warrior, and have never had the freedom for such things."

He saw something—resignation or disappointment—pass over her face. She nodded.

Nay, I did not mean—

He sighed and rubbed the scar by his eye. His temple throbbed. This exchange felt like trying to walk with bare feet upon sharp fragments of pottery, and he was afraid he would botch it more than he already had. "When I turned nine, I was sent to my father."

Her eyes betrayed shock. "I have heard warriors are best started young, that it makes them savage as boars."

"I didn't begin fighting at nine. I followed him about like a puppy, and was tasked with learning how to read, write, and hunt. How to obey orders. I took up arms at sixteen. But it would be true to say that I moved directly from childhood into the disciplines of war, and have known little else, but for the short periods I spend here, with my mother and sister. Only here do I know peace."

Her gaze was intent, prompting him to add, "I want to show it to you. The forests, the mountains, the bay that lies not far from my mother's citadel. These island people have never had to fear war or invasion. On winter nights we dance before bonfires, and the heavens dance with us. Here, I am a different man. Maybe here, things can be different for you, too."

Why had he told her that? He realized he was picturing her with her own hearth and children, and a husband who loved her.

The back of his neck prickled. He had broken Meraud's strictest rule by bringing Eamhair here.

What would his punishment be?

Chapter 6

After Eamhair convinced Cailean that she could take care of herself for a day, he went off with a group of village men to hunt "in the wildwood" and catch up on all he had missed during his absence.

"The wildwood?" she said. "Is it dangerous?"

"No, just...wild."

She decided to try and walk from the bed to the hearth—maybe even farther. Earlier, as Cailean carried her back to the bed from outside, she'd noticed a basket of walnuts on the table. If she succeeded, she would shell them.

Sitting on the edge of the bed, she pushed the sole of her foot against the mat and tucked her broken wrist against her stomach before rising and stepping off the dais. Vita rose as she did, watching every movement she made.

There was some discomfort, but nothing bad enough to make her abandon her goal. The worst was not her ankle but still the rib, which protested if she breathed too deeply, sneezed, or tried to lift anything.

She limped to the table in the main chamber, sat on the bench, and shelled the walnuts with a mallet. From that task she placed three speckled eggs in a pot of leftover broth and took them to the hearth to poach in the embers, thinking Cailean might be hungry when he returned. Once there she studied the suspended stone circle above it. It was hollow inside, and somehow pulled in the smoke, keeping the main room fresh. How ingenious! The floor was constructed of hewn wood rather than packed earth, and there were several woven rugs. As bothies went, this was quite the nicest she had ever set foot in.

She looked around for something else she could do and made her way from one end to the other, tidying and sweeping as best she could, wincing occasionally when she strained her healing injuries, but generally pleased with the improvement she felt.

The sleeve of one of his tunics was ripped; she mended it with a bone needle and thread she found in a bronze coffer, but was dissatisfied at the result. It was hard to stitch with a splinted hand. She almost ripped the thread out again, but in the end left it.

Through it all she kept glancing at the unsheathed sword he'd left propped by the doorway—a grim yet breathtaking thing. Shadowy patterns ran up and down the blade like worm sign. She would swear that when she wasn't looking directly at it, the runes moved.

How many men had it killed? As if hearing her thoughts, Vita whined, yawned, and dropped near the hearth with a sigh.

Holding the tunic, she crossed to an oak chest against the wall and opened it, thinking that might be where he kept his clothing.

For several heartbeats she could only stare, but the treasure was too intriguing to keep her still for long. She eased down to touch the surface of a heavy shirt, fashioned not of wool or linen but iron rings, each linked through the next. It flowed in her hands like poured water. If a man wore this along with padding or hardened leather, it would surely protect him from all but the most prolonged attack.

Beneath the ringed tunic was a folded banner, the wool dyed a rich dark gold with blue trim, and in the center, an embroidered falcon in flight, wings unfurled, talons extended. Each feather was detailed and symmetrical with the next, fanning out in a way that suggested the wind streaming between them. A talented seamstress had created this.

Her mind dredged up eager gossip from Bericus's hall.

The warriors who fight for the Bear of Britain wear armor they have taken from Saxons—mail shirts woven into tunics and neck guards.... The Blue Falcon is always at Artorius's side, steeped in a glow no weapon can penetrate.... He can fell three separate targets with three arrows shot from the same draw.... It is said he alone has killed over a thousand men.

A shiver ran over her skin.

Cailean, the scarred warrior—*a few weapons have penetrated that glow*—knew Artorius. Had *fought* at his side.

More shivering. Cailean was the Blue Falcon.

Rumors of Artorius had traveled to Dunaedan for years, brought on the lips of bards and merchants, with the men who came to vie for Eamhair's hand, and most recently, by Bericus's returned warriors.

It was said he never released a warrior except to death, and his army was far, far away—almost beyond fathoming, well beyond the old Roman wall.

Why would a man of his come to Dunaedan? Had Cailean deserted his overlord? Was he in hiding?

She pondered whether to confront him or pretend nothing had changed and let him tell her, if he ever chose to.

The curiosity was relentless, like the nip of midges. It wasn't long before she delved again into the chest.

A small wooden coffer held the kind of tools a surgeon would use. She recognized them all—a cauterizing iron, a fleam, an assortment of knives, and long linen strips wound into balls. There was also a clay pot, its opening sealed with a daub of wax. She pried it out, smelled the contents and poured a dab of viscous golden liquid onto her fingertip. Honey. Why would Cailean have honey tucked in with his bandages and medicines?

There were more trappings of war—a thick hide buckler covered with nicks and scars, an iron helmet with a neck guard of interlocked rings, and a heavy double bladed axe. Beneath it all lay something wrapped in lambskin. She picked it up and unlaced the ties.

A tingle radiated through her blood much like what happened the day Cailean took her hand at Dunaedan, or the night Taranis placed his palm against hers. The surprise of it nearly caused her to drop the thing.

A reddish glare pulsed. She thought she saw it infuse the entire room—a translucent cloud smelling of smoke—but it vanished almost as quickly as it appeared.

The lambskin fell open and a double-bladed seax gleamed up at her. She had never seen a weapon like this—lethal yet artistically beautiful.

Holding it in her right hand, she touched one of the cutting edges with the two middle fingers of her left, instantly drawing back with a curse as blood welled. To open her flesh at so slight a touch!

Looked at directly, the curved blade was black, but when angled, it reflected a rich purple sheen. The hilt was ivory. She knew that because of a comb Ula treasured, a present from her father long before she was wife to Bericus. The knife hilt was carved into the shape of a woman.

An owl—unmistakable in its detail—perched upon the woman's shoulder.

It fit her hand perfectly, with indentations set at exactly the right spots for each finger.

She rose, brandishing the weapon, fantasizing about defending herself like a warrior. The reddish light brightened.

As she thrust the blade outward, picturing Nemausus's vulnerable stomach, the leather door curtain swung to the side and Cailean entered.

He stopped and she stared for a long moment before finding her voice. "I—I ask your forgiveness. I mended your tunic and was putting it away, and…and…." She straightened, swallowed, and lowered the knife.

He removed a bag from his shoulder and placed it on the table as she hastily bent to retrieve the knife's sheath. But it was far too late to pretend she had been doing anything other than snooping. The armor was draped over one side of the chest, the banner over the other. The buckler lay on the ground next to her, and the knife was in her hand.

This was how she rewarded all he had done for her. By burrowing through his possessions like a common thief. Her cheeks flamed.

He crossed to her and took the knife, saying, "Here, let me." She stared at the ground, hardly breathing, her shoulders hunched, waiting to hear his voice raised in anger.

But all he said, rather dryly, was, "My mother insists I take it along when I leave the island. She thinks I need it as a reminder of my oblig- ation to her." He wrapped the knife, bent, and placed it in the chest. As he straightened, he saw her hand. "It cut you?" He seized her wrist. The tips of her middle fingers still bore a smear of blood.

His tone brought her gaze up—she was surprised to see no anger in his face, only fear. "Barely a graze." She pulled her hand free. "It doesn't even hurt. See, it has nearly stopped bleeding."

He examined the two cuts. His expression cleared and he gave her a long, all-encompassing stare, but let it go.

"I see that you are, in truth, a heroic warrior," she said. "I only meant to place the tunic in the chest. I did not intend to—to do this." She gestured at the scattered items. "I could not help myself."

He picked up the ringed shirt. "This is Saxon made. Most of my father's men have this armor now. It has changed our fortunes."

"It is a marvel. And—the knife. What is it made of? There is a shine around it that brightens and dims."

"Aye."

"What causes it?"

"I cannot say. It has always done that. The knife was found in a distant land. Many men died to acquire it. The blade is made of a kind of rock, fired at such high heat it was transformed into what you saw— a substance the Romans called glass. They made all kinds of things out of glass. My mother has a mirror of glass—you can see yourself reflected in it perfectly. Legends claim this knife is older than we can imagine—yet the blade is not notched or damaged in any way."

"I wonder what it has seen?"

"More than we can fathom."

"When I touched it, it was like…like the way it feels when I am afraid. I shivered. My heart raced. My fingers stung."

"As though the blade is alive, and filled with lightning."

"Yes, that is it exactly."

She picked up the buckler, running her fingers over the pitted surface and dented iron boss in the middle. "You have seen much of war, I think."

He sobered. "Will there ever come a time when we won't be fighting each other? I long for that day but I fear we will destroy ourselves before we reach it. I have lost brothers I love, and the fighting never ends—not for long."

She met his gaze, not knowing what to say.

But he gave a shrug to dismiss such a dismal subject and moved on. "Are you hungry? We brought down a fine stag and split it among us —I have the loins and meat for stew. I also snared four doves. They wouldn't take long to cook."

She turned to the task of putting away his war gear. "Yes. I'm so tired of doing nothing. I could roast them."

"No need. I am happy to do it." The birds were already plucked; all he had to do was remove the spines and entrails. While the plump torsos roasted over the fire on two spits he cleaned the livers, hearts, and gizzards and placed them close to the fire with onion and more of the morning's leftover broth. Soon the bothy filled with the mouth-watering odor of sizzling fat. Eamhair cut two helpings of bread from the loaf without much trouble, and poured ale. When she turned the meat, she remembered the eggs she had poached, and carried the pot to the table.

They feasted. Cailean tossed a few bits to Vita and the cat. After some time of silence, of watching the fire and the cat cleaning its fur,

Cailean gently asked, "Will you ever tell me what happened? From the first day I came to Dunaedan, I was warned repeatedly that you were to be married to Drost Gocinecht—had been betrothed to him since you were born. Yet, while I was gone, your father married you to another—and not just any man. Drost's own brother."

"Fathna is Drost Gocinecht's brother?" Eamhair reared back, her breath catching when her ribs reminded not to move so abruptly. She took careful breaths until the ache subsided. "I did not know that."

"Forgive me, I've upset you."

"Now I understand why my father was so angry when I refused, and in front of the proxy."

Picking up a whetstone from the corner of the table, Cailean turned it over and over in one hand, watching it instead of looking at her. "Why was there a proxy?"

"I don't know. I suppose Fathna did not care to stay and wed me himself."

Cailean's head tilted in that way he had, as though he thought something was unusual, but kept his gaze on the stone as he ran his thumb along the edge.

"You may well wonder," she said. "I did not understand it. I understood *nothing*, and no one bothered to explain anything to me. Bericus did not care that I was his child. I was simply something to be sold for his own profit."

The hand she had placed over her ribs slid to her stomach as she remembered the midwife's declaration. *She could be with child, but there is no way to tell—not for a few months.*

Ossian had flown into such a rage he had beaten Eamhair until she lost consciousness, but before that happened, he told her he would enjoy snapping every bone in her body if she did, indeed, spit out a mongrel fathered by any man other than Fathna.

She shivered. Cailean dropped the stone and reached across the table to cup her forearm, his eyes reflecting the firelight in a mesmerizing blue gleam.

Was Taranis's child living and growing inside her? She only knew she'd had no monthly bleeding since she woke from her injuries, and she wasn't about to ask Cailean if she'd had any while senseless.

His touch was a distracting comfort, but this was something she needed to know. She turned her head, pretending to watch the embers in the hearth, and tried to work out how much time had passed since she woke in Cailean's bed. Should she not have bled by now? The realization tightened her stomach into a knot.

To give birth without being wed was the worst thing a woman could do. The only thing more sinful was becoming a whore, and somehow, the two were linked, for all women who bore children without being properly wed were considered whores, no matter the cause.

Cailean had saved her life. She could tell he cared about her, but that would not last, not if the midwife's warning proved to be true.

He still watched her, quietly waiting until she was ready to speak again.

So she did. "In losing me to Fathna, Bericus lost the gifts and wealth he has taken for years from other suitors. And if Drost ordered his brother to wed me, it would explain why Fathna had so little interest that he let another man represent him. Perhaps Drost found out what my father was doing, and did this to punish him."

"How did you come to be bound to Drost?"

"I can only tell you what I have been told—that long ago, Drost and his father overthrew all the tribes around Dunaedan, including ours. I was just days old when he and his warriors defeated the last of the Caerini. All my life he has been our overlord. Bericus is still called chieftain, but only at Drost Gocinecht's continuing pleasure, and only as long as Bericus fulfills the tributes demanded of him—the best of our crops, our finest bulls and calves, slaves, and anything else Drost wants. He also makes free use of Bericus's men—they are obligated to quell any uprisings or other trouble throughout the western districts, and are, of course, duty-bound to respond when Drost calls for fighters." She paused, thinking back to that dim morning when she had come upon Drost and the whore Luned at Dunaedan's north gate. "As my mother explained it, Bericus killed a young warrior during the fighting. Later they found out he was Drost Gocinecht's son. After my father surrendered and was forced to beg for his life, Drost ordered that my mother and I be brought out. He inspected me and gave Bericus a choice—to watch Drost butcher my brothers, or give me to him when I came of age, as payment for his son's death."

"Ah," Cailean said. "I see."

"When I was eight years old Drost made one of his annual visits." Her teeth locked and she had to wait for the fury to subside before she could continue. "He went into the hall and reminded my father of his obligation. Humiliated him before his men. Knowing my father and brothers as I do, I am certain that is why I have been paraded like a prized sow. It is hatred, resentment, and childish revenge. Drost stole much from my father—his prominence, his lands, even the bride price he could have expected from marrying me off. Bericus's revenge was to make me into a fable and reap the bride price that way, many times over. *The girl promised to a king.* I am a shred of mist, words turned to song, composed to extract silver from gullible men. They come to Dunaedan thinking they have a chance to win this beauty they have heard of—that is why he always kept my face covered, so they wouldn't realize how they'd been deceived. He didn't want them to see that I am a woman like any other, just an ordinary woman after all."

Cailean's fingers tightened and she felt that prickling sensation. The firelight illuminated a mist of color around him again, blue, white, and pale purple. She half suspected she was imagining it, but there was no denying how she felt—that she stood near a mystical bastion guarded by swords of flame.

"You have spent your life imprisoned without committing a crime."

"No one argued for my release but my mother, and all she ever received for it were beatings. Sometimes I could see through the cloth my father tied over my eyes when he led me through the hall. I could tell by the way some of those men stared that their only thought was to replace my father's prison with one of their own. They never saw *me*, but the idea they brought with them of me."

Cailean still said nothing and for some reason, his silence emboldened her. "I *hated* them. I hated my father and brothers. I was so...*angry*. Is it wrong for a woman to speak this way? I know few women, only the village wives, Dunaedan's whores, and the slaves. Not many ever speak of being unsatisfied. Even my mother is resigned. Women are expected to serve, to be of use to their fathers, brothers, and husbands. Otherwise, they have no worth at all." She swallowed the lump in her throat that she feared might become a sob. "Will we ever be given a choice in anything? My brothers often declared that women have no souls—that they are barely above pigs in nature. If that is true, why am I so angry? Pigs are not angry. Sheep are not *angry!*"

"Eamhair...Eamhair."

With a deep breath, she said, "There was a man at Dunaedan. He told me about his country, where kings are less important than queens. His wife fought in battles—not as a mere warrior, but a leader."

"Who told you these things?"

That story had bewitched her at the time, but it was ruined now. She couldn't forget or forgive the promises Taranis had made and broken, or what he had done on the beach.

She whispered, "Just one of the suitors who thought to purchase me."

Taranis never meant to save her. Perhaps he simply wanted to triumph over the others—to win the maidenhead of the famed Eamhair. He was probably far away now, laughing.

Yet he had not acted or sounded triumphant. Rather, he had seemed quite miserable. Still, he'd left her to be beaten or killed, hadn't he? Stinging tears blurred her sight and she could not meet Cailean's gaze. Dunaedan's baron did not know. He still thought her Bericus's untouched daughter. If he discovered the truth—if her stomach swelled up, would he be sorry for rescuing her? Would he despise her?

Cailean rose and came around the table. He sat beside her and pulled her to his chest. She rested her head against his collarbone, closing her eyes, and gradually, rage subsided into warmth and the comfort of his palm stroking her hair. The movement of his muscles against her closed eyelids was like a dance between their hearts.

She felt his voice reverberate through her cheek. "If there are such things as souls, I would wager it is women who have them, not men. I wish I could take this anger from you, Eamhair, but you are right to be angry. I, too, am angry. I am thinking of going to Dunaedan and killing your father and brothers."

She lifted her head and placed her wounded hand on his chest, where the beat of his heart was now quick and hard. His left hand tightened upon her shoulder. She felt a tremor of violence coursing through him.

"Never think such a thing. You would be hunted. Tortured. Promise me, Cailean. You won't seek vengeance on my account."

His jaw clenched and he broke her gaze.

Vita growled.

She brought his face back with a finger on his chin. "I am alive. My bones will mend. I do want to go to your land in Armorica. Promise we will, as soon as I can walk. As soon as you remove the bandages. Except—I would like to meet your mother first. And your father, if that is possible."

His gaze remained distant. Swallowing, she forced herself to go even deeper. She would say anything to turn him from this deadly resolve. "My mother came to me before all of this. Right after you left to search for the prisoner. She told me Bericus was going to give me to you." She paused as she watched the blue in his eyes darken and his attention slide away from thoughts of murder to center wholly upon her. "I danced. I danced and I laughed, because I was so happy. I know it is all spoiled now, but for that one day, I knew joy. You don't need to kill anyone on my behalf, Cailean. I am here, I am alive, and I am free —because of you."

She held her breath. He would now reject her in his thoughtful way, but at least she had diverted him from his earlier intent.

"Eamhair." He placed the palm of his hand on her cheek.

She could not bear to hear any excuse he meant to say and pulled back. "Whatever they have done, they are my family. Bericus is my father. Nemausus and Ossian are my brothers. They live because my mother gave birth to them, as she did me. If you kill them, it will be the same as if I killed them, for I will have driven you to it. Do you want me to suffer the guilt of that?"

He dropped his hand to his lap. "As you wish, Eamhair."

Her shoulders relaxed and she sighed. "I am so tired." She stood, hoping she had not pushed their companionship into something unnatural and stilted. "Will you take me to the sand dunes tomorrow? I do want to be able to walk again without limping."

Placing his hand lightly on her elbow, he escorted her into the room with the bed. And, as she had known he would, he quickly retreated. The bed had become a perilous symbol. It had been one thing when his concern was keeping her alive. Now it was something else.

She pulled the furs up to her throat. "Sleep well, Cailean."

"And you, Eamhair," he returned from the shadows by the fire. "Sleep well."

I SHALL MAKE THEE SHARP, QUICK, AND TERRIBLE. THOU WILT BE MY BULL UPON THE EARTH...

~~~THE PROPHECY OF ATHENE

Arcturus Beckons

ARTUR LIFTED MERAUD OFF HER FEET. "A CHILD! YOU ARE CARRYING A child? My child?"

"Yours and mine together."

"This makes me happy!" He shouted to the heavens with the kind of unabashed, puppy-like delight that only children and young men possess. He was sixteen, but living much of his life in the wild, solitary hills of Gwynedd had sculpted him into an imaginative, thoughtful youth, full of lust and love and honesty. Caring for his goats and sheep, hunting, and working his garden had molded his body into that of a powerful man, and he was uncommonly tall. Meraud felt almost dwarfish when he encased her in his arms, though she too was tall. For a brief, joyous interlude, she closed her eyes and pretended she was as young as he.

She returned his smile, though she knew the road ahead would be difficult, and that there would be much arguing, and in the end, she would break his heart.

STAY. BE MY WIFE.

I must go home.

Let me go with you. Your home will be my home. I know what is happening. The loss you suffered is terrible. Because of it, you're afraid to love me, or to let me love you. Do you want to cause me the same pain? Don't deny me my child, Meraud, don't.

It was all so hard. How to tell him he would not be allowed to set foot on her island? How to make him understand?

There was more. She had seen in the fire that he had a destiny of his own. If it weren't for that, she would find a way. But she would not rob him of his glory, or the chance to save this land.

So she stirred poppy juice into his stew and left after he fell into deep, dreamless sleep, pausing only to whisper in his ear. *If I have a son, I will send him to you when he comes of age.*

The stars kept her company, glistening, humming, sometimes darting and flashing, but one in particular pulsed, almost crimson, *beckoning, beckoning.* She knew it well, for she had been taught the movement and meaning of stars when she was a small child.

She curtsied. "Arcturus." It flared as if pleased to be noticed.

I will miss you, my herdsman. You saved my life and brought me happiness when I believed I could never be happy again.

Chapter 7

Meraud left the beloved dream with reluctance as a cool, lavender dawn poured through her open window. No one knew it, but she still missed her herdsman, though it had been nearly twenty-two years since she'd seen him. Cailean's age plus seven months.

Cailean looked almost exactly like his father, except for his eyes. Perhaps that was why she couldn't release the past, why it remained so vivid she could still catch the scent of the dusty thatch hanging off the edge of the shepherd's hut, remember the softness of their bracken and sheepskin bed, hear the crackle of the ember fire in the hearth.

His young, eager face was so clear in her memory, his joy at hearing he would be a father.

She had not seen him since the night she had drugged and abandoned him to return home...to her obligations.

But she had kept her promise. She sent him his son when he turned nine, and ever since, Cailean spent most of every year at his father's side.

She rose and washed her face at the water basin. Not bothering to call her handmaid, she combed her hair and plaited it, perusing herself in the Roman-made looking glass hanging on the wall. Her hair was long and thick, and it took time. Her fingers wove by rote as she indulged in reverie.

At least in Artur's memory, she would be forever young. He would never see the lines extending from the corners of her eyes and across her forehead, or how her hair, once glossy brown, had turned silver. Growing older didn't bother her, but after one of these dreams, she had just enough vanity left to be grateful for that small boon.

She had been old then too, of course. Her fecundity had been a shock, but all her children had come after she left her youth behind.

Artur had no idea. Meraud had cast a glamour that made her appear as young as he. He had seen what she wanted him to see.

Her fingers paused. Her head turned. She closed her eyes, breathed in slowly, and smiled. For an instant she saw her son as he'd been at nine, the ardency and trepidation and eagerness when she told him he was going to his father.

She stood and called her maid. This was an occasion—she must dress accordingly. And food—there must be the best mead, wine, and roast goose. Cailean loved goose, basted to keep it soft and flavorful, swimming in her own special cream and mushroom sauce.

Her rebellious son had finally had enough of living in a primitive hut on the farthest corner of the island, enough of hurling his independence in her face. He was coming at last, and bringing the girl.

Her smile faded. She concentrated, hard enough to cause a stab of pain through her temples. She couldn't see things as effortlessly as she had when she was young.

The girl had a baby inside her.

Was it Cailean's? No matter how hard she tried to bring it into focus, the father's face refused to form, and there was something else.

A pall surrounded this girl, stretching out from her body like tendrils of smoke that grew murkier and thicker near Cailean. As though it sought to engulf him too.

All joy foundered as she saw what it was.

Chapter 8

A HAND PRESSED AGAINST EAMHAIR'S SHOULDER. SHE OPENED HER EYES, blinking in the glare from a tallow candle.

"It's time—unless you'd rather stay here and sleep?"

Cailean's face was indistinct in the gloom beyond the flame. He sounded almost hopeful.

Fighting off grogginess from the poppy juice she was still using at night, she pushed herself into a sitting position. "No, Cailean. I'm awake. Now go on. I can dress myself."

"Are you sure—?"

"I'll call when I'm done. You can lace me up."

He went out, leaving the candle, and she quickly pulled on the shift and gown he'd brought her yesterday—a real dress, much nicer than the shapeless tunics she had been wearing.

The gown was a bit too big and too short. She was distressingly tall for a woman, and still thin from her battle with death. But at least she didn't have to strain her neck to look Cailean in the eye. She tightened the leather belt he'd provided then slipped her feet into soft deerskin boots, which folded painlessly around her broken ankle.

A few days ago, he had suggested she might be well enough to meet his mother, and she had eagerly agreed. Explaining that the island was large and it would take most of the day to reach his mother's home, he asked if she would mind waking and leaving early.

After Cailean laced up the gown, he draped his cloak over her shoulders. "It will be cold on the water," he said, pulling the soft badger fur close around her throat.

She chose to walk, but had to lean a little on his arm. They went outside. A saddled mare awaited them, digging a hoof through the dirt as if eager to be off. Vita gave herself away by whining, though Eamhair couldn't see her.

"This is Leila." Cailean gentled the mare before gripping Eamhair at the waist on her right side, and under her arm on the left, hoisting her onto the saddle before swinging up behind her. As he settled her into the crook of his left arm, a shadow separated from the wall and approached, speaking quietly.

Eamhair knew the voice. It was Molle, the elderly healer who had been helping Cailean take care of her. Besides treating her wounds and providing poppy juice, the woman had come every morning and evening to help her dress and undress, and assist with her intimate daily needs. She had always spoken Eamhair's language before, but now she spoke something else and Eamhair understood not a syllable of it. Cailean replied, his words lending themselves to the fascinating accent that tinged his speech.

Molle placed her hand on Eamhair's forearm. "May the Celestial Goddess go with you, lady."

She was so much like Ula that a miserable pang shot through Eamhair's heart. "Thank you for all you've done."

The shadow squeezed her arm and stepped away; Cailean prodded the mare forward into the night.

"How far is your mother's home?" she asked.

"A long way."

Eventually the mare halted and Cailean swung off, bringing her down with his big hands carefully placed to avoid causing her pain. She heard the sea lapping nearby.

He insisted on carrying her and took her down an uneven, slippery path to a beach, where a raft was waiting. A man stood upon it, holding a pole or long oar. Beyond him, a boat rode at anchor.

The boat. Or, she amended as she studied it, one eerily similar to the white boat she had dreamed of, and illuminated by some kind of radiance, though there was only starlight.

Rocking upon the waves, the vessel was a beautiful thing, with a center mast and three oar ports. The stern resembled the curled tail of a sea creature and carved at the prow was a form she recognized—a woman's head, neck, and breasts. A braid dangled over one shoulder. All that was missing was the crown of spindrift.

Eamhair stared, afraid to blink, but this woman did not turn. There was no comfort emanating from luminous eyes. It was a lifeless wooden figurehead.

Cailean placed Eamhair on her feet. "Wait here," he said, in the same soft tone he used with his horses and his wolf. "I'll come right back."

Blindfolding his mare, he led her, nervous and snorting but willing to trust, onto the raft. Adventurous Vita bounded next to her without hesitation.

The oarsman pushed off and guided them to the boat. A plank was lowered. Leila was coaxed up, along with Vita.

The raft came back and Cailean held out his hand. Again Eamhair had trouble breathing as she anticipated what he would say.

"Are you ready, Eamhair?"

She felt her mind and heart surge forward, but she forced herself to give him her hand with a measure of outward calm.

Leila had regained her serenity with a nosebag and blanket. Vita lay near her front hooves.

The plank and raft were pulled in and stored, the sail unfurled. The boat leapt away from the shoals. Cailean settled Eamhair on a pile of sheepskins with her own blanket, and went off to speak to the sailors.

The heavens here were brighter than at Dunaedan. Stars glittered from hottest white to yellow to red and finally blue, large and small, some in clusters and others solitary loners.

At first she was fascinated but confusion soon took over. They were different. Ula had taught her the names of the stars when she was small. But she couldn't find any of them here.

Impossible. They were there—she had just never been on the ocean at night. Or perhaps it was a lingering effect of the poppy. No matter how often she blinked, the stars remained slightly blurred.

What would she discover if she could fly up to them? Were they open doorways, allowing light from other lands to shine through? What kept them from falling?

Cailean returned and dropped beside her, putting an arm around her shoulders. She nestled against him, thinking she had no desire to keep aloof, as perhaps she should. He was not any man—not a stranger. He was the man who had saved her life, in more ways than one.

Something else changed. Flowing sheets of green formed in the northern sky, towering ribbons that widened and stretched before softening into shades of purple, blue, and red. Eamhair had observed similar heavenly spectacles since she was a child, but these were more intense, and while the sky-ribbons she had viewed from Dunaedan remained distant, these drifted closer until they enveloped the boat, plunging them in a wash of shifting color. Eamhair reached up, feeling heat against her palms, watching in awe as rainbows curled around her fingers. She left Cailean's side, forgetting her injuries as she spun in wild circles. When she closed her eyes she still saw color eddying, and with her eyes closed she felt it drawing into her lungs so that even inside, she was filled with color. She felt as though she was *becoming* color.

"Glorious!" she shouted, through humming that sounded like the paean of a multitude.

Cailean joined her. "It prepares you for landing."

What a puzzling thing to say. But she was drunk on color, and so asked no questions.

At some point the seamen worked the sail and slowed the boat's progression. They entered a small bay, and this time the boat itself was driven up onto a shingle beach. Vita leaped off the side and Eamhair followed Cailean and his mare down the plank.

The sky brightened as the sun crowned the eastern horizon.

He lifted her onto the mare and leaped up behind her. Leila, twitching her ears, started off across the beach, over a wide stretch of sandy slopes covered in bentgrass, and into a forest. The sailors followed on foot, leaving two of their number with the boat.

This wood was like nothing Eamhair had ever seen, being confined all her life to the bare expanse of sea cliffs that was Dunaedan, where the few trees that sprouted never grew much higher than scrub.

Here, sunlight made shifting patterns through tall leafy trees. The leaves fluttered and sighed in a dance with the breeze. Eamhair fancied the trees were bending down in welcome, and there remained that hum in her ears, now so muted she could scarcely detect it.

She squinted. "What is that, Cailean?" she asked, pointing.

"What? I don't see anything."

"There is color around the leaves, between the branches. It's faint, but—are my eyes lying to me?" She twisted so she could see his face.

"Oh," he said, glancing at the trees. "I only notice that for a day or two after I've been gone a long while. It's just the way the air is here.

We call it Æythral—you would call it rays. The island gets quite a lot of rain. It could be sunlight through water in the air. Or it could be connected to the sky ribbons—that is what I think."

Cailean's island was a strange place, more like Ula's faery tales than an unremarkable chunk of earth and rock rising out of a turbulent sea.

As the sun ascended, the spaces between the trees grew hazy with green-tinted mist. Ula's whimsical stories took precedence in Eamhair's mind. She began to believe she might see a unicorn, or a red-bearded giant, or a herd of galloping kelpies—half-beast, half-sea foam.

The path, which had been a gentle incline, became steep; the leaves gradually turned gold, scarlet, and yellow. The air grew cooler, crisper, as if autumn had descended between one breath and the next. Leila's hooves sent piles of dry fallen leaves rustling. And always, around them, the gossamer mist, now tinged gold instead of green.

She had always wished she could see the vast forests her mother often described. This journey through Cailean's homeland felt like a dream come to life.

Cailean quickened the pace and they soon emerged onto a high, rocky ledge. The mare stopped.

Beside them, carved into the rock face, was an enormous figure of a woman in a wonderfully detailed gown. She wore a warrior's helmet, pushed back from her face. An owl perched on her shoulder. Her right hand brandished a spear and her left stretched out, palm up. Her gaze was fixed on the vista below, which came into view as an ocean of retreating clouds exposed it.

Eamhair craned her neck to see the woman's face. She towered, indeed dominated the landscape. Eamhair had no doubt she could easily be seen by the people in the village she'd just spotted, so far below she could make out nothing other than clusters of buildings, tendrils of smoke here and there, and in the center an enormous fortress with two square towers at each end, rising above everything around it. Beyond the village, on the far side of an orchard, was a steep hill—she discerned a path winding around it, up and up to the wide, flat summit, which held a circle of standing stones, and beyond the hill lay the sparkle of the sea.

Off to their left, the nearer peaks of a mountain range were covered in sunlit green, the farther ones violet-blue. The white froth of a water-fall tumbled off a ledge similar to the one they were on—and there was another statue, another woman, or perhaps the same woman, also gazing down into the valley.

"That is the woman on the hilt of the knife," Eamhair said, remembering.

"Yes."

"Who is she?"

"Our mistress and guardian. It is said that if ever these statues are destroyed, the island will sink, never to be seen again. It is also claimed that they are thousands of years old, yet as you can see, they have hardly been touched by the elements."

"My mother's stories feel as though they have come to life. She spoke of miraculous places, where we can go beyond our ordinary lives and find something of the gods."

"I miss it when I'm gone."

All the reserved aloofness from Dunaedan had vanished. Cailean's eyes were incandescent; he made no attempt to hide his pleasure.

As he urged Leila onto the downward path, he said, "That village below is where we're headed—where my mother lives. It's called Gilraidha Soi. 'Fortress of Bright Water' in your language. I was born there."

Soon after they reached the valley floor, fifteen riders galloped from the village and crowded around them, shouting and laughing. Cailean returned their shouts; Eamhair could only assume they were exchanging greetings. They slapped him on the back, glancing at her before politely looking away. One woman, dressed like a man in trousers and a tunic topped with a leather jerkin, and possessing an uncommonly beautiful combination of blue-black hair and arresting green eyes, grinned at her in a way that implied they knew each other, but Eamhair was certain she had never seen her before.

This boisterous group rode with them, sending up a large dust cloud as they neared the village. People ran out of bothies and work-shops, forcing the horses to slow, and Cailean's mare was soon hemmed in. All of these people spoke the foreign tongue Eamhair likened to the sound of milk spilling from the lip of a pitcher into a wooden cup—each vowel flowing into the next—but she could tell by their expressions that they were mightily pleased as they smiled and touched Cailean's calves.

The crowd pulled back, clearing a path. Leila pranced forward towards a woman, dressed in a gown of purple and silver. A gold and silver coronet studded with pearls and faceted purple stones threaded through her grey hair. Eamhair could tell by her bearing and the way the villagers regarded her that this was a person of power and respect.

"I sent no word, yet here she is, letting me know I can never surprise her." Cailean leaped off his horse, ran forward and caught her, lifting her and swinging her in a circle. The younger woman who had grinned at Eamhair dismounted and joined them, and all three shared an embrace.

He escorted both women to his mare and brought Eamhair down from the saddle. Through it all he grinned in a way that made him appear no longer an intimidating warrior but boyish and happy. Placing his hand over the elder woman's, he said, "Meraud, my mother. And this is my sister. Rhalanse."

Eamhair realized she hadn't done anything with her hair that morning other than tie it with a strip of cloth, and she became acutely aware of her ill-fitting gown. They might not like a strange woman appearing out of nowhere with their Cailean. But both embraced her, murmuring, "Welcome, Eamhair, to Inis Tearmann," with that smoothly curving accent she had first heard in Cailean's voice.

"What—what does that mean?"

"'Sanctuary.'" Cailean lifted a brow and his smile turned markedly sardonic. "Since my mother obviously knew we were coming, I'm certain she has arranged a repast."

"You may be assured of it," Meraud replied. "I have not forgotten the demands of your stomach, son."

Rhalanse looped her hand around Eamhair's right forearm. "It is gratifying to see you so recovered. I helped a little when you first came. You probably don't remember. I see Cailean and Molle have taken good care of you. Why, you are hardly limping."

She waved off Eamhair's apology for not remembering and led the group beneath a stone arch into the fortress's courtyard. It had no gate at all—Eamhair saw no guards or guard towers, and the palisades were lopped off rather than pointed.

"It reminds me of Dunaedan," she said, "though it is much bigger and the towers are square." They made their way into the fortress. "And I have yet to see any defenses."

"No need of them," Cailean said. "I have suspected from the first that the man who built your tower must have had a few drops of *aes sidhe* blood in his veins."

"*Ae shee....*"

"It is what we call ourselves. We call your lands the Dominion of the Seventh Age. In our language, you are a *Ystoula*, a woman of the Seventh Age."

"Es-tola."

"You have an ear for it."

"The Seventh Age...I don't understand. What does that mean?"

"There are seven great bodies of land where you're from, and an old belief that seven ages is how long those lands will last. But I cannot tell you the length of an age. That calculation was lost eons ago."

"But we are in the seventh? The last? What will happen after?"

"No one knows. It is a story without an ending—perhaps deliberately."

"Cailean, teach me your language. Teach me...everything about this place."

"I will." He was almost too tall even for these lintels. His grin lingered as he added, "I think the blood of your forebears will help you learn it easily."

If that possibility meant Cailean would continue to look upon her with such affection, she was happy to let him believe it.

Her father and brothers seemed far away and small, like buzzing flies caught in the corner of a room, annoying but not dangerous.

Chapter 9

TARANIS CONSUMED BARELY ENOUGH FOOD TO SURVIVE. GRIME WAS CAKED beneath his fingernails. His hair was lank, his beard dirty. Before coming to Dunaedan, he'd been a fastidious man, scrubbing his hands and arms every evening and bathing every few days. Now, he didn't notice or care.

He sat in the lonely tunnels beneath Dunaedan's fortress most of the time, ignoring the squeak and scrabble of rats, losing all conscious thought in the distant rhythmic heaving of the ocean.

He only roused when hunger or the need to relieve his bowels forced him to, and that happened less and less. When he did steal food, he always climbed to Eamhair's deserted bedchamber, to lie on the bed and lose himself in grief.

Her scent lingered on the pillow for only a few days; after that, no matter how hard he sought it, it was gone. The flowers she had pressed and preserved were scattered on the floor beneath the table, crumbled near to dust. Maidservants took away her clothing, the illustrated Bible, and the wall hangings. The brazier was never lit, so the room grew permanently cold and smelled like a place that had long been uninhabited.

There was nothing to keep him here. He should return to the south, to his mother. She was getting old; someone was bound to take advantage of her.

But every time he tried to rouse himself to leave, he failed.

It was his fault Eamhair was dead. He had caused it. Again. It was only right that he rot in the tunnels, never to be mourned by anyone.

"WHERE HAVE YOU BEEN?"

Taranis heard Bericus's distant, irritated roar and paused from his theft of a stale oatcake the maids had tossed in the pig basket.

Despite the general apathy that consumed him, the chieftain's enraged tone sparked his curiosity.

Half a month back, the village priest had sought audience with Dunaedan's lord. The man had bravely chastised Bericus for what he had done to his daughter. The entire village had turned against him, the priest claimed, and most of them believed Bericus's actions would draw the anger of Christ himself. The priest warned that Dunaedan was doomed to bad fortune and decline if he did not offer penance, right his wrongs, and give his child a proper Christian burial. And what, the priest asked, would Drost Gocinecht think? What about Drost's brother, who was Eamhair's husband? Had Bericus thought of how those two men would react to what he had done? When Bericus gave his daughter to Fathna of Innse Orc, it became that man's responsibility to punish Eamhair if she needed punishment, not Bericus's.

At first Bericus reacted in his usual manner, shouting denials, refusing to listen, and issuing threats at those who criticized him. Taranis, listening from the passageway, sighed in annoyance.

But the priest had not backed down. Why, he asked politely, had Fathna not yet returned? The proxy had warned Bericus of his master's temper. What if an enraged Fathna was even now gathering an army? What if he descended upon Dunaedan and slaughtered all who lived here?

The priest's words inspired Taranis. He would frighten Bericus into bringing back Eamhair's body. Then there would be a grave he could lie upon, where he could beg forgiveness of her decomposing corpse and bodiless spirit.

A small nagging voice in the depths of his mind suggested he would do better to ask forgiveness of Athene. But that was going too far. He would never again bow to her. *Bitch!*

Taranis set out to haunt Bericus. He keened behind the wall outside the chieftain's bedchamber. He stole items from where Bericus left them and put them somewhere else.

Finally, deep in the night, shrouded in a large pale cloak, he entered Bericus' chamber and woke him with moaning. When the man sat up in his bed, wheezing and terrified, he melted away.

Bericus grew wan and contrite.

He ordered his sons to go and retrieve Eamhair. "We will bury her lavishly," he said. "We will sacrifice fifty—no, twenty sheep to soothe the outrage of the old gods, and spend a fortnight on our knees, asking forgiveness of the Christ. We will smear our foreheads with ash and wear hairshirts. Whatever must be done to rid Dunaedan of Eamhair's evil spirit."

Nemausus and Ossian set out to fulfill his wishes. Everyone expected them to return within a few hours, but the day passed, then the night, and still they did not appear.

Taranis realized they must have just now returned and were answering to their father. Chewing on the cake and wincing at the pain in a loose tooth, he climbed the steps to the chamber where Bericus conducted private business.

"The mist was so thick we could not see our horses' ears," Ossian was saying.

"We were afraid we would stumble over one of the cliffs," said Nemausus.

"Do you expect me to believe you have been out riding through the countryside all this time?" Bericus was shouting and there was a sudden thump. "Admit you stole that Chian wine we were given last year and went off to get drunk."

"Nay, Father." Ossian sounded almost pleading. "Before the fog descended, we searched the cliffs where she—fell. There was nothing, I swear. No sign of her body. Not a single bone—"

Nemausus interrupted. "Cailean of Dalriada was there that day. He tried to stop us from punishing her. But he never returned to Dunaedan as we ordered him to."

"We decided to go to that hovel he lived in," Ossian said. "We thought he might have taken her body away and buried it himself. Anyway, you never released him from his bond to you. We meant to force him to return and answer for the loss of the monk, whether he had anything to do with Eamhair or not."

"And?" Bericus prodded impatiently. "Where is he?"

Taranis pressed his ear to the wood.

"That is when the mist came." Nemausus sounded hesitant. "We couldn't tell what direction we were going. Once we did nearly ride right over the edge of a cliff."

"You are trying to tell me you have been lost in a fog all night? A fog that I, nor any other man living here, ever saw a wisp of?"

"It's true," Ossian said. "It did not lift until this morning. Somehow we had gone around Uisge Bealach, and were close to the hovel. We went there, but all is deserted. He must have gone away again. He has abandoned you."

Now Nemausus spoke with righteous anger. "Would you like us to hunt him down, Father? I know we can find him. Give us a few hours and we will have him on bent knee before you. Or, if you prefer, we will cut off his head for desertion."

"I have more important matters to settle," Bericus said. "What are we going to do to appease the priest, the villagers, and the cursed gods, with no bones to bury? How can we save ourselves from Fathna?"

His sons remained silent, perhaps choosing not to aggravate him further.

Taranis went away. It was the first he had heard of Cailean's return. Nor had he known his half brother had been witness to Eamhair's murder.

There was something wrong about this. Taranis did not believe Cailean would leave the area where Eamhair lived—not if he had been drawn here because of her as Taranis had, and Winoc.

Even with her dead, Cailean would not be able to leave. Taranis was certain of it. Taranis could not, though he had tried any number of times.

Resolve gave him purpose. He would find this hovel. Perhaps Bericus's sons were wrong. Even if they were right, there might be a clue to Cailean's whereabouts that they, being loutish and lacking the wit of four-year-olds, had missed.

THE RUIN DID HAVE AN ABANDONED FEEL. THE LEATHER DOOR CURTAIN was ripped. A thick layer of dust covered the rough board table and bench. The pit hearth contained more bird and rat droppings than it did ashes, and a pile of sheepskins in the corner was spotted with mold.

Taranis inspected it carefully, but found nothing.

He studied the ground outside. The footprints he saw were fresh—

left by Eamhair's brothers. He walked away from the lonely structure, disappointed, but as he glanced back a final time from a knoll, he saw a flash next to the doorway, as swiftly gone as it appeared.

He returned and scuffed through the sand until the source was revealed.

The necklace.

He picked it up. The air whirled away, leaving him suffocated in helpless rage and agony.

Alive!

She must be....

She is alive!

Chapter 10

CAILEAN GAVE MERAUD HIS STERNEST REGARD. "YOU HAVE ALWAYS SAID no one can know about this place. Your spells keep it hidden even from those who sail across our breakers. Why is she different? Why did you allow her to come here?"

He didn't miss her pause. "She was in danger and so were you."

"I have been in danger before, and was left to live or die by my own devices."

One of her shoulders lifted. "I feared you might forget your obligation."

"Have I ever? Well—other than last year. And that was deliberate. I did not forget."

"It seemed all too similar to last year. You did not come, though you have lived near the beacon point for many of their months. Do you deny there was some distraction keeping you there?"

He couldn't stop a wry shake of his head at her reminder that she always knew his whereabouts.

He picked up his goblet, hammered from copper with a rim of gold, and sipped the wine, a dry, heady vintage from black grapes cultivated on the island. "Will you force her to stay, or send her back with a hole in her memories?"

"She is all I imagined, and more."

"That is your answer?"

"I agree with you, son. She is different. You feel it. You did not have to tangle yourself in the affairs of that place. You certainly didn't need to allow that brute—Bericus, is it? authority over you. You could have spent time with Eamhair and used the forgetting—you could have used the forgetting on all of them. But, Cailean...you did not do that."

"What are you keeping from me? You know something."

"All will become clear in the Infinite Lady's own time, for both of us. Look." She placed one hand on Cailean's forearm and pointed with the other.

Eamhair, using a silver-topped shaft of oak to keep weight off her ankle, had entered the hall at his sister's side.

The gown of twilight blue complemented her hair, its split, gold-lined sleeves sweeping off her wrists and falling almost to the flag-stones. The belt resting on her hips was made of interlocked golden rings. Blue and gold—his war colors, though she couldn't know that. The wide scooped neckline skimmed the outermost rim of her shoulders, making it hard to not imagine it sliding off. Her hair was elaborately arranged with braids and tuckings, and capped with a net of gold filigree studded with beads of lapis. It did not so much cover her hair as set it on display.

Her skin was luminous, her eyes alert and rested. Taken as a whole, this was a startling transformation from how she had always appeared at Dunaedan, worn and weary, dressed in stifling layers of clothing that hid everything and which rendered her as shapeless and colorless as the abandoned skin of a lizard.

This is how she should always look. Appreciation washed over him, as though he hadn't seen her in days, though she had been taken from him just hours ago to rest.

He came out of a brief trance to the realization that other men were also staring. Some spoke among themselves as they perused her and one half-rose from his seat. His expression could only be described as predatory.

Her uneasiness was clear in the way her gaze flitted everywhere and her teeth worried her lower lip. Feeling more than a little preda-tory himself, Cailean rose and crossed to her, bowing and holding out his arm.

"May I escort you, lady?"

Her frown vanished into a relieved smile. Giving the staff to Rhalanse, she allowed him to place her hand on his forearm and he led her to his mother, adding, "You appear rested."

"I slept. The bed was so comfortable. As though I was floating in a cloud."

"Yes, we too have engineers."

"The most talented of engineers, to construct beds that make one never want to rise!" Upon saying this she blinked; a charming flush bloomed over her cheeks and she dipped her head.

He managed to keep from laughing—just. "We stuff our mattresses with goosedown. It is no more a marvel than that." He paused at the bottom of the dais so she could lift the hem of her tunic and step up. "Here she is, Mother," he said as he pulled out a chair. Once she was seated, he resumed his own seat at the head of the table, which lay in a pool of shadow between the cressets and candles. It was a good place to observe without being obvious.

Meraud and Rhalanse pointed out some of the hall's features, the high ceiling reinforced with massive beams of black oak and lined with narrow openings along the upper edge that pulled away smoke, the arched heavy doors made of the same wood, the elaborate candelabras that could be lowered and raised with hooked rods, and sunken hearths where men turned spits and women basted the meat.

A contingent of serving maids carried platters of food and pitchers of wine, ale, and mead to the tables. Cailean watched Eamhair's eyes widen as she took her first sip of wine. He leaned forward. "Be careful. It is potent, and we do not water it."

"Winemaking is an art we have long cultivated," Rhalanse said. "Perhaps I could show you our vineyards."

"I've never seen a vineyard. We seldom have wine at Dunaedan. Only what is gifted to us, or what we get in trade. My mother and I once tried to make it from rowanberries, but it turned out very bitter."

Rhalanse sipped from her own goblet before bursting out, "There is so much I want to show you. Our chamber of maps and scrolls. That's where we keep histories of the places we trade with. And our bird-house—we've collected birds from all over the world. There is one especially—hardly bigger than a moth, with feathers bright as gems. They come to me and hover, their wings beating so swiftly you can't see anything but a blur. And, oh, our steam room and mud baths. The mud will help heal your injuries and soothe your bones. Cailean says you have hardly any color where you come from. Would you like to see our dye house, where we fashion the dyes for our fabrics?"

"Mud baths?" Eamhair's brows drew together.

"There is time for all things, *anoshla*," Meraud said gently. "Let her rest a little."

Rhalanse slapped a hand over her mouth and laughed. "Forgive me," she said. "It's just nice to at last have someone new on the island." She stocked a plate for Eamhair, choosing the most succulent morsels of partridge simmered in a broth of leeks and wine, and herbed venison, stuffed pies, spiced eggs, soft white cheese, and sweet juicy pears, which she cut into slivers with a small silver knife.

"And I-I am happy to be here," Eamhair said, but Cailean didn't miss the hesitation, that odd catch in her voice, and wondered if she was telling the truth.

The hall was crowded, noisy with laughing and chatter.

While Eamhair ate, Rhalanse entertained her with various descriptions of life on the island. Cailean watched as the gown did slide off one shoulder. She quickly pulled it up again, though. Being dressed like this must feel odd, maybe even wicked.

He had seen her without clothing of course, for when he carried her away from the cliffs, she had been wearing only a sleeping smock, which was torn, bloody, and soaking wet. He'd ripped it off to look for wounds, not thinking beyond staunching the blood and keeping her alive, and couldn't even remember clearly what she looked like.

He did remember seeing his ring—bound to her right forearm in a braided twist of leather. His search for injuries paused when he came to it, and he nearly wept for failing her when she so manifestly trusted him not to.

Gede and his wife appeared at dusk that day, bringing food. Gede's wife also produced a tunic of plain wool and a stringed coif like the village women wore. She dressed Eamhair, clucking disapprovingly over the chieftain's daughter being naked and alone with a man, but her judgment fled once she saw the extent of Eamhair's injuries; chastisement turned to sympathy and worry. She thanked her god for Cailean's abilities, and asked many questions about the honey he'd rubbed on her lacerations.

The musicians began playing. Dancers took their places, linking arms; each one mimicked the next in an interplay that blossomed and shrank across the flagstones. Soon they brought out their gauzy banners and moved into the island's traditional ribbon dance.

Eamhair's delight as she watched helped him see it with new admiration. It was always that way with her—she'd done the same thing with his pergula, with Vita, Inis Tearmann's white boats, the color in the air and even the ribbons that carried one from the Dominion of the Seventh Age into his mother's country.

If he didn't know better, he would never imagine she had plummeted from those deadly cliffs. He gave little credit to his crude medicines or bandaging, and almost all to Inis Tearmann. He had never fully understood what the sky ribbons did, how they merged with the body and healed it, or if it was already healthy, infused it with vitality. The island's inhabitants remained lucid and strong into extreme old age. His own mother was rumored to be several hundred years old. The air here, crisp and scented of pine, instilled tingling bursts of euphoria. He was certain the air and the ribbons had worked a profound rejuvenation on her.

The wide timbered doors stood open to draw in cool evening air and offset the heat from the fires. Cailean meant to coax her out there as soon as she finished eating. Impatient eagerness initiated a shiver though he was also sweating. It was being here, with *her*. Being here, looking at his home with her wonder.

He reached down, letting Vita pluck a partridge leg from his hand. Anticipation strengthened. The first time he ever saw Eamhair he'd imagined that he knew her. The fancy returned, even more strongly, when Bericus introduced them in his dim, smoky hall. Never before had he experienced such a sense of intimacy, of knowledge, of shared experience with a woman.

Seeing her here, laughing with his mother and sister, filled him with hot, exhilarating intoxication.

Meraud smiled in her enigmatic way. "Look how the men watch her. You would think they had never seen a woman before. And Inis Tearmann has many beautiful women. I think each one is imagining being her lover, don't you? I suppose it could be that she is new and so is a novelty." She angled her head. "Is something wrong? You look like your Vita. Quite...territorial."

He kept his face as neutral as he could.

Her smile diminished and she leaned in a little. "Prepare yourself, son."

An instant ago she had been laughing, thoroughly enjoying pricking him with her barbs. Now she was grave, pensive. She had seen something, something she feared he would not like. "There is more here...than is evident."

His mother often saw things that were invisible to others. She knew things no one else knew. Her warnings could not be taken lightly.

"Why?" He kept his words low so they wouldn't be heard over the music, the rumble of dancing feet, the laughter and chattering. "Why did you allow her to come here, Mother?"

"Would she not have died had you not brought her?" Her smile returned, no longer teasing but sincere. "Cailean, she is welcome."

"Why? Why is she different? I thought no one from the mainland could ever see or know our ways."

His mother sighed. "The more I give, the more you want. Much is kept from me—the Infinite Lady withholds her trust, but she does guide me. I have failed her before, and I do not intend to fail her again. Eamhair walks a path none of us can fully know, but I will help her as best I can, as you have done." She took a small bite of bread. "Look."

Eamhair's head was swaying in time to the music. Cailean couldn't see her eyes, for she was watching the dancers, but he knew they would be brilliant.

His mother lifted her brows. He shook his head, rose, and went around the end of the table, holding out his hand. "Will you dance with me, Eamhair?"

She had just taken a bite from the slivered pear and was licking juice from her fingers. There was more juice at the corner of her lower lip.

This girl would be the death of him.

"How?" she asked, even as she rose and placed her hand in his.

He swung her into his arms and carried her into the midst of the other dancers, where he circled to the lively drumbeat, never letting her set a foot on the floor. She was soon returning his laughter and wincing at the same time. Shifting her to his left arm, he pressed his palm, warm and damp, against hers.

When he couldn't hold her anymore, he fetched them both a goblet of wine. She drank deeply, forgetting to be careful. Her eyes were soon glazed.

"Take me outside and let me walk, Cailean," she said. "You have done enough."

He brought her the staff and they went out, away from the noise and heat, into the night's dewy coolness. He led her farther, wanting the dance of the heavens to be as vivid as possible, not washed out from the light showering through the open doorways. The music receded and was replaced by the tranquil thrum of crickets.

Her hand tightened upon his arm as they neared the edge of the apple grove. "Cailean," she said in a severe tone, "did you not tell my father that you came from Dalriada?"

"Nay, lady, I never said that. Only that I had fought in the conflicts."

"But—but my father...he and all his men believed—"

"Your father likes to make assumptions, and I did not correct him."

"But why?"

"I made a vow when I left this place for yours, that I would never speak of it to anyone."

She leaned the staff against a tree trunk then leveled him with a gaze that brooked no evasion. "It wasn't because you are the Blue Falcon? Because you know Artorius? You fight for the Bear of Britain. Admit it."

Ah. Now he understood those glances she had been giving him ever since the night she had explored his war chest. He was surprised by the relief he felt. He could not lie to her and did not want to. "He is my father."

"Your *father!*"

"But my mother is not his wife."

"O-oh."

"What exaggerated stories have you heard? I am a common warrior like any other. Many men fight for him. I am but one."

"A common warrior? The Blue Falcon charges as swiftly as a falcon dives upon its prey—"

"That is Bharosa. He's the one doing the charging, you know."

"And a glow surrounds you, a blue glow, protecting you from injury—"

"I could show you the scars to prove that wrong, but I hesitate to strip before a maiden."

She bit back a grin. "It would not be the first time."

"You—what? You lie."

"I do not. You and Bran and Owain. It was...overwhelming."

He stared, half shocked, half entranced by this new, bolder girl. The wine had obviously—*the beach! The sea cave!*

"You were *watching?*"

There was laughter in her eyes, like those of a child who has pulled off well-planned mischief.

"And you never let us know you were there. Nor did Vita give you away."

"I did not want to shame you."

He turned his head up and laughed even as he inwardly groaned. What man wanted to be seen that way by a woman—especially the woman he loved? But two could play this game. "Mind you that first morning I came to the cave? You were asleep."

"Yes."

"I knew you were there. I only pretended to be surprised. I watched you. I watched you all the time."

"You are a devious, sly-hearted cur. My lord."

He returned her smile.

"But you have not yet satisfied my curiosity about the Blue Falcon. I have heard he is the only man as tall as Artorius—"

"Two tall parents will usually beget tall offspring."

"But I have heard he is as tall as a giant. As tall as a one-hundred-year-old tree."

"He is tall."

"Does he really command an army of dragons that spew fire at the Saxons?"

With a snort and a shake of the head, Cailean replied, "Would that were true."

She hesitated as though she was contemplating her next question. "It is said you can strike three different targets from three arrows shot at once, and that you alone have massacred over a thousand Saxons."

"Loosing three arrows at once would lessen the force of all and cause them to fly wildly. I can assure you I have never done that. And my father would take issue with your second claim." His smile widened. This was a side to Eamhair he hadn't yet seen. He'd had no idea she could be mocking, and he liked the way the starlight twinkled in her eyes. "He states such numbers for himself, and would not tolerate being outdone by his bastard son."

"Oh, Cailean. You are the son of *Artorius*."

"Does this give me new standing?"

"I-I have heard stories of him for years. It is said he is the most accomplished warrior who has ever lived. But of course he is my father's enemy, due to being Drost Gocinecht's enemy. If Bericus knew, he would be angry. So angry." She gave in to helpless laughter. "Cailean," she said. "You have been right under his nose!"

"How have you heard of Artorius?"

"I listen. I have always listened. My father never knew. Such tales! Men gladly die for Artorius. He has triumphed over every enemy who seeks to break his shield. I have even overheard a few of my father's men plotting to desert and go to fight with the brave Bear, where glory and adventure is abundant. Oh, you must tell me everything. What is he like? What is it like, to *fight* for him? To be his son?"

"Is there a part of you that yearns to be a warrior?"

"Not—not to destroy, but to stand and...demand respect. In that way, yes."

He clasped her hand. He wanted to kiss her, more than he had ever wanted anything, but he checked himself, for as the evening progressed, his desires had crystallized. He wanted Eamhair to accept him as her husband. He would wait until the vows were spoken and she knew the full truth. He would not trick her.

"Eamhair, I am a killer," he said. Four simple words that could not convey the enormity of what he had done.

The light in her eyes dimmed. Her gaze moved over his face as though she might peel away his skin and expose what he couldn't describe. But she didn't release his hand.

He expected questions. Or perhaps she wouldn't want to know. She might cringe, instinctively comprehending the blood in which he had bathed.

But he didn't expect what happened. "Oh, look!" She pointed.

The heavens were dancing.

Ribbons—swaying, floating, stretching like gigantic tapestries, enveloping them in wave after wave of humming color.

"It is magic!" he heard her cry.

He breathed deeply, reveling in the spark that began at the top of his head and raced through his blood. Ah, he had missed this. It somewhat resembled the effect of strong wine, but more. Much more. This third immersion in Inis Tearmann's curative ribbons might even complete Eamhair's healing.

"Am I dead?"

"What?" He opened his eyes, coming back to his own feet on the ground.

"My mother used to tell me stories of an enchanted isle where the faithful go after death. Is this that place?"

"No, Eamhair. The island is real—enchanted, aye, maybe, but real. I was born here. I grew up here. It is as real as Dunaedan. You are not dead."

She regarded him as though trying to decide if he was lying. He returned her gaze and laughed. "I swear. You are not dead."

Turning her face up, she said, "Tonight they are your colors."

"Mine?"

"Blue, white, purple. The colors I see around you. Here, they are in the sky."

She sees it? In truth, she is different. "Artorius gave me the name Blue Falcon. He said the way I leaned against my stallion's neck as we rode into battle reminded him of a falcon. And he always said he saw me through layers of blue."

"Of course—he saw your colors. Your eyes—they are the gravest I have ever seen, and the bluest. They are like lightning; I am certain they strike terror. Yet, when I look close, I see purple, like spring wildflowers or those stones in your mother's crown, and that makes them welcoming—not fearsome at all. But I understand why he called you that, for you are swift and lean, and your eyes see everything."

She lifted a hand and traced the air near his cheek and for an instant, he felt sure the gleam of the ribbons came not from the heavens but from her skin.

"Donnah," he said. "My donnah."

"You said you would tell me what that means."

"Beloved." Wedding be damned, truth be damned. Drunk from this night, from wine, from *her*, he pulled her against him. She released a small gasp as she resisted, then her arms crept around his neck. He kissed her and it was everything he had dreamed for so long, the opening of her lips against his, the wine and pear-sweet taste of her, the movement of her fingers in his hair. It was familiar in some indefinable way. Oddly, he saw in his mind a balcony above a courtyard, a marble table filled with delicacies, and a talisman in the likeness of a scarab beetle.

But all too soon her hands came back around to his cheeks—her right hand tracing over the scar beside his eye and down to his chest before she pushed away.

"I—I cannot." A tear fell from her eye, reflecting the rainbow colors springing and swirling around them.

He refused to release her. "Why can you not? Seeing you, in that dress, makes me dizzy. The whole world is spinning from the way you look."

She met his gaze, frowning, her eyes glistening with tears.

"What is it, my darling?"

"I...cannot...trick you, lie to you. I cannot."

"Have you lied to me?"

"I...have not...told you...all."

"Tell me now." He kept his tone light, but inside, foreboding stirred.

"Please let me go."

His arms tightened. "I will not let you go. I have told you my secrets. Now tell me yours."

She rested her cheek against his chest and wept. He stroked her hair, kissed the top of her head, and waited.

"I—am married."

"I know that. To Fathna. I do not accept it."

"Nay!" She lifted her head and faced him, her face wet with tears. "To—another."

"Another?" He remembered what Gede had said, how she had refused Fathna because she was already wed.

"He is called Taranis."

At first there was only a certainty that he had heard the name before. Then it came back. *The monk who murdered Drost Gocinecht's baby daughter.* The man he had gone in search of, foolishly hoping Bericus would keep his empty, worthless promise.

"The *monk?*"

He was so shocked that he allowed her to break free. She backed away several steps. "He is no monk," she said. "He is a seolh."

"A seolh." He tried but failed to keep his brows from lifting.

"A being from the sea—one who can change his form. I-I was on the beach, and there he was, coming out of the water. He declared he would take me to his province. But when I asked him to save my mother as well, and—and *you*, he seemed to change his mind. He said that coming onto land stripped him of his powers, and he was afraid my father and brothers would kill him."

Cailean could only stare, aghast.

"When I was little, my mother promised the seolh would someday appear and save me. *He* is my husband." She put her hand over her mouth. Tears fell as she struggled to speak. "I—I may be—his child may be growing inside me."

Cailean fought a choking urge to deny every one of her words, to banish them from this night, which had been so perfect.

Prepare yourself, son, Meraud had warned.

When he said nothing, Eamhair looked at the ground. He felt her grief like a cold ocean wave. "I am sorry," she whispered.

He drew in a deep breath and clenched his hands. "Eamhair, he is the escaped prisoner I was sent away to find. He killed Drost

Gocinecht's baby daughter. He is no seolh. He is a criminal. A murderer. He lied to you."

She frowned and shook her head. "He had no care for humans and our dilemmas, except for me. Why would he murder a child?"

"He is a master of trickery. I do not dispute that."

"No, Cailean." She shook her head. "He came and went through the walls of my bedchamber—never through the door. I heard the ring of truth in his voice and saw it in his manner when he spoke of his country, where queens rule, not kings—he was the queen's consort, and I saw how much he loved her. There is more. My mother dreamed when she gave birth to me. She dreamed that a powerful king would come out of the sea for my sake, to protect me, to save me. And that is how he came! I have seen color around him too, Cailean. Like you, he is not an ordinary man."

"I don't understand. He has a queen, but you are his wife?"

She did not answer immediately. Her gaze lowered again. "I suppose I say that because—because I do not want to think of myself as a whore."

She gave herself to that murderer? "You love him."

"No, no! *No.*" She brushed at the tears on her cheeks. "I was bewitched, I think. His voice ebbs and flows like the sea, like the secrets it holds in its deepest chasms. I was charmed by the stories he told of his sea fortress. I trusted that he would take me, and my mother, away, and that we would be free." Her hands fisted. "The king of the seolh people. Who could not be dazzled? He was—my friend and protector. But after I asked him if he would save you, too, he—he became angry. I still cannot understand how it happened. I was on the beach, after they married me to Fathna. I had run away…and Taranis was there. Everything changed. I…will not say what he did."

"You do not need to." Fury and ice roared through Cailean's veins. All he could see was a haze of blood.

"It is too late for us, Cailean. I am ruined. I am one man's wife and another man's whore. I…am not worthy of you."

"Eamhair! This man lied. He used your innocence to his own advantage."

She was silent for a long time. When she spoke, she sounded hoarse, as though her throat hurt. "I will remember this night all my life, and in every life to come. But it doesn't matter. It is done, and there is no repairing it." As she spoke, she was tearing at the strap around her arm. When it unknotted, she pressed the silver ring into his hand and quickly started away, forgetting her staff. After a few steps her ankle failed. She cried out, faltering.

He jumped towards her but she thrust out her arm to stop him.

She stumbled to the stone tower, leaving him to watch helplessly.

Chapter 11

EAMHAIR OPENED THE SHUTTERS IN HER CHAMBER AND SPENT THE DAY observing the people of the village, who went about their business unaware they were being watched. She listened to the language as it was spoken, the words reliant upon o's, and y's, and e's. It was a fluid, gentle vocabulary that brought Ula achingly to mind, as it seemed to hold within its cadences the natural softness of love. She watched a plump woman lean down to a small child with crimson cheeks and bright plaits, and murmur *"el anoshla"* as the girl lifted her arms to be held. The girl snuggled against the woman's shoulder, and Eamhair remembered Meraud using that word when speaking to Rhalanse. Perhaps it meant child, or baby, or dear, or daughter.

She wiped away the burn of tears.

A maidservant, who curtsied and introduced herself as Nyfain, brought a platter of warm barley cakes spongy sweet with heather honey and dotted with white, nutty seeds. Tucked in among them was a wedge of firm yellow cheese and a jug of ale that she declared was the best of the season, with a taste of sunlight and morning dew. Setting that down, she returned to the corridor and carried in the silver-topped staff, saying she'd found it on one of the tables in the hall. She went away, telling Eamhair to strike the little bronze bell if she wanted anything.

She was halfway through the cakes and cheese and had finished two cups of ale before she realized something was different. Sitting back on her stool, she looked down.

There was no pain—no aching, but for the one gnawing in her heart.

She stood and put her weight on the broken ankle. It felt strong and sure. She turned her broken wrist in a circle. It moved easily, without grinding or protest.

The night before, by the apple grove, the sky ribbons had enveloped her, bright and vivid and warm, suffusing her body inside and out. Had they worked this miracle?

Thinking of the ribbons brought back Cailean's shock and anger. His disappointment.

If her revelations hadn't turned his stomach, he would have followed her to her chamber. He would have told her it didn't matter. Cailean was not meek. His silence, his absence, made it clear she would not be forgiven.

She had never been in love before, but still she recognized it for what it was. She'd fallen in love long before she knew him—before he came to Dunaedan, through stories about Artorius and the Blue Falcon. She had never imagined she would ever meet that mythical hero, yet it had happened. He had kissed her. Called her his donnah. He had loved her too, until he learned her secrets.

She had not only lost her home, her few companions, and her mother. She'd lost Cailean as well.

At dusk, Nyfain came to help her dress and Eamhair roused from misery. She would not hide like a petulant child. It would be better to get the confrontation over with. Garbed in another of the lovely gowns from the clothes chest, she left the chamber, taking along her walking stick in case this newfound strength abandoned her.

She was startled to discover Vita stretched outside the door. The wolf rose and pressed her cold nose against Eamhair's hand.

"She has been here all day," Nyfain said with a snort. "Would not move. Forced me to step over her."

Oddly comforted, Eamhair walked to the feasting hall, Vita hugging her right leg as if to lend support.

She paused outside the entryway, closed her eyes, and pressed her bandaged hand to her stomach, trying to calm the knots and turmoil.

Movement in the air was enough to make her realize someone had approached. She caught a trace of the scent she'd grown to know. Her eyes flew open.

Cailean's face was unreadable. "I have been worried."

Her mouth was too dry to answer. What could she tell him? That she'd been hiding like a miscreant from an angel?

"You must be hungry."

He bent, intending, she saw, to pick her up and carry her. She swallowed. "My ankle is much improved, Cailean," she said. "I can walk."

He straightened and gave her a somber glance, but obediently moved to her left elbow and accompanied her into the hall, his hand resting on the small of her back.

"Sit beside me, Eamhair," said Meraud as they approached. Rhalanse poured a few splashes of their rich wine into a goblet.

Eamhair propped her stick against the table and sat. The scent of food made her mouth water, but her stomach was still knotted, and she wasn't sure she could eat. To hide it, she sipped wine until Cailean had gone around the end of the table and seated himself across from her. Picking up her knife, she ate just enough to keep from being questioned about it.

After the meal, two men carried in a heavily carved and ornamented chair, and set it in the center of the hall. A tall, grey-bearded man made himself comfortable upon it, painstakingly arranging his elaborate crimson robes embellished with feathers.

He handed his staff to a herald, took up his harp, and proceeded to tell a story, one that caused the people in the hall to forget the food before them and beat the hilts of their daggers against the tables.

"It is one of our favorite tales," Meraud told her. "Dwyn sings it in your language specially, so you can follow."

The saga described a battle between Artorius and the Saxons at a faraway place called Badon, how the famed leader slew nine hundred with his own blade, and how the enemy was so thoroughly routed that peace had been the order of the day since, may it continue, with the grace of the gods, until the end of time.

The story was told in the manner of bards, in song and poetry, using phrases designed to heighten the emotion of the audience, punctuated by both brief and long pauses to allow his listeners to build the scene in their minds. Eamhair saw the Britons charging. She smelled the blood and heard the screams, the deafening clash of weapons, as if she were a raven soaring over their heads.

A warrior lifted his sword like a banner and called to his men. Bending low against his stallion's neck, he became one with his warhorse...and Eamhair realized whose face she was seeing.

She turned. Cailean watched the bard impassively, his arms crossed over his chest, but when she looked at him, his gaze met hers.

"Were you in this battle?"

With only candlelight nearby, his thoughts remained safely unreadable, but he gave her a brief nod.

Meraud leaned close. "It was his last campaign with Artorius. My son was badly wounded, both in body and spirit. The Bear tried to heal him but in the end, was forced to send him back to me." She traced one of Eamhair's coiled braids with her index finger, sighing. "Cailean loves his father. He did not want to leave him, but Artorius ordered it. He said Cailean needed to go away and recover his soul." She paused before adding, "He wandered aimlessly—not even returning to us for last year's harvest—until the Ivory Lady brought him to you."

Eamhair blinked away the burn of tears.

The bard left his chair to quaff ale and rest his throat, and Rhalanse took his place. The hall, which had been lively with talk and laughter, fell silent again. She stood beside the chair, waiting, her head bowed, until the atmosphere in the chamber was weighted with anticipation.

Rhalanse's voice had incredible range, and hit each note with absolute purity. She sang without assistance from harp, pipe, or even a drum until the end, when the drummer joined in with faint, resonating emphasis.

Her song told of a queen who loved two brothers, how she saw each in his own right and loved their different strengths and weaknesses, but jealousy spoiled it; the love affair along with the queen's country degenerated into rivalry and murder. One hero offered his life to save his love. The other grasped at life so he could remain at her side. *Which one made the better choice?* the song implored, and suggested that not even the gods could decide.

When she finished and her voice tapered into silence, dagger hilts thundered against the tables.

Eamhair wiped her cheeks, embarrassed before she saw that many others wept as well. "The faithful at Dunaedan would say she sings like an angel. Did she invent that story? Is it from a dream?" Ula's tales had often been crafted from what she had dreamed the night before.

Meraud shook her head. "It is ancient history told to us by that queen's descendants. They live on an island much like this one. They insist the queen was real; after her death, the island was overrun and eventually the culture vanished but for what is kept alive through song and legend."

Again Eamhair stole a glance at Cailean. His arms were no longer crossed but resting on the table, palms down. As her gaze met his, he leaned across and took her hand, threading his fingers between hers. The noise in the hall, the heat of the fires, the fragrances of onion and ale and meat became distant distractions.

Eamhair wanted to say something that would ease the torment of that bloody battle. But, never having been in a battle or even seen one, she struggled to find the words. "Cailean," she began, but got no farther. Had she helped him heal somehow, as Meraud suggested? How could she have? Their exchanges at Dunaedan had been rare and fleeting.

I am a killer. His bald statement had brought a glimpse of something —misery, perhaps—to his expression.

The weight of her ignorance turned Eamhair's tongue to lead.

Meraud rose from her seat and rang a bell. Rhalanse and Cailean joined her in the center of the hall.

"Tomorrow is the Seventh Year Sacrifice," she announced. "All our labors and prayers build to this night, when we put ourselves and those we love into the hands of the Infinite Mother. Our rites keep Inis Tearmann hidden. They keep our fields flourishing, our livestock healthy. They prevent evil from finding us." She paused. "Prepare yourselves and your families," she said, "as I will prepare mine."

The silence that fell over the hall was heavy and solemn, and sent cold wisps of dread down Eamhair's spine.

Cailean, his mother, and his sister left the hall together.

Chapter 12

FROM THE INSTANT THE NECKLACE WINKED AT HIM, TARANIS FELT
through every blood vessel and every nerve ending that Eamhair was
alive. He knew there could be some other explanation. Someone might
have taken it from her and later lost it—like that devious, flaxen-haired
maidservant, Viviana. Or Eamhair could have dropped it before she
was thrown over the cliffs. But neither of those options made much
sense. She had never been allowed out of her bedchamber after the
night she defiantly refused to be Fathna's wife. And the hovel was so
remote. Why would anyone, especially a maidservant, go there?

When he was nine years old, this necklace brought revelations so
bleak he had tried to gouge out his eyes. He had begged for death.

Now he breathed on it, kissed it, and prayed to it. *Bring me a sign.
Show me Eamhair. Where is she?*

But his exhausted dreams showed only the past. He saw the night
he'd seduced Aridela in the Cave of Velchanos. How she had
responded without shame or deceit. How she had gazed upon him, a
barbarian, without fear.

He saw fire and ash and the world pitching. Heard Aridela's
screams for mercy. Burning air seared his lungs and again he watched
the dead at Phaistos swell and burst. That hideous memory dissolved
into the beautiful white shrine by the sea, and Helice blessing his
union with her daughter.

He saw the Oracle, Themiste, at first shy and blushing, yet so eager once he touched her. He relived their second joining, trapped in lust and Poseidon's inscrutable demand.

Alexiare's mournful face swam through his dream, informing him that Themiste had given birth to a daughter. Menoetius staggered up the steps in the oak clearing and offered his blood to Crete—to Aridela. Alexiare confessed to the murder of Selene.

Aridela vowed to reveal his crimes, and hers, to the council.

Her neck, snapping in his hands.

He rose from the pallet, groaning, and threw the necklace against the wall.

But within ten breaths he was holding it again, carefully brushing dirt off the stone.

I beg you. Show me where she is. Take me to her. I will do anything. Anything.

Chapter 13

For most of the night Eamhair lay awake, staring at the flicker of a candle. What was this sacrifice? Why did it cause all within the feasting hall to grow silent and grim?

At some point she heard chanting. Throwing a mantle around her shoulders, she climbed down the staircase and went outside. Far away on the other side of the apple groves, a line of torches ascended the path up the hill. At the summit, a multitude of torches leaped and capered in some kind of dance.

She returned to her chamber and fell into fitful sleep, dreaming of Cailean as he looked back at her from the boat the day he sailed off to find the escaped criminal. Taranis.

The dream slid to the beach, and Taranis's halting whisper. *Forgive me, Eamhair.*

Again the dream changed shape. She was falling through an ocean of crystals that shot rainbows as far as her eyes could see. A voice gently urged, *Go and live as all women do. Make their stories your story, so that someday they will know you as one of their own.*

Birdsong woke her. She spent another day mostly alone except when Nyfain brought spiced wine. She was offered no food; Nyfain explained it was a day of fasting and reflection.

Eamhair wanted to ask about the sacrifice, but something stopped her. She wished for the comfort of Vita's company, but the wolf remained absent.

Rhalanse and Nyfain appeared together at dusk. "We have come to lead you to the place of ritual," Rhalanse said. "But first, you must be painted. Don't worry—Nyfain is one of our finest artists."

They placed Eamhair on a stool where her face was well lit by candlelight and the brazier. Nyfain laid out clay pots and an assortment of small brushes, mortars, and pestles. She ground pigments, scooped out paint, and went to work as Rhalanse watched, every now and then suggesting a color or pattern.

When Nyfain was satisfied, Rhalanse handed Eamhair a mirror made of polished silver. It was the first time she had ever seen her reflection in anything other than water, but the novelty of that quickly switched to astonishment. Her brows and eyelids were darkened. Deep blue feathers in the shape of wings ran from the outer corners of her eyes across her temples and over her cheekbones, where the blue was joined with a dusting of gold. Her lips were now red—nearly the same shade as the Inis Tearmann wine. As she stared, Nyfain positioned a coronet that came to a point in the center of her forehead, punctuated with a highly polished, blue-violet stone, crisscrossed with golden seams and cut into the shape of a teardrop. It reminded her of the stone in Taranis's necklace, and once again she felt a stab of sorrow. There was something about that ornament—its loss left her grievously unhappy, even though every thought of it always brought back the rape.

For the first time she saw the scar on her forehead, an uneven white mark, wide at one end, shrinking as it vanished into her hairline. She touched it, but it didn't hurt.

"I..." She turned the mirror around. "This is me?"

Both women laughed. "It is indeed," Rhalanse said. "Now, shall we rid you of these splints and bandages? Are you weary of them, Eamhair?"

"Oh, yes," Eamhair cried. "Utterly sick of them."

Rhalanse unwound the linens and removed the splint from Eamhair's wrist. The joint was somewhat shriveled. She moved it experimentally.

"Well?" Rhalanse asked.

"There is no pain. It's stiff because I haven't used it. Please, the ankle."

She couldn't wait to test it without the bindings. Rhalanse tried to assist her, but she refused. "I can walk. Ah, it is good to move." She twirled around the chamber, rising up on her toes and holding out the edge of her gown. "Are we going to paint your faces too?"

They both laughed and exchanged a glance. "That is only for you," Nyfain said.

"But—why?"

"We're late. We must hurry." Rhalanse pulled a mantle from the clothes chest. "It will be chilly. Put this on, Eamhair."

Eamhair was glad for the fur-lined cloak as she followed the two women through the deserted village and apple groves, and around a ripened field of grain.

It was a clear night, the heavens replete with a thousand bright trails. "I don't understand it," she said as they started climbing the path up the hill. "The stars are different. I recognize none of them."

"We are some distance from Dunaedan." Rhalanse pointed. "We call those the Three Stallions. Can you see?"

"I...think so."

"And the Faery. See her wings?"

"That one is easy."

"Now follow the tip of the Faery's wing, down and to the left."

"Oh—there is the Guardian. I missed it somehow."

"Cailean told me he saw it at Dunaedan. It creates a channel between your Dunaedan and our Inis Tearmann." She linked her arm through Eamhair's. "My mother calls it Arcturus, the Bear."

The path led them in an upward spiral until it eventually deposited them on the summit.

An immense crowd—surely every man, woman, and child from Gilraidha Soi and many, many more—was gathered around the standing stones. In the center were three piles of brush and wood, ready for lighting, and a slab, like a table, set upon wooden supports, higher at one end than the other.

Nyfain left to join her family but Rhalanse stayed with Eamhair.

No one else had painted faces. Why? What was the paint telling them? Everyone who saw her talked about her; she saw it in the murmuring and glances. Her cheeks heated with embarrassment.

Men used torches to light the fires. Sparks flew, and the hill was illuminated in cheerful light. Children were hushed and soon the only sound was the crackle of burning wood.

A tall figure advanced into the empty space. Eamhair had no trouble recognizing Meraud, though she, too, was painted. Her face and bare arms were covered in flecks of gold; three bold blue stripes angled from her right temple to her left jaw, and a blue stripe stained the center of her bottom lip. Tassels, feathers, and bones laced through an imposing headdress made from her own plaited hair; a mane of brightly dyed feathers fell in a lavish deluge over her shoulders.

In her right hand was a knife—*the* knife, the one Eamhair had discovered in Cailean's war chest.

"Let us begin," she said in the language of Inis Tearmainn. Rhalanse, putting her mouth close to Eamhair's ear, quietly translated.

In the silence that followed, Meraud bent her head and regarded the ground. When her gaze lifted, she looked straight at Eamhair.

Eamhair's nerves frayed. Why were she and Meraud the only two people wearing paint? Why was Meraud holding Cailean's knife?

She felt the crowd press closer.

A man led a ram into the clearing, a large, proud creature with snowy white fleece, gilded horns, and crimson-dyed hooves. The bell around its neck rang with every step.

Relieved, Eamhair took what felt like her first breath of the night. She was accustomed to the butchering of animals. Inis Tearmann was not so different from Dunaedan after all. The ram would be killed and roasted on these fires, the meat shared in a feast. She searched the crowd, hoping to see Cailean.

Movement and a renewed hush drew her gaze to the center.

Two men guided a third into the circle. He wore nothing but a loin-cloth and a band of blue material across his eyes. A headdress made of ram's horns rested on his head. Set between the horns was a white crescent moon, carved of stone, or bone, or white wood. His hair was loose. Though his eyes were covered, his stance, so tall, straight, and proudly unflinching made him instantly recognizable.

Vivid designs were painted on Cailean's body—complex knotwork twining with stylistic bears, serpents, wolves, herons, and raptors.

Why was he blindfolded? Seeing him like this revived the parading at Dunaedan, the silence of the staring men, the drumbeat, the fear. Cailean knew firsthand what that felt like.

The men led him to the slab and helped him lie upon it, face up. They bound his wrists and ankles to hooks at each corner.

Fear wound tighter as Eamhair watched firelight play across his chest and legs.

The two serving men retreated and Meraud lifted her voice so that it rang across the hilltop. "Once every seven years, I tell the story of the sacred knife of Inis Tearmainn." She held up the knife, blade pointed to the heavens. "For it was given to the aes sidhe long ago, during a time of cataclysm in the Dominion of the Sixth Age. Our wisewoman saw it, hidden in a cave where crystals shine as though carved from stars. She sent explorers to retrieve it and bring it here for safekeeping. As they approached, the earth woke and tried to shake them off. Lightning struck. Three ravens attacked. But they were not swayed, and their courage was rewarded. A fissure opened before their feet and disgorged a casket with this knife inside."

Rhalanse translated smoothly along with her mother's speech, adding, "The wisewoman was Meraud. She is much older than she appears."

As Meraud crossed to the slab, Rhalanse explained further. "Boys draw lots to be named our *kira*. Every seventh year, the winner and the knife become blood brothers. The kira serves, and possibly dies, in honor of the Lady of the Moon."

"Kira?"

"It means *the poet sons*. They are the royal, glittering gifts of Inis Tearmainn. Our priceless treasure. The Lady of the Moon takes them. Some she keeps and some she returns. We never know which it will be. Those who return to us are forever changed by what they have seen and experienced. This is what makes boys willing to risk their lives, for the changes are profound. The kira who live are the wisest among us, the bravest, the most heroic. They are mysterious and magical, revered above all others. The kira are champions who transmute death and disintegration into life and blessings."

"Cailean?" Eamhair asked, though she knew the answer.

"He is the only kira who has also been Inis Tearmann's prince."

Meraud circled the slab, looking down at her son. When next she spoke, she sounded different—uncertain. Twice her voice broke as though she fought weeping. "Through the passage of time, the aes sidhe learned the secrets of the knife, how even the most negligible graze kills, yet at its own determination a few are spared. No kira knows whether he shall live or die. It is the knife's choice."

"The knife cannot be swayed," the villagers chanted.

"In our legends," Rhalanse said, "the reason the kira are known as the poet sons is because of one boy who was restored to us. He described being in a cavern with an old woman. She asked for a poem, and was pleased with his effort. She laughed and sent him home. Since then, the kira study the work of our poets for months before they offer themselves. And since those days, the kira cannot share their experiences, for fear of tainting the purity of the offering. Most don't remember anyway—not in any fashion they can share. What they hear and see is buried deep within."

Meraud turned to Cailean as soon as Rhalanse finished. Again she lifted the knife. "Behold," she said. "I present our treasure to infinity and the Infinite Lady."

She brought the knife down. Her body blocked Eamhair's sight, so she could not see where it struck, but she did see Cailean's thigh muscles flex, and the one hand she could see clenched into a fist.

The hilltop and fires vanished in exploding bursts of color; all she could hear was the call of swans, and rustling, as of tall grain in a rising wind. A man emerged from the darkness of her vision holding a sickle-shaped blade. He brought it down as Meraud had done and blood was everywhere, and a beloved voice cried, *Aridela, Aridela.*

Arms went around her. Rhalanse spoke urgently, "Have faith, Eamhair. He is blessed."

Eamhair realized she had screamed. No one else was screaming. Everyone was silent, staring at her. Horrified, she smashed both fists against her mouth.

Meraud was staring at her too, anger etched upon her face.

Rhalanse stroked Eamhair's hair. "What our prince does, he does willingly. After the death of the last kira, he drew lots with the other boys and he was chosen. He was elated about it."

The strength in Eamhair's legs failed. She slumped to the ground, still weeping but careful to stifle all but the smallest whimper, for she was afraid of Meraud's anger and the palpable hostility in the crowd.

Rhalanse held her close; so close that Eamhair felt it when she nodded towards her mother.

Meraud turned back to the slab. Again her blade lifted and descended. Eamhair covered her face with her hands.

Absolute silence fell. Eamhair's ears rang with it.

After only a moment or two more, Rhalanse squeezed her shoulder. "It is done."

Eamhair lowered her hands and opened her eyes. Meraud had stepped away from Cailean. The cloth covering his eyes was drenched in blood. Crescent-shaped slices were cut into his wrists, throat, and chest. His blood ran into grooves in the stone slab, followed the slant to the lower end, and dripped into silver basins.

His hand was no longer clenched. He didn't move. She saw no sign of breathing.

"There are kira who cannot leap the chasm between life and death," Rhalanse said. "The last time I witnessed this was fourteen years ago, and lots were drawn for the next boy. Cailean joined in, though he was only seven. The rite is somber, but weeping and fear is not allowed. It implies a lack of trust in the wishes of the Celestial Lady, and we believe it could affect what happens."

"I—didn't know." Eamhair shrank with remorse and new fear—fear that she would be responsible for anything that happened now. *Move,* she ordered. *Move!* She stared at his chest, but saw nothing—not the slightest rise or fall.

"The cuts are not deep," Rhalanse said. "They bleed freely because of something he drinks before the rite."

Eamhair was relieved to hear it.

The crowd began chanting. "Anathema. Anathema."

Meraud returned to the slab and released the bindings. His arms fell limply over the edges. Blood continued to drip from his wrists onto the ground.

Eamhair detected new tenseness in Rhalanse's voice when she spoke again. "In ordinary years, we sacrifice rams. The meat is cooked; we feast and make merry. But every seventh year this is what we do. The kira dies in place of the ram, or at least he comes so close that we cannot feel a heartbeat or detect any breath. We never know if he will return. When he doesn't, terrible things happen—droughts, blights, the rise of despots, or catastrophic wars. Not here, on Inis Tearmann, but in the lands you call home."

Meraud removed the cloth from Cailean's eyes and retreated a few steps. She stood with her head bowed, tracing a design in the air with the blade.

Who was the goddess of Inis Tearmainn? Was she like the Christos, or Ula's gods, or maybe something else—something too exotic to imagine? Was she brutal, requiring blood and death to be appeased?

Eamhair stared at Cailean, longing to wake him through the force of her will.

Rhalanse helped her stand. She guided Eamhair forward, right up to the stone where she could look into his face. Rhalanse placed one of Eamhair's hands on Cailean's chest and the other on his shoulder. "Call to him, Eamhair," she said.

Hardly realizing what she was doing, she moved her hand from his shoulder to his hair, at the temple. Her palm came away wet and red. Meraud had opened the crescent shaped scar beside his left eye.

She'd always thought the scar was a battle wound—now, she wasn't sure.

"Oh, Cailean," she said. "Come back."

She waited, blinking away tears. She grasped one of his hands and brought it to her chest. It was cold. She massaged it, but there was no response.

"Come back to me," she whispered, lower than before, no more than a movement of her lips.

There was no flutter of eyelids or slow intake of breath. His eyes simply flew open. He sat bolt upright and stared at her as she released him and stumbled backward. "Aridela," he said hoarsely.

Eamhair was only half aware of the exchange of glances between Meraud and Rhalanse. "He spoke that word last time as well," Rhalanse said.

Taranis called me that. Uneasiness sparked. *Are Cailean and the seolh connected? Do they know each other?*

Though he stared into her face, it was clear he wasn't seeing her, or was seeing someone else in her place.

He spoke. "What seems...the end...."

He grabbed her arm. Leaning forward, he pressed a kiss to the red mark at her wrist. "So long," he muttered.

Eamhair was torn between two nights, two places, this night on Inis Tearmann, listening to Cailean, and another night at Dunaedan, when Taranis had said the things Cailean was saying, had done the things Cailean was doing.

His gaze traveled over her face, her hair, and he spoke again, still in that hoarse mutter. "I will be with you.... Nothing...nothing will ever separate us."

"Cailean, can you see me?"

His eyes widened. He frowned. Abruptly, forcing her to take another step back, Cailean leaped from the stone and advanced upon her. Blood ran still from his wounds. But he was standing, closing in on her, and his face blazed.

"I see you, Eamhair."

She blinked up at him, instinctively recognizing what she saw—a primal, sexual gaze. Her cheeks grew so hot she wanted to fan them. But within, her heart and body answered in kind.

Meraud stepped away and poured the blood from the silver bowls onto the ground at the apex between the three bonfires. As she poured, she chanted.

"The earth shall taste the beating heart of She we have forgotten," Rhalanse translated before she, too, stepped away, giving Eamhair a knowing smile.

Someone swatted the ram. It bolted between the fires and into the night, bleating, never to know Cailean had taken its fate upon himself. The beast's many wives and offspring raced after him.

All around Eamhair, the crowd was embracing, shouting, leaping. Rolled-up banners were unfurled, corn dollies tossed. Drummers sent a deep primordial beat into the night. Women shook gourds and out came the flutes and pipes. Everyone sprang into wild dancing, and mead or wine or some other brew was passed around in fat leather skins. Tables were brought forth, heavy with bowls of fruit, bread, cheese, and berries, and under cover of the drumbeat and rejoicing, a few couples slipped away.

Cailean never took his gaze from hers. "Of course I see you," he said.

She could think of no clever reply for this blood-streaked man whose desires were so clearly written on his face, and feared she was staring like a mute imbecile. But before it became too uncomfortable, his attendants pulled him away and he was lost in the crush of revelers.

Rhalanse circled back to her side. "The kira feel life...deeply, when they return."

Eamhair turned to face her. "I ask your forgiveness."

"You understand now?"

"I think I am beginning to. And I thank you and your mother for allowing me, an outsider, a stranger, to be part of this sacred rite. You have given me more honor than I deserve."

"It used to be different. The chosen had to die, but we saw that was not the way. Our land is graced and we live in plenty. Because of him— because of my brother and the kira who have gone before him. And you, Eamhair, are no stranger to us. We have looked for you for a very long time."

"What—what if something were to happen to Cailean when he is with his father?"

"If he were to die? Boys would again draw lots."

Eamhair shook her arms, stretched her neck, and drew in an energizing breath. She, too, felt life streaming through her body with fiery heat. It was like rising from a tomb, the grave-clothes falling away, and it lent her new bravery. "Would you think me mad if I told you I have seen you before...in another place? Your heart was broken. I promised to watch over you, but I...I failed. It must have been a dream, yet it feels so real."

A groove formed between Rhalanse's fine black brows. "Eamhair, I have had that dream. I think you and I are woven like wool on a spindle. You are my sister. My friend. But more."

Eamhair nodded. "I feel the same way."

"I often dream of a woman," Rhalanse said. "I know her—in fact, I am certain I was her in another life. You are always in the dreams, Eamhair. Your hair is different—it is as black as mine—but it is you. Every detail remains clear after I wake. Whenever I dream of this woman, she says the same thing. It has happened so often I know it by heart. May I tell you?"

"You can tell me anything, my sister."

"'Mist shrouds our eyes and stoppers our tongues, a grey, damp silence broken only by the softest sigh, like a dawn breeze. We know not how many centuries pass: we feel not the flow of time, until She turns her far-seeing gaze to us. When we gasp and draw our first breath, we are newborns who never fought great wars, or loved deeply, or brought harm upon one another. So the journey begins. We are become Athene's wanderers.'"

She drew in a breath and released it almost reverently. "We transcribed these words and placed them in our chamber of maps, with our other scrolls and books. I often read and ponder them. My mother believes it a foretelling of some kind."

"Athene." A thrill soared through Eamhair's senses. "Athene's wanderers...."

"It is the name of a goddess. There are places and people in the east who tell stories of her. Our scouts and traders brought knowledge of her from Athens, an ancient city of learning named after her."

Nyfain brought a flask. Rhalanse sipped from it and handed it to Eamhair.

The liquor burned Eamhair's throat but steadied her and halted the shuddering. She drank more, wanting to dull this raw emotion she didn't know what to do with.

Rhalanse laughed. "Careful. You are not accustomed our spirits."

"I am happier than I have ever been. But for...."

"Yes, Eamhair?"

"I would be perfectly happy, if I knew my mother was safe. If I could tell her I survived. That I am well."

"Ask my mother about her. She knows things—sees things. Perhaps she could help."

Rhalanse sounded so certain that Eamhair felt a spark of hope. "Will Cailean come back?" she asked.

"Look."

Rhalanse pointed and Eamhair saw him—barely. Women held his arms and hands. Men formed a laughing, haphazard guard. A girl rode upon his shoulders, her legs dangling over his chest. She squeezed a skin, sending streams of liquid into his mouth, making him twist and bend to catch it. He grinned at her giggles.

Eamhair thought he had again been blindfolded before she saw that now the band across his eyes was blue and gold paint, extending from one temple to the other and halfway down his cheeks in the shape of a raptor, its wings spread wide. It was remarkably similar to the design Nyfain had painted on her.

"He is our Harvest God," Rhalanse said proudly.

"Har—harvest? This is...harvest time?"

"Yes. It is our festival of Lughnasadh. Did no one tell you?"

Eamhair knew of the old religion's harvest festivals through her mother, though Bericus had put an end to those traditions at Dunaedan when she was still a baby. The place where Ula was born had celebrated Lughnasadh, and through Ula's tales, Eamhair had grown to love the hero Lugh, with his terrible sword, his charmed spear and boat, his stallion and hound.

"But—but that would mean—"

"What is wrong, Eamhair?"

It was winter when my brothers threw me off the cliffs. "How long have I been here?" She put her hands on her stomach. *My blood time has not come since I woke on this island.*

"My mother said a child is alive within you. She told me that the first day you came to Gilraidha Soi. She said she didn't think you knew."

Through dizziness and disbelief, Eamhair said, "I was sure I was not. At least, I told myself...."

"Whatever happened in the Dominion of the Seventh Age can be left there."

"How? If I am—with child?"

"This is not Dunaedan. This is Inis Tearmann. We treasure our children."

Eamhair knew she was saying too much. But her mouth kept

forming words and speaking them; she couldn't stop herself. "I dared believe that here, I could leave behind the misery of that place...of that night. The...shame of it."

"What shame?"

"The shame any woman suffers for bearing a child to a man who is not her husband. And Fathna. He could kill me and no one would protest. He would be praised as a strong leader. No one would believe I was taken against my will. No one would care. They would deem it my fault—they would say I had enticed him, or I was not pure enough, or some other thing."

She gazed at Cailean as he advanced between the bonfires. His skin had been cleansed and his wounds bandaged. He was smiling at his admirers, allowing the giggling girls to pull him along. How innocent they were. How...lovely.

"Do you think Cailean does not know?" Rhalanse said. "He knows. He is kira, Eamhair. He knows."

"Then he must despise me."

Rhalanse laughed and hugged her. "You have allowed your father too much influence. It is no wonder. Sent to his church every day, being told of your sin and weakness. Those teachings have been carefully established. The religion of the Christos keeps you guilty and meek, always asking forgiveness for sins you cannot help committing—like smiling. Bleeding. Being female, like their most famous sinner, Eve. The priests want control over everything—especially us, because of the power we once wielded. I have many stories I can tell you of how things used to be. The priests strive to prevent those days from ever returning."

"Where I am from, it is believed that only men—the Christian leaders, the priests, the abbots and monks—can hear God and speak his commands. My mother said that was how she knew they were liars, for the earth gives of its bounty freely to anyone who asks. She told me once that she overheard Bericus telling the priest what to say."

"Every year, your world drifts farther into shadow. The old truths have all but been forgotten there."

"How do you know so much, Rhalanse? About my home? About me?"

"Cailean has told us. Eamhair, give up trying to mold yourself into what those men want. Their demands will never be good for you— only for themselves. Seek what *you* want. Stay with us here, on Inis Tearmann. Become one of us. Be my sister in truth."

259

She placed her hand on Eamhair's cheek. *"What did it mean when I lost the soft hills? Time melts into mine, jewels and ancient forgiveness."*

"What is that?"

"It is the poem the kira told the old woman in the cave. He said she laughed and patted him, and said, *You shall go back, young poet, and live your life, and have many babies."*

Eamhair watched Cailean and contemplated.

His chest was still bare, but the loincloth was gone, replaced with leather trousers and soft skin boots. He appeared stronger than ever, taller than before—tall even among these tall people.

"He knows this is part of his fate as it is yours," Rhalanse said.

Eamhair forced herself to wait. He must choose—especially if he knew the truth. He must choose even as she had to. It was his right, and hers.

She shivered. Her thoughts grew as clear and pure as a running stream.

In the old days, his life would have bled away as we watched. There would have been no other choice. He would have been lost, and I would weep, and face a lifetime without him.

His head turned. He was looking for something.

Not one more breath will I waste trying to please men who give nothing but cruelty and spite. I will not form myself to their idea of purity. I reject Bericus.

When his gaze found her, he stopped searching and stopped walking, though the girls tugged at his hands.

I reject Fathna.

His admirers pulled and called in an effort to regain his attention, but his gaze remained locked upon her.

I reject Taranis.

She did not smile or beckon or speak, but inside, something new crept from darkness into light.

He took one step. His head tilted.

From this day onward, things will be different.

He was striding through the crowd. Leaning down, he said something to the man beside him, never taking his gaze from her. The man veered away.

Something close to fear crept through her body. She had to physically resist the urge to run. She knew what was coming and couldn't stop images of the beach, and what Taranis had done. It had hurt so much. He had pressed down upon her, making her feel crushed and suffocated. His head had loomed in black silhouette, blocking out the stars. The absence of light had rendered him faceless, an incubus, and his harsh breathing had been a sound she never wanted to hear again.

Cailean reached her. Eamhair was bombarded by unmistakable disappointment from the women accompanying him. This was the foreigner who cried out and wept. She alone among them had shown weakness.

The cut by his left eye had been stitched with flax and swabbed with golden honey.

She lifted her chin. *I will never again be weak.*

His mouth lifted in a slow smile.

The other man returned with Leila. He handed the reins to Cailean, bowed to Eamhair, and went off.

The glow in Cailean's eyes was changing now, so swiftly she could not name each color before it slipped into another. It must be due to the mingling of his blood with the alchemy of the knife, the lonely journey to death and back—and perhaps something else, something no one would ever know but Cailean.

He brought her to the mare, lifting her in that deliberate way he had, around the waist on the right side, under the arm on the left, so he wouldn't press against the ribs that had broken. The women surrounding them drew back, laughing now in good-natured surrender, waving and turning away to find entertainment elsewhere.

He leaped up, taking the reins as he passed his free arm around her and pulled her against him.

As he kicked the mare's flanks and they cantered into the night, a fire sparked within, warm like the grass on the moor in the summer and scented like flowers, but flowers she had never before seen or smelled—flowers that lived out of reach.

The mare carried them to a far-off grove where the ground was cushioned with bracken and the only sound was the music of a lonely night bird, and the only light came from stars.

And then she learned what was possible between a man and woman, and that not all touches hurt—some touches could be craved. She put aside Luned's misery, Nia's warnings, her mother's hatred, and that night on the beach. She stepped outside of all she had ever known to enter Cailean's realm, knowing she would never again be Eamhair of Dunaedan, Bericus's daughter.

For a moment that was both endless and too brief, she felt the beating of her heart become one with his as their palms pressed together. The shape of their grove merged into the filigree of the tree-tops and the immutable cliffs and riotous sea at Dunaedan, the slow wheel of the starry heavens, and even beyond that, to a place of rainbows that shimmered like a waterfall.

A new Eamhair burst free of her old stone walls, and found that everything beneath was gleaming and vital and eager. She threw open the secret places she had kept closed and safe all her life—places not even Taranis, with his tricks and deceit, had come close to touching.

Chapter 14

Rhalanse told Meraud about Eamhair's grief over her mother and so, two days after the harvest festival, Meraud spent the night in her scrying chamber, a holy place built inside a cave deep in the bowels of Gilraidha Soi's southern tower, where the veil between worlds was porous enough to see through on occasion.

She lit a fire in the round hearth and flung the dust of iron, lead, and copper on it. She ground a larger than usual dose of dried dreamer's cap with her pestle and for good measure, mixed in a pinch of laurel. As the visionary power washed over her, she stared into the polished sheet of green obsidian that almost always showed her what she wanted to see, but this time, it threw back no more than her own reflection. She switched to the faceted beauty of a fist-sized ratnaraj stone from the Far East, but it, too, remained silent, offering nothing but muted crimson flames from the hearth.

It wasn't until dawn, when her eyelids were drooping with exhaustion and her heart with disappointment, that things changed.

Light haloed one of the gems in her basket, a rare oblate crystal permeated with gold veins. She pressed it to her forehead, closing her eyes and sending her mind into the stone. As she stood inside it, surrounded in golden filaments like spider webs, figures took shape at last—either in the embers of the fire or in her imagination, she wasn't sure.

But it wasn't Eamhair's mother she saw. It was Cailean and Vita, waiting beside the beacon fire as the sailors arrived. The four of them raced to the bothy, phantom sparks flying off their bodies, where they gathered up the girl and Cailean's war chest. Using both sail and oars in an effort to reach Inis Tearmann before it was too late, they set off from the Dominion of the Seventh Age.

She kept watching, hardly daring to blink.

They rowed strongly into the sky ribbons that flowed down to envelope and hide them from the other place.

Faster, she saw Cailean shout. *Faster.* She heard the echo of his desperation an instant after his mouth formed the words. He brought Eamhair up off the rain-washed deck, holding her, and turned his face to the heavens, weeping.

As Meraud watched, the grey-black vapor coalesced around her body.

The boat burst free of the ribbons and flew into the bay by Cailean's bothy on the other side of the island.

Eamhair was only partly visible, like a girl glimpsed through mist. And worse—while the pall around Eamhair had begun to fade as she returned to good health, the subtle cloud she had seen reaching out for Cailean had thickened.

Death was greedy. It would not relinquish one it had tasted, not easily. It would try to right the imbalance by whatever means it could.

She started to retreat but finally, there were the cliffs of Dunaedan.

Meraud stilled, longing to give Eamhair good news. But she saw only a disheartening image of Ula, sobbing as she stumbled along the cliffs.

All hope plummeted as she saw that same cloying shadow around her, too.

Meraud turned away from the hearth, which by now had died down to a few radiant embers. Her head was aching. She climbed the stone steps to her bedchamber, where she quenched her thirst with a cup of spiced mead and unbraided her hair, wanting only to sleep, to put off trying to decipher what she had seen. But shouts, laughter, and eager barking drew her to the window. She opened the shutters and looked down upon the courtyard.

Eamhair was there, playing with some village children. They were tossing a leather ball for one of the dogs. Vita was there as well, disdainfully refusing to take part in a game of fetch; she lay behind Eamhair, her muzzle on her front paws.

Eamhair had healed quickly at Cailean's bothy. Too quickly for such injuries. Meraud didn't think the sky ribbons had that much power. They did impart health, vigor, and long life, and they may have revived Eamhair, who had only expired a breath or two before the boat churned into Inis Tearmann's waters. There may have been enough of a spark left, even if Cailean believed her dead.

Or...not. Everything about this girl was puzzling. But something had brought her back.

In the courtyard, Eamhair paused in her play. She looked up. Her gaze locked with Meraud's.

What would happen if Eamhair wanted to go home? Meraud had desired an answer to this question more than any other, but it remained hidden.

She didn't want to frighten the girl. But she had to protect her...and Cailean.

Perhaps the overlay was not a lingering aftereffect of death. Perhaps Meraud's ability to see was being deliberately hampered.

"Is it you, Lady?" she asked.

But she had received her allotment of answers, and there was only silence.

Eamhair tried to compose a friendly, natural smile as she approached Cailean's mother.

"Sit with me, Eamhair." Meraud motioned to a nearby chair on the dais.

No one but the cleaning women were presently in the hall, and Meraud's chair was removed from their activity. It was a perfect time to approach this busy monarch. Eamhair had worked everything out that morning while Cailean slept, but it all depended on Meraud. Meraud must grant her the use of a boat, and a maybe few men. If she agreed, Eamhair would go to Dunaedan, enter the fortress somehow, find her mother somehow, and somehow get Ula out. If Ula's gods showed them favor, they would make it back to the boat undetected; Ula would be saved and Dunaedan could be forgotten.

Well, it was not a very good plan. But it was better than nothing.

"I am so pleased you have come," Meraud said. "I have wanted to spend a little time with you—whatever time Cailean allows, of course. He is so selfish."

Eamhair dragged the other chair over. She sat, pinching the

armrests before she realized what she was doing and relaxed her hands.

Meraud motioned to a serving maid and soon they had wine and a plate of sweetmeats made of almonds, honey, and pastry. "Are you hungry?"

Eamhair shook her head. "Lady, Rhalanse said you could tell me about my mother. She said you might know if my mother lives."

Curse it, she hadn't even asked Meraud how she was feeling, or complimented her gown, or any of the other niceties she had been taught.

But Meraud showed no sign of offense, other than a slight lift of one brow.

"I-I am so happy and grateful to you," Eamhair said quickly. "But my mother—I worry for her. She is—not treated well."

"Ula lives." Meraud placed her hand over Eamhair's. "Your mother is alive."

There was a frown though, between her brows. Eamhair noticed it and it made her afraid. Somehow, she had to make Meraud agree to let her—

"Eamhair, is it true that you are happy here, with us?"

"Oh yes, lady. I-I love Rhalanse, and the children, and...Cailean. Everyone. All of you are so kind." Could she tell Meraud she loved her, or would Meraud think she was toadying?

"Good." Meraud sipped and grimaced. "This wine is sour," she said, and had a bite of pastry. "I want you to be happy on Inis Tearmann." Her hand tightened over Eamhair's. "I searched. I have done everything I can think of, but truthfully, I worry more for you than your mother. I can never see what would happen if you were to return to Dunaedan. I cannot see *anything*. Not for you...and not for Cailean."

"Not...for Cailean?"

Meraud leaned forward. "There is something about that place. It is veiled from my sight. I feel certain that if you were to go back, it would be...a mistake for both of you. It is only a feeling, but I have learned to trust these feelings, Eamhair, in my long life. If you can, it would be best to find happiness in knowing your mother is alive. Would she want you to take such a chance for her, especially as you are with child? I think she would want you to stay here where you are safe, to give birth to a healthy baby and be happy."

Eamhair hardly heard what Meraud was saying. She was trying so hard not to weep, to keep her face expressionless, to not burst into argument.

"You cannot go back," Meraud said. "Perhaps, in time, we could send her a message. Or, when things have settled, perhaps a few of my men might try to help her. I will have to look again, at some point."

Eamhair couldn't remember later how she came to be in the chamber she shared with Cailean. He asked her what was wrong. She replied that nothing was wrong, and only afterward thought she might have sounded brusque.

She understood what Meraud hadn't said. If she insisted, Cailean would also insist. He would demand to go with her. She couldn't put Cailean's life at risk. Nor could she risk the lives of any others.

Ula's grief and loneliness would forever scrape at her daughter's happiness. But to protect Cailean, Eamhair could live with that, as Meraud so obviously wanted her to.

Chapter 15

EAMHAIR GROANED, LOATH TO WAKE UP, BUT THE DETERMINED KNOCKING went on and on.

Cailean appeared to be sleeping peacefully, his face tucked into a pillow stuffed with feathers, one arm flung across her stomach—an arm that only seemed unresponsive. She knew from experience that if she attempted to rise, that arm would tighten. He would wake. There would be kissing, and other things.

Sunlight filtered through the half-open shutter on the east wall, illuminating the scar by his eye, which was still angry, though nicely knitted beneath the stitches.

She lifted his arm, hoping this time she would defy his instincts, but again she failed. His eyes opened and his arm clamped down.

"Someone is knocking," she said.

"They'll go away." He pulled her closer.

Rhalanse called through the door. "Cailean? I have been most patient."

"She *has* been patient." Eamhair brushed her fingers through his hair. It was thick and straight, and reminded her of a waterfall.

"Curse her." Throwing back the furs, he rolled off the bed and pulled on trousers, lacing them as he went to the door, the tunic he'd swept up from the floor slung over one shoulder.

There was a consultation. Cailean said something impatiently, but after a muffled answer, Eamhair saw him nod.

He closed the door and returned, yawning. "My mother requires our presence at tonight's feast." He nuzzled into the space where her neck met her collarbone, his morning stubble prickly. "Rhalanse swears we won't regret it."

"Dare we show our faces? The gossip...."

"My mother rules this place. Oh, she would say she does not, but she does. If we do not go, she might burn us in the next bonfire."

Eamhair startled away and he pulled her back, laughing. He sobered as she winced. "Did I hurt your rib?"

"It has been better since before Lughnasadh." She gave him a sly smile. "Could you not tell?"

"You have been...engaged. Where did you learn how to do those things?" He squinted.

She laughed. "My only friends were the whores at the brothel. Do you think I have lived over a score of years without being told a few tricks?"

"Ah." His features relaxed. "Someday, I will find a way to thank them."

"My rib might be fine but you're pulling my hair—again."

At his request, she'd been leaving it loose at night, though it was driving her mad with its weight and the way it went everywhere, and tangled, and often got pulled when he rolled over on it. But he liked it; he teased that it could be used as a blanket, and she teased that his could as well, and she sometimes braided his hair with hers, light and dark woven together.

"How did you first get this scar?" she asked languidly after he pulled her close and kissed her for a long time in all the places she loved to be kissed. She touched the skin next to his eye. "Was it from the black knife? Did your mother do it?"

He rubbed it as if it itched. "I became a kira when I was seven, and entered the land of the dead for the first time when I was fourteen." His gaze wandered to a spot beyond her shoulder but he kept her close, and soon returned to nuzzling the skin beneath her ear, which sent shivers clear to her feet.

"Yes?" she said. "You entered the land of the dead when you were fourteen."

"No one is allowed to ask what happened there," he said with a mock frown.

"Oh—I forgot. I am sorry. Forgive me."

He traced her cheekbone. "How you blush," he said softly. "Such lovely blushes."

Her face grew even hotter. She had always hated the way her skin betrayed her feelings.

He gave a low laugh and brought her closer yet, so their chests pressed together and she could feel all of him, and know beyond doubt what he was contemplating.

"How far does this blush go?" He pulled away to examine her, running his finger over her throat and down to the lacing on her shift. "You and your tiresome clothing. Why is this not on the floor where it belongs?"

Curiosity drifted away. It was difficult to think when warmth followed the path of his finger, layer after layer of heat, drowning out everything else. "Oh, Cailean," she whispered.

Surprisingly, it was he who returned them to the question. "I was fourteen," he said, next to her ear, "flying on the wings of the mushroom. They soak them in wine to sweeten the taste."

"Yes?" She turned her head to encourage him to kiss the side of her neck again.

"I saw nothing for a long time, then, far away, a circle of light. It came closer and closer until it surrounded me and I was standing on a rocky outcrop with another man—a man who called me his brother. There was a cave mouth not far from us, and from inside, we heard growling."

Eamhair lifted her hand, pressed it to his palm, and wove her fingers between each of his.

"The man was angry. He ordered me to flush out the beast hiding in there. I was angry too. I called him a coward. I turned—I was going to leave him—and he shoved me into the cave mouth. Next thing I knew, I was being shredded alive by a lioness."

"A lioness?" She drew back from him a little. "It hurt you? You said I was like a lioness."

"Sovereigns of the wild, as fearless as they are proud."

She blushed; he laughed and twisted a lock of her hair around his finger.

"A lioness," she said, wonderstruck. "Was it a dream?"

"Well, I was bound at the time on the stone slab. My mother hadn't cut me beside the eye. Yet when I woke, this wound was there. She said it appeared as if an invisible knife was slashing me. It healed and left the scar. She thought it important. It was the first time any kira had returned physically changed, other than the eyes. She decided she was meant to open it again every seven years."

A thought struck her. "I would never harm you. So I am not like a lioness."

He laughed against her skin. "It was odd, though. As that beast savaged me, I heard a woman telling me it was my punishment, and the mark would remind me never to make that mistake again. But I don't know what crime I committed, so how can I avoid doing it again?"

They kissed. Eamhair thanked him for telling her and promised never to reveal his secret from the land of the dead.

When they rose, he laced her dress and plaited her hair, though it took longer than it ever did with a proper maid, and she thought it quite messy.

They went for a stroll through the village, Vita hugging their legs.

All the village dogs hated Vita, though none had courage enough to attack her. They skulked in a wide circle, barking, but every time Vita's ears cocked towards them, Cailean spoke her name and she subsided.

"You have such control," Eamhair said. "It must be maddening for her."

"I will tell you something about Vita." Cailean fondled the wolf's ears as they walked. "One time there was a dog who would not leave her be. It followed us wherever we went and barked all night outside my chamber. I grew so weary of it, but Vita obeyed me and left the hound alone. One night when I'd had more wine than I should have, the dog kept me awake. I said something about wishing someone would put an arrow in its throat. Next thing I knew, there was a yelp... and blessed silence." He sent Eamhair a half-shamed glance. "Vita killed it. Since that night, I've been more careful about what I say around her."

"She understands you?"

"It seems she does."

One of the village women approached with a curtsy. "M'lady, will you come with me? We have been instructed to measure you for a dress."

"Lady Meraud has been most generous. I have no need of clothing."

"Mistress Rhalanse asked us to make this one, and she wants it done immediately."

"Go on." Cailean kissed her temple. "My mother wants to see me, anyway."

Eamhair reluctantly allowed herself to be pulled away and taken to the first bedchamber she'd been given, which she hadn't entered since the night of the harvest festival. Why did she feel she must spend every breath with him? Surely they had a lifetime together.

Ula's sad, aged face reared into her mind. How she must be suffering, believing her daughter murdered, thrown off the cliffs by her brothers, at the order of her father. Eamhair knew this grim image would haunt her for the rest of her life. But she must learn to bear it, to trust that someday, Meraud might deem it safe enough to send Ula a message, or rescuers.

If you can only live, Mother. Live until I come for you. I swear I will, someday.

Her hands unconsciously moved to her stomach, and the maid who was measuring her hips asked her to please lower them.

"You have gained weight," the woman said. "Your hips are wider than they were last time I measured. It's good to see you regaining your health." She blinked. "Have I offended you, lady?"

"Nay." Eamhair breathed deeply. "I feel a little sick."

The maid grinned. "Wider hips and a little sick. We all know what that means."

Eamhair proffered a weak smile and said nothing. The seamstress and her two assistants got what they needed and left, promising a new gown for this evening's feast.

Nyfain came in as the other women were leaving and advised Eamhair to rest, for, she said, this night would be a long one.

"Are we celebrating something?" Eamhair had sensed a hushed excitement in the air all morning.

Nyfain's brows lifted. "Inis Tearmann needs little excuse to celebrate. Our harvest was bountiful. Our prince touched death and returned triumphant. That is enough, surely?"

"Aye, surely."

Eamhair obediently got into bed; Nyfain drew the bedclothes over her and fastened the shutters. She tiptoed out, closing the door behind her.

Again Eamhair rested her hands on her stomach. She had felt the movement of many babies in their mothers' wombs, but she felt nothing in her own. Since the night Taranis had forced her, she had known there was a possibility—only a possibility—but had held on to hope that she would be spared. Now that hope was destroyed. Rhalanse had suggested that Cailean was aware. But what if he wasn't? How would he feel about his lover giving birth to another man's child? If he did know, why had he said nothing?

No man at Dunaedan would accept such a thing.

She didn't think she could sleep, and so was surprised when Nyfain returned. Twilight was upon them.

The finished gown was brought in—a heavy dark green over-dress stiff with gold embroidery and lacing, made even richer by a cream colored under-tunic that edged the neckline and peeked through splits in the skirt and sleeves. The wide, dangling sleeves were banded at the wrists with luxuriant rabbit fur.

With the final addition of the belt, gold disks that draped her hips, they stood to admire their work.

"I have never even imagined a gown of such beauty," she said.

The women smiled and told her it was a pleasure sewing for her. They must have worn their fingers out to accomplish so much in one day.

Nyfain escorted her to the feasting hall then left to join her husband and daughter. Musicians were playing, dancers were dancing, and the trestle tables were weighted down with food. The air was redolent with mouth-watering aromas. Maids carried wine and ale from table to table, and there was much laughter.

She had only begun to search for Cailean when he appeared at her side. He must have been watching for her.

He too was finely dressed in a black tunic made of some exquisitely soft material, black trousers, and a sleeveless cream-colored over-tunic edged in gold. An engraved golden band ran around his forehead.

He held out his hand. "Dance with me?"

Her feet had already begun tapping. "Happily!" She pulled him to the center of the hall.

They danced several jigs and reels, drinking the potent Inis Tearmann wine whenever they paused. The music and laughter began to echo, and the color grew bright at the outer edge of Eamhair's vision.

"The bracelet I made would go nicely with that gown."

"What bracelet? Was it in my chamber? I didn't see it, Cailean."

"No, not here. At Dunaedan. I had some dried rowanberries—"

She stopped in mid step, nearly causing a nearby couple to collide with her. "*You* made that?"

"Did you like it?"

"I thought—I thought because it was in the sea cave, that it came from Tar—from the seolh. Why did you never tell me? It's still in my coffer, I suppose, if they have not stolen or destroyed everything of mine."

"Do not be sad, donnah. I will make you another. I will make you a thousand if you wish." He brought her hand to his mouth and kissed the red mark on her wrist then swept her back into the dance.

It was not her imagination. People kept glancing at them. There were expressions of anticipation...of resentment...of amusement...of joy. She smoothed her gown and felt the placement of her braids. "Is something wrong with my dress? My hair?"

"Of course not."

"Why is everyone staring?"

"How can they help themselves? You are beautiful."

She laughed. "It is good to be young, full of heat and passion!" She put her palms on his cheeks. "And here, no one calls it a sin."

He started to smile and she added, for his ears alone, "My destiny was set the day I walked into Bharosa's nose."

He bent his head and kissed her, right there in the midst of the reel —something that could never happen at Dunaedan without dire consequences—and lifted her off her feet. Holding her in one arm, he adroitly pulled the pins and ties out of her hair with his free hand, causing it to fall about her shoulders and down her back. She gasped and scolded, and everyone who saw stopped to raise their fists, or their cups, or their daggers, and cheer.

She pushed at his chest as he laughed at her. Over his shoulder, she saw the crowd part, making way for the approach of a woman —Meraud.

Cailean set her on her feet and Eamhair tried to school her expression into something more dignified, though her mind ridiculed her for it—who on this island did not know how she and their kira prince had been spending their time since Lughnasadh?

But Meraud looked pleased and happy. Her hands were overflowing with a profusion of ribbons and flowers.

"For you." Meraud held out the object. Eamhair saw with astonishment that it was a wreath, thick with fresh blooming flowers and shiny green ivy, the front a spectacle of gold. In the center was fashioned a golden bull, horns lifted in a proud and dominant crescent, flanked by birds—falcons—with outstretched wings, each feather exquisitely detailed, and rich gold weaving in the Caledonii style. Hundreds of ribbons in more shades than she could readily count were woven around and between the greenery and gold, and gathered together at the back, where they tumbled in a colorful cascade.

She stared, speechless.

Cailean took it from his mother and placed it on her head. The ribbons mingled with her hair and her senses filled with heady perfume.

"Will this do?" he asked.

She tried, but no words could pass through the choking sensation in her throat.

He took her hands and Meraud spoke, something about giving birth to Cailean, and how she had envisioned this day for her son.

"You are my chosen woman," Cailean announced, "and I will defend you with my life." He slid his silver ring upon her middle finger. "Never remove this again, my lady," he said with a glare that would put Bericus to shame.

She laughed and threw her arms around his neck. "Never."

Next to her ear, he said, "My destiny was set the day I agreed to become Bericus's lackey just to be near you."

Cheering and toasts proceeded, and Eamhair realized that in this place she was now Cailean's wife, princess to his prince.

She had told him, that first night at Gilraidha Soi, that she might be carrying Taranis's child. Yet here he was, making their union formally complete.

Rhalanse pushed her way through the throng and seized Eamhair in a tight embrace. "I couldn't tell you before and ruin it, but the paint at Lughnasadh was part of our wedding rite—an announcement of intent, if you will. You were painted with Cailean's colors. Everyone but you knew this night was coming. We just had to make the bridal wreath. Cailean insisted."

Eamhair smiled at him, hoping he could read the happiness in her eyes, for she had no words to express it. Nothing could make it more perfect.

Except having Ula here.

Three women with baskets full of flower petals laid a path of blooms from the center of the hall to the open arched doors.

Leaning in close, Eamhair said, "I see only purple in your eyes tonight, my lord. Only purple...and they want me."

He kissed her fiercely; sweeping her into his arms, he prowled over the scented path and out of the hall, saying things in his own language she knew were love words, though she didn't understand them all. He took her far from Gilraidha Soi and they spent that night making love and dancing, drenched in the ribbons the heavens sent to celebrate with them.

PART III

Stealing Ula

Chapter 1

MERAUD WALKED BY THE BAY WITH EAMHAIR'S BABY, STOPPING EVERY NOW and then to dribble a little seawater over his hair and rub it in. "Your mother is the fulcrum and you are the force," she said. "I will keep you secret and safe."

He pushed a corner of the blanket into his mouth and laughed.

"You will have all the adventures a boy needs, I promise, but the ribbons will hide you. No one will see you coming, my eidolon, until it is too late."

The baby stretched out a hand; Meraud pressed her finger against his palm and he closed his fist around it. "Look at you," she crooned. "So strong. And you will grow stronger." She kissed the tip of his nose. "Stronger and stronger, until lightning and thunder cower from your anger."

She traced the red mark on the inside of his wrist, shaped exactly like his mother's. "We are at the beginning," she said. "There is more to do, and much farther to go." She contemplated the calm, blue-green water in the bay. "I have asked the Infinite Lady why this must happen. Do you want to know what she said?"

The baby blinked. Meraud whispered, "'For a dream.'"

Cailean had appealed to Meraud for help in wrestling out what was wrong with his wife. He'd noticed something no one else had, including Meraud—that Eamhair did not seem quite right. There were sighs hidden beneath her smiles, and she spent too much time sleeping.

Eamhair had steadfastly denied this, and claimed she was as happy as it was possible to be.

Cailean sent in the queen's healer, who declared Eamhair healthy—at least in body. What he really feared, and reluctantly told Meraud, was that the child was causing it—that the poor thing revived the unspeakable act that began his life. Cailean had done his best to convince her he didn't care who the father was, but there was nothing he could do to erase the memory of the rape. No matter how she tried to hide it—perhaps because she tried to hide it—his altered kira senses recognized a subtle decline in the girl who had so mesmerized him the first day he encountered her on Dunaedan's cliffs.

"Shall we go see your mama? She is surely missing you."

Meraud and the baby traveled back to Gilraidha Soi and went along to the couple's chamber. Cailean was hunting; it was a good time to ferret out Eamhair's secrets.

She let herself in. The chamber was dim, the shutters closed. Eamhair lay in bed, motionless. Meraud crossed to the basket and placed the baby inside, still snuggled in his blanket. He had drifted off to sleep on the ride back and didn't wake, but Eamhair did. She sat up, stretching. "He is asleep?"

"Yes." Meraud sat on the edge of the bed. "How are you feeling?"

"Very well." But Eamhair's gaze darted to the window—just for an instant—a clue so negligible Meraud was ashamed to admit she probably would not have taken any notice of it without Cailean's confessed concern. "A little tired."

Meraud picked up the pitcher by the bed and poured a cup of apple cider. She handed it to Eamhair, saying casually, "Has Rhalanse ever told you the story of her brother?"

"She is full of stories about Cailean. It drives him mad."

"Not Cailean. There was another."

Eamhair's brows lifted in surprise. "No…she's never said anything of a brother other than Cailean."

"His name was Ruadan."

Meraud saw the question in Eamhair's sudden frown and stillness. *Is he dead?*

"I lost him to the knife of Inis Tearmainn."

"Oh, Meraud. Two of your sons have been pledged to the sacrifice?"

"Nay." Pain weighted Meraud down like tree roots. "But the knife took him, nevertheless. It swallowed him in darkness."

"I grieve with you. It must make Rhalanse even more cherished."

"Yes. At least I have her." She pictured her son, his strong small legs, slightly bowed, and the shadow that never left his eyes. She should have known. She should have taken steps—

Dismissing old, useless recriminations, Meraud explained. "As you know, the knife has been with us a long time. I think we were led to it so we could keep it safe. It would be catastrophic if it fell in with those who would use it for evil."

"Cailean said it is made of something called glass."

"Once it was stone. Heat changed it. Heat gave it life. It can and does kill on its own volition. It seems to enjoy killing. The hardest task I have ever had to do is use it on the kira at the seventh year sacrifice."

"Do they die? You truly don't know if they will come back?"

"We never know. It is agonizing. They are not dead, though. Not like others the knife kills. I have stood above so many of the kira on the ritual stone, and watched them. They do breathe. I suspect they lie somewhere between life and death. Some cross the abyss and do not return. Others, perhaps pulled by a strong enough will, do."

"Cailean was so worried when I cut myself with it."

"The knife cut you?"

"Yes, but it healed long ago, before we came to Gilraidha Soi."

"Show me."

Eamhair held up her left hand, revealing fine white scars across the tips of her two middle fingers.

Meraud was stunned. *It tasted your blood and allowed you to live.* She looked at her son's beloved with new eyes. *This means something.*

She had to drag her thoughts back to this moment, to the girl. "Like you, el anoshla, I am a mother. I am your honorary mother, and I love you as if I gave birth to you. We are connected—by Cailean, yes, but more as well. We are both women, both mothers. In the loss of a child, I have endured the worst pain imaginable. Can you tell me what you have been feeling, what has been marring your happiness, more easily than you can tell Cailean?"

Eamhair was quiet a long time. "It is your love," she said at last.

Meraud was shocked and hurt. She did not give affection easily.

"It is a never-ending reminder of what I have lost."

Understanding glimmered. "What have you lost, Eamhair?"

"Every time he smiles or laughs, or takes my finger in his hand, I

281

realize I can never share my son with his other grandmother. It hurts so much. I still forget, sometimes. I think, 'Oh I can't wait to tell my mother about this!' before I remember."

It was not the rape causing her sadness. It was Ula.

Meraud should have realized this, but Eamhair hadn't mentioned her mother in so long.

Reaching out, Meraud brought Eamhair into an embrace and held her as she wept, feeling the girl's agonizing sobs clear through her chest.

"I was given to her late in life," Eamhair said, "and was her last child. She lost several. She released my brothers to my father, but she kept me for herself. I was the one thing in her whole joyless life that made her smile."

Meraud wiped Eamhair's eyes with her sleeve.

"I have tried to let her go, as you wanted. I have tried to forget her. But it only gets worse."

Meraud had to fight to keep from weeping herself at Eamhair's sorrow.

"If she still lives, she believes me murdered in the most horrible way, by her own sons. How I long to see her, if only to let her know I am well cared for and loved."

"Why can you not share this with Cailean?"

"If he knew, he would set sail for Dunaedan the same day, the same hour. If he were captured, or...." She drew in a breath. "You said we could never go back. I have not forgotten. I would never willingly send my Cailean into danger. What good would it do, when I don't know if she is even still alive? She was not in good health." Another indrawn breath. "I will be happy again, Meraud. In time."

"She lives."

Eamhair blinked and her cheeks reddened.

"Remember, anoshla, time passes differently on Inis Tearmann. We have told you this before, but it is hard to remember when you can't see it happening. Inis Tearmann lies in a void where the passage of time is like water, ebbing and flowing, advancing and retreating. It can even be shaped, somewhat. When Cailean goes to his father, time here slows. Otherwise Cailean might have to leave Artorius as soon as he arrived. Your mother has suffered your absence for a sennight, I think, or at most a month. Once, the difference in time between our two lands was quite large. Centuries. But we have been drawing closer together, and I suspect that soon, time will always pass more slowly here. For what reason, I cannot say. I don't know."

Now she was lying, but it couldn't be helped.

Hope transformed Eamhair's face in a way Meraud had not seen in a long while. It affected her deeply. As much as she wanted to keep her children close and safe, she never could. It was frustrating. But that shining light in Eamhair's eyes gave her the strength to force through her uncertainty. "I have not been completely truthful. Please forgive me, Eamhair. I see now that you must know everything in order to freely make your own wise choices." She hesitated, trying to find the right words. "The name of this island in your language is Sanctuary. Inis Tearmann truly is that for you, Eamhair. I suspect that as long as you stay here, breathing our air, you will remain healthy. If you return to Dunaedan, you may die. I cannot predict what will happen. I cannot see it, Eamhair, because...." She cushioned Eamhair's hand between hers, "because you did die. When Cailean brought you here, you died, but you were close enough when it happened that the sky ribbons revived you. At least...I think that is what happened. The ribbons of Inis Tearmainn impart stamina and strength. Sickness is rare and we live a long time. I myself, according to your ways of counting, am well over four hundred years old. Do you understand? I don't *know* what will happen if you go back. But I suspect that at Dunaedan, you are dead."

Eamhair was silent for a while. Then she asked, "So the threat is to me, not Cailean, nor anyone else? Only me?"

"That is hard to say. I have not been able to see him either. I can see him, somewhat, when he goes to his father. But when I try to see him at Dunaedan, everything is hidden. Foggy. Just as it is when I try to see you. It has not always been that way, and that worries me." *Only since you came into his life.*

The girl's thoughts were easy to read. If she believed she would be the only one to suffer or die, she was willing. Her silence had been to protect Cailean and her baby.

Meraud felt her heart breaking as she realized how Eamhair must have been inwardly ripped apart over the last year as she tried to let go of the one she had loved since birth in order to protect those she loved now.

Gently, Meraud said, "Cailean is not as helpless as you believe. He is a gifted warrior who has survived many battles. His father values his abilities as a strategist. He will not run off blindly to please you. He loves you, but he is not a dimwit. Cailean deserves to be told how you feel. And…together we will think of something. He has spent so much time in the Dominion of the Seventh Age, and months at Dunaedan. He might…know of a way."

The poor girl was nearly beside herself.

I thought I was done with that miserable place. No, that is not true. I want to be done with it. But I am not. Not yet. I am bound until the Seventh Age comes to an end.

"You should talk to us, and not keep things hidden, child."

Meraud returned Eamhair's smile, praying her face was not so easy to read.

Chapter 2

"THINK OF OUR SON, IF NOT YOURSELF. WHO WOULD TAKE CARE OF HIM?"

Meraud knew this argument would fail even before Eamhair answered.

"I have arranged everything," Eamhair said. "Hollan has milk enough to nurse two babies instead of one. And I could easily name at least five couples who would take him if the worst happens, and love him as their own. I *am* going with you."

"No."

"My mother does not know you—not well enough to go with you willingly. Besides, how would you find her? You know not where her bedchamber is, or how she spends her time. You have never been in the tower. I have to go."

Meraud decided to interject when she saw the subtle glow in her son's eyes intensify, as it always did when he was caught up in the throes of strong emotion. "Your wife makes a good point, Cailean. Eamhair has learned how to handle a bow, and can accurately throw a knife. And this is her mother. Have we not kept them apart long enough?" *Against her will,* she did not add, as Cailean had not been told how Eamhair tried to forget about Ula for his sake. Nor did he know about Meraud's concern for their safety. Eamhair had insisted, and, perhaps out of guilt, Meraud had agreed.

Before he could argue, Meraud added, "The fewer who go, the better, as I see it. Eamhair knows the fortress and her mother. She knows the habits of all who live there. You, my son, will be the one to find a way in without being detected."

He relented eventually, once he extracted Eamhair's promise that she would follow his orders without question.

His eyes began to gleam in a different way. He had been stuck on Inis Tearmann much longer than usual, having stayed at Eamhair's side through her gravidity. He must be chafing for excitement. "Maybe I can get Bharosa away somehow," he said, and Meraud suppressed a smile.

Eamhair armed herself with a long, leather-handled seax, and her bow, of Scythian design, and a quiver of arrows she could strap over her shoulder. All through the months the baby grew inside her, Cailean and the other archers on Inis Tearmann had taught her about weaponry and fighting. Every day she practiced until she went into labor; by now, she had developed a skill, especially with the bow, that pleased her instructors. They compared her to her prince, and said she had the true eye of a falcon, as he did, which pleased her.

She was dressed for a fight, if need be, in trousers the handmaids made for her so she would not be handicapped by skirts, a long-sleeved wool tunic covered by a heavily bossed leather vest, forearm bracers, and boots. Nyfain wove her hair into a single tight braid to keep it out of the way.

Eamhair ran along the corridor and down the steps. She had given the baby one last kiss and was on her way to join Cailean, Rhalanse, and Meraud in the courtyard. But as she reached the main floor, she hesitated, overwhelmed by an inexplicable urge.

She passed by the arch leading to the courtyard and descended to the shrine, where the sacred, glass-bladed knife was kept on a bronze stand. It made her shiver to touch the lethal thing, but she wanted it—needed it—with her on this perilous mission.

It wasn't hard to believe the knife was compelling her to its will. Meraud claimed it lived in some fashion. Eamhair felt she and the blade had a connection; she wasn't sure why—perhaps because twice, it had savored Cailean's blood. But there was something else. Every time she thought of the knife, she saw the face of Fathna.

She knelt, bowing her head to the exquisite ivory and gold likeness of Inis Tearmainn's heavenly Goddess, and spoke into the silence.

"What did it mean when I lost the soft hills?
Time melts into mine, jewels and ancient forgiveness."

She looked up, blinking tears from her eyes. "Lady, I ask you to bring us home safely, and give us many babies."

Rising, she crossed to the doorway. "You restored me to life and have given me happiness. I will never forget you, or this place. Whatever you want to do to me, I accept. Just let me save my mother."

EAMHAIR LEANED OVER THE PROW, STARING AS THE INIS TEARMANN currach emerged from its spell-cast cloak of sea mist.

Before them lay the cove where Dunaedan's fishermen moored their boats. It was not yet even Lauds; this was the quietest, most deserted part of the night—the safest time to slip into the fort with none the wiser.

But instead of neatly tied currachs ready for their fishermen to take out at sunrise, the glint of light from the thin crescent moon showed six much larger boats nearly blocking the way into the cove. Six boats, all with the black boar insignia of Innse Orc.

Only charred skeletons remained of Dunaedan's fishing boats. The scent of scorched wood hung in the air.

The sailors threw their oars into a hasty reverse stroke. Without a sound, the boat retreated into its disguise and disappeared.

"Fathna!" Eamhair whispered. "Why, after all this time?" Filled with dread, she backed away from the prow and put her arm around the mast. "Has he overthrown my father? Is Fathna Dunaedan's master now?"

"Remember donnah, about the difference in time," Cailean said. "He might have just now returned for you, or is here to confront Bericus about the monk."

She shivered. "Dunaedan's boats were burned. Something terrible has happened."

"We should go home," one of the sailors suggested. "Allow more time to pass."

"My mother is in danger. We cannot leave her here."

"What about landing at that wee beach east of here?" said the other sailor with a jerk of his head. "It's likely empty."

"The beach of the seal-people?" Eamhair's voice trembled. That place, once so beloved, now offered only memories of Taranis.

Cailean frowned, but said, "Let's try it," and the sailor went off to the tiller.

His regard was steady. "Will you agree to stay on the beach long enough for me to see for myself what's going on? If Dunaedan is over-run, we might have to postpone our rescue."

She started to argue, but she had promised to obey. She reluctantly nodded.

TARANIS SET OUT THROUGH THE LONGEST TUNNEL, TIMING HIS ARRIVAL SO that he could spend an hour or so at the hovel beyond Uisge Bealach and return before the local fishermen began their workday. Though the king of Innse Orc and his men had vanquished Dunaedan, had butchered those who fought them, had pulled down part of the fortress, burned much of the village and many boats, had raped more than a few women and enslaved all that were left, still these outlying fishermen went about their daily work, accustomed to the fighting between powerful men and knowing they still had to eat.

Every time he approached the deteriorating bothy, he was flooded with emotion. He couldn't stop it any more than he could stop taking his next breath. Finding the necklace felt like a promise. Not from that bitch goddess Athene. He knew now she never meant to help him. Perhaps some other deity had placed it there, had caused it to sparkle at the instant he was looking.

As always, he watched and listened before leaving the tunnel. The entrance was perfectly hidden at the rear of one of the deep clefts created through the ages by wind, tides, and erosion, and was additionally concealed by dense clumps of bentgrass, thistles, thorny furze, and stunted trees. The hardest part was getting through the thorns, but once that was accomplished, all it took to reach the boats was a quick icy wade around the point of a sheer bluff that protruded into the inlet.

Since finding the necklace, he had gone to the hovel every night, needing to spend time at the place where Eamhair had, at some point, mysteriously been. Nemausus had moved Viviana into Eamhair's tower bedchamber, so the hovel and the Cretan necklace were his only remaining connections to her.

It was never difficult to get across Uisge Bealach. These country folk followed a rigid community schedule of work, meals, and sleep.

Dusk was a good time to commandeer one of the currachs, as was the silent, sleepy hour before Lauds.

Once across, he made his way over the low hills, stopping at the top of the knoll where he had first glimpsed the reflection of the necklace. Below, the bothy was a barely discernable layer of deeper shadow.

Where are you, Aridela? Is my brother hiding you?

He descended and circled the hut. All was deserted, as usual. He sat awhile in the doorway, listening, but the only sound was the single haunting call of a curlew.

He turned the necklace in his hands, watching the glimmer of silver, admiring the lapis bead, which gave off a luminous glow even in the absence of light. He held it against his cheek, absorbing the ever-present heat in the metal. "I miss you," he said. "I wish I could ask your forgiveness." He stared up at the starry heavens. "She will never use or deceive me again. I swear to you, even if you and I return a thousand times to this miserable world, no matter what happens, she will never again trick me into hurting you that way. If only you will give me one more chance."

He returned to the inlet, his feet shuffling heavily through the sand. He had a long, tedious walk back to Dunaedan, and at the end there would be no Eamhair to make it worthwhile.

Just as he started to enter the groove where the tunnel entrance lay, he changed his mind and decided to walk along the cliffs. At this time of night, it was unlikely he would see anyone, and the heavens were resplendent. Far away in the north ribbons of color undulated slowly from side to side.

He stopped above the little beach. *This is where I raped her. Rape was her last memory of me.*

Grief sent him spiraling into despair, but before it could devastate him, he blinked and stepped backward, for a boat was sliding out of the black ocean, grating as it beached. Two men jumped out; Taranis dropped to his knees. Another form leaped from the boat—a dog. Taranis flattened into the bentgrass, hardly daring to breathe.

The two spoke. He heard no more than wordless murmuring, but as the taller man left, calling the dog to his side, the other one reached out and stopped him. The night wind carried words to Taranis's ears. *Just hurry.*

He recognized that voice. And now, as *she* turned back to the boat, he saw the swing of the long plait of hair falling down her back.

Eamhair!

Silently praying the dog—*wolf*—would not catch his scent, he forced himself to remain still. The wind was in his favor, blowing from the north.

The man—*Menoetius*—and his creature climbed the slope to his left and set off towards Dunaedan. Taranis waited until they were lost in the gloom before leaping to his feet and sliding down to the beach.

CAILEAN ORDERED THE SAILORS TO REMAIN ON THE BOAT. IT WOULD WAIT, disguised from the eyes of men, off the coast, ready to pick them up as soon as they received the signal.

He and Eamhair beached in a dinghy. Cailean examined the land with suspicion, but all was silent. Deserted.

"I will reconnoiter," he said. "Should I leave Vita with you? She gives good warning of danger."

"You might need her to do that for you," Eamhair said. "I will be fine. Just hurry."

"We will run." He kissed her. "Stay here, my princess. Be patient."

Hoping her obedient nod could be trusted, he said, "Come, Vita."

He and his wolf raced into the night. *At least she is armed.*

But as soon as they came to the mooring place, Vita froze. She faced back toward Eamhair and the beach, still as stone, her ears perked. They flattened against her skull. She growled once and was gone, running as fast as he had ever seen her run.

Sweet swiving balls. Something has happened already? Cailean set off after her.

"WHERE HAVE YOU BEEN? I THOUGHT YOU DEAD!" TARANIS STOPPED A few steps away.

Eamhair stared as if he were a demon disgorged from hell. "Taranis."

"Yes, it is I." His hands clenched. "How are you alive? Your brothers threw you from the cliffs. Yet here you are, without even a limp. Did they lie to Bericus? Did they help you escape?"

"Nay. They gleefully threw me to my death."

"Eamhair! You cannot imagine how miserable I have been!" He

came closer, longing to reach out and take her in his arms. To breathe in her scent, to feel her skin against his.

She is not dead! Not dead!

But she backed away. "Cailean will return. He will kill you. You must go."

"I will not go, not unless you go with me. We will leave this place together." He held out his hand, palm up. "You are mine, Eamhair. I don't know what lies you have been told, but I do know you have suffered—in no small part because of me. Let me take you from here. I will give the rest of my life to protecting you."

"As you did before?"

He clenched his hands to keep from shaking her. Cailean would, indeed, return soon. Damn him, and damn his wolf! It would be able to track them. "I know you thought I abandoned you, but I did not. I needed time to make certain I could get you away safely. I can do that now. I did not leave, even when everyone thought you dead, because in my heart I knew—*I knew*—you lived. Come with me, I beg you. Come with me and be safe forever. Be my queen."

"You already have a queen. You told me about her, remember? You love her so much. Perhaps she is lost to you, but I will not be her replacement. Nay, Taranis, I am here for one reason—my mother. As soon as we have her, we will vanish. You will never see me again after this night."

His mind churned, one idea after another forming before falling away. If Winoc were alive, he would advise against revealing the truth to Eamhair. His Mycenaean slave had always given wise guidance. Every time Chrysaleon ignored it, he had paid a price.

But he was out of time, and out of choices.

"Eamhair, *you* are my queen. Those stories I told—they are true. You are Aridela. You were the queen of Kaphtor and I was your consort—"

At that instant a bolting shape exploded at the edge of his vision. He threw up his left arm instinctively, and that saved him from having his throat torn out.

The wolf's teeth closed on his forearm, snapping the bone. Taranis fell with an involuntary cry of horror and pain.

"Vita," he dimly heard Eamhair shout. "Stop—away!"

The wolf obeyed immediately. Growling, it released his arm and retreated to stand in front of her.

Cailean ran up, sword unsheathed. He advanced, pointing it at him. "Well well," he said. "The murderer. The rapist, slithering about in the night. On a search for defenseless women?" Starlight writhed through the blade as it inched nearer and nearer to his face. "You will never have that chance again with Eamhair, I promise you."

Taranis scrambled to his feet, holding his mangled forearm against his stomach. He fought to keep his voice from shaking. "I will admit to being a rapist—sorry as I am for it—but I am no murderer. Why would I kill Drost Gocinecht's daughter, and draw his wrath? You—you have been keeping my wife from me."

"Your wife? Priests may marry, but when were monks given that privilege?"

"I was never a monk, and she is my wife."

"Not even Bericus would consider what you did to me a marriage contract," Eamhair said tightly. "Everything about you is false. I recognize none of it."

Taranis saw Cailean's regard veer to her and he hurled forward, throwing Cailean off balance in an attempt to knock away the sword. With that weapon gone, he might have a chance.

But Cailean kept his sword and shoved him backward with it. Taranis felt the blade slice through his tunic and into his chest as he sprawled, groaning.

Vita leaped again. Now he would die, either in the wolf's teeth or by Cailean's blade, but he would not be so easily defeated. He snatched up a heavy stone and threw it as hard as he could at the wolf's head but it missed and struck Eamhair—Eamhair, who was standing behind the beast trying to pull it off him. She cried out and stumbled.

Even as she bent, she shouted again. "Vita, no! Cailean, do not harm him!"

She straightened and lifted something in one hand—a blade as black as the heavens above, yet outlined in a flicker of red.

His throat went dry. The knife from Crete. The knife Aridela had used to kill Harpalycus. *Here*, somehow…here.

He had hidden it, along with the necklace, in a remote cave half a world away, trusting they would remain undiscovered for all time.

Through the humming in his ears he heard her say, "He has fiendish power. I don't want him to hurt you."

Cailean laughed. "Donnah," he said mockingly. "He will not."

Taranis remembered that long gone night in the oak grove on Crete, when he battled Menoetius in a desperate attempt to put off his own death and make an offering of his bastard brother instead. Pain ignited into fury.

He used to respect me at least!

Using Cailean's distraction, he jumped up and barreled into the man's stomach as he had that night centuries ago.

This time, the sword did fly from Cailean's hand.

Taranis heard Eamhair shout as he punched Cailean in the face with his good right hand. Some part of him knew he would not win this fight, but he had gone too far, and would not stop—not until one of them was dead.

He hadn't counted on Eamhair. His head jerked backward as she seized a handful of his hair and yanked, brandishing the Cretan knife. She spoke with grim intent. "If I cut you with this—even a little—you will die."

He had no time to react—blinding radiance flashed around the blade. Releasing a wordless cry, Eamhair dropped it.

It landed near his hand. Instinctively, he gripped the hilt as Cailean kicked him.

Both men rose; Cailean retrieved his sword, but now Taranis was armed. They moved in a wary half-circle. Taranis jumped, knowing he had only a heartbeat or two before Eamhair released the wolf.

He never reached his foe. As he raged forward, agony exploded— its nexus the hand holding the knife. Like lightning it spread, bringing with it a groan that escalated into a helpless shriek. Every bone in his body felt as though it was shattering. His legs buckled.

He dropped the knife and fell, only now smelling the charred flesh of his cauterized palm. Unholy pain sent him spinning into blackness, where he could hear nothing but his own echoing prayers for mercy.

EAMHAIR STARED AT THE COLLAPSED MAN. HE MOANED, THOUGH HE appeared to be unconscious. Her gaze moved to the knife just beyond his fingertips.

"We cannot go through with this." Cailean swiped blood from his lip and held up two fingers. "Two warnings. Fathna's boats and now *him*. We will return to Inis Tearmann and wait for a better night."

Her heart sank. He was right. But they were so close. "Can we not even try?"

"How did this pus in a boil know we would be here? He has probably told others. I will risk much—but not you."

"No one—no one knows." Taranis's legs twitched, and he moaned again.

Cailean shook his head. "What is wrong with him?"

"The knife," Eamhair said, low. "It burned me. That's why I dropped it. Look at his hand—it burned him too. I think it did something else to him. I have never heard a scream like that."

"No man deserves it more."

"Please, Cailean. We came all this way. Can we not try? I beg you."

Barely above a whisper, Taranis said, "I can help." He drew in one hoarse gasp after another.

"You. You're as trustworthy as an adder."

"There is—a way in. No-no one will see you. There are...tunnels. No one knows."

Cailean scoffed. "A secret tunnel leading into Dunaedan? More likely straight to Bericus."

"I live there." Taranis broke off. He struggled onto one elbow. "There are three. And hidden doors—into every chamber—including Lady Ula's."

Cailean turned to Eamhair. "You promised you would obey me, and I am telling you we cannot do this tonight."

Eamhair was staring fixedly at Taranis.

"What is it, donnah?"

"When I was a child, I found a hidden door, and stairs leading to an alcove in the hall—behind that old bearskin. I used to stand in there and eavesdrop."

Cailean's head leaned to the side in that way he had, as though picturing it.

"I told you Taranis entered my bedchamber without ever coming through the door." She placed her hand on his forearm. "I believe him."

"You should—listen to her." Taranis spoke haltingly. His eyes closed. "It is true. I—have just lost all my power over her by telling you this...secret."

"How do we find this tunnel?"

"The cove—where the fishermen keep their boats. Climb the—rocks on the side closest to the fort—to a sea cave."

"I know that cave," Eamhair said.

Taranis worked to catch his breath. "The back wall. It is sealed—with mud. You can break through easily enough."

"And then?"

"There is a...tinderbox and lamp. Follow the tunnel. Climb the ladder to the stairs. Lady Ula's is the—sixth door."

"I'm going with you," Eamhair said. "The tunnel will hide our movements, even if Fathna has a guard at every corner. I'm certain no one knows of them. Not Bericus or my brothers. They would have bragged about it had they known. And Taranis would have been caught."

"I won't leave you here with *him*, you can be sure of that."

"Wait—" Taranis reached out a faltering hand. "By the time you get her, it will be nearing Prime. Too—too dangerous to leave the same way. You will have to use the long tunnel—to Uisge Bealach."

"A tunnel, from Dunaedan to Uisge Bealach? That would take centuries to build. I think you want her to be sent to Innse Orc as Fathna's plaything."

"No—*no*."

Eamhair realized she was slanting her head the way Cailean so often did, and for the same reason—because she was picturing it in her head. "It would take years to build such a thing, but with many men—slaves—maybe not centuries. He could be telling the truth."

"Watch for—fishermen," Taranis said hoarsely. "Go around the cliff—wade. Hides the opening from the—the currachs on the—beach."

Confidence drowned out disappointment. Eamhair smiled. "She will be in her chamber, sleeping. We won't even have to search for her. Oh, I cannot wait to see my mother!" She threw her arms around Cailean's neck and laughed.

He put her gently away. "We will fetch her together. What has happened to your other knife? And your bow?"

"I left them in the boat. I know I should not have done that. You taught me better. I promise to be more careful." She left to get them.

Taranis drew in a gasping breath. "The tunnel...has barricades. There are—handles—in the wall. Pull them. Tunnel will fill with—rocks—if anyone comes after you."

Cailean crossed his arms over his chest. "What to do about you? You seem to be recovering. Will you scurry back and betray her...again?"

"Nay." Taranis shook his head weakly. "I will not."

Cailean looked at the arm his wolf had rendered useless. Taranis had it pressed against his stomach, and he was shuddering. "Well, perhaps not. Should I leave you here, Vita, to keep him out of mischief?"

The wolf yipped and displayed her bloodstained teeth. "Very well," he said, stroking her head. "You will come with us."

Taranis dropped onto his side and closed his eyes.

Chapter 3

TIME PASSED. TARANIS SLOWLY REALIZED HIS BONES WERE NOT FRACTURED after all, but for the forearm Vita had snapped in her jaws. He clenched his hand, the one scalded by the knife. The blistering, pain, and swelling were subsiding.

It had all been some kind of trick to stop him from harming Cailean. The cursed bitch goddess had intervened, had made him believe he was injured when he wasn't.

He worked himself to his knees, took several breaths, and wobbled to his feet. For a while he remained bent, forced to wait out waves of dizziness. His mouth was painfully dry.

"They'll succeed," he said to the sand. "With the tunnels to aid them, there is no reason they would be caught. They will spirit Ula away and Bericus will never know what happened for the rest of his days."

He straightened carefully.

You will never see me again, Eamhair had promised. It was true. Other than the inability to leave Dunaedan, which he'd blamed on lethargy and grief, he'd not experienced any perception of her after the day her brothers threw her off the cliff. Wherever she had been, it was completely hidden from that preternatural obsession that had compelled him to journey to Dunaedan.

They would go through the tunnel to Uisge Bealach, steal one of the currachs, row it out to sea, and be gone forever.

As his mind cleared and his body grew more limber, he was haunted by his latest mistake. He hadn't used the time before Vita attacked to tell her how much he regretted what he'd done. He should have been on his knees begging forgiveness. Instead, he'd been accusatory and demanding. Now she would disappear and he would never have the chance. His lies...the rape. They would be all she ever remembered of him.

The pain of such thoughts almost sent him back to the ground. Desperately he turned his mind to Cailean, and stirred the fires of his rage.

Cailean, insulting him. Making threats. Mocking him. Anger seethed and he embraced it, for it obliterated guilt.

With each step he took, his fury intensified. *Spiriting her away where I can never find her. He has made her hate me, and if I don't do something, she will hate me for the rest of her life.*

Cailean didn't even know she was Aridela. Spineless, cursed mongrel. The fool didn't know what he had.

Christos! I have helped you. Now help me.

The need for vengeance sent him forward, at first wobbling like a drunk, but little by little, his strength returned. He picked up speed, breathing fast.

He has triumphed over me as he did on Crete, even after he was dead. She always kept him between us, a wall I could not scale.

He moved on instinct, with no more than a vague idea of confronting them in Ula's bedchamber. He would call Cailean's bluff and force him to slink away like a dog. He would beg Eamhair's forgiveness and lead both women to safety.

But they are armed, and there is that wolf.

He knew his plan was folly. But no matter. Something would come to him when he needed it. In the end, he vowed, it would be Cailean who screamed in agony.

Being Nemausus's lover was unpleasant, but even so, Viviana found it worthwhile. He had finally given in and allowed her to move into Eamhair's bedchamber, which was indescribably nicer than the thin straw pallet in a smoky chamber off the kitchens, crowded in with six others. A room to herself. Her own brazier. A bed—a real bed. He only did it for his own convenience, so she would be close by and not reeking of onions and smoke when he wanted her, but she didn't care about his motives. When he didn't want her, she slept beneath warm sheepskins on an actual bed, and imagined herself a lady.

He hadn't yet given permission for her to sit with him at the high table, which made her simmer with resentment. She was forced to continue serving as though nothing had changed. The other women laughed at her for it.

Earlier, at the evening meal, with all of Dunaedan's warriors and Fathna's watching, he'd ordered her to attend him, slapping her on the behind and eliciting derisive snorts from the men who heard. Now she was stuck in his bedchamber, listening to him snore after he'd used her.

She stared at the ceiling, tapping her fingertips together and plotting how to improve her circumstances. There had to be a way to make the sotted cur treat her with more respect.

His snore broke and he stretched. He sat up, yawning.

"Do you need something, my love?" she asked.

"Can you piss for me so I don't have to get up?" He had drunk himself into a stupor, and his breath turned her stomach.

"I would gladly do so if I could." She concocted a loving smile.

"Go get me something to eat. And more wine." With a grunt, he swung his legs over the side of the bed, rose, and blundered out, leaving the door swinging.

"Bastard," she said.

He was always ordering her to go and fetch things for him in the middle of the night. Did he not care that the hall was filled with Fathna's men, brutes who would rip her arms from their sockets as they all took turns raping her? No. Or he thought they wouldn't dare interfere with his plaything. But they would. They were animals, and had stolen all the power for themselves. If they wanted to rape Nemausus's woman, they would laugh in his face while they did it.

Though she hadn't seen it herself, she had heard about some of their atrocities. Bodies of women had been found, horribly torn and mutilated with bite marks, knife wounds, and bruises. What they'd suffered before they died...she could not think about it for long, not without unbearable terror.

She rose and threw a furred wrap over her nightshift—a garment she'd stolen from Eamhair's clothing chest before the maids took away her things. But she put nothing on her feet. She was so afraid of going past the hall by herself, she always went barefoot, no matter how cold it was. She went in darkness too, fearful that even a single candle flame might wake one of them.

It was freezing tonight—Nemausus would have to be satisfied with whatever she could find in the storeroom, for she would not go to the kitchens. It wasn't like he would thank her for her efforts no matter what she brought.

She tiptoed down the winding stairs, pausing at the bottom to peer into the hall. Nothing moved, not even a dog. The fires were low. She heard snoring, but nothing else. Taking a deep breath, she flitted across the exposed space and back into the welcoming shadows on the other side, where she paused to listen again. All remained still. Her confidence picked up as she padded along the corridor.

Once in the storeroom with the door closed behind her, she lit a candle so she could take stock of what had been left over from the earlier meal. There was a hunk of rye bread under a cloth, and some cheese. The mice hadn't even got to it yet. There was no wine, though. Maybe she could find some ale.

From the corner of her eye she glimpsed something looming. She pivoted, her heart pounding, her hand shaking so much she nearly dropped the candle.

But it was not a man. Part of the wall stood open, like a doorway. She stared, poised to flee if a demon or ghost or some other hideous creature appeared, but nothing happened. There was a chilly draught and the smell of earth, like a freshly dug grave. Shiver after shiver crawled across her neck.

Curiosity triumphed over fear; she reached out to touch the edge of the door. It responded by swinging smoothly, silently. Holding up the candle, she tried to see what lay beyond the portal but could make out no more than a landing and a few steps.

As long as she had lived at Dunaedan, this had been a solid stone wall. No one had ever mentioned a doorway. What lay beyond the candlelight? Had it always been here without anyone suspecting?

She wasn't about to enter that yawning breach. Just standing so close caused her heart to lurch.

Step by soundless step, she backed away, and eventually felt the surface of the door leading into the corridor against her spine. Blowing out the candle and leaving it on the floor, she felt for the latch, lifted it, and went out. It took several deep breaths to recover a semblance of calm before she could start back to the stairs.

She'd taken at least ten steps before she realized she'd forgotten the food. But she wouldn't go back. Not even knowing he would beat her for disobeying his orders. She might never enter that room again.

She came to the archway. Fathna's men were still asleep. Gathering up her shift, she flitted past the opening, her bare feet making no sound.

At the bottom of the stairs, as she placed one half-frozen foot on the first step, she looked up and nearly screamed. Right before her stood a man—more of a shadow really, but she knew from the shape what blocked her way. Her mouth opened but before she could do more than suck in a breath he had her smashed against the wall with the edge of a blade nicking below her chin.

For some time he did nothing but hold her still, leaving her to imagine what was about to happen. He pressed against her, preventing her from making a sound or struggling, even if she dared struggle with a knife pricking her throat.

If this was one of Fathna's men—and who else would it be—she could only hope he wouldn't wake his companions to take their turn upon her. One man she might be able to forget, in time.

No new sounds came from the hall. Apparently this swift, nearly silent confrontation had not awakened anyone.

He slid behind her, scraping the point of the knife down her body until it jabbed just below her ribs, and prodded her up the stairs to the first door—the chamber where Bericus conducted private meetings. The man opened the door and pushed her before shutting the door behind him. Light from a dying fire in the brazier outlined the table, chairs, and stools.

He had the knife at the nape of her neck before she finished stumbling. "I don't want to hurt you," he said, next to her ear. "I am not here to hurt you. Will you be quiet?"

At her nod, he removed the knife. She turned to face him and backed away until she felt a chair against her legs. "Sit," he said, and she did.

He pushed one of the candles on the table towards her. "Light it."

She carried it to the brazier and lit it in the embers. When she brought it back, the first thing the light showed her was that he was injured. His left arm was pressed against his stomach and crusted with blood. Perhaps if she struck him there she could get away.

Her gaze lifted to his face and awareness dawned. This was not one of Fathna's men after all. It was Taranis, the monk Drost Gocinecht wanted so badly. Taranis was the reason Fathna of Innse Orc was here at all—it was his fault they'd been crushed and now lived in fear for their lives—those who were still alive.

He had discarded his religious robes for the clothing of a normal man—trousers, boots, and a belted wool tunic that had a bloody slice down the middle as well as the rips and blood on his sleeve. So...two injuries at least.

She kept her mouth shut. If he realized that she knew who he was, he might want to be certain she could never speak of it.

"Where were you just now?" he asked.

"With a lover. Please don't tell Nemausus. He will kill me."

"Or I could kill you. I can see you know who I am."

She dropped her gaze and sucked in a frightened breath. "I-I am a servant. I have no grudge against you. I will say nothing, I give you my vow."

"I want you to say something."

"W-what?" She met his gaze, which was, she realized, striking. The candlelight illuminated the green of his eyes and played over his wide shoulders. But for his lank hair and dirty fingernails, this man would be handsome.

"I want you to go to Bericus, my lady," he said, bowing. "He will reward you for the information I carry."

She liked being called "lady." She liked being bowed to. She nodded to show she was willing to listen.

"His baron has returned. He is here right now, in Lady Ula's chamber—or was, not long ago. That is not all. Bericus's daughter is with him. Yes—she is alive. They have come to spirit Ula away. Their plan is to flee to Uisge Bealach and steal one of the boats. They mean to sail off and disappear. You must go now, before any more time passes —or they will succeed." He stepped back, giving her room to stand. "Fly, my lady—Viviana—before it is too late."

How in the name of the Christos did he know who she was? "Is this really true?" she asked as she rose.

"I vow it. Lady, I beg you not to tell them of me. They will ask no questions before killing me, and I swear I did not do what I have been accused of."

"I won't."

He stood to the side, leaving an open path to the door. She could hardly believe it—she had been certain she was going to be raped at least, possibly killed. But instead she had been given the kind of information that would rid them of Fathna and his despicable men. Taranis was right—Bericus would reward her most generously if this all turned out to be true.

She'd never had any use for priests or monks, but Taranis the man was a different matter. "Do you need help getting safely away? Perhaps I can help you."

He hesitated before bowing again. "I am most grateful," he said, "but I know a way out."

He left the chamber with her and they parted on the stairs, her going up and him going down—she had no doubt he was headed for the storeroom and that opening. He'd probably been hiding behind that wall ever since he escaped from the pit just over two months ago, and had been right under their noses this entire time.

"Hurry, mistress," he said, "or it will be too late." He vanished in the gloom.

VIVIANA WAITED, LISTENING, BUT HEARD NOTHING OTHER THAN SNORES from the hall. Breathing a sigh of relief, she ascended the stone stairway, passing Nemausus's door. The chamber above it was Ula's. She put her ear to the wood. There was shuffling and a woman's soft sobs. Was that whispering?

"A tunnel?" she heard. "To Uisge Bealach? How can that be?"

"It is true. Come, Mother. Collect your things."

Eamhair! The chit hadn't been gone so long Viviana would forget her voice. *Taranis spoke the truth and Nemausus and Ossian lied. They said they killed her.*

There was more low conversation. At first she didn't recognize the deeper voice, then she did. It was Cailean of Dalriada, Dunaedan's intriguing baron. "You have no need of extra clothing, lady," he said. "Come, we have a long way to go, and the tide will be turning against us."

Viviana heard a few more muffled sounds but soon there was only silence. Carefully, she lifted the latch and opened the portal just in time to see another hidden doorway in the wall close, leaving no sign of its existence.

Glancing about to make certain she was alone, she stepped into the room. The lid to the clothes chest was flung open. Several tunics were spilled onto the floor. She crossed to the wall and placed her hands on it. The stones were cold. Nothing moved as she pushed and prodded.

She brought a candle to inspect it more closely. There, and there, and there—cracks in the mortar. Or were they seams?

What was the trick to open it? Taranis obviously knew. So did Cailean or Eamhair. How many of these disguised doors were there?

Viviana studied the wall. Nothing, *nothing*, suggested an entry.

Taranis was right—she had to hurry. She left Ula's chamber and headed down the stairs.

Finally, she would win Nemausus's gratitude. He would stop hurting her. She would sit at the high table, and more. He might give her silver, and ribbons, and fine tunics. He might even make her his wife. She could be the true lady of Dunaedan, with both Ula and Eamhair gone.

Her steps slowed. Bericus could reward her far more abundantly than his son, and he would want to know what mischief his wife was up to.

Nemausus was a beast. She felt hardly any incentive to help him, especially as she wasn't at all certain she would get anything out of it.

An idea struck. Fathna was a *king*, and he was furious over the events that had robbed him of his new wife and the criminal his brother wanted. He had promised to lay waste to Dunaedan, and had done much damage since he brought his holocaust of fire a fortnight ago.

He was the one to tell.

Taranis left the tunnel the same way he'd entered—at the mooring place above the burned boats, where Cailean and Eamhair had broken through.

The woman on the stairs had given him the perfect solution. With her help, all would unravel exactly as he wished, and Eamhair would never suspect he'd played any part in the betrayal.

He stole a pony from one of the barns in the village and prodded it across the moor as fast as it could gallop.

Cailean and Eamhair would not make good time through that long tunnel with Ula. The old woman would have to rest.

It would also take time for Viviana to wake Bericus, to explain what Cailean was doing, and maybe longer for him to believe her. They would then wake Fathna and the explanations would commence again. More time would be required to rouse the warriors, and most of them would be sleeping off drunkenness from the previous night. It might be sunrise before they were armed and the horses saddled—and there weren't as many horses as there were men. Most would have to march on foot.

Of course Bericus might believe Viviana immediately, and manage to capture the three before they left Ula's bedchamber. But it was a small concern. Cailean would hurry Ula along. No doubt they had already vanished into the tunnels by the time he and Viviana parted ways on the stairs.

He laughed.

When he reached Uisge Bealach, he would sink all the currachs but two. One he would take to the other side, leaving only one for Cailean and the women. Those small boats could not hold three people—and a wolf. He knew what would happen. Cailean and Vita would remain behind. Cailean would send Eamhair and Ula across. He would probably try to go on foot around the southern end of the inlet and meet them on the other side, but that would be difficult, as the west side of Uisge Bealach was a tangle of trees and brush, of promontories, drifting sand and encroaching seawater. Skirting all that would cost him. Like as not, Cailean would be caught and slaughtered.

Meanwhile, Taranis would already be on the far side, ready for Eamhair and Ula to drift into his arms. Without their champion, they would not be so quick to reject his help. All they had to do was evade Bericus's men for one day. When night fell he would take both women into the tunnels and there they would remain, safely hidden, until the search was abandoned.

When that day came, he would escort them to a new life of freedom.

If things did not go smoothly—if Eamhair and Ula were captured and returned to Dunaedan, he would enter Eamhair's bedchamber from the tunnel and again offer his help. She would surely accept, for her mother's sake if not her own. Together, they would rescue Ula. The end result would be the same—they would wait in the tunnels until Bericus gave up.

In time, Eamhair would forget Cailean—in time, after he enthralled her with the best stories from Crete, after he found more of Eseld's mushroom. Winoc—*Alexiare*—be damned. If Eamhair could remember the past, he knew she would love him again. She would forgive him. But most of all, she would understand why he'd forced himself on her.

She would no longer view it as an unwanted assault, but the headstrong passion of the man who still loved her after two millennia.

Fathna might even prove useful. Eamhair hated him for some reason. She hated him so much she had chosen death over marriage to him. If they were captured and Fathna of Innse Orc still wanted her, she might be much more willing to go with Taranis. He would truly be her savior.

What a stroke of luck, running into Viviana on the stairs.

It wasn't until he'd galloped down the slope to the inlet, shining like a silver ribbon beneath a burgeoning dawn, that he remembered the obsidian knife. He cursed roundly. Perhaps it was for the best—he did not want to relive the agony it had wreaked. But the idea of it being lost forever, or of some crofter or fisherman stumbling upon it was intolerable.

He dismounted, letting the exhausted pony stagger away.

Perhaps he could recover the knife later, if all went well.

The currachs were not easy to destroy, especially with one arm. But eventually, using the knife he'd taken from Dunaedan and one of the oars, he successfully staved holes in them. One by one, they sank.

Wiping sweat from his forehead with the back of his good arm, he dared close his eyes and rest.

There was no sound but the softest wash of water. Even the birds were still sleeping. He finally had time to catch his breath and think.

Eamhair had flaunted the obsidian knife without difficulty until she threatened him with it. Only then did it burn her.

He inspected the crusted blisters on his own palm. They were more like half-healed calluses now, rather than new wounds. The knife hadn't scalded him right away either. Not until he leaped at Cailean. The physical sensation of breaking bones had seemed so real. By Christ's sacred blood, it would be a long time before he forgot that. He had been so enraged, so intent on killing his half brother, nothing less than that would have stopped him.

He pondered. *Only when I attempted to kill Cailean. And Eamhair was only burned when she attempted to cut me.*

The eastern horizon lightened to the coral blush of a seashell. He rose, taking a deep breath. He must go.

It wouldn't be long now.

Chapter 4

"No!"

Meraud woke with a violent jerk, her cry ringing through the bedchamber. She was covered in clammy sweat and her heart stuttered so badly it frightened her; she pressed her hand to her chest, trying to slow it down.

A dead woman—someone she loved. She saw herself weeping bitterly as she washed the body and garbed it in a gold-encrusted gown. There was a red birthmark on the wrist, shaped like a bull's head, but the woman wasn't Eamhair. Her hair was black.

The woman had been murdered, but everyone believed it a tragic accident.

It was the murderer's face that brought her out of the dream, nearly screaming.

Never, in all her long life, had she heard the name *Chrysaleon*. Yet as she tried to speak it, it felt familiar to her tongue. And those eyes—as familiar as her own hand.

Betrayal cannot birth from nothing. It weaves backward and forward, into and out of the thread of life and death, of faith and love, of envy and desire.

For the first time in many years, Meraud wept. She rose from her bed sobbing, and struggled to light a candle. Then she went along the corridor to collect Rhalanse.

VIVIANA FEARED FATHNA WOULD PUNCH HER AS SHE TRIED TO EXPLAIN about the wall openings. The way his jaw clenched and his lips tightened suggested he might.

She saw Jocosa cowering in the bed behind them, and knew she'd interrupted something—something Jocosa's tear-streaked, bloody face made clear was not to her liking.

But when she said that Eamhair was alive and in the fortress, his expression changed. He ordered Jocosa out—she jumped from the bed and slipped past the king and Viviana, pressing herself to the doorjamb as though touching either of them might poison her.

They will all be more respectful soon, Viviana told herself.

"Show me," Fathna said, "and I hope for your sake you weren't dreaming."

She led the way to Ula's bedchamber. He examined the wall. He pushed. He tried to pry the tips of his fingers underneath the stones, but nothing happened. It remained firm and unmoving.

He roared for Bericus. Viviana went off quickly and soon brought the chieftain, disheveled and rubbing sleep from his eyes. Nemausus and Ossian came too, crowding in behind their father. Nemausus scowled at Viviana and she began to doubt whether she'd made a wise choice.

"This mangy female of yours claims there is a passageway behind the wall. Is it true? If so, how do you get into it?"

Bericus blinked. "I-I know nothing of any passageways." He turned a half-bleary, half-furious gaze on Viviana. "What have you been telling Lord Fathna, wench?"

"A man came to me." Viviana curtsied, only slightly regretful about breaking her word. It was either Taranis or her. "He told me all I have told you. Before I disturbed you, Lord Fathna, I listened outside Lady Ula's chamber. I heard Eamhair speak. I saw the opening in the wall. I also saw the way the man got into Dunaedan—there is another door in the storeroom behind the hall."

"Man? What man?" Bericus peered at her, blinking, red-faced.

"The one who escaped two months ago. The one Drost Gocinecht wants."

Fathna's gaze upon her was now as sharp as a knife blade. "The monk?"

"Aye, lord." Sweat ran down the back of her neck. "Taranis."

"Where did he go? Where is he now?"

She didn't answer quickly enough to suit him. He clamped her upper arm so tightly she almost screamed. "I don't know! But I'm sure he was going back to the storeroom. Maybe that door is still open."

He and Bericus squinted at her. Her skin went from hot to cold and hot again as she awaited her fate.

"I do remember hearing rumors of hidden tunnels when I was a boy," Bericus said, "but I have never seen anything that would make me believe they are real."

"There are those old scrolls," said Ossian. "The plans for the tower, with the other archives."

"Get them," Bericus said. "And check the storeroom." Ossian bowed and left.

Bericus went up to the wall and examined it for himself. He and Fathna pulled, pushed, and prodded. Bericus stood back, shaking his head, and sent Viviana a look that promised retribution.

Ossian came back, his hands stained with yellow dust. He said the plans had crumbled away when he unrolled them, and there was nothing different about the storeroom.

Fathna, with an angry growl, struck the wall with his fist, and before their eyes, it clicked and swung open.

Viviana stared, half disbelieving. The others seemed equally stunned. After a moment Fathna stepped into the darkness. "There are stairs. I cannot see where they lead. Someone light my way."

Viviana scrambled to hand him a candle. He took it and climbed down the steps, Bericus right behind him.

When they returned they studied how the thing worked. Bericus started bragging about Aedan, the engineer of Dunaedan.

Fathna interrupted him. "You are wasting time. Your slippery little daughter is getting away with your wife. Call your men!" He turned to Viviana. "They are going to Uisge Bealach? The inlet?"

"Yes, lord. Taranis said so, and I overheard Ula say it as well."

"This doorway must lead to Uisge Bealach somehow," Nemausus said.

Fathna leveled a baleful glower at Bericus. "I will take my men on horseback to Uisge Bealach. You and your men follow through here in case they double back. They cannot be allowed to escape. If they do—" His eyes narrowed—"you will suffer for it. My brother will raze every stone and timber of this place as though it never existed if you make things harder than you already have."

Viviana fought back a smile at the fear that blossomed across Bericus's face.

Dunaedan's cowering chief bowed. "Ossian, wake the men—the villagers too. All who live under my standard will bear witness to what happens to a traitor, even if she is my own offspring."

HOLDING THE LAMP HIGH, CAILEAN LED HIS CHARGES PAST THE FIRST IRON handle they came to. Someone had already released the rubble on one side. Taranis, probably. Cailean didn't pull the other handle. There was no need. No one had seen them except Ula. These tunnels were ingenious.

Nevertheless, he pushed them along at a fast pace—as fast as Ula could go. The sooner they were away from the Dominion of the Seventh Age, the better.

Ula was already breathing hard, but she had questions and did not seem inclined to wait for answers. "Where are we going? Where have you been? How did you escape your brothers that day?"

Eamhair held her mother's arm to give her aid. "We're going to Cailean's island. I didn't escape them. They threw me from the cliffs, Mother. Cailean saved my life."

Ula's steps slowed. Breathing heavily, she frowned, first at Eamhair, then Cailean. "How—how did you survive?"

Cailean urged them on. "There will be time for this later."

But now Ula stopped. Her hand lifted to her throat.

"Lady Ula, we must go." Cailean tried to see through the gloom stretching before them. He was not at all sure Taranis wasn't playing another trick. The tunnel might simply end for instance, trapping them. He would not breathe freely until they were on the boat, surrounded in Inis Tearmann's sky ribbons. "What was that?" He strained his ears to hear over Ula's gasping.

Voices. Echoing footfalls.

Vita growled and started forward until Cailean ordered her to stay.

"We have been discovered." His teeth grated. How else but Taranis? He had betrayed them. "Hurry. Hurry."

They ran, and soon came to the second set of handles. Instructing the women to get safely beyond, he pulled down on them both. The portals opened with shrieking rusty protest, releasing an avalanche of rocks and rubble. Clouds of dust filled the already stuffy air. More and more and more poured out of the walls. The tunnel was soon blocked from floor to ceiling.

"This is good," Cailean said. "It won't be easy to dig through that. Come along, *el caelwyn*."

But even as Ula waved at the dust and coughed, she clutched Cailean's arm. "You...you are the dream. You, Cailean of Dalriada. You are the king sent to protect my Eamhair."

"What is she talking about?" Cailean glanced at Eamhair, uneasy. She, too, was staring.

"Nay, Mother," she said slowly. "The seolh-king already came, but he was not the savior you envisioned. When I most needed his help, he abandoned me."

"Eamhair, don't be thick-headed. Cailean is the king I dreamed of. Do you think I could forget? From the first time I saw him I knew there was something...and now it is clear. Look at his eyes, blue upon blue. Like bilberries and seaweed. I see it all around him. I can *taste* the blue."

After a long pause, Eamhair said, "He—came in a small white boat, from Inis Tearmann. He came from the sea."

Cailean wanted to be kind, and struggled to control his impatience. "Lady Ula, the sun will be rising by now. There may be fishermen already at Uisge Bealach. Whatever it is—whatever you see, can be discussed later."

Ula went on scrutinizing him as if he hadn't said a word. "He saved you when your need was desperate, did he not?"

"You said he would be a seolh."

Ula waved a dismissive hand. "I didn't see that. I just thought it made the most sense. Do you *know* he is not one?"

"Yes. My Cailean is a ferocious warrior. He is the Blue Falcon, son of Artorius the Bear. He is my husband, and the prince of Inis Tear-mainn. He is a kira, one of the rare and holy poet sons. He is many things, Mother, but a seolh is not one of them. If you had not told me that part, I might have seen this long ago. I might have...done things differently."

It was not only her words but also the tone of sadness that brought back the memory of their first night at Gilraidha Soi. Eamhair had told him of her mother's promise that a king would come out of the sea—a seolh-king—a being who would protect and save her. The being she had placed her faith in and who rewarded that faith with lies and rape.

He drew her into the shelter of his arm and she rested her cheek on his shoulder.

"I was only trying to bolster you," Ula said. "You were a frightened little girl."

"Please," Cailean said. "If we continue to stand here, they will dig through and find us."

Vita growled and paced as though agreeing.

"Come, Eamhair," Ula said. "Your sea-king wants us to run. So let us run!"

Not long after, they were all relieved to see a suggestion of light ahead.

Vita, who had been loping easily alongside Cailean, now pricked her ears; she stood perfectly still then peered up at Cailean.

"What is it?" he asked. "Do you hear something?"

She yipped.

Cailean stroked her neck. "Go on. Find it, whatever it is. Keep Eamhair safe."

She licked his hand and took off, vanishing almost instantly.

Cailean put his arm around Eamhair and kissed her. "Not much farther, donnah." He turned back to Ula. "Can you make it, lady?"

"For you I can," she said with a smile.

Chapter 5

PAIN RADIATED FROM EAMHAIR'S ANKLE. IT WAS SHARP ENOUGH THAT SHE was forced to limp, and she failed to hide it from Cailean.

He slowed, staring at her foot. "Something's wrong."

"That rock Taranis threw. It hit me in the ankle—the same one that broke when my brothers threw me off the cliffs."

He stopped her and cupped his hand around it. "It's swollen." He cursed. "And it's bleeding. Damn him!"

"I can run." To prove it, she set off, but almost immediately stumbled in a divot that turned the ankle; pain shot up her leg and she fell. Cailean gave the lamp to Ula and swept Eamhair into his arms, ignoring protests.

She held onto his neck as he ran on. "I will tire you."

"You weigh hardly anything," he said. "Look, here we are."

Before them lay the small round opening. One by one they crawled out and forged through the thicket into a pastel dawn. Taranis had predicted truly. Puffy clouds hugged the eastern horizon and the unruly water flashed white and silver. Eamhair's confidence soared.

"Cailean, I think I know how you feel when you go to your father. This is an adventure like I never thought I could have. We *will* triumph, I know it. I cannot wait to go home and tell our son stories of how we rescued his grandmother."

He smiled and kissed her cheek. "I'm going to see to it that you have more adventures. No more tedium for you, my warrior lady."

Ula threw down the lamp as she emerged from the thorns and brush and stepped onto a strip of wet sand. Breathing hard, she followed as Cailean carried Eamhair to the edge, where water lapped against the shore.

"This must be the cliff Taranis warned us about. Can you make it?"

"I think so."

Holding her arm, he stepped onto the shelf of sand beneath the water and they inched around the jutting pinnacle. Once she stood on dry land on the other side, he returned to help Ula.

"The monk who is not a monk is apparently honest sometimes," Cailean said as he assisted Ula out of the water.

Eamhair didn't answer. She had just spotted Vita. The wolf was half-crouched, the thick fur on her neck bristling, her teeth bared. She was holding a man at bay—a man Eamhair had believed she would never see again.

Taranis brandished a knife in his good hand and an oar lay on the ground beside him, but wisely, he'd taken a defensive stance. He turned as they approached.

"Who is that?" Ula asked.

Eamhair didn't know what to say, and so settled on, "A liar."

The glance Taranis sent Cailean was venomous. Clearly jealous. Eamhair's earlier elation plummeted. He was here to cause trouble, and they had no more time for trouble.

Vita's ears went down and she pressed against Cailean's legs, growling. "Is this what you heard?" he asked the wolf. "And you let him live?"

She whined.

"What are you doing here?" Eamhair asked bluntly.

"If I am never to see you again, I had to at least say farewell." Taranis took a step towards Eamhair but stopped when Vita snarled and snapped at him. He carefully placed his knife on the sand. "I had to see you once more," he said, straightening. He took another step and this time, Vita allowed it. "Eamhair—I am to blame for all that has happened. If only we could go backward and rework our mistakes."

"If only we could do that," Cailean said. "Each day would be sunny. Rivers would flow with ale. There would always be ripened fruit upon the vine, ready to pluck."

Taranis scowled but would not be distracted. "Do you remember the stories I told you of my queen? How she fought alongside me, how she saved my life? Eamhair, she was you. She used that very blade—

314

the black one—to kill the man who tried to kill me. You were Aridela, Queen of Kaphtor, and I was your consort. You said you wanted to help me find her. You are her!" He reached for her hand but she quickly put them both behind her back. "That is why I did what I did on the beach! I was taken over by what we shared so long ago. In those days, you welcomed me as husband and lover—as the man prophesied to be at your side. Our love was rare. Extraordinary. I have loved you —only you—for centuries—and will, for as long as the pyramids stand in Egypt."

Eamhair was speechless, certain he was a madman and wondering how to be rid of him, until that last line.

He saw her reaction and his face lit. "You remember. I made you that promise. It's still there, in your heart from long ago, from another life. You have loved me since the earth was new, even if right now you have forgotten—if vengeful gods have stolen the memories from you."

"No. No." She shook her head forcefully. But there was some-thing...like a half-forgotten dream. Clay lamps. A cave. A bull and a lion dropping from a ledge and stalking towards her.

No man will have you but me. Only me. For as long as the pyramids stand in Egypt.

Eamhair pulled herself out of that murky place, though she couldn't stop an uneasy shiver.

Cailean shoved between them, severing what had felt like pure hot lightning from Taranis's eyes to hers. Taranis stumbled as though he'd forgotten Cailean was there.

A violent jumble of fists, of cursing, of grappling and twisting, of elbows and strikes and spattering blood ensued. Cailean shouted, "Let's see how you deal with *me*," and Taranis, his head thrust back-ward by a punch to the cheekbone, gruffly returned, "You don't understand."

"Nor do I wish to understand the excuses of a rapist," Cailean said, just before Taranis caught him in the jaw with his own fist.

Eamhair swallowed, feeling sick. Taranis had brute strength, even with a broken arm. Cailean was experienced in all methods of fighting. She felt as though she had witnessed this scene before...somewhere.

But it no longer mattered, for a wave appeared on the summit of the slope to the west. A wave pouring over the lip like a cloud of mayflies.

"Look!" she cried.

The two men parted, swiping at the blood each had drawn, and looked to the west. Cailean turned to her and held out his hand.

As she took it, she said, "We are going. You should go too. Quickly. Before they see you. Forget about me, Taranis, and put your lies behind you."

Taranis stared from the horizon to her. He bent and retrieved his knife as Cailean plucked her off the ground and set her on her feet inside the nearest boat. He did the same with Ula before turning on Taranis so abruptly that Taranis stepped back. "We were followed. Our plan was discovered—as was the tunnel you swore was a secret. How did that happen?"

Eamhair watched him closely. Was that a flash of guilt? It was so swiftly subsumed into shock or anger she wasn't certain. Shaking his head, he stated, "I told no one of the tunnel. I would never reveal that secret."

"You revealed it to us," Cailean said tightly. "You sent us in there, then you sent the rest of them after us, didn't you, knowing we might be finished off like rats."

"No. You cannot believe that," Taranis said to Eamhair. "You cannot. It's not true."

"What are you doing?" Eamhair asked as Cailean moved away from the boat. He retrieved the oar and gave it to her.

"Row to the Point and light the beacon fire. The boatmen will come for you. I will hold off your father and brothers."

"I will not go without you."

"Eamhair, you promised you would obey me."

Taranis came closer. "Go, Eamhair. Think of your mother." His eyes glistened. Bowing his head, he muttered, "I have harmed you before. I cannot seem to stop harming you, *anwyl*, though you are the only woman I have ever loved."

She couldn't deny a frustrating instant of pity. Though he was now able to stand and walk, he must still be suffering terrible pain from the events at the other beach. Yet, even with such injuries, he was here. The chance of being captured and given to the merciless Fathna increased with every breath yet he remained, as if nothing mattered but her condemnation or her mercy.

His voice exerted its power. That mesmerizing, husky cadence sent an inexplicable spark over her skin even now.

There was good in him. Wasn't there? Or did she only wish for that to be true?

"The first time I saw your eyes," he said, "I knew you. I *knew* you, and my fate was fixed. All I have done has been in servitude to you. You are my destiny, Eamhair."

Anger flared; she glanced at Cailean and saw that he, too, was angry. How dare Taranis try to weave himself into her shared fate with Cailean, as if he were part of it as much as they? How dare he imply that trickery, lies, and rape were nothing more than helpless servitude, or forced by love?

How dare he claim to love her? Everything he had done proved otherwise.

Let him suffer guilt for the rest of his days. She remembered the fear and pain of that night on the beach. Yes, she had a son, a beautiful son, and she loved him. But loving him did not excuse how he had been conceived.

"That is unfortunate," she said, hardly recognizing her own voice. "But you alone have caused your misery, and you alone will have to endure it."

He looked up, his expression so anguished that she added more gently, "Go, Taranis. See them coming? In another moment it will be too late."

Then she turned to Cailean and instantly forgot him.

"My brave wife," he said softly. "Think of our son, before you throw your fate in with mine."

She hesitated. It was almost enough to convince her. But not quite. "What would life be without you? A bleak, barren, lonely place."

He had no time to reply, for Fathna and his mounted men galloped down the sloping turf in a thunder of hooves and whooping shouts.

EAMHAIR HELD ULA AS THE HORSES SPREAD OUT, BLOCKING THE BEACH and leaving only one path to freedom—Uisge Bealach. She looked them over; there were fifteen men besides Fathna, mostly armed with axes. She saw no bows or spears, and only a few swords. Clearly these warriors had been hastily roused and sent here. Some probably didn't even know why. Those that did must have thought three fugitives, two of them women, were not much of a threat. Not many had even bothered to don armor or helmets. It was a small blessing. They would last longer, but the sheer numbers facing them promised eventual defeat.

There was no one she knew in this throng. They were all Fathna's men from Innse Orc.

Cailean made a low hissing sound. Eamhair followed his gaze, realizing that Fathna, the bastard, was riding Cailean's beloved warhorse. Tall Bharosa, easy to pick out among Dunaedan's sturdy ponies, was snorting, half-rearing, jerking against the reins as Fathna cursed and yanked so hard the stallion's mouth was bloody.

Fathna raised a gauntleted hand and barked an order. His men stood back, lowering their weapons.

Eamhair heard faint shouting. Her hopes, slight as they were, sank. The tunnel pursuers had dug through the blockade. And now the men following the horses on foot were descending from the western slope.

Cailean turned his back to the enemy and pushed at the boat. He meant to force it into the water.

She shoved the wide end of the oar into the sand to anchor it.

"Eamhair!" He faced her and she was nearly undone by the doom in his eyes.

"I will not leave you," she said.

He drew in a shaky breath. Then he drew his sword from the scabbard at his hip, and a snarling Vita took her place against his right leg.

All too soon Bericus and his men discovered where their prey had gone. He, Nemausus, and the hastily assembled warriors of Dunaedan splashed through the water and crowded onto the beach with Fathna's men. None of them wore armor—not even boiled leather. There was no armor at Dunaedan since Drost Gocinecht had conquered them. He didn't allow it.

She had no armor either but for her hardened leather vest, but she was armed, and apparently the only one—*thank the Infinite Lady*—with a bow and quiver of arrows. She shoved Ula behind her, slid the bow from her back, and nocked an arrow.

Fathna, she noticed as she lifted the bow, remained at the rear, behind his men. Even so, he positioned a shield in front of his chest as he glared at her.

Cailean shifted so that he stood between their attackers and Eamhair. Taranis hesitated then took up a defiant stance beside him. With only a knife and one good arm, he would not be much help, but it appeared he meant to try, and was throwing his lot in with theirs.

Even more people appeared—village men armed with sickles, scythes, gaffs, cudgels, and pitchforks, followed by the women and a crowd of boys who could barely contain their excitement. Finally, her brother Ossian and the serving woman, Viviana, waded around the crag and onto the beach. Viviana's cheeks were flushed, her eyes bright. She was brazenly wearing one of Eamhair's tunics and... Cailean's rowanberry bracelet.

Safely positioned in the midst of his men, Bericus shouted, "Put my wife out of that boat—I want her to come to me, now!"

"I will die here with my daughter rather than spend one more night at Dunaedan!" Ula screamed.

"It will be my pleasure to grant that wish, you slut," he said before turning towards Eamhair. "I thought you were dead. My sons lied to me." He cuffed Nemausus in the face, knocking him off balance.

To Fathna, he shouted, "I did not lie to you, lord. I believed her dead. But here she is, alive after all. Punish her as you wish for her defiance. Brand her on the forehead. Kill her and grind her corpse into the sand—I care not. Give her to your men. That is what I would do."

He laughed at Eamhair, making her realize she had allowed her horror and hatred to show. She quickly controlled her expression.

Nemausus straightened, rubbing his cheek. "We did throw her over the cliff," he said plaintively. "How *could* she be alive? Cailean did this somehow, Father. He is the one who betrayed you."

Finally, Fathna spoke. "Perhaps a deity softened the fall."

Cailean made an impatient gesture. "The tide is rising. Come and take her if you think you can."

Eamhair's growing resolve solidified. This was what she had seen on the cliffs after her forced marriage to Fathna. A crowd of warriors, weapons flashing. She knew how it would end—how it was meant to end.

She met Ula's calm gaze.

"All I ask for is Bericus," Ula said.

"I understand."

"I am happy, Eamhair. Soon we will be together again, in that magical place where the faithful go when they leave this miserable world. Know that I have loved being your mother."

"And you put joy into my life every day."

Eamhair unnocked her arrow. She gave her knife to Ula and placed a restraining hand on Cailean's shoulder as her mother stepped out of the boat.

Ula pointed to three crows drifting in a circle above the tableau. "The Morrigan and her sisters are witness to what happens here," she announced into the silence.

She walked towards Bericus's warriors. One by one, they parted for her.

"You will not face these men alone," Eamhair said next to Cailean's ear while everyone was transfixed by Ula.

He didn't turn, but his shoulder tensed. Eamhair climbed over the side of the boat and took her place at his elbow.

"The babe will be safe and loved on Inis Tearmann with your mother and sister." She prepared an arrow, speaking quietly so Taranis wouldn't hear. "Let us give him a story that will make him proud. My heart and my life are woven through yours, Cailean. I will not slink away like a coward, leaving you to defend me." She breathed deeply of the clean morning air and wondered, for an instant, how many more breaths she had. "Something is wrong with this time and place. Let us leave it together. Let us be done with it, together."

There was no response other than that tilt of the head for a few heartbeats. "Fathna's men will have no honor," he said. "They'll try to trick you—blind you with sunlight, or throw sand in your face, or attack you three to one. Keep your balance. Don't let them distract you. You have a score of arrows—no more. Breathe."

She flexed her hand then tightened her grip on the bow. "I will remember."

He faced her at last. "I see Vita in you. You have the same heart. The same spirit. The first time I saw you, I saw a wolf who longed to be free."

She returned his gaze, memorizing the irrepressible stubble bristling across his cheeks, the white scar and gleaming blue eyes. "Soon I will be with my mother, and soon after that, you will join me. This adventure has unfolded in a way I may not have expected, but I am happy to die in your company, Falcon Blue." She had to swallow hard before she could add, "Death had a taste of me at the bottom of the cliff. It has sought me, like a wolf on the scent, ever since. No living being has ever defeated that particular adversary, but for a little while, I did." She smiled. "Because of you."

He clasped her head between his hands, and for all the prickly harshness of his face his mouth was incredibly soft. "Not this, nor anything else can separate us," he whispered. He looked into her eyes —his as violet as the most delicate wildflower on the moor—before he returned his attention to their enemies and his eyes flamed deadly blue.

Everything else receded into insignificance as he transformed before her eyes, becoming as keen and hard as a stone carving. His body was perfectly motionless, yet the space around him almost vibrated, and the sword in his right hand, gently wafting to and fro, promised swift, bloody death to whoever was willing to test his resolve. No one from Dunaedan was willing. They knew from living with him how this quiet, contemplative man could turn violent in an instant, lethal without remorse. But this was a new Cailean for Eamhair. This was the Blue Falcon. He held his sword—Ravange—almost carelessly, but his eyes were as much a cold-blooded predator's as Vita's.

Eamhair, I am a killer. She had dismissed that statement. Now her breath hitched as she saw the truth, and she was glad she was not his enemy.

Without even glancing at her, he said, "I have never told you I love you. I have never said the words."

His voice broke through her hypnotized fascination and brought her back to the moment. She turned her head and watched her mother as she stepped through the crowd of warriors. "And yet," she said, "I know you do. I did not need the words."

Bran caught Ula's arm as she passed, and murmured something. Ula patted his hand. "You are a good man, and you have my blessings." She removed his hand from her arm and continued on until she reached Bericus, who jerked her off balance and slapped her, full force.

She nearly fell, but recovered. Head high, she stood next to her husband, blood running from her lip. Everyone, even Fathna and his men, stared at her as though spellbound.

Ula met Eamhair's gaze and nodded. Then she brought out the knife and sank it into Bericus's throat.

Blood spurted. His hands rose. He fell, choking and gurgling.

Nemausus tugged his sword from its sheath with a roar and ran his mother through.

There was a suspended interlude of dumbfounded silence.

Nemausus screamed, "Kill them!" as he pulled his blade from Ula's body. But before he could take a step he slumped to the ground, Eamhair's arrow lodged in his eye.

Chapter 6

TARANIS GLANCED AT EAMHAIR IN THE CONFUSION AFTER NEMAUSUS screamed his order and died. Tears ran over her cheeks; her skin was pale, her mouth grim, but she had another arrow ready.

Love and pride surged through him. He'd told himself he came here to see Cailean defeated, but now he realized another motive had wormed in underneath—one he'd refused to acknowledge. He wanted to fight for her. Die, if necessary, for her. To truly earn her forgiveness. The wolf, in preventing him from taking one of the currachs and leaving, had made it possible. If he had really only cared about saving himself, he never would have come to this beach at all.

Yet it was also true that if he had not interfered, she and Ula would have escaped. Their disappearance would have been a mystery for all time. It was due to his duplicity that she was now forced to fight an overwhelming number of trained men. He had brought this end upon her.

Of the three, he was by far the weakest. Any attempt to move his broken arm caused incredible pain; his only weapon was a knife, and his woolen tunic would stop no blade. Moreover, in this life, he had never wielded a sword or trained as a fighter. The most he had ever experienced were a few drunken brawls. He'd been an accomplished warrior for Mycenae, but though his mind remembered, his body was out of practice.

He tucked the knife into his belt for later when the fighting came close and hefted the oar Eamhair had dropped. Using all the power in his good shoulder and arm, he successfully battered two men to the ground in the first wave of attack. Still, he knew he wouldn't last long.

As he knocked away one warrior's sword, he felt another blade come up, aiming for the vulnerable area beneath his ribs; a hiss whined past his ear as he twisted just in time to see the opponent flail and fall, one of Eamhair's arrows lodged in his back.

It feels as if we are on that beach at Amnisos again, fighting Harpalycus. When did she learn to use that bow? How is she even alive?

It was a puzzle he didn't have time to explore. He dropped the oar and armed himself with the fallen warrior's sword.

The wolf brought down man after man. She moved like a gust of wind; no blade could touch her. Her jaw, muzzle, and chest were matted with blood as she ripped out body parts from those who didn't see her coming or could not stop her.

"If we can kill Fathna, we might still walk away from this," he heard Eamhair say. "Ossian is a coward. He will flee if Fathna is gone."

But those two kept themselves at the back, behind layers of armed men.

Taranis and Cailean spread out, giving Eamhair room to nock, aim, and loose her lethal arrows. Every so often she darted under the guard of her companions and recovered arrows from the fallen.

Most of Bericus's men weren't putting much effort into defeating them. Especially Bran. He was a giant and a skilled fighter, yet he hung back. He and Cailean were obviously avoiding each other.

Good. If Cailean had friends among their attackers, it would work in their favor.

However, row after row of Fathna's men rushed the three, their swords and axes singing. Taranis was already tired, and he saw no end to the numbers attacking them.

The fight grew thick and hot. Moaning and screams provided gruesome background noise.

Two warriors attacked him simultaneously. He writhed when one man leveled a blow against his broken arm, and the other bashed his cheekbone with the hilt of a knife.

He barely knew he was falling, or when his face hit the sand. A shadow loomed over him and he closed his eyes, waiting for death. But then sunlight struck his face again. Eamhair had brought the warrior down.

Pain took over, and the battlefield faded away.

"You did it. You hit him."

Taranis heard Cailean as his consciousness wavered. He opened his eyes.

"But he is not dead," said Eamhair.

Awareness was returning, along with agonizing spasms in his broken arm. Through a haze of dust and sand, he saw warriors lowering their weapons, peering backward.

Men shuffled. Wind whistled, cold against his face. He shivered.

"Stop the attack!" he heard Fathna shout. "To me!"

Fighting waves of nausea, Taranis struggled to his feet, determined to die standing rather than on his stomach.

The warriors were retreating towards Fathna, who wore an expression of pure fury, and no wonder. An arrow shaft protruded from his left shoulder. He motioned; one of his men broke the shaft off and quickly backed away.

Now the leader of the enemy was wounded—not fatally, but enough to make him dangerously vindictive.

Dead and wounded men lay everywhere, but neither Cailean nor Eamhair had any wounds that he could see. Cailean appeared fresh and strong. Eamhair, too, stood straight, her bow ready, her expression resolute.

Cailean called Vita to his side. She came, favoring her right foreleg.

Why had Fathna ordered his men to stop? Cailean would have soon tired and been overwhelmed, leaving Eamhair alone. When her arrows were gone, she would be helpless.

Could Fathna be giving up? Perhaps he had lost too many men to Cailean's sword and Eamhair's arrows, and didn't want to risk losing more. Perhaps the pain in his shoulder was more than he could bear.

Then he noticed that Eamhair's quiver was empty. Her last arrow was nocked, ready to release.

Several moments of silence passed. Then Fathna yanked on the stallion's reins, causing it to rear and scream. "Can you hear me, monk?" he shouted.

Taranis started. Warily, he looked over the warriors' heads at the leader.

"Are you listening, Chrysaleon of Mycenae?"

Taranis's senses reeled. *Who—who is this?*

The king of Innse Orc grinned. "I did not think I would ever see you fight on the same side as *him*." He pointed at Cailean. "Did you forget he had her, the night you cut him open and spilled his blood for the barley?"

His warriors exchanged baffled glances.

The malevolent smile. The eyes that missed no detail. Even the way he sawed at the bit, causing his poor mount's mouth to spill blood and froth—all this gave away the man's true identity. Taranis searched for the prince of Tiryns in the Pictish king's face, but saw nothing overt. Struggling to speak evenly, he said, "How can you be here? How are you alive?" Vertigo flowed, wave upon wave, as though all the blood in his head had drained away.

And how, in the name of all the gods, could Harpalycus know who he was? How could he know who Cailean was, and Eamhair?

Fathna went on grinning and watching. Missing nothing. Thoroughly enjoying himself.

The necklace and the knife. Aridela. Menoetius and Alexiare. Now Harpalycus. Chrysaleon's past was coming to destroy him—but not before an interlude of torture.

He remembered the day his guards at the palace of Labyrinthos reported that Rusa—Harpalycus—was dead. That he'd expired from thirst, starvation, and injury, caged in the Knossos marketplace.

One by one, Chrysaleon asked each guard if they had allowed anyone to touch the man before he died. They all shook their heads and swore none had. He'd believed them, like a halfwit.

The bastard now spoke to Cailean. "That man fighting alongside you as though he is your ally, came to this wench—" he motioned toward Viviana—"and told her where to find you. Maybe he intended to strike a bargain—ask for the girl as a reward?" He returned his gaze to Taranis, laughing. "The great king of Mycenae. The illustrious ruler of Labyrinthos, reduced to a woman's petty betrayals and trickeries."

Sweat broke out on Taranis's forehead. He couldn't help glancing at Eamhair and Cailean. Cailean returned his gaze impassively, with no surprise and only mild disgust, but Eamhair was livid.

She will never forgive me now.

"So you and the king of Innse Orc know each other." Cailean swung his heavy sword in a beautiful arc as though it weighed no more than a feather. "I saw this when I was in the world of the dead. At the time, I did not understand. I should spill your guts," he added, his voice cutting like flint.

Through lips so numb he could hardly force them to move, Taranis said, "I will be dead soon enough. We will all die here." Simple breathing was suddenly difficult. "Do not let him take Eamhair. No matter what you have to do."

"He will not take her." Cailean continued the lazy swinging of his sword, back and forth, as though inviting someone to come and test it. He smiled at Fathna's warriors.

"I believed you a hero," he heard Eamhair say. He didn't look at her. He couldn't. "But there is not one truth within you. You have accomplished nothing but destruction and misery. I hate you, Taranis. Every benevolent god looking down upon this world hates you."

You are right about that, my queen.

Fathna turned his attention to the villagers. "You there," he said. "You boys. What would you do to please me? To win a place at my side and the right to warrior training? To have a life of glory, adulation, and all the women you could ever desire?"

They stared, open-mouthed. Taranis estimated their ages from about seven to twelve.

"I will give all this and more to the one who brings down the traitor, Cailean of Dalriada, and Eamhair, whore of Dunaedan. Show me your talents. Earn honor, wealth, and respect. You will change your circumstances and sit with me at my high table."

He pointed to the smooth rocks tossed up on the beach by countless tides. "My warriors, with their swords and axes, have failed. What can you do with those stones? Show me."

There was hesitation. The boys looked to their elders, but Taranis saw fear etched on far too many faces, and knew these people didn't dare defy Fathna.

But for the priest, who stepped up to Fathna and Ossian and said something Taranis couldn't hear. He did hear Fathna's succinct reply. "I dislike Christian priests. Back away from me, or I will have them stone you as well."

The priest hesitated, but only briefly. He bent his head and retreated, the coward.

Slingshots were the first weapon young males learned to use. These boys would be proficient slingers, and would carry their slings everywhere. Taranis knew from his eavesdropping that Bericus held annual competitions to encourage the skill—boys as young as five took part.

"Decide," Fathna said. "I am hungry and bored, and I want a surgeon to remove this sliver from my flesh."

Several boys ran to the water's edge, collecting stones. As he feared, most had already pulled out their slings.

They filled their arms and came closer, dumping stones into piles. Fathna's men made a half circle around them to prevent an attack by Cailean or Taranis, and Eamhair had only one arrow. When Taranis glanced at her, he saw her shock. She had probably known these boys all their lives.

But the promise of glory, riches, sex, and plenty to eat must be too tempting to resist.

Cailean crowded in front of Eamhair and held his sword ready, but he ordered Vita to keep at his side. Why? Taranis had no doubt she could decimate the majority of Fathna's newest fighters and, even wounded, would move too fast for their stones.

But the fool could not stomach releasing his finest weapon upon children. His scruples were going to get them all killed.

More joined in, including the younger ones. Taranis and Cailean deflected as best they could, but the sheer number of stones meant a few hit their mark. One struck Taranis on the sternum and for a long instant he couldn't breathe. He heard cheering and saw blood spatter from a gash on Cailean's cheekbone. The boys had drawn blood where no warrior could.

Being cheered by Fathna's men encouraged them to try harder.

"Put the wolf on them!" Taranis shouted, but Cailean ignored him.

Working in tandem, two boys sent stones whipping at Cailean, forcing him to duck. Immediately a third succeeded in striking Eamhair on her bow arm, and that stone was quickly followed by another that collided with the side of her head, knocking her half over.

She straightened. "Bastard! Coward! Using children to fight for you! Come and fight us yourself!"

Fathna merely laughed.

Vita yelped as she was pummeled, but she would not leave Cailean's side and he could not protect her—not without exposing Eamhair. A hefty stone crashed into her spine and her hindquarters dropped.

Eamhair struggled to lift her bow. She prepared her last arrow, but her aim was unsteady, wavering between Fathna and Ossian.

Ossian pinned Viviana in front of him like a shield just before Eamhair released the arrow. He held her there, though she twisted, shrieked, and clawed his face.

The arrow veered off course from Fathna and sank into Viviana's chest. Her head sagged and Ossian shoved her to the side.

Two rocks pounded Taranis, one in the bicep and another against his temple. Pain throbbed. His eyesight blurred as he toppled to his knees.

Another rock struck Eamhair in the head. Blood gushed and she dropped like a snapped tree branch.

Cailean knelt beside her, his back to the boys and their slings. He picked her up in his arms.

And then, finally, the boys stopped. All was silent on the beach at Uisge Bealach except for the washing tide and rising wind.

Vita dragged her broken body next to Cailean's leg. She rested her muzzle on his thigh and her tail fluttered as he stroked her.

One of the younger boys threw down his sling and ran to a village woman. He buried his face in her apron, sobbing.

Taranis swiped blood from his eye. The boys appeared stunned, as if they just now realized what they had done.

They killed their lady. May they rot in blackest hell for it.

Eamhair's voice brought his head around. It was amazingly strong and even. "I see a forest," she said, placing her hand on Cailean's cheek. "There is a girl. She holds out her hand. She is my sister, donnah. And my mother...my mother is there. I am not afraid."

Her hand slid down Cailean's chest, her eyes closed, and Taranis knew she was dead.

He remembered his arrogant resolve to destroy Cailean. He had vowed he would hear Cailean scream, but here, at the end, the scream lodged in his own throat, choking him.

Cailean lowered his forehead to Eamhair's before placing her on the sand. Picking up his sword, he stood, keeping his back to Fathna's men and the boys who had killed her. He faced east, to the rising sun. He closed his eyes and stretched out his arms. Taranis saw his lips move.

A whining rush of air pulled Taranis out of desolation. Fathna had taken one of the slings, loaded it, and was whirling it in his right hand, once, twice, and a third time. He released it; it hummed like a strike of lightning and hit its objective perfectly—the back of Cailean's head.

He crumpled, falling across Eamhair, and did not move. Blood seeped through his hair, over the nape of his neck, and dripped onto the sand.

Taranis saw Menoetius as clearly as though it was the night of the holy king-killing all over again. *I will make the sacrifice*, Menoetius had vowed. He never faltered.

They were caught in the same circle, Menoetius the champion, Chrysaleon the sinner, again relying on guile and deceit to achieve his desires, and again failing.

He glared at Fathna and tried to rise, but vertigo sent him sprawling. If only he could kill that vile, cursed bastard. He would give anything—*anything*—to rip the flesh, strip by strip, off his ancient antagonist.

"Bind him," Fathna said.

Two warriors hurried to secure Taranis's wrists and ankles. They yanked his broken arm and he couldn't stifle a groan.

He looked again at Eamhair. A lock of her hair had come loose from the braid; the wind lifted it like a bright banner.

With Taranis safely disabled, Fathna approached Cailean and Eamhair. "Now I see why she was thought beautiful." He bent and sliced off the lock of hair, held it up as if to admire it, and tossed it into the wind. "Bring him here," he said. "Shackle him to her." As he gave the order, he booted Cailean's body off Eamhair, onto his back.

His men did as he commanded and Fathna looked down upon his foes with satisfaction.

A pungent stench drifted from him—like the smell of ashes in a cold, dead fire. Taranis remembered that smell from when he was Chrysaleon. Odd, that it hadn't changed, though Harpalycus lived in another man's body.

One of the straps was wrapped around Taranis's throat, making every breath onerous. More straps tethered him to Eamhair. There was no reason for this, no purpose other than Harpalycus's love of torture.

Fathna faced the warriors and villagers. He pointed at Taranis. "This man murdered Drost Gocinecht's baby daughter. Imagine what he did to her first. So if any of you think he deserves pity, know the truth."

His gaze ran over the tight leather straps as he added, "I am reminded of the cage at Knossos. Boys are the same everywhere, in every time—they love to throw rocks. I remember how it felt, how helpless I was to stop it. I never thought an opportunity for revenge would come; yet here we are. The gods offer me their favor." He stared avidly at Taranis's gasping. "Do not worry. I will not leave you here to perish. When the sun sets, I will return. I plan to take you to my brother."

Taranis longed to mock him, but it was hard enough to breathe, much less speak.

Fathna strode away, ordering everyone back to Dunaedan.

There was more scuffling and cursing. Taranis craned his neck as far as he could. Three of Fathna's men were trying to catch the tall black horse but it lashed out with its front hooves and ran off. Fathna finally gave up and took one of the ponies. They all left, his men on horseback and the villagers on foot, carrying the wounded.

Dunaedan's blacksmith approached. "The baron was a good man," he said. "And her, poor child. She never had a happy day her whole life." He wiped his face with his sleeve before kneeling and loosening the leather around Taranis's throat. Taranis gratefully drew in a full breath.

"I will come back and free you if I can," Gede said, "and somehow, I will see these two get a Christian burial."

He shuffled away.

The cawing of crows, the moaning wind, and the rhythmic wash of the tide disrupted an otherwise silent morning. Taranis rested his cheek on Eamhair's shoulder and touched her hair with his fingertips. He closed his eyes and concentrated on breathing, on overcoming waves of vertigo and pain.

But before long he heard more footsteps. This time it was Ossian. The man stood over them, glowering.

"Bastard," Taranis said, though his voice was hoarse and weak, the word an ineffectual curse.

Ossian kicked him in the shin. "See those crows? They're just waiting for me to go, then they'll be down to feast on your eyes."

Cailean's hand lifted, quick as a serpent strike. His sword blade sank into Ossian's stomach and twisted before he pulled it free.

Ossian fell with a horrific scream. His blood pumped out as he writhed, releasing one grating gasp after another. Eventually his breaths slowed, turned to wheezing, and stopped.

Cailean's eyes were open, staring into the sky. Tears ran across his temples.

"You're alive, my brother," Taranis whispered.

Chapter 7

COLD WIND TEASED A FEW MORE STRANDS OF EAMHAIR'S HAIR FREE. Taranis watched them lift and float, and was reminded of a long-ago day when he'd gone into a smithy and the floor was awash in copper dust lit by the sun.

Shouldn't her hair have lost that sheen when she died? It was cruel, the beauty of it, implying she was still vibrant with health and life.

Cailean said nothing.

Bharosa came up, nickering, and nuzzled Cailean's face. Cailean placed his hand on the stallion's jaw.

A sudden conspicuous reflection flashed on the hill north of the beach. It continued to flash as it glided along the slope and skimmed down, coming nearer, softening to a shimmer full of watery rainbows. The shadowy outline that stepped from it became a woman, tall, straight-backed, her grey hair plaited and fastened with silver pins. She was arresting, as regal a female as he had ever seen in either of his lives.

This is what Aridela would have looked like, had she survived to old age.

Another woman joined her—a much younger woman with loose black hair. She was sobbing.

A group of men followed. They kept their distance.

The older woman walked up to Cailean. Anguished but dry-eyed, she knelt and caressed his hand. "Oh, son. My son."

"I knew what would happen," Cailean said. "I regret nothing. I would do it again."

He is ever this way. Why can I not be more like him? Would it make a difference?

Cailean didn't look at his mother. He didn't look at Eamhair, or Taranis. He went on staring at the sky.

Taranis had just begun to wonder about this when he spoke. "I cannot see, Mother. Eamhair—is she dead?"

"Yes."

Behind her, the younger woman's sobs grew more miserable.

"And Vita?"

"She, too, is dead."

Cailean lifted his free hand and swiped angrily at his eyes.

Taranis glimpsed a delicate aura of color burgeon around Cailean's mother—a subtle cast of green.

Beneath the grey hair, age lines, and sorrow, lay another. Themiste, Oracle and High Priestess of Crete.

Shudder after shudder ran through him, but he forced himself to remain silent. It was all too much, and he could no longer think coherently. This time, he would wait to see if the woman who had hated him in the past recognized him in the present.

She mopped blood from Cailean's face with her sleeve then at last turned an impassive gaze to him.

For a moment she studied him, her expression weary. Then she said, "Nearly thirty years ago, I gave birth to twins. A boy and a girl. From the beginning, my son was a mystery, consumed by inscrutable darkness. It became evident to all when he had lived but five winters. He stole the holy knife and deliberately cut a child—a small graze, but she died. When asked why he had done it, he said he wanted to see what would happen."

Taranis bit his tongue. Why was she telling him this? Dread crawled through his stomach. He didn't want to know.

"The dead child's mother and father, and the village elders, demanded that my son be exiled. I was compelled to take him away. We journeyed by boat and on foot to the lands of the Britons, and there, we were caught in a violent summer storm. Ruadan was swept from my arms and I lost him. After I returned home, I used every method of sight I had ever learned, but there was no sign of him—not even a glimpse. Nevertheless, I knew in my soul that he lived."

The woman leaned across Cailean and drew the necklace out from beneath Taranis's tunic. "Still with you," she murmured, "Just as it was when I placed it around your neck."

"You—you gave birth to me?"

"Even without it, I would have known you. You have not changed so much that I would not recognize you, son."

"I am a twin?"

She glanced over her shoulder and held out her hand. The young woman stepped forward and knelt beside her.

Taranis looked into his own eyes, as green as new fronds of bracken. But was there not a subtle difference? Traces of blue, turning her eyes to the color of the seas around Crete?

This woman, his so-called *twin*, was Selene. He could not explain how he knew, any more than he could explain how he recognized any of them, but he was certain. Somewhere inside this young woman Selene lived on.

"I have dreamed of you my whole life," she said, but her expression was indifferent.

Before he could think of something to say to this woman who was not only his sister but also the one person who had seen through every lie he had ever told, she turned her gaze to Cailean and he knew she had no interest in him at all.

She was a stranger to him. He was a stranger to her. Her eyes offered nothing, except perhaps anger.

"What is your name?" he asked, shrinking beneath the burn of humiliation.

"I am Meraud," the older woman said, "and this is Rhalanse."

"My sister. My mother." Shock caused his voice to crack. "I remember nothing of what you say. But I do remember...rage. I harmed myself and others, if they got in my way, until I turned nine, and my mother—Breda—gave me the necklace. She said I was wearing it when she found me in the ruin of a flood. After that, my anger was focused like a spearhead."

Deciphering her expression was impossible, but she appeared only distantly sad, as if hearing a story about someone she didn't know, or didn't feel responsible for.

"He is your son?" Cailean asked. "He is my brother?"

"Your half brother," Meraud said.

"This does not please me," Cailean said roughly. "He lied to

Eamhair. He forced himself upon her. And he betrayed us this day. It is because of him she lies here, dead."

Taranis was consumed with grief and shame, but soon bitterness made it possible to again breathe. "You could have saved her long before Fathna ever came. Before I came. You failed her as much as I did."

"Treachery still has you in thrall, son," Meraud said. "Your path is lined with stones and thorns. You have a long way to travel upon it yet." Her expression softened, very slightly. He almost missed it. "But when you ask, you will have the forgiveness you crave."

Athene's words! She made that promise in the labyrinth! But it was a lie. Fury erupted. "I *did* ask! And was refused."

I will never again ask, never. I won't be one of those frightened little mortals who cower and beg for my own death.

Meraud motioned to the men. They approached and released Taranis from the rest of the bindings. Two of them helped Cailean to his feet and supported him, for he swayed dangerously. Two lifted Eamhair. Another carefully picked up Vita; the last man spoke gently to Bharosa and was allowed to grasp his bridle.

Rhalanse and Meraud rose and turned away with the others.

This was all they meant to give? An old story? Why tell him at all, if they intended to leave him here? Using his good arm, he tried to push himself up but got no farther than kneeling. Dizziness made everything spin. "You're leaving," he said bitterly. "Why am I surprised? You abandoned me once before."

Meraud stopped but didn't turn. "When you ask it, you will have forgiveness," she said, almost too quietly to hear.

The others retreated to the wavering rip in the air and one by one, crossed through. He watched, stupefied, as they kept on walking, growing smaller, more distant, until only insubstantial ripples were left.

When they were gone, Meraud faced him again and he gritted his teeth, trying to quell the spark of hope.

"I am sorry I lost you," she said. "I have thought of you every single day." A tear tracked down her cheek. "But it will do no good for you to remember." Bending towards him, she reached out and placed her palm on his cheek. He swallowed and clenched his good hand into a fist, fighting how much he wanted to lean into that caress. His eyes closed of their own accord.

"Forget, my son," she said. "Forget."

He felt the loss of her touch viscerally. When he opened his eyes, she was following the others. As soon as she entered the tear, it closed upon itself and vanished.

There was nothing now but the lapping of water against the shore, the soughing of wind, and the thin, reedy cry of a curlew.

Chapter 8

How much time did he have? Taranis blinked at the sun. Fathna had promised to return, and he would want vengeance. He would make certain death came only after unbearable torment.

Ages upon ages ago, Chrysaleon, king of Mycenae and Kaphtor, had died. Looking back, Taranis remembered how Chrysaleon fell ill and vomited away his strength and finally his life.

Poison. Harpalycus could have hidden himself in any of the slaves who served him.

The dizziness gradually lessened and he was able to stand. He left the torn, bloody sand, the silent, staring corpses. But he didn't take a currach and row out to sea. He returned to the other beach. The boat Eamhair and Cailean had landed in was gone; no doubt the knife was gone as well. But he climbed down and searched anyway, digging and scuffing through the sand. He was surprised when he found it.

He picked it up gingerly, but it was no longer hot.

The ivory hilt was not even yellowed. There were no chips in the blade. It was a miracle of gleaming perfection.

There was something about this knife. He heard hints of voices. Faces appeared in the obsidian and vanished too quickly to place.

The woman on the cliffs, Eamhair had said at Dunaedan's gate. *She told me you changed my destiny.*

Why remember that now? *I thought you could save me,* she'd said, *but you cannot, or will not. Now I will die.*

The skin on the back of his neck crawled. She had a vision of her own death, and it had come true.

There were so many unanswered questions. How was Harpalycus still alive—and with his memories of Crete intact? What was the mist of color around Eamhair, Cailean, and Meraud? How was he able to recognize the people they used to be, when they could not themselves?

He could swear he saw a vague cloudiness emanating from the blade. A deadly, malignant power—almost a consciousness, wavered before his eyes. He felt the movement of air, in and out, like breathing. He heard laughter at the edge of his awareness.

Without warning, the blade flared as it had before, so brightly he was blinded. He smelled his skin burning just before he fell.

WHEN TARANIS WOKE, HE WAS LYING NEAR THE WATER. HE WATCHED AS IT swelled forward and retreated. Farther out, the waves thundered.

He sat up and started to stretch, but pain stopped him. His left arm was injured—broken in fact. It throbbed and was coated with dried blood. There were punctures that looked like bite marks from some animal. He realized he had other injuries as well. Bruises. Cuts. One eye was swollen closed and there was sharp, shooting pain in his temple.

With concentration, he remembered finding Eamhair at this beach, Vita snapping his arm, betraying Cailean, and finally, the battle at Uisge Bealach.

The sun was now a huge scarlet sphere, resting low in the west. Fathna—Harpalycus—had promised he would return to Uisge Bealach and collect him. But this was a different beach. Somehow he had escaped the straps lashing him to Eamhair.

How had he come to be here? Who had freed him? It must have been Gede, the blacksmith, but he could not be certain.

Was Cailean still lying at Uisge Bealach, clinging to life? Did Eamhair's body still rest beside him?

The knife lay next to his foot. He picked it up, turning it over and over, watching translucent red sunlight creep up and down the black blade.

He felt the weight of the pendant around his neck, and now he had the knife. He knew what he would do.

THE MOORING PLACE WAS NEARLY DESERTED. ONLY TWO MEN WERE THERE, pulling the burned shell of a boat out of the water, and they hardly glanced at Taranis. Perhaps the rest of the village was celebrating Fathna's victory in Dunaedan's hall, or maybe they'd been sent out to search for him, or they were huddled in corners, trying to come to terms with this day's cursed doings.

He climbed to the cave and entered the tunnel. It, too, was deserted, and much colder now that the mud wall was no longer keeping out the wind.

Once, on one of his forays into the fortress, he had stolen a silver casket banded in iron, thinking it would be a good way to protect food from rats. It still sat, undisturbed, by his sleeping pallet. He threw out the stale bread and placed the knife and necklace inside, cushioned in a bit of wool, and carried it back to a place where one of the stones in a support arch was loose. He worked the block out and deepened the hole, set the coffer inside, and replaced the block, taking his time to make sure it was indistinguishable from the other stones around it.

No one will find you this time.

He searched for a stone with a fine edge and scratched on the face of the block. It was barely discernable, but served its purpose.

Eamhair

Taranis

Even in death

Long, long ago, when the bull-king Damasen cursed him, he'd sensed that his life would go on—that he would become immortal or be brought back some other way, and he had been—into a life many centuries removed from all he had known. Damasen had promised he would remember, and he did. He remembered the citadel at Mycenae. His first glimpse of Crete's amber cliffs. Aridela coming out from beneath the awnings with her women and later, her dance with a bull. Winning the Games. The terror of the earthshaking. Killing Menoetius. Killing Aridela.

Another dismal, empty future loomed before him. He was condemned for a second time to live with nothing but recollections of his atrocities. *What would life be without you?* Eamhair had asked Cailean before she perished at his side. *A bleak, barren, lonely place.*

He had lived a similar existence on Crete, until the poison killed him. He knew exactly how she felt when she said that.

He could not do it again. Not again.

He'd squandered his second chance. He had tricked and raped the woman he loved. Attempted to kill Cailean, and when that failed, betrayed him, hoping someone else would kill him.

He could not expect to be given more chances.

But Athene was nothing if not inventive. She might want to make him suffer another time or two—until she grew bored.

Brave Eamhair stood on the edge of a cliff, her hands curled into fists. *My fate is my own!*

As he left the sea cave, he noticed the two men had stopped hauling on the boat. They stared into the sky, holding onto each other.

He looked up and stilled, frozen with awe. A long streak of light, flashing halfway across the heavens. Near the tip a halo billowed, blue-white like an ornament of ice, so bright he could hardly look at it straight on.

It appeared to be motionless, but as he watched, he saw it slowly lengthen until it stretched across the entirety of the blue bowl in which it swam.

Shivering, he dropped off the boulders, climbed the slope, and walked westward. Soon Dunaedan's palisades and tower came into view.

Two guards challenged him at the main gate. He heard someone say, "It is the monk."

The gates were opened and more men emerged. They prodded him inside with their swords.

"Fathna was so angry when he found out you and the other two were gone, he killed the man who told him," one of the guards said. "I am glad I am not you, monk."

Cailean and Eamhair were no longer at Uisge Bealach? The blacksmith must have taken them away for that Christian burial he'd promised.

Fathna was leaning against one of the iron bound doors to the hall, his arms crossed over his chest. "So," he said. "Here you are, begging someone to put you out of your misery. Just like last time."

Taranis said nothing. There was no more need to speak.

Fathna straightened and spread out his arms. "Miserable Chrysaleon of Mycenae. I will be happy to again serve as your deliverer."

THOU SHALT BE CALLED EAMHAIR OF THE SEA,
WHO BRINGS THEM CLOSER...

~~~THE PROPHECY OF ATHENE

A Gift Of Hope

"SHE IS PASSING," MERAUD SAID. "JUST BENEATH THE WINDOW."

Cailean heard the shuffle of feet and low chanting. The grating of wheels being drawn along the road came to his ears easily, as did the crackle of torches.

But he saw nothing.

"The people are putting flowers in with her. They are piled high."

His nose caught the tantalizing mingle of floral scents. She would like that.

"Bharosa is pulling the cart," Meraud said. "He is draped in blue, and there are gold tassels on his bridle. Vita lies next to her, son. Eamhair holds her close."

Cailean stroked his baby son's hair. It had been dark at first, but over time had lightened until it was the same color as Eamhair's. Every day of his life, this boy would remind the islanders of their dead princess.

"I placed her bow and three arrows upon her breast, as you asked. She is a singular woman, Cailean. A warrior. A mother. A lover. A pure soul. Your perfect match."

"Why do you say 'is,'" Cailean asked wearily. "She is dead, Mother."

"Only in this life." Meraud rubbed Cailean's forearm. "Her destiny has not yet been fulfilled. In fact...it has hardly begun."

Cailean wanted to believe, but his grief was as heavy as logs strung around his neck. He feared believing. He feared the pain of Meraud being wrong. How could she know such a thing? She was simply trying to make him care about something again.

"It is time to follow. Are you ready?"

"Aye." He allowed a handmaid to take the baby.

Two men guided him down the steps, through the courtyard, and onto the road behind Eamhair's funeral procession. He walked between them, his hands on their shoulders. He heard people speaking; there was murmured sympathy and people touched his arms.

He wished he could see what was coming. He could imagine it, because he had witnessed other funerals on Inis Tearmann, but none as grand as what Meraud had planned for Eamhair.

They came to the horses and he mounted. He and his guides, followed by Meraud and Rhalanse, rode to the lovely hoof shaped bay where the water was nearly always calm.

"Mother!" Rhalanse cried.

"I see it," Meraud said.

"What? What do you see?" Cailean had always taken his acute eyesight for granted. This blindness was intolerable. The Blue Falcon, forever hooded.

"The water is blue." His sister's voice was hushed. Awed.

"The water is always blue," he said.

"We are coming up to the shore," Meraud said. "The beach is glistening—it is blue like I have never seen, except in your eyes, Cailean, and the eyes of the other kira."

"The bay—the water—it looks like—like blue sparks in a fire!" There was more life in Rhalanse's voice than he'd heard since the day Eamhair died.

"It is the jellyfish," Meraud said. "They have come into the bay. There must be thousands. They are making the light."

Soon the horses halted and Cailean was assisted to the ground. He was guided forward. He could tell he was close to the water by the sound and scent, by the breeze.

"You are standing in the midst of the glow," his sister told him. "It is all around you. I have never seen this before."

Cailean felt the presence of many people. The entire island had come to say goodbye to their kira's princess.

"They are being taken to the top of the pyre," Meraud said. Cailean heard his son give a small sigh. Meraud must be holding him.

She had described the pyre during its construction so that he could picture it. It sat in the middle of the bay, a high trellised structure with space at the top for the litter. He could smell the pitch used to make it more flammable.

"They are there now," Meraud told him. "The men are returning." After a moment, she said, "The fire is being lit."

Cailean's enhanced hearing picked up sounds from the cliffs at the mouth of the bay. The order being given. The drumbeat. The sputter of ignited cloth. The seething whisper of arrows followed by thudding strikes. Soon the pyre was roaring. He felt the heat.

Donnah.

Vita.

I am lost without you.

"Everyone is releasing their tokens."

These were small clay shells, each with a round center turret. A candle was placed inside, the lid set; candlelight glimmered through four holes. The shell-shaped hull kept them floating for a long while.

"The heavens mourn her loss with us."

There was the humming that always came with the ribbons.

He remembered how she had danced and laughed and shouted as she experienced their healing influence on the boat.

"Your son, Cailean." Meraud stopped, catching her breath. "He is watching it all, taking it in. And his eyes—his eyes are as blue as yours."

Everywhere people were crying out and weeping. Eamhair's funeral seemed more a gift of hope, beauty, and love than loss and grief.

If only he could see it.

Chapter 9

THE SENTRY SHOUTED THAT SOMEONE WAS APPROACHING. "A WOMAN, alone!"

Coarse laughter and lewd talk met this announcement. Artur ignored it. He left his worktable and companions and stood outside, watching. Listening.

The guards sent out a challenge. There was some indecipherable reply. The gate opened, squealing and grating, and there she was, framed on each side by massive timbers.

His Meraud. She was still tall, slim, and straight shouldered. But her hair was silver now, and her face bore signs of a life lived.

What must she think of him? So grizzled and scarred. So much older. But her face told him none of that mattered.

He took a step. Another. Then he was running, embracing her, picking her up as he had done so many years before, swinging her and kissing her cheeks, and she was laughing and putting her hands in his hair.

"Oh, how I have missed you," he said.

"And I you."

"Why have you come?" He shook his head. "Nay—don't tell me. Not yet." Setting her back on her feet, he pulled her into the crumbling Roman fortress, hardly taking his gaze from her face as he called for ale and food.

Only after the loaf of bread, the knife, and flask of ale was placed beside them and they were alone did he lean forward to cup her knee. He said nothing, knowing that only the most momentous of news could have brought her.

She sipped her ale and set down the cup. "Cailean is blind."

Not dead. He realized he had been dreading those words. Relief coursed through him.

"He fell in love," she said softly. "He married a woman who fought and died at his side. He was blinded in the battle by a slinger."

Artur stared at her. Then he put his hands over his face and wept.

She rose and embraced him, and wept with him.

"My son," he choked out.

"He will always be your son. He adores you, Artur."

"Still, he is lost to me, spirited away to that place where I can never go. But…I am happy he found love. Worthy love, like I did."

"Eamhair gave birth before she died."

"Cailean has a child? A boy or girl?"

"A boy. His mother gave me the honor of naming him."

"And? What name did you choose?"

"Adamantinus."

"Adamantinus," he whispered, and wept again.

"We call him Adam." Smiling faintly, she added, "Eamhair had difficulty with Latin."

Meraud returned to her stool, wiping her eyes with the heel of one hand. "Cailean may not last. He has lost his joy and his will, and I have failed to revive them. Perhaps I was not meant to."

"You have very little good news, Meraud."

"There is one thing I can tell you." She gripped his hands. Hers felt as soft as ever, like a child's. "A war comes—not in your lifetime, or mine, but soon. A fearsome war, the most terrible ever seen. It will be won not with swords and spears but in the heart and mind." Her lips tightened as she struggled for control. "I have seen them there, at the forefront. The Infinite Lady prepares her warriors even now, for this battle will engulf every country and every living being in our world."

Meraud read the question in his eyes and shook her head. "I have looked and looked, but the fight is tangled and long, shrouded in shadow, and I cannot see the outcome. What I do know with certainty is that your son is as brave as you could desire. Triumph or defeat, my love, you can be proud."

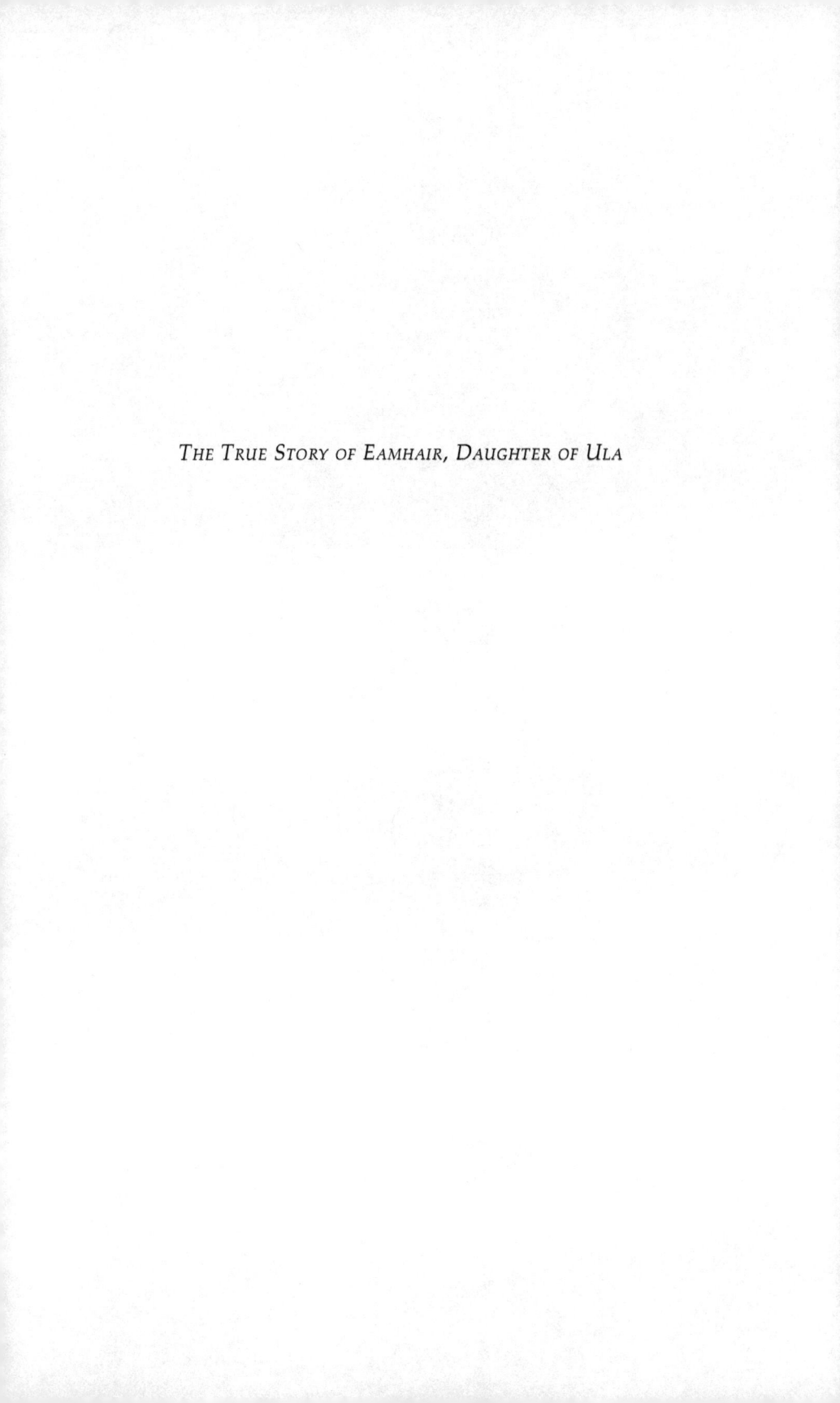

The True Story of Eamhair, Daughter of Ula

Historical Notes

There's a ton of stuff I could write about here, but I think I'll keep it short. Here are the highlights!

Eamhair – Ee mer
    Rhalanse – Rhalanz

The Round Towers of Ireland: the merchant who "happens" upon Taranis and Breda mentions seeing round towers in Hibernia (Ireland.) These towers may not have yet existed at the time of *Falcon Blue*, however, one at least *was* built near my time setting, and the construction date of others is unknown. It's safe to assume they were built after Saint Patrick made history, and he died in 461. So it's possible some may have been built by the time of *Falcon Blue*, which is set in the year 502. Hey, that rhymes!

Whithorn: I decided to use the name "Whithorn" for clarity, even though the priory wasn't called that right away. It was called The White House. Whithorn was founded by Saint Ninian in 397 AD.

The Judgment Stone: East of the town of Durness there is, or was, a place called Ceannabeinne. One of the legends attached to this place is the "Clach a Breitheanas," or "Judgment Stone," where criminals were tossed off the cliffs to their death.

Sorcha, the White Seer: Ula tells Eamhair about her ancestor, Sorcha, who was gifted with a life of ten thousand years. Some readers might remember that Sorcha the White Seer was Menoetius's mother, the mysterious slave who vanished after her son was born.

In *Falcon Blue,* I used as inspiration for her the story of Tuan mac Cairill, a truly fascinating character from Irish mythology.

Theoderic the Great: he didn't have any sons, at least none that are recorded. I made Harpalycus his half-forgotten bastard, which seems believable. Theoderic did have one recorded concubine, and even the names of his actual daughters are not certain, so it's not too far out there to suggest he might have had more children who didn't make it into the history books.

Innse Orc was an old name for the Orkneys.

Dhu Rinn was an old name for the town/village of Durness.

Sgathag Creag (Dread Rock) is my name for the actual Pictish fortress of Craig Phadrig, which is located on a hilltop near Inverness. It would not have been called Craig Phadrig during the setting of my story, because Saint Patrick hadn't yet gone up there and converted everyone.

And Drost Gocinecht is listed in a few Pictish king lists as ruling the Picts during the years in which my story is set.

As is the other king I mention but once: Domangart Réti, from Dál Riata/Dalriada.

Uisge Bealach (gap of water) is my name for the Kyle of Durness, a sea inlet near Cape Wrath.

Bharosa is a Friesian stallion, for those who don't know about their history and so don't catch the clues.

My inspiration for the people of Inis Tearmann are the Aes Sídhe. Wikipedia's description is what got my mind working on this. It says:

"The *aos sí* older form *aes sídhe* is the Irish term for a supernatural race in Irish mythology and Scottish mythology (where it is usually spelled Sìth, but pronounced the same), comparable to the fairies or elves. They are said to live underground in fairy mounds, across the western sea, or in an invisible world that coexists with the world of humans. This world is described in the *Lebor Gabála Érenn* as a parallel universe in which the *aos sí* walk amongst the living."

I was especially inspired by the idea that they live in an invisible world that coexists with ours, and walk among us. More, I cannot say, as it would be getting into spoiler territory!

The word "pergula" is Late Latin, so I felt okay about using it.

Titles in The Child of the Erinyes series

About the Author

Early on, Rebecca Lochlann began envisioning an epic story, a new kind of myth, one built upon the foundation of the Greek classics and continuing through the centuries right up into the present and future.

This became her life's work, though she didn't exactly intend it to be that way when she started.

The Child of the Erinyes series is mythic fantasy, inspired by the Greek tale of Ariadne, Theseus, and the Minotaur. As one reader put it, "Loads of testosterone, slaughter, and crazy magic," with a love story (of course.)

Though the story is fiction-fantasy, it still took about fifteen years to research the Bronze Age segments of the series, and encompassed rare historical documents, mythology, archaeology, ancient religions, and volcanology.

The Year-god's Daughter is her debut novel: Book One of *The Child of the Erinyes* series. It has been utilized as a study guide in an American university, named a B.R.A.G. Medallion honoree, and was a finalist in the Chaucer Historical Fiction awards. Book Two, *The Thinara King*, a First Place winner in the Ancient History category of the Chaucer Historical Fiction awards and a Next Generation Indie Book Awards finalist, continues the saga. Book Three, *In the Moon of Asterion*, wraps up the Bronze Age segment of the series and leads into the middle trilogy, set in Scotland. These are: Book Four, *The Moon Casts a Spell*, Book Five, *The Sixth Labyrinth*, and Book Six, *Falcon Blue*, which jumps backward in time to the Early Medieval Era.

The denouement comes in the final three books: *When the Moon Whispers, First and Second Chronicles*, and *Swimming in the Rainbow*.

Rebecca has always believed that certain rare individuals, either blessed or tortured, voluntarily or involuntarily, are woven by fate or the Immortals into the labyrinth of time, and that deities sometimes speak to us through dreams and visions, gently prompting us to tell their lost stories. Who knows? It could make a difference.

Connect with Rebecca at her website, BookBub, Facebook, or in a review at your point of purchase.

Attributions

Cover design: Rebecca Lochlann, Erinyes Press

Original Front Cover Warrior: Eve Ventrue, eve-ventrue.com
Blue falcon & wolf: Jozef Klopacka, Shutterstock
Standing stones: Ivan M Munoz, Shutterstock

Back Cover Print Edition:
Northern Lights, Depositphotos
Labyrinth, EcOasis, Shutterstock
Design Elements: A-R-T-U-R, Depositphotos

Big Crescent Moon with Triple Moon, Infinity Loop and Little
Goddess. Pagan and Wicca: Christine Krahl, Shutterstock

Labrys Axe graphic © "Labrys-symbol" Licensed under Public domain
via Wikimedia Commons http://commons.wikimedi-
a.org/wiki/File:Labrys-symbol.svg#mediaviewer/File:Labrys-
symbol.svg

Crescent moons, necklace, & Erinyes Press logo: Lance Ganey: free-
lanceganey.com

Author website, maps, bibliographies, etc: rebeccalochlann.com

I probably never would have written any of my books without my
mother's influence. She took me to the library religiously every two
weeks from the moment I learned how to read. She fought for my right
to read whatever I wanted when others would have censored me. All
my life I've known what I wanted to do because of her.

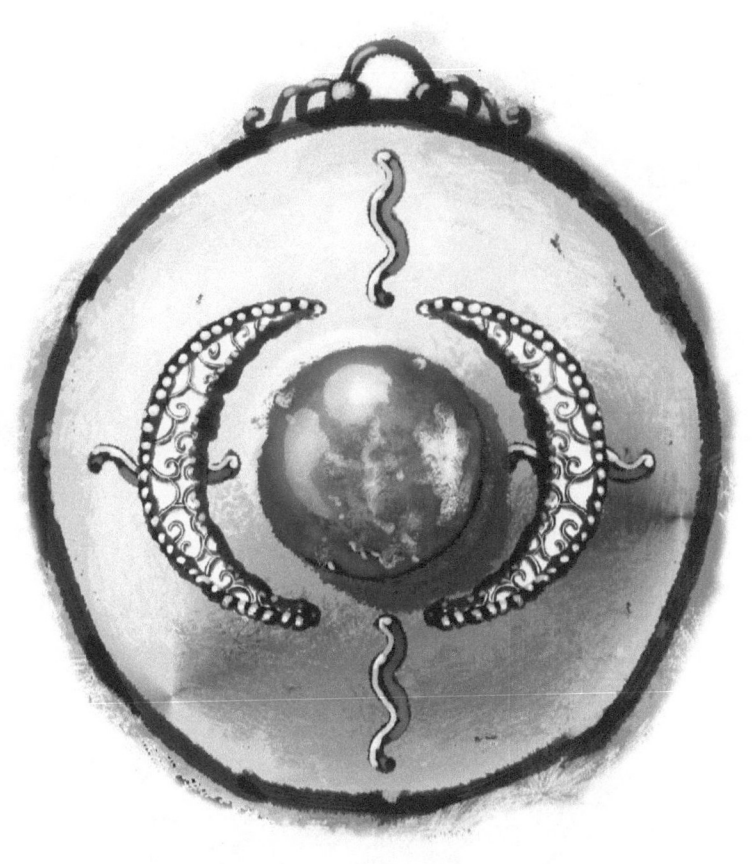

www.ingramcontent.com/pod-product-compliance
Lightning Source LLC
Chambersburg PA
CBHW051213120726
47905CB00004B/1099